ONE COMMANDO

"THE BIG RED"

By the same author:
Song of Death

Published by Covos Day Books, 2001
Oak Tree House, Tamarisk Avenue,
P.O. Box 6996, Weltevredenpark 1715, South Africa

First published in 1997 by RLI Publishing

Photographs courtesy Lt-Col. Ron Reid-Daly who
provided access to the RLI Regimental records

Cover design by JANT Design
Design and origination by Nick Russell

Printed and bound by United Litho, South Africa

ISBN 1-919874-35-6

One Commando

The Author

Dick Gledhill was born in Kenya in 1951 and lived in Nairobi, where his father was a lawyer during the Mau Mau uprising. He finished his schooling in the UK before working as a commercial diver off the English coast and travelling to Australia, where he joined the army and was posted to the Second Battalion, The Royal Australian Regiment.

After serving for three years he joined the Queensland Fire Service as a regular firefighter, and took up recreational skydiving.

In the mid-1970s he returned to Africa, enlisting as a trooper in One Commando, The Rhodesian Light Infantry. He saw action on Fire Force operations inside Rhodesia and on external raids during the bush war.

Gledhill later transferred to the Rhodesian Air Force where, as a sergeant at the Parachute Training School in Salisbury, he instructed Rhodesia's paratroops.

He left Zimbabwe after Independence in 1980 and returned to Australia, where he resumed his firefighting career — a job he still enjoys.

He has more than 2000 parachute jumps to his credit.

One Commando

Dedications

"They went through the gates and flew upward to feast with Odin in Valhalla, those warriors slain in battle." *Anon*.

This book is dedicated to my sister, Pam, who has always believed in me.

It is also dedicated to the officers and men of my regiment, The Rhodesian Light Infantry, a small but brave group who held at bay, for a while at least, the forces of terror.

And for those who died in the fight — especially Mark Ellis. A good mate and an extremely switched-on machinegunner.

Acknowledgments

I would like to thank the following people:

Heidi Daniel who patiently corrected my dismal spelling and atrocious punctuation, **Kerry Corrigan** who gave up her valuable time to input the script, and **S.O.** whose skill and patience knocked off the many rough edges.

Richard Allport and **Professor JRT Wood** for the use of extracts from their published works.

Lieutenant-Colonel Ron Reid-Daly who gave much of his valuable spare time to ensure the terminology and radio procedures I used were correct. The passage of time had dimmed my memory — but not "Uncle" Ron's!

My deep gratitude also goes to a couple of mates; **N.M.** and **C.K.** who lived, breathed and fought for their country, Rhodesia, with distinction. Without their assistance, this book would not have happened. They have their reasons for not wanting to be mentioned here, even though our little war ended a long time ago. As Stevie Wonder sang, "Peace has come to Zimbabwe", but my shamwaris need to keep their heads down for a while yet.

Author's note

Although this story is fiction, it is very much based on fact. Rhodesia went through fourteen years of bitter struggle in a terrorist war which claimed an estimated 40,000 lives.

I make no apology for the terminology used; it was in common use during that time and I have kept it for authenticity.

I have tried to describe the Fire Force contacts as accurately as possible from memory. There were many big battles against the terrorists in their camps, both inside and outside Rhodesia. An attack on the air base at Grand Reef happened. I know, because I was there.

The scenes I have tried to describe at the kraals, farmhouses and compounds in Rhodesia were not isolated cases. They happened with sickening regularity, on thousands of occasions.

The character of Sergeant Hunter is a composite drawn from the many men of many backgrounds who made up the Commandos of the Rhodesian Light Infantry. The clearheaded, aggressive and forward-thinking qualities I have attributed to him alone have been made to make the story easier to follow. There were, in fact, men like Hunter to be found in every troop of the RLI — uncompromising, professional soldiers at the peak of their skills.

Rhodesian Light Infantry troopers, comprising, in the main, 17 to 24-year-old conscripts, were fearless in combat. ZIPRA Commander-in-Chief Joshua Nkomo, later Vice President of Zimbabwe, said this of the Regiment: "The ones who use the helicopters, they are formed completely of mercenaries. They wreak havoc on us."

The part about being formed by mercenaries was a lie told to gain favour in the political arena. True, there were men from other lands fighting in its ranks on normal soldiers' pay and subject to the standing orders of the country's long-established, professional army.

But the majority of the Regiment's soldiers were young men from Rhodesia.

The part about wreaking havoc was accurate.

This is the story of a few of them.

Dick Gledhill
Queensland, Australia
February 1997

FOREWORDS

LIEUTENANT-COLONEL R.F. REID-DALY, CLM DMM MBE
First Regimental Sergeant Major; Officer Commanding Support Commando, The Rhodesian Light Infantry, and the Commanding Officer of the Selous Scouts Regiment

As a founder member of the Rhodesian Light Infantry, it gives me great pleasure in writing a foreword to this book. The RLI, as it was generally known, was an all-white professional soldier unit and was formed in February, 1961. I was chosen to be its first Regimental Sergeant Major.

Forming a new regiment is no easy task, and, to add to the very considerable teething pains we experienced, we had to endure the taunts and jibes of the older regiments of the Rhodesia and Nyasaland Federal Army — all of whom were black — but white officered.

I can remember entering the Warrant Officer's and Sergeant's Mess at the end of a particularly bad day where everything that could possibly go wrong had done just that. Rhodesia had never had white professional soldiers before and the citizens of Bulawayo were shocked to encounter these well-trained, but highly aggressive soldiers, in the various places of entertainment around the city.

This was a time of peace in Central Africa, and the absence of an enemy to fight meant that the civilian population, and the police in particular received the brunt of the RLI's aggression. Indeed, the situation became so bad that a prominent Bulawayo newspaper publicly called for the RLI to be disbanded.

Seated in a corner of the Mess as I entered was Sergeant Major Paddy McEever, a retired Irish Guardsman, and an honorary member of the RLI Warrant Officer's Mess. Paddy took one look at my face and asked what the problem was. When I told him he said "Sir, these are early days. I am telling you that this Battalion is going to earn a great reputation as a fighting regiment. I know — I can feel it in my bones."

Prophetic words indeed, for when winds of war swept over the Rhodesian landscape, the RLI became the cutting edge of the Rhodesian Army. As a Fire Force their professionalism and martial skills were unsurpassed, as hundreds of insurgents were to testify with their lives.

One Commando — The Big Red — established, I believe, a world-record by parachuting into battle three times in one day.

But perhaps the most apt description of the RLI came from a grizzled African Warrant Officer from the Rhodesian African Rifles who was involved in a major contact alongside the RLI. He was wounded in the contact and, while recuperating, had this to say about them. "We in the RAR used to laugh at your soldiers, for to us, they looked like boys. But today you have shown us how to fight. They have the faces of boys, but they fight like lions."

This book, although fictionalised, portrays a very real picture of these men and the tasks they carried out — always with great success.

I am proud, honoured and privileged to have been a member of The Rhodesian Light Infantry.

Johannesburg, South Africa
January 1997

SQUADRON LEADER DJG DE KOCK
Commanding Officer
The Rhodesian Air Force Parachute Training School

While reading this book, memories of the hundreds of tough, dedicated young men, both black and white, who passed through the Parachute Training School, came flooding back.

In 1961, five Royal Rhodesian Air Force volunteers, including myself, were sent to RAF Abbingdon in England and underwent training as Parachute Jump Instructors. Later that year, with the help of four Royal Air Force secondments, the Rhodesian Air Force Parachute Training School at New Sarum was in business. Initially we only trained "C" (Rhodesia) Squadron of the British 22nd Special Air Service, with a limit of twenty men on each course.

After Rhodesia's Unilateral Declaration of Independence from Great Britain in November, 1965, our RAF secondments went home and nothing much happened until 1970. At this time the Rhodesian SAS were operating outside our borders and it became evident that High Altitude Low Opening (HALO) Free Fall training was required. It also became apparent that it was necessary to deploy more troops into Fire Force contacts and the only way this could be achieved in Rhodesia was by parachute.

The RAF had left us with a book of parachute rules but, by the early 1970s, with our bush war escalating on all fronts, these became obsolete and new methods had to be employed to gain the upper hand. The methods devised by us subsequently changed the way paratroops are deployed the world over.

Our staff grew to five officers and over 75 PJI sergeants and despatchers. The number of men trained in each course increased from 20 to 240 and three Fire Forces were permanently in the field (each with a PJI and two other despatchers).

Static line drop heights were reduced from 1000 feet to 500 feet, and, on many occasions, as low as 300 feet. HALO drops were increased to over 20,000 feet and often conducted at night with the navigation being done by a PJI with his head sticking out of the door during the final run-in, map reading the way to the target. Trees were deliberately used as drop zones as they provided cover on landing and open ground was avoided. Yet the injury rate remained below 0.7%.

During my last year as the Commanding Officer of the Rhodesian Air Force Parachute Training School, over 14,000 operational jumps were recorded and some troops of the RLI and the RAR recorded three operational jumps in one day. Most were done from DC3 Dakotas but on occasion troops, fuel and ammunition were dropped from a DC7F.

The staff of the Rhodesian Air Force Parachute Training School came from all corners of the globe including British, Welsh, Irish, Scottish, Australian and American.

I was privileged to lead such a diverse, multicultural band of dedicated instructors, one of whom was Dick Gledhill.

Melbourne, Australia
January, 1997

ONE COMMANDO

CHAPTER ONE

THE ATTRACTIVE AIR hostess welcoming the passengers aboard the Air Rhodesia flight from Johannesburg to Salisbury wouldn't have taken much notice of the stocky man with the broad, powerful shoulders, if she hadn't noticed his eyes. They were cold and hard and they frightened her.

As he approached to present his boarding pass, she steeled herself for the moment when they would meet. He seemed absorbed in his own thoughts – what they were she could not guess. As he handed her his pass, their eyes met. For Bridget, that brief moment seemed an eternity. Then she got her second shock. The eyes were now warm and friendly with a hint of mockery, not directed at her but rather at the world in general. He knew secrets not privy to others.

The rapid transformation caught her unawares and for a split-second she dropped her defences. Just as quickly, she put them up again, adopting the cool, professional manner of air hostesses the world over. But that brief look had been enough. It was as though she had bared her soul to him and he had seen into the very core of her being.

"Welcome aboard, sir. Ninth row, and to the left," Bridget said, handing back his pass with as much aloofness as she could muster.

The meeting had jangled her nerves and it was all she could do to maintain her normal worklike manner.

The flight north to Rhodesia across the great Limpopo River was uneventful, in spite of the savage guerilla war raging in the Rhodesian bush far below the Viscount aircraft. However, Bridget found herself wondering about the passenger in seat 9A. If ever she had seen a fighting man, it was him. Few words had passed between them during the course of her duties, but she had noticed that he spoke with a slight Australian accent. There were many foreigners serving in Rhodesia's army – some for the adventure and others because of their belief in the cause. In which category would 9A fall?

ALTHOUGH RAY HUNTER had lived in Australia for many years, he was in fact African-born — in Kenya to be exact. The son of a prominent lawyer and his wife, Raymond, as he was christened, inherited his father's lively intelligence and sardonic wit, and his mother's dogmatic, stubborn resilience, countering the easygoing flippancy which ran through the long line of affluent Hunter males. For him, there would be constant inner turmoil and self-searching between the analytical thirst for knowledge from the legal minds preceding him, and a theological bent from the priests and God-fearing men of his mother's side. From both parents he received the gift of physical strength and endurance, although he was given to bouts of quick temper.

Under normal circumstances there would be a bright future for the boy; a secure and respected place in society, influential friends and family. In short, all the attributes to forge ahead. But life and events were to dictate otherwise.

IN THE EARLY 1950s, elements of Kenya's predominant Kikuyu tribe rebelled against the whites who had settled the country and the terrorist movement known as the Mau Mau was born. Their murderous campaign on an unsuspecting population was conducted with a fury and savagery so intense that the country was left reeling with shock. Not only the whites were subjected to the horror in their midst. To ensure loyalty among their own people, many Kikuyu suspected of harbouring goodwill and faithfulness to their white employers were forced to endure hideous "oathing" ceremonies where it was not uncommon for them to be forced to butcher members of their own families and eat certain body parts. To the Western mind, these acts were incomprehensible and abhorrent. To the Mau Mau, it was an invaluable tool in their fight to oust the white man. In the African psyche, steeped in witchcraft and magic, these oathings, however unwillingly taken, were more binding than any oath or law a European could devise.

More binding, in fact, than life itself.

Of all this, Raymond knew nothing. Young children have no place for adults and their politics. Theirs is a world of chasing butterflies and magic, warm sunshine and lemonade. Parents and servants alike loved the young boy, whose constant questions amused them. He learned as much about the Africans and their ways as he did about his own people. The household servants would cluck and fuss and laugh hysterically at Raymond's antics as he delved and explored and experimented. Black and white alike admired his frank open-ness and trusting ways.

There was only one exception to this; perhaps in a strange foresight of events to come, Ray had a secret hideaway in the roof. It was surprising that the African servants, normally very observant, had not noticed his surreptitious comings and goings as the youngster secreted odd bits and pieces into his hiding place. Entry to the roof had been gained by shinning up the tree near the house and climbing along a branch. The deft removal of a couple of tiles and he was in. With cast-off pieces of timber and cardboard left in the attic space, Ray had fashioned a comfortable platform from which he could watch activities in the living room through a tiny opening next to the lightfitting in the ceiling.

Lately the Africans had become increasingly surly and moody. Not just the servants, but everyone in the area. Even Mugo the cook, who was genuinely affectionate to the Hunters, had become distant and uncommunicative. Ray did not know why his friends wouldn't play with him, so he played on his own more and more.

The Mau Mau came for Mrs Hunter and her son one afternoon a few days before Raymond's sixth birthday. The residence, situated far enough from Nairobi to be reasonably isolated but near enough for Jack Hunter's daily commute into town, suited the Hunters well. It also suited the terrorist gang's purpose. The choice of the Hunter family had not been by chance. Jack Hunter had been instrumental in the conviction and execution of several Mau Mau members and they had a very large bone to pick with him. The timing of the attack was not coincidental either. Much as they hated Jack Hunter, they were afraid of him. He was as tireless in the hunting down of the Mau Mau in his spare time with the local militia, as he was in bringing the same men to justice in the courts. Many a Kikuyu gangster had good cause to rue the day they came up against him.

The attack was to take place while Jack was at work in town and Maureen and her son were alone.

Ray was playing in the large garden, emulating his hero, Allan Quartermain — Rider Haggard's hero from "King Solomon's Mines" — which he had seen at the drive-in cinema two nights earlier. He was busy fighting a huge, ferocious lion — a large stuffed toy bear — with his bare hands. Gradually, he became aware that something was wrong. Nothing tangible, just a sense of foreboding. Perhaps it was the stillness. Where were the servants, going about their business? There seemed to be nobody about. Where was Jomo, their big Rhodesian Ridgeback? The dog was usually somewhere nearby. Although the sun was shining, the air seemed cold.

It was the sounds coming from the servants' quarters that gave the source of the trouble away. He did not know what they were, but even in his young mind, Ray knew something was wrong, terribly wrong.

They were, in fact, the sounds of the messy slaughter of Mugo.

Mugo had been sitting by the fire in the cooking room for a while. He was in a quandary. He knew of the plan to murder Mrs Hunter and the boy. He did not know when it would take place, but that it was imminent. He wanted to warn them. They had treated him well and he was fond of them — but he was afraid of the Mau Mau. His superstitious mind told him that the Mau Mau would know if he warned them. If only there was some way he could pass the information without actually telling them. It was a big problem and he had been pondering over it for days. Mugo heard the door creak open and silhouetted in the frame stood Kamau, his sister's son.

"Hello Uncle, we have come to pay our respects," said Kamau. The words were in keeping with the formal greeting, but there was malice in the voice. Kamau's eyes were glazed and Mugo knew what the panga in his nephew's hand was for.

Kamau had been an easy recruit into the ranks of the Mau Mau; young enough to be torn between two worlds. On the one hand, his uncle's world, with thousands of years of tradition, unchanging, with the dignity and respect of one who has his place in a well-ordered society. On the other, a tantalising new world with glittering possessions and wealth. After a smattering of education, Kamau began to covet the white man's ways and belongings which, until now, had been beyond his reach. The Mau Mau gave him the opportunity to take that about which otherwise he could only dream.

It had been decided that Mugo must be eliminated. His loyalty to the cause was in question. Who better to do it than Kamau, his own nephew, and the leader of this particular band. Although Kikuyu on his mother's side, Kamau had Matabele blood from his father, who had travelled to Kenya from Southern Rhodesia with a missionary named Taggart. This mixed ethnic background had stood both for and against him in his rise to prominence in the Mau Mau. The Kikuyu viewed him with slight suspicion because he was part foreigner, but his natural leadership qualities, derived from his Matabele warrior lineage, overrode the xenophobic tendencies of his half-relatives. He had gained the respect of his comrades through ability alone.

The date of the attack had been withheld deliberately from Mugo, who remained seated on the floor of the small pole-and-dagga hut. He knew why Kamau had come and accepted his fate with the stoicism of his race. He remained squatting as his nephew raised the heavy panga. "Goodbye Uncle," hissed Kamau as the blade flashed downward, splitting Mugo's skull open like a ripe watermelon, spilling brains and blood to the earthen floor. The frenzied, awful assault continued until the air was heavy with the sweet, unmistakable smell of fresh blood and all that remained of Mugo was a dozen or so sticky lumps of flesh and bone.

Meanwhile, Raymond was making his way back to the house. Fearing instinctively that he might be seen, he crawled and darted from cover to cover until he reached the back door. Once inside, he raced to his mother's sewing room where Maureen was busy making a dress.

"Mummy, Mummy, come quickly," he urged, tugging at her arm.

"Not now darling, you can see I'm busy," she admonished.

"No Mummy, please come," he persisted, tugging at her arm again. If Maureen hadn't been so preoccupied with her own thoughts that day, she would have sensed the urgency in her son's voice. As it was, she dismissed the cajoling as another of his games.

"Raymond, I've told you about interrupting Mummy when she's busy. Now go and play like a good boy." Ray turned away, but at the door, he tried again. "Please Mu...," he pleaded. Maureen's quick temper rose. "Raymond, go to your room now, and think about what I've just said."

Ray slammed the door and ran into the corridor. He didn't know what to do. Should he obey his mother and go to his room? He was torn between a child's ingrained trust and obedience to his parents, and the need to flee from the danger he sensed but could not understand or explain. The decision he made was to save his life. He scaled the tree next to the house, lifted the two tiles, slipped into the attic, replaced the tiles and lay still in his ceiling hideaway.

Maureen heard the soft knock at the front door. A short time later she heard the knock again. Mugo usually answered the door, perhaps he was over at his quarters.

"Just a minute," she called, putting her sewing on the hall table. "Now, who could that be at this time of the day," she thought to herself. The knock came again, polite but insistent.

"How am I ever going to finish this dress with all these interruptions?" she muttered under her breath as she opened the door. She vaguely recognised the tall Kikuyu as a relative of Mugo.

"Yes?" she asked, annoyed at the insolent smile on his face.

"Jambo, Memsahib," replied Kamau, his sly grin showing even white teeth. It was then Maureen noticed the panga in his hand and the fact he was not alone. There were several other Africans standing behind him. A stab of fear shot through her and she realised she should have remembered the pistol tucked away in her handbag.

"Yes, what do you want?" she asked again, backing away from the door and kicking it closed as she turned and ran. Before the terrified woman could take more than a few steps, the door burst open and she was knocked to the floor. Maureen tried to get up but Kamau was on to her. He grabbed her neck in his big hands and pulled her into the living room.

"Get your hands off me, you filthy bastard." Maureen's fear was tinged with anger now. His only reply was a slap that sent her spinning to the floor. "Go and find the boy," Kamau ordered three of his men. "Find him quickly, there is not much time." They left, disgruntled, not wanting to miss out on the sport they knew was about to begin. Kamau turned back to Maureen.

"Do it," he commanded. The Africans grabbed the struggling, and by now terrified, woman and held her on the floor while they tore the clothes from her body. Maureen, in her mid-thirties, was still very attractive, with firm, round buttocks, strong, lithe legs and a narrow waist that would make any woman half her age envious. Her walk was bouncy and invigorating. She knew men stared at her when she passed by. She enjoyed their admiration even though she was fiercely loyal to her husband. Some Africans wanted white women because they were unattainable. Most men wanted Maureen because she was desirable. Kamau was no exception. He had watched the white woman often and dreamed about the day he would have her. The Mau Mau gave him that chance. It was Kamau who had pushed for and planned this particular raid.

From his ceiling hideaway, the boy looked on in silent horror as the Africans took their turn at Maureen. He watched his mother writhing and thrashing around on the floor as, one by one, they knelt between her legs and rammed their swollen members into her, the only lubrication coming from the previous assailant's semen and the blood flowing from her torn membranes. He watched the others, laughing and trembling with excitement as they forced her legs apart and held her down. When her struggling became too violent, they would stun her back into submission, not enough to render her unconscious, that would defeat the object, just enough to make their fun easier.

Then came Kamau's turn. Here was the woman he had wanted for so long, lying on the floor in front of him, naked, bleeding and helpless. No longer unavailable. He had been watching the scene unfold with mounting excitement. His eyes were hot with lust, his mind and body burning with desire. He shook like a man with a fever. His member, rigid and engorged with blood, felt as though it would explode.

"OFF," he shouted to his men. His breath was coming in short, ragged gasps and his chest felt so tight it might suffocate him. As they let Maureen go, he kicked her in the stomach, grunting in satisfaction as she doubled over. He flipped her on to her front, exposing her round, white backside. Using his feet, he spread her legs wide apart. With eyes fast glazing over in ecstasy, he plunged himself into her vulnerable anus, tearing both it and a scream of pure agony from the woman writhing on the ground beneath him. It lasted only a short while until Kamau spent himself savagely into the body of the now unconscious Maureen. Unsteadily he stood up, his mind reeling from the enormity of what he had just done while roughly wiping the blood, faeces and semen from his half-erect penis with a piece of torn dress. Gradually, his eyes began to focus again; he was slowly coming back to reality.

The three men returned from their search for Ray and stood in front of their leader.

"Where is the boy?" Kamau demanded.

"We can't find him," answered Kathigi, the second in command. "He must have got away and is going to warn others."

"Why can't I leave you baboons to do even a simple job," snapped Kamau. "How can one small boy escape three grown men?"

"We looked everywhere," defended Kathigi. "We can't even find spoor. He is gone."

"Never mind. We don't have much time left," he answered. "Right, you know what to do. Do it. "NO, there is no time for that," snapped Kamau to one of the men who was looking expectantly at Maureen. They had missed all the fun.

"The white men will be coming shortly, so hurry." While the rest of the men ransacked the house, Kamau began on his speciality. He rolled Maureen on to her back and his panga began its work: first slashing the insides of her thighs, sending bright spurts of arterial blood in all directions. The next stroke was in-between the legs, cleaving the pubic bone in two, destroying the genitals. The fourth slash was a disembowelling stroke, opening up Maureen's stomach, spilling her entrails up over the gaping bloody wound. As he started on her breasts, Maureen's back arched and she gave a great shudder, her head thrown back in a silent scream. At the same moment, she seemed to stare straight at her son, hidden in the ceiling. Ray was transfixed as he watched the life leave his mother's eyes, to be replaced by the cold emptiness of death. Still Kamau's panga flashed up and down, up and down, until Maureen's body was hacked into almost unrecognisable pieces. Only then was he satisfied.

When the house was well and truly ransacked, the gang prepared to leave. Before they departed, they had one more task to complete. This was left to Watoto, so named because of his small size. The man called "Child" had two British army hand grenades, stolen from the barracks some months before. He had been briefed on how to set up a simple, but effective, booby trap. The M30, or "pineapple", grenade is issued in a close-fitting cylindrical container. If the safety pin comes out accidentally while the grenade is still in the container, the firing level remains held in place. If the grenade slips out of the container, the spring-loaded lever will fly off, detonating it in seconds. Rigging up the booby trap was simplicity itself and Watoto went about it with great relish. It made him feel important to be entrusted with such a task. First he discarded the lids of the containers, next he tied them horizontally to the legs of the heavy chair next to the door. A thin, almost invisible, fishing line was tied to the neck of each grenade, strung across and tied to the bottom hinges of the door. The lines were now stretched across the door through which Jack would enter. The last task was to ease out the grenades just enough to pull the pins out, then push them back in. The trap was set. Two grenades were used where one may have sufficed, but then Jack Hunter was a cunning adversary and they wanted to be sure.

Finally, the *piece de resistance*. The phone call to Jack's office in Nairobi. "Hunter and Associates, Jack here," said Jack after the receptionist had put the call through.

"Bwana Hunter, there is trouble with Memsahib Hunter at the house," said Kamau in his best servant's voice. "Please come quick, bad trouble." Kamau hung up.

The gang hardly heard the whining of the big black dog at the back door as they left. The dog knew Kamau and had come trustingly up to him for a pat. Somehow, the dog had survived the savage blows to the head and the disembowelment, and had tried to get into the house, dragging its entrails behind it.

Meanwhile, Jack was busy. He hurriedly dialled a number. "Kenya Safaris, George Selby here," said the voice at the other end of the line.

"George, this is Jack. I've got trouble at home. Get hold of the police and the rest of the boys from our AT unit and get out there quick."

"OK you got it. We'll be there ASAP. Be careful." The phone went dead and Jack was gone. Cursing at every delay as he weaved through the traffic, Jack hurried through town. Once on the outskirts he accelerated until the car was racing along at breakneck speed. Even so, it was thirty-five minutes before he came to a screeching halt in front of the house.

JACK HUNTER BOUNDED out of the car, knowing something was wrong as soon as he saw the front door ajar. Caution returned as he entered the hallway and he began using the skill that had earned him the respect of friend and foe alike. It took him only a few seconds to locate his wife's remains, lying in the blood and gore that covered the living room. Just when he needed them most, his legendary coolness and self control under adverse conditions abandoned him. He gave a choked cry as he rushed through the door to look at Maureen's mutilated form. Such was his horror, he didn't feel the tripwires as his leg swept through them, pulling the grenades out of their containers. He did, however, hear a sound with which he was all too familiar — the "ping and crack" of the levers as they sprung off and detonated the little M30s. Even then, his mind and body refused to work coherently. He stood dumbly, looking at his wife and back to the grenades lying on the floor. The few precious moments left to save himself were lost and the four-second fuses did the job they were designed to. Jack Hunter's body was flung across his wife's corpse, shattered and broken.

George Selby had wasted no time in getting the Anti-Terrorist unit together, arriving only fifteen minutes after Jack, and a few before the police. He stood at the door of the living room, fighting a wave of revulsion that swept over him.

Cautiously, stunned by the scene they had found, the police and Jack's friends began searching the house, looking for young Ray.

While they were sifting gingerly through the living room, a soft moan could be heard from above. George looked up.

"Quick, get a ladder, the boy must be up there somewhere," he said to one of the policemen. They soon found the half-conscious child in the hiding place that had saved him. Although badly concussed and with the wind knocked out of him, the layers of cardboard and timber had saved Ray from serious injury. They carried the battered and traumatised child to a Police Land-Rover for the drive to Nairobi Hospital.

The last thing Ray saw before falling into a shock-induced sleep was the merciful putting down of his beloved Ridgeback.

THE PLANE TOUCHED down at Salisbury airport and the passengers began to disembark. Bridget was standing on the tarmac, bidding farewell to people as they reached the bottom of the steps.

"Goodbye, Mr Jones. Bye, Mr and Mrs Hart. Hope you enjoyed the flight. Goodbye, Mr Hunter. Thank you for flying Air Rhodesia."

This time there was a cheeky grin on his face which made him look like a naughty schoolboy.

"Thank you, Bridget. It was a wonderful flight," Ray replied. Bridget found herself smiling back at him with a genuine warmth. He certainly was a mixture, this one.

"A girl would have to be careful with him around," she thought. He gave her a flirtatious wink and he was gone. Later, when the crew had completed formalities and passed through customs, they were driven to Meikles Hotel, where they were booked in for the night. Bridget rang her parents, who lived in the small town overlooking Lake Kariba in the country's north. She wouldn't have time to go up and see them as she was on the early flight back to Johannesburg in the morning. After a shower to freshen up, Bridget went down to the lounge area to wait for her friend Mary, the other hostess on the flight. They planned to dine in the hotel's restaurant and then see a movie in town. She didn't have to look up to know who the man standing beside her was.

"G'day, could you spare a bit of company for a lonely boy who is far away from home." The Australian twang was unmistakable, although she thought she detected something else in the voice. A hint of breeding? There seemed to be a bit of culture buried in the background. She looked up into his direct gaze, slightly annoyed by his presumptuousness.

"Thank you, no, I am waiting for a friend."

"Would it hurt to converse with one who is already smitten by your great beauty? One who would gladly be your slave, at your beck and call?" She couldn't help smiling at the obviously insincere flattery.

"I won't bite and I promise I'll be a good boy and shove off as soon as your friend arrives."

"Oh all right, but I warn you, you are wasting your time."

"Any time spent in your company, beautiful lady, cannot be a waste," Ray replied, giving her one of his most disarming smiles.

Even though she was wary and on guard, within twenty minutes Bridget was completely relaxed and feeling comfortable with his easy manner. They fenced lightly with each other, a verbal thrust and parry, and she found him to be knowledgeable on most subjects, with an extremely sharp wit that had her laughing often. She realised she was enjoying herself and was almost sorry when she saw Mary approaching their table.

"Ah here's your friend. I'd better be off then," said Ray, standing up.

"Hi, Bridget, sorry I'm late," said Mary. "I just had a call from my boyfriend. He's out of the bush and in town and is coming to pick me up shortly, so I won't be able to have dinner with you. I can't disappoint him, haven't seen him in ages."

"Oh okay, you lucky thing. Have lots of fun. See you in the morning."

"Fully intend to. Why don't you two go out for dinner?" Mary said in parting, casting a glance in Ray's direction. Then she was gone.

"Yes, what a good idea, a pity to waste an evening," Ray said, looking directly into Bridget's eyes.

"Boy, you don't give up do you?" Bridget retorted. But she was smiling.

Dinner was a pleasant affair. The Manhattan restaurant, famous for its Portuguese steak cooked with olives, lived up to its reputation. Afterwards, Bridget showed Ray around some of the night-spots, where they danced the hours away. Even though he was polite and stuck rigidly to correct social etiquette, Bridget could sense the animal magnetism in him. At first it disturbed her, but he was not pushy and she gradually began to relax and drift with it, enjoying the unhurried sensuality. Feelings that she had kept in the background for the more than twelve months since her last relationship, began to well to the surface. She started to respond to him and the warm closeness of their bodies made her feel heady. Later, when he walked her to her hotel room, she was past caring about her usually strict code of moral behaviour and left the door open for him.

Their lovemaking was urgent and completely consuming. Ray seemed to know every little thing that would arouse her as though by instinct. He brought her to the peaks of ecstasy, playing her like a finely tuned violin. She was too far gone, too euphoric, to realise that this man did not know real love and lust was the nearest he could come to it. She only knew that he seemed to make her a complete woman, something which had definitely been lacking until that night. When at last they fell into an exhausted sleep, she felt fulfilled.

The early wake-up call jangled harshly in her ears and she groggily answered the telephone. After putting the receiver down, she looked over to where he had lain. He was gone. In his place was a rose. She wondered idly where he had got it. It was then she realised with certainty that she would probably never see him again.

"Oh God, what have I done?" she thought. "I've given myself to a guy I don't even know." But as she lay there reflecting on last night's happenings, she knew that both in and out of bed, he had made her feel the most important woman in the world and had certainly given her something she would not forget for a long while. She just hoped she would not be disappointed with the future men in her life. She knew she should feel guilty, but relaxing in the afterglow of what had been really beautiful lovemaking, she could feel nothing but peaceful serenity. She couldn't help wondering, however, about the contradictory nature of the man who had been her lover for so short a time. He was well versed in all the social graces, he was polite and attentive, which seemed totally at odds with the hardness of him. She had felt it at times throughout the night. It was not just the hardness of his body, but his spirit. Perhaps that was part of his attraction. Whatever it was, she knew that he would be dangerous.

THE BOY WAS put in the care of John and Mary Winter, the couple who had agreed to become his Godparents at a party one afternoon when the booze was flowing freely and goodwill to all men and eternal friendships were sworn in the false sense of well-being that comes from gregarious get-togethers.

The Winters were a mismatched pair: he an older, successful toy manufacturer; she much younger and attractive in a decadent sort of way. She had married John for his money and the plush lifestyle it offered. Their sex life was almost non-existent and Mary sought solace in the beds of anyone who took her fancy. They were a selfish pair and bought their friends with constant parties and free booze. They took the boy unwillingly out of a grudging sense of duty. Neither had wanted children because it would have cramped their lifestyle. Ray grew up more or less on his own.

He did not lack for material things, Jack had provided adequately for his future. But the Winters simply didn't have time for him. He was a nuisance. After the Mau Mau had been quashed, the servants came back and life went on as before. The Africans took Ray under their wing and he had, in a small measure at least, someone who cared about him. He learned about the African and his ways. What it had taken from him, Africa gave back in another form. Knowledge. Knowledge that would stand him in good stead later. His schooling suffered through lack of interest and when he was sent to one of England's top boarding schools, as his father had planned, it was a wild colonial boy who was thrown into a bastion of English society. Because he was different, the other boys picked on him. They tormented him and hounded him. Later on, when the fists started flying, he had no defence. He was always outnumbered and the punishment was frequent. He became withdrawn, sullen and reclusive. A young boy, lost in a cold, wet and hostile environment. His African mentors had taught him the art of hiding inside and he became good at it. He could withdraw from the taunts and the jibes, but he was afraid of the fists. It was not so much the pain as the concussion that often followed a heavy blow from one of the bigger boys. The disorientation and memory lapses were frightening, especially when there was no one to turn to. Stoically, he accepted the canings from teachers when he came to class with black eyes and split lips, and the further punishments when he refused to tell them who had done it. They could not get inside this strange boy, and what people don't understand, they don't trust. So there was no rapport between Ray and his teachers either.

There was one brief burst of sunshine that came into his life one weekend — his Aunt Tatt. The Hunter clan was scattered widely, with only one family anywhere near enough to the school to visit. Mick and Tatt Croft were in their forties. Mick had been battling illness for many years and could not get about much. Tatt, out of curiosity as much as anything, decided to visit the nephew she had never seen. A plump, round-faced, homely woman, she recognised the hurt, confusion and loneliness in her kin straight away and took him into her heart. She did not coo and cluck and fuss, she sensed it was not what Ray needed. But she was there for him. She visited often and they went for long walks together. She let him talk when he wanted to. He did not seem to be able to cope with too much close physical contact, so she did not press it.

They quickly developed a strong spiritual bond and would sit together on the river banks, happy in the warmth and peace of each other's company. Ray spent his first holiday in England with his Aunt and for the first time in many years, felt happy and reasonably content.

But the school of hard knocks had not finished with him yet. One Saturday, he was waiting at the front gate for her. The afternoon was cloudy and overcast, cold drizzle hinted at worse weather to come. The touch on Ray's shoulder was firm but gentle. It was the maths teacher. Mr Baker had seen something of the potential in the boy, but like the rest of the staff had been unable to get through to him. Instead of writing him off, however, he had at least kept trying.

"Ray." His voice was gentle. "Your Aunty won't be coming to visit you." He paused, not wanting to carry on.

"She has been in an accident."

Ray stared ahead as if he had not heard.

"I'm afraid your Aunty died on the way to hospital.

"She won't be able to visit you," he added lamely, trying to say something of comfort but not knowing what. The boy simply shrugged the teacher's hand off his shoulder and walked away into the drizzling rain. No tears, no words, nothing except a numb emptiness. The teacher watched him helplessly, there was nothing he could do.

Normally, Ray would have taken another way back to the dormitory. He seldom went past the shelter near the cricket oval because that was where Robert Knight and his cronies loafed about. Robert was big and solid and attracted the normal sorts that hang around bullies. It was he who took most delight in baiting the "kid from the colonies".

"Hey, look who's here. It's the monkey from the trees."

"BAHOO, BAHOO," his gang shouted in chorus, imitating the sound of a monkey.

"Where are you going, you little ape?"

Ray just kept walking.

"Hey, I'm talking to you, you white jiggaboo."

Ray kept walking. Robert jumped in front of him, raising a fist. What he saw stopped him in his tracks. Instead of the meek, frightened little boy he expected, he saw white-hot anger blazing in Ray's eyes. At the same time, he felt all the breath go out of him, as a powerful punch drove into his solar plexus. He felt teeth break and blood spurt as that same fist drove upwards into his mouth with a savage uppercut, as he doubled over in pain from the first blow. As with many people who use their size to intimidate, Robert had no real substance. He had never had to back his claims. This showed all too clearly as Ray continued to rain blow after blow into his head. Skin split and blood began to flow freely as the bigger boy went down, trying vainly to cover his face with his hands.

The other boys, initially taken as much by surprise as Robert by this sudden turnaround, kept their distance. But they soon realised Robert was going to get hurt badly if they didn't do something. They went in to pull him off. What they found in their midst was a snapping, snarling whirlwind of angry fury as Ray punched, kicked and headbutted into them.

By the end of the fight, everyone was scratched, cut or bruised to some extent. By now, the anger had left the young boy but he stood, chest heaving, bloodied but still defiant in the middle of his suitably awed antagonists.

After the fight, the other boys left him alone, even treated him with respect. He never became particularly gregarious, seeming content with his own council, but a gradual change came over him. He began to assimilate the English middle class's manners and courtesies. Although never more than average academically, he excelled at sport. The teachers believed they were winning with their previously difficult pupil. But it was not they who were winning. Those few moments of blinding anger had taught Ray a valuable lesson. He had learned to fight back. For most of his life, he had been dealt a dismal deck of cards. A deck of cards he had not known how to deal. Now, it was as if knew that he was destined to have to push against heavy odds, and to survive was going to have to push back. Hard. He had also begun to realise that being an out-sider was going to get him nowhere, so he blended in with his sur-roundings and became successful at it. A bit like the boy who was made to sit down against his wishes by his mother. He said: "I might be sitting down on the outside, but I'm standing on the inside."

The boy whose heart was in the warmth and wide open spaces of his native Africa became, on the outside at least, a well-spoken product of English gentry.

Allowed to return to Kenya for school holidays, by the time he was approaching his sixteenth birthday he noticed that Mary was taking quite a bit of interest in him. Naive as he was, he knew it was not the interest of a mother to son. She was always seeking him out, wanted to be near him, touching him. He did not understand the longing in her eyes. Innocent he might have been, but his healthy young body began to react to the signals Mary was sending and when she seduced him, he was putty in her hands. There was no love, just lust. To Mary, he was a new and exciting toy, to be played with and enjoyed. His inexperience made him easy to mould.

Being a selfish woman, she was demanding. In her naked greed and hunger for his body, she unwittingly taught him many secrets until she became an open book. The tables turned swiftly and it was she who was now putty in his hands. Once Ray had started to learn life's lessons, he learned them quickly.

He soon became an artist in the game of love. He could read subtle gestures, nuances and take what he wanted from women. It is possible that he was never fully aware of the power he had. He never flaunted it or became boastful. He just knew that when he wanted something, he usually got it.

After finishing school, Ray wandered around the UK doing odd jobs with no particular purpose in mind. After a while, longing for warmth and open spaces, he requested and received from his foster parents the last of his inheritance, with which he bought a one-way ticket to Perth, Western Australia. It seemed to be the obvious choice.

Africa did not have any promise for a single, white boy. At least Australia appeared to hold a future.

Ray found the sunshine and space he was seeking, but lacked the skills and maturity to obtain a job. Within two months, his remaining money was gone and he found himself hocking the last of a few belongings to pay for food. He exchanged a boarding house for a sleeping bag in which he rolled a couple of pairs of underpants and a toothbrush.

He slept in the bush for several weeks, only going into town to look for work and to buy food when he was very hungry. He washed when he could find a tap.

On one of these sojourns, he happened to walk past an army recruiting office. On the off chance, he went inside.

"Yes, mate. What can I do for you?" asked the recruiting sergeant behind the desk. Ray almost blurted out the truth and said, "I'm hungry and I need a job". Instead he replied, "I am looking for adventure and travel. I understand this is the place to come".

The army took the fit young man into her ranks and moulded him. On the parade ground and in the bush, she taught him the demands and challenges of a soldier. He passed out as the outstanding recruit of his intake, attentive in the lecture room and skilled in warfare at basic training at Kapooka in New South Wales.

As an infantryman, he was posted to the Second Battalion, Royal Australian Regiment, where for the remainder of his three years' service, he practised and honed the skills taught to him by the military.

After serving his time, Ray became a civilian again, travelling around the country working at odd jobs; once more without direction. He adapted well to the Australian way of life and although he developed the nasal twang of the Australian, he still maintained the slightly polished speech and manners of the English gentlemen he had been as a teenager.

He also became adept at the Australian custom of hard drinking and barroom brawling, and before long was known as being a good bloke to have around in a rough and tumble. With women, however, it was different. His English sense of correctness and manners was a hit with them, a fact that got him into more trouble than he would care to admit.

He took up parachuting, revelling in the danger and feeling of freedom it brought, and quickly notched up several hundred freefall jumps.

Carefree and happy-go-lucky though he seemed on the outside, Ray Hunter was becoming increasingly frustrated. He needed a sense of purpose, and there appeared to be none. That is, until the bush war in Rhodesia began to become more and more newsworthy. Visions and nightmares that had been forced into the background started to crowd back into his consciousness. The easygoing, light-hearted manner changed.

There was now a determined set to his jaw and the lights of amusement and humour that often twinkled in his eyes were replaced by a hard, cold stare that frightened people.

One Commando

Ray quit the fishing trawler where he had been working as a deck hand and purchased another airline ticket. This time back to the land of his birth. Africa.

Chapter Two

For two months the Rhodesian Army had been patrolling the dry, sandy, sparsely populated area to the south of Malvernia, a few kilometres from the Mozambique border.

It was a vast, hot, inhospitable place. Home only to flies, elephants, a very few people and, lately, terrorists. Reports had been coming in on a regular basis that the terrs were infiltrating into the area from Mozambique. It was ideal country in which to move with little risk of detection. For the most part flat and featureless, in many places thick scrub made it easy to hide from searching eyes. Water was scarce and unless one knew where to find it, it was a foolhardy place to be. Death would come easily and swiftly to the unwary.

Yes, it was ideal country to move through to get to the more populated areas north to spread the doctrine of terror. For the most part the terrs had come into the country from further north, through more populated areas. That, coupled with the hilly terrain, had made it easier to locate the terrs as they moved from village to village. The observation posts on the hills had been able to pick them up from their vantage points and bring them to contact.

Most of the groups had been poorly trained and not very motivated. But lately, a new breed of terrorist had been emerging. These were better trained, more motivated and aggressive. It was these men the Rhodesian Army was hunting down. They were determined and elusive. These "hard core" terrorists, as they were becoming known, were giving the Rhodesian security forces a tough time. Although they were obeying their Russian and Chinese instructors' directions to "strike at soft targets" (civilians and farmers), then disappear "like fishes in the sea" and blend in with the local population, they were fighting back when cornered instead of running or giving up. The security forces knew they had been in a fight when up against these blokes.

A Rhodesia Regiment territorial section of four reservists, led by Lance Corporal Dave McEvoy, were at the end of a 10-day patrol of a sparsely populated area 20 kilometres from the Mozambique border.

They'd seen bush, bush and more bush; an occasional elephant, startled kudu and mopane flies — millions of them. These tiny, black insects, actually a species of native bee, got into hair, eyes, up nostrils and down throats in an effort to sip moisture. Dave's territorial section was hot, thirsty, tired and bored. Call-ups for part-timers were becoming more and more frequent, meaning that men like McEvoy and his section had to leave jobs, businesses and families to spend a large chunk of the year traipsing around godforsaken corners of the land.

"Why can't the regulars do this shitty work? They're volunteers and get paid well for it," complained Tony Scott. He resented being separated from his wife and kids more than the rest of them. It was his favourite gripe, and he started up as soon as they sat down to rest from the midday sun in a scrap of shade under a scrawny acacia.

"For fuck's sake, Tony, put a sock in it," snapped Dave, who was as tired and irritable as the rest of them. "We're here because we're told to be here. Now shut up and let me work out our possie for the SITREP (Situation Report)."

Noting the grid references, he picked up the radio handset. "Hello Three, this is Three One. How do you read? Over."

"Three One, Three, reading you strength four, over," came the scratchy reply.

"Roger, Three. Sitrep as follows." Dave gave the section's grid reference and signed off with, "November Tango Romeo (nothing to report), out."

The four men rested in the shade until the midday heat had passed. "OK buggers, let's move out," said Dave, getting to his feet and hoisting the heavy pack to his shoulders. Grumbling and complaining, the others kitted up and moved out in single file.

They almost missed the tracks in the sand. Steve Grobler, in the lead, was looking at tree level and missed them. Dave almost stepped on them as he checked the compass, but his peripheral vision over the edge of it stopped him in time.

"PSSST," he hissed a warning and gave the silent signal for spoor. The rest of the section went to ground in the nearest cover. After checking the area thoroughly, Dave positioned Nick, the big, burly machinegunner, to cover the direction of the tracks. The other men were placed in covering defence.

"Three. This is Three One. Do you copy?"

The reply came almost immediately. "Three One, Three. Reading your fives, over."

"Three. Located spoor of approximately eight within 100 of last LOCSTAT, heading north-west. Spoor checks like Charlie Tangos. Commencing follow up to get a more definite direction, over."

"Roger. How old? Over."

"Difficult to tell," said Dave. "A few hours perhaps. Over."

"Roger. Follow up, but avoid contact, I say again, avoid contact.

We'll send India Alpha Foxtrot (*that week's code word for the RLI*) to assist you. Copy?"

"Roger, copied that. We'll keep you informed on any developments. Over."

"Three, good luck, out."

JASON NCUBE CAME from a long line of warriors, the Matabele, who are direct descendants of the Zulus. During Shaka's reign, one of his lieutenants, Mzilikazi, refused to pay his tribute of a percentage of cattle after a raid. Shaka sent his Impis (fighting units) to bring him to heel. Mzilikazi fled northwards, eluding Shaka's army, and eventually settled in the Matopos Hills in what is now south-west Zimbabwe.

The name Matabele means "he who hides behind a big shield". During their exodus, Mzilikazi and his followers waged war with everyone in their path, gradually absorbing other tribes as they went along. These tribes were new to the Zulu method of fighting, which was to crouch down behind their large cowhide shields as their enemies threw their spears, before rushing them and killing them with the short stabbing spear made famous by Shaka himself.

The Matabele were as warlike as their southern cousins; the 1896 rebellions in the new colony against Rhodes' British South Africa Company forces bore this out.

Jason Ncube was no exception; like many of his tribe, he was tall and broad-shouldered, with aristocratic good looks that spoke of a long line of good breeding. Brought up on a Catholic mission, he soon saw the hypocrisy of a people who expected him to copy their ways and behaviour and yet, with a naive arrogance, demanded him to kow-tow and be subservient. He learned their ways, but it was not for the glory of civilised man and his God that he was getting to know his enemy.

In December 1961, the non-tribal Zimbabwe African Peoples Union (ZAPU) movement, led by Joshua Nkomo, began a deliberate campaign of rioting and rebellion in Rhodesia. The party was banned, but gangs of political thugs roamed the townships and intimidation was rife. British South Africa Police units did well to contain the growing unrest as it spread to rural areas, where crops were burned and cattle maimed.

Disorganisation was rife and compounded in August 1963, when the Reverend Ndabaningi Sithole led a breakaway faction and formed the mainly Shona Zimbabwe African National Union (ZANU). This split was to dominate African politics and the course of the struggle in Rhodesia/Zimbabwe until the late 1980s.

In the 15 months to November 1965, rioting and banditry escalated. Then, five days before Ian Smith's Unilateral Declaration of Independence on November 11, a National State of Emergency was declared.

For the next three years, the flames of African nationalism in Rhodesia were fanned by events taking place elsewhere in post-colonial Africa. Small groups of Chinese-trained guerillas began to enter the country across the Zambezi Valley near Mana Pools in the north of the country, and below Victoria Falls from their bases near Lusaka, the Zambian capital.

Some penetrated to the centre of Rhodesia and even as far as Chiredzi in the extreme south-east. But for the effective police containment of the supportive, though small peasant *Zhanda* (people's militia) groups in some rural areas, these early guerillas might have been more effective.

On April 28, 1966, seven ZANU guerillas were killed in a contact with security forces near the northern town of Sinoia — an event later commemorated by the Zimbabwe African National Liberation Army (ZANLA) as "Chimurenga Day" — the start of the second armed rebellion against the white settlers. It was the beginning of an on-off guerilla war that was to last nearly fourteen years.

For Rhodesians, the bush war really only started in December, 1972, when two European farms in the Centenary district of north-east Rhodesia were attacked by a small but ineffective group of terrorists led by the man who would one day head ZANLA, Rex Nhongo.

In these early days, Jason Ncube was a willing and eager recruit. His natural talent and ability as a leader were soon recognised and he was sent to Tanzania for training. The Chinese Red Army instructors, in turn, recognised his intelligence and capacity to learn and under their expert guidance, he quickly became well versed in the art of terrorism.

Talented though he was, Jason Ncube still had to learn the realities of war the hard way. In these early days, the terrorists were being badly mauled by Rhodesia's security forces as they moved through populated areas. Observation Points (OPs) spotted them easily from hilltops, and the unpoliticised locals informed the authorities on a regular basis. Posters outlining rewards for the successfull capture of terrorists and arms of war brought great results and made the insurgents' work that much harder.

They found themselves up against a small but highly efficient, well-disciplined and extremely motivated army and those first years were fraught with danger for the infiltrators. As the Mau Mau before them, they soon found that a low-scale guerilla war was not popular with rural peasants. They were hard pressed getting recruits and lost many men in combat. At that stage, the Rhodesians were winning.

Jason Ncube had been up against the security forces many times. On nearly every occasion, he and his men were severely hit by their opponents, whose superior training, motivation and weaponry outmatched those of his rag-tag unit. He had been wounded twice but somehow managed to get away each time. But the tall Matabele's survival skills were honed with each day he survived and he attracted a cadre of men who, like himself, were skilled and dedicated to the cause. In time, Jason's name was familiar to the Rhodesians. He was a thorn in their side.

The period between 1968 and 1974 was characterised by ineffective and sporadic hits on soft targets; the indiscriminate mining of farm roads and border areas and infrequent clashes with the security forces as the terrorists quietly, but effectively, consolidated their support in the north-east and south-east rural areas close to the Mozambique border. A short-lived ceasefire in mid-1974 only added to the overall perception of the country's white population that there was little to worry about.

In mid-1975, General Spinola's coup toppled the government in Lisbon and within days the Portuguese beat an undignified and hasty retreat from their colonial outpost. Samora Machel's FRELIMO guerilla army was handed the country on a plate and soon ensconced in Maputo, the newly-renamed capital. Soviet tankers and aircraft arrived in droves with several thousand "advisers".

ZANU's hierarchy, now safely based in Maputo following bitter, internecine fighting and a split with ZAPU — Joshua Nkomo's predominantly Matabele army in Zambia — stepped up their infiltration of small groups into Rhodesia.

IF THERE WAS one thing Jason Ncube had learned, it was to keep an eye out behind him. The Rhodesians were great ones for following up. It didn't matter how hard they hit the freedom fighters, they would always follow up if there was even the slightest chance that any had got away.

For this reason, there was a rear guard watching the track they had come along. Jason and his boys were in no hurry. For one, it was too hot to move about during the middle of the day; and moving too rapidly through the country increased the chance of detection by the security forces. Most importantly though, they had to move from water to water as it was the dry season and the precious life-giving fluid was scarce.

This was why he had shanghaied the two wiry Shangaan tribesmen as guides and trackers. They knew the area and where to find water. Jason's group had been resting up a lot longer than Dave and his men, and it was one of the Shangaans detailed to watch the rear who spotted the four whites as they came on to the spoor.

Jason was summoned urgently. Even with his excellent eyesight, it was a while before he picked up what the little tracker was pointing at. He was amazed at the Shangaan's incredible skills and eyesight, even though he was no slouch himself. Jason watched the white men for a long while as they slowly followed the spoor towards them. He was tempted to scatter his boys and meet up at a rendezvous later, as was the custom when approached by security forces, but something made him change his mind.

The Rhodesians were doing everything right: straddling the spoor in extended line, spaced well apart and keeping their dressing. But something told him that these men were inexperienced in combat. He didn't know what it was, perhaps they were too hesitant, too unsure. Whatever it was, he knew his chances were good against them. One thing he knew, their tracking skills were dismal, they were very slow. He quickly rejoined the main group.

"There are four Boers following us," he whispered. "We are going to ambush them. Follow me." With that he took off, still going northwest, but before long doubling back in a wide semicircle to a thick clump of bushes not far from where they had originally rested. He placed his men with care to give them good fields of fire, but well concealed.

"Do not fire until I start firing, and don't fidget," he ordered. He then went and lay down in the middle of the group and waited. Even then, it was a while before the four approached the area.

"Psst," hissed Dave. He gave the signal to go to ground in all-round defence. He could see that the terrs had laid up here.

SOME DISTANCE TO the west, at a little dirt airstrip near Malapati, three Alouette helicopters whined into life as the three sticks of men from One Commando, the Rhodesian Light Infantry, clambered aboard. They had been briefed on the situation and were itching for a fight.

The Rhodesians had learned the value of having quick reaction troops dotted around the country. These quick reaction forces, or Fire Forces as they later became known, were developed to such a degree of skill by the Rhodesian Light Infantry that they devastated terrorist groups all over the country. As the helicopters clattered their way towards Dave McEvoy's position, three more sticks were climbing on to the back of a two-five truck, also heading towards the sighting.

"Right buggers, listen up." Sergeant Merv Wells shouted to make himself heard above the noise of the helicopter's engine. "When you get on the ground, you bloody switch on. Walk with your safety catches off. Those eight terrs down there are hard core. That's our intelligence report, so don't think they will be easy meat. Got that?"

"Roger Sarge," shouted the three troopers.

It would be another twenty minutes before they arrived at the scene, so they tried to relax. But they were keyed up and tense. Waiting is always the hardest part.

JUST AS MCEVOY was pressing his handset to report the latest development, the air around them was filled with a sound like a swarm of angry hornets. A red dot appeared on his right temple and a gaping hole on his left cheek as a bullet tore through his head, knocking him lifeless to the ground. Tony Scott felt a hard thump as though someone had punched him in the chest and he also went down. He tried to get up and looked slightly puzzled at the bright gushes of bubbly blood spurting from his rib cage. Bob Woods, a quietly spoken, bespectacled man, balding prematurely, also died before he hit the ground, his throat torn and spinal cord snapped by the passage of a high velocity 7.62 intermediate AK round. Nick the machinegunner had reacted a bit faster than the others. Aggressive by nature, a barroom brawler by nature, he was used to responding to violence. He was returning fire before the other three had even realised there was something wrong. His return fire caught Jason's men off guard; they had expected a quick, easy one-hundred percent kill. Now bullets were coming back thick and fast. They broke and ran. Two of them didn't get far as bullets found them and they went down.

"Get back here you gutless hyenas," screamed Jason. But it was no use, they had gone. Withdrawing steadily, firing as he went, Jason retreated.

Nick hardly felt the round that hit him in the right thigh, he was too busy. As soon as he realised the return fire had ceased, he stopped. It was only when he went to get up he realised that something was wrong. Then the pain started. He crawled over to Dave's inert body and picked up the handset.

"Three, Three One. Fuckin' Jesus, we've been hit, we need help."

TEN MINUTES LATER, the barely-conscious Nick called the choppers onto his position. The RLI medic administered a saline drip and injected two ampules of morphine into the bag. Nick lapsed into unconsciousness as the medic splinted his shattered leg before he was loaded on to the waiting helicopter with the bodies of his stick.

"Right Errol, I want you to go back with the casualty" ordered Sergeant Wells. "We have enough drips and morphine, so we won't need you."

"OK, Sarge" replied the medic, "I'll look after him. I hope you get those bastards."

Sergeant Wells walked back to his men as the chopper lifted into the sky. "Right boys, we've got some terrs to catch. Trooper Zietzman, I want you on those tracks. Corporals Kirk and Carr, I want your sticks to flank. Extended line. I want those gooks caught, and fast."

"Roger Sarge. Okay ouns, you heard him, let's move."

A short while later, Trooper Zietzman called back. "Hey Sarge, these buggers have bombshelled, the tracks are all over the place."

"Okay find one set and follow, they will join up eventually."

The spoor was leading them in a southerly direction towards the Mozambique border. "Hey Sarge, I used to hunt in this area. I think I know where those fuckers are heading," shouted Bob Swart.

"Well, spit it out man."

"About two kilometres the other side of the border there is a water-hole. It's the only water in the area and there's a big baobab tree near it. It is the only recognisable feature in the area. I scheme it must be the obvious place for them to join up."

"Right, I'll get on to the boss and tune him. Zero Alpha. This is One One Alpha. Do you read? Over."

"Reading you strength threes, over."

"Roger. We think we know where the Charlie Tangos are headed, over."

"Roger, give us a grid reference, over."

After he had radioed the position, there was a short pause.

"One One Alpha, Sunray speaks," said the voice of Major Hill, the officer commanding One Commando. "You've given us a dicey one there. It is out of our area. Copy over?"

"Roger, but it is only just out of the area and if we hurry, we will catch them. Over."

"Roger. We have a small problem, there's only one Cyclone Seven (helicopter) available at this time. One is taking the casevac to Base and the other is u/s."

"Copied Sunray. There are only six Charlie Tangos left. One stick could do the job."

"Okay, wait five."

The Major began to pace the tent. Crossborder raids were a strict

32

no-no. But as Sergeant Wells said, it was only just over the border and the terrs had killed three Rhodesians.

"Right," he said. "Colour Sergeant Wilson. Who do we have on those trucks?"

"Just three sticks, sir."

"Who's in charge?"

"There are no NCOs, sir, only troopers."

"Fuckit. Have any of them got the experience to do this job?"

"That Aussie bloke Hunter seems to know what he's doing," said Sergeant Wilson.

"He hasn't been with us long, has he?"

"No, sir, but he did serve three years with the Australian army."

"Right, send him. But you make sure he knows what he is up against."

Three-quarters of an hour before last light, the lone G Car carrying the four-man RLI follow-up stick swooped in low over Mozambique territory to land in a small clearing four kilometres from the waterhole — as near as he dared get without alerting the quarry.

"Good luck, guys," smiled the gunner, and gave the thumbs up as they clambered out. "Right, take her up, sir," he said into the headset. The little Alouette lifted off and headed for home.

"Rather them than me" mused the pilot.

"They're RLI, sir, they're born to it."

RAY HUNTER LED his men off at a jog. They had only 30 minutes of decent light left to cover the distance to the waterhole. Panting, he led them to a small rise about three hundred metres from the waterhole, facing Rhodesia, ready to intercept the incoming gang.

"Mark, I'm going to put you here, in the middle," he said to the lanky machinegunner. "Johan, I want you over here," he told the rugged South African. "Koos. You here, facing the rear. In case the sons of bitches sneak up from behind."

When he had finished, the small group had the capacity for all-round defence, with the main firepower facing the expected direction of the enemy.

"Now, no sleeping at all tonight. Hardcore gooks are coming our way, so let's not have them catching us napping. Stay switched on. Okay." Ray went back to his position and lay down. "Zero Alpha, One One Bravo. We are in position."

"Roger, One One Bravo. Best of luck, out"

They lay in silence, waiting. Gradually, a feeling of unease began to creep over Ray. He felt he was being watched. He tried to dismiss the thought, but it persisted. He looked across at Mark and could see in his eyes that he felt the same.

SAMSON NDHLOVU AND his men had been making for the waterhole and the border from their camp deep inside Mozambique when they heard the faint sound of a distant helicopter. They went to ground and waited. His group were the next due to be infiltrated into Rhodesia and this waterhole was the last stop before crossing the border. He wondered why the Rhodesians had come. Why so few, and into Mozambique? He knew why when he saw them take up position to the west of the waterhole. All the section commanders in this area were briefed to scatter and make their way back to this point if engaged by the security forces. So he knew that Jason must have bumped into the white men, and was making his way back.

He didn't know how they had found out about this place, but he knew he had to warn his comrade. He withdrew his men to a safe distance and turned to one of the wiry Shangaan trackers.

"Do you know where the holes in the fence are, near the broken tree and the skull of the elephant?"

"Yes, I know of that place."

"Tonight, some comrades will be coming through there. I want you to go and warn them that there are Boers waiting to kill them at the waterhole. Then I want you to lead them to me here."

"Yes, I will do this thing."

"It is dark, go now and warn the comrades."

The Shangaan melted into the night and Samson went back to brief his men.

WHEN IT WAS quite dark, Ray quietly went to his men in turn and gave the order to move out. "I think we have been seen," he whispered to each man. "So we are going to choose a possie to ambush our ambush possie."

In the dark, he didn't see their smiles at his joke, but knew they'd be there. Before moving out, Ray rigged up a couple of little surprises. He first carefully took the tin mug from his waterbottle pouch and, using a piece of string, tied it to the branch of a small tree. There was a slight breeze blowing and hopefully the occasional sound it would make would keep the terrs thinking they were still in the same spot. The next trick he had seen used as a child. The grenade had no container, so he wedged it between a fork in the shrub and fed a toggle line from the grenade to another shrub. He felt the anger rise in him as he recalled the time he had seen his parents butchered. He had to control his shaking hands as he put the finishing touches to his work.

"This'll sort you bastards out," he thought with grim satisfaction. He had put his anger aside and was now thinking clearly as he went to each man and signalled them to move out.

He led his men in a semicircle until he was east of the rise in the ground. Once again he positioned the stick to his satisfaction. They lay down in the sand and waited. Every so often there was a faint metallic sound as the metal mug gently touched the tree. "I hope it fools them," Ray thought to himself.

It was almost midnight before the Shangaan led Jason and his section to Samson. They had moved far enough away to be well out of earshot of the RLI stick; even so, they talked in low tones.

"We will have to find another way into Zimbabwe," said Samson. "This way is blocked."

"Why do you say it's blocked?" asked Jason. There was scorn in his voice. "Did you not say there are only four of them?"

"Yes, but our orders are to avoid contact with the white soldiers."

"Comrade Samson, let me tell you this. Today we killed three and possibly even a fourth Boer in Zimbabwe," Jason said with pride.

The word Boer was used by the terrorists to describe white Rhodesians in general because Joshua Nkomo and his rival, Robert Mugabe, were telling the world press the same thing. By classing the Rhodesians with the Afrikaners, it was hoped the naive Western world would see them in a more unfavourable light. Ploys like that did, in fact, work and a gullible world believed what they were being told by the "Freedom Fighters" who butchered innocent civilians, both black and white, on a regular basis.

"The white man is not invincible. We have proved that," said Jason. "There are only four of them and they are expecting us to come from the west. We will attack them from the north and wipe them out."

Still Samson was not sure.

"Listen," Jason said forcefully. There are fourteen of us and only four of them. And don't forget that they killed two of the comrades. Just for that we must kill them."

There was no moon to see by but the RLI stick heard faint noises as the terrs moved up, and knew that an attack was imminent. The fourteen terrorists crept to within fifty metres of the slight rise in the ground. Once or twice they had heard the soft sounds of the billy can, so the whites must be there, waiting. "Silly fools," thought Jason. "There are four of them and they think that six of us are going to walk

35

blindly into a trap. Instead fourteen of us are going to surprise them. Tonight there will be four more dead whites. One of them is stupid, he keeps shifting to get more comfortable. These white men are soft."

A ragged volley of small arms fire split the silence of the night. The green tracer rounds lit up the gloom. Still the RLI held their fire. Ray had warned them not to fire until he gave the signal.

"AYEEE, my brothers. See we have killed them, or they have run away. Charge," shouted a hothead.

Some of them had mistaken the lack of return fire as a sign of victory. Six terrorists leaped to their feet and charged the rise.

"No, you fools. STOP!" screamed Jason, realising that something was wrong. But it was too late, they were almost there.

This was the moment Ray had been waiting for. As they reached the incline he started firing. A split-second later Mark's machinegun opened up, the heavier boom of the Belgian-manufactured MAG in marked contrast to the higher crack of the communist AKs and RPDs. The six were bowled over like skittles. Two of them had their legs shot to pieces, the momentum of their charge propelling them past the rise and down the other side. The man nearest the RLI stick had his heart and lungs ripped from his chest while a further terrorist was half-disembowelled from a round at waist level. The last two ran into a hail of bullets which jerked them like puppets on a string all the way to the ground.

It was all Jason could do to stop the rest of his men from running. Somehow he managed to get them under control and return fire. He had seen from where the enemy's fire came and directed return fire towards the RLI stick.

Johan emptied a magazine and was changing it for a fresh one when he saw winking lights to his right and opened fire towards them. Koos wriggled around to get a field of fire and also started shooting towards the remaining terrorists. The bang of Ray's booby-trap was hardly heard in the chaos and it only killed dead men. The three badly wounded terrorists crawled away on the far side of the rise. Africans can withstand an incredible amount of pain. They will often survive wounds that will would kill a European.

Jason knew he would have to withdraw his men and he did so, fighting to keep them from a panic-stricken route. He cursed and cajoled them into orderly retreat, making them give each other covering fire as they went.

When the firing had stopped and it was obvious that the enemy had gone, Ray checked his stick.

"Anyone hurt?"

"No we're fine," came the reply.

When they were ready, he called softly, "follow me" and led them away to a safer spot. He did not know how many they had been up against, but he realised their leader knew his job and that to get complacent now would invite disaster.

When they had reached a safe distance, Ray again directed them into all-round defence. Then he went round to each of them.

"How much ammo have you left, Mark?"

"Six belts."

"How much, Johan?"

"Six mags."

"Koos?"

"Seven mags. Ray." He had come into the firefight a bit later than the rest.

Ray went back to his place. That they had given the terrs a hiding there was no doubt, but he was worried about their leader. How determined was he? Would he try to find them and counter attack? They say that attack is the best form of defence. Would it be better to find them and have another go. Keep them off balance?

As they were flying in by chopper, Ray had noticed a depression in the ground some two thousand metres to the north-west. He had filed it away as a likely place to go to ground. It would be ideal; it was out of sight and it might muffle sounds to a degree. If they were licking their wounds, that would be the logical place to go. He brought the stick in close so he could talk to them.

"I think I know where our friends might be laying up," he said in a low whisper. "It might be risky, but I wouldn't mind having another crack at them. I am not going to order you to do this, but I think we will scare the shit out of them. They won't be expecting something like this. What do you think?"

Mark, Johan and Koos had come to respect the stocky, powerful man with the nasal twang. He had only been their leader a very short while, but already they trusted his judgment.

"Ja, okay Ray. Let's fuck 'em up."

"Okay, here's the plan."

TWO THOUSAND METRES away, Jason Ncube was thinking hard. How had those cursed Rhodesians known they were there? They hadn't seen them, he was sure of that. One minute the white men were lying in wait for six comrades from the west, then when the attack went in they were ambushed themselves. The superstitious side of his nature made the hair rise in the nape of his neck. Maybe the white man in charge had the magic, perhaps he could see into other men's minds, how else could he have seen in the dark? He tried to control his thoughts and concentrate on matters in hand.

If you had asked Ray Hunter how he knew he was being watched, he could not have told you. Perhaps seeing his parents butchered had shocked into his subconscious a sixth sense that civilised man discarded long ago.

Jason was in a quandary. By rights they should have been safe in Mozambique by now. Normally the Rhodesians did not cross the border but these four had, and they were good soldiers. Very good. He would have to discuss these latest developments with his sectorial commander back at base. He would have liked to try another attack on the whites, but his men were jittery and he would be hard pressed to get them to follow him into another firefight. Plus he had lost five men today, with another three wounded. The one with the stomach wound would be dead before the sun came up. The other two would survive if they got medical attention in time. The Shangaan had gone out and brought them in after the contact. He had been tempted to leave them behind but remembered his Chinese instructor's teaching. "Try and take the dead and wounded away with you so the enemy won't know how successful they've been."

Although they were bearing the pain well, the three wounded men's breathing was ragged and hoarse and every so often a low moan would escape their lips. Jason hoped the noise would not carry to the Boers, although they should be well out of hearing range.

"As soon as stretchers have been rigged up to carry the casualties, we will go," thought Jason, at last coming to a decision.

"YIPP YIPP, YAAA YAAA!!! WHOOP WHOOP!!"

Jason started in horror at the voices howling at them from the dark. Orange tracer began to lick at them, seeking them from the blackness. "AYEEE!!!" They were devils.

"Run my brothers, run," shouted a voice near him.

Jason found himself running with the rest of his men. He heard a meaty thunk and fell over the prone body of one of the comrades who had been shot in the head. Angrily, he scrambled to his feet and kept running into the night as fast as his legs would carry him.

Chapter Three

"JESUS H. CHRIST. You boys have been busy," mused Sergeant Wells, suitably impressed on surveying the night's work. The three choppers had flown in not long after first light to reinforce the four-man stick and to take back to Rhodesia the bodies of the dead terrorists and their weapons for photographing and ballistics testing.

Although it was a war, during the long years it lasted the Rhodesian conflict was classified as a police action; the terrorists were considered criminals and dossiers were kept on them. Fingerprinting, photographing and ballistic records of terrorists, dead or captured alive, were used to tie them in with whatever activities they might have engaged in, whether it was robbery, murder or sabotage.

The sweep through the terrorist position by Ray Hunter and his men had been very successful. The shouting and screaming had served two purposes. One, it had severely put the wind up their opponents as had been intended; and two, it gave each man in the stick an indication where the others were, ensuring the sweep went through cleanly, without confusion. The noise the wounded terrorists had made, although not loud, had been enough to give their position away.

While the bodies and weapons were being ferried to the trucks waiting across the border, Sergeant Wells had organised a thorough search of the area, looking for any clues that might be of value to the security forces in the future.

"Hey Sarge, there's two wounded floppies here," called Trooper Jannie Potgieter. "Want me to shoot them?"

Jannie and his stick had been following a large and messy spoor that spoke of badly wounded terrorists. They found them only a few hundred metres from the last contact area.

"Shit, no," called back the Sergeant. "We'll take them back for questioning. They might have something useful to tell Special Branch."

As they were waiting for the three choppers to pick them up, Sergeant Wells said: "By the way, you four, congratulations on your good shooting last night. You buggers did well. Ray, the Major wants to have a talk with you when we get back."

The helicopter with the engine trouble had been fixed during the night. Using spotlights, the mechanics had worked tirelessly until the thing was fixed, knowing the RLI boys might need it desperately.

After a clean up and a late breakfast, Ray and his stick were taken to Major Hills's tent for the debriefing. Already in the tent was the 2IC,

Captain Watson, and the Commando Sergeant Major, Warrant Officer Gerr. Also present was Sergeant Wells.

"Congratulations, men. You did a bloody fine job out there last night," the Major said, a touch of pride in his voice. "Sergeant Wells has briefed me on yesterday's contact and follow up. Tell me about this other group that was near the waterhole."

Bit by bit, the facts were pieced together until a complete picture formed. "What standard of soldier were you up against, Ray?" asked the OC.

"Well, sir, some of them were a bit of a rabble. But a couple of them seemed to know what they were about. Someone was trying to lead them properly and if the rest had had any real soldiering ability, last night might have been a different story."

"It might interest you to know that we are pretty sure the leader of the group was Jason Ncube," said Major Hill. "He is a bad bastard and is giving us a headache. We are not sure who was in charge of the group that was already near the waterhole, but we are of the mind that they joined forces and Jason took overall command. If that was the case, then you boys did extremely well."

Captain Watson spoke: "It would appear from these latest developments that we've discovered one of the main infiltration points in this area. We are lucky insofar the terrorists don't seem to have maps or radio communication and have to rely on written orders and that creates a certain degree of inflexibility. Also, it would appear that they have to rely on certain prominent landmarks, which in this flat terrain is difficult as they are few and far between. If we could locate more of these, we might be able to pin them down as they come into the country."

"Trooper Swart knows this area," said Sergeant Wells. "It might be a worthwhile exercise to pick his brains."

"Good idea, Sergeant. We will do just that," said the OC. "Right, is there anything else?"

"Yes, sir, there is one question I would like to ask," replied Ray. "All these gooks (Ray was using the term the Australians and Americans used for the Viet Cong during the Vietnam war, which became common usage during the Rhodesian war) are coming into the country from Mozambique. They must be basing up somewhere and unless they are being transported a long way, there must be camps not too far from the border. Why can't we go and find them and take them out?"

"Good reasoning, Ray. We know there are camps over there and, yes, it would be great to locate them and wipe them out.

Unfortunately, what's bleeding obvious to us at the sharp end doesn't seem to have reached the dizzy heights of the hierarchy just yet. They're still trying to come to grips with the fact that there's really a war going on. They're still working with peacetime attitudes which are slow and ponderous. Plus, our politicians are loath to upset the outside world any more than we're already doing. We are fighting a holding action only at this point, Ray. Right, is that all?" asked the OC, looking around.

"Sir, I would like to ask one more question."

"Yes, Trooper Hunter, what is it?"

"Our helicopters, sir. They are just being used in a troop-carrying role. They are all mounted with machineguns in the door, why can't they take on a more aggressive role? We know the terrorists bombshell (scatter) as soon as they are contacted. What's to prevent us putting Stop Groups in the area to cut off the escaping terrs and possibly have a helicopter circling around with someone controlling the scene?"

"You are asking questions that are already being dealt with, trooper. You aren't the only one with a brain around here but I'll tell you anyway. The helicopter pilots and gunners are all for it, but the high-ups have deemed the helicopters too expensive to risk in an aggressive role. Believe me, we are pushing for it. Now, will there be anything else? I have work to do."

"Dismiss," ordered the CSM.

After the four had left, Major Hill said: "Keep an eye on young Hunter, we are going to need men like him."

BOB SWART'S KNOWLEDGE of the area proved invaluable and the terrorists found themselves being hit at every crossing. The helicopter pilots and gunners, against orders, took on a more aggressive role, not only putting the troops into likely areas, but actively searching out insurgents and shooting at them.

Major Hill tried controlling the scene from a prowling helicopter, and it worked. In fact, it was so successful, the powers that be had to sit up and take notice.

The terrorists were being stopped in their tracks. They had tried moving through populated areas and that had not worked — mainly because they had expected the African population to rush up and welcome them with open arms. This had not been the case. The majority of the population were from Shona-speaking tribes and the Shona are usually fairly peace-loving. They were not unhappy with life and were left alone most of the time. They were just not interested in the war of liberation that the guerillas were waging. The Rhodesians were now wreaking havoc on them in the unpopulated areas. They had to devise another method of gaining control of the country.

To wage a guerilla war successfully, it is necessary to have the support of the local population: it is hard to find the enemy if they blend in with the locals.

Chairman Mao's theory of "moving through the people like fishes in the sea" could not be utilised if the people were offside. If the locals would not back them willingly, then they would have to support them unwillingly.

Achieving this was simplicity itself. Abject terror. It works. It is simple and it is effective. If members of your family have been beaten or shot to death and you are told that if you don't comply you will be next, the chances are that you will be only too willing to do as you are told. Threats of dire punishment if you "sell out" to the enemy or fail to support the "freedom fighters", were stark reality.

When an area was thoroughly subverted and the people cowed, the terrorists could move through it in comfort. With the locals feeding you, hiding you and giving you information, it is easy.

Recruiting young men into the terrorist ranks was along similar lines. They were abducted from villages and schools as in 1973, when 295 pupils were abducted from St Albert's mission near Mount Darwin in the north east. These youngsters were sent to Tanzania for training and then infiltrated back into Rhodesia. The sweetener was the promise that when "Zimbabwe is liberated", they would have all the white man's possessions and be able to use the white women for "your mattresses at night". These new terrorists also found that just pointing their weapons at someone gave them the right to take what they wanted. The adage "power grows out of the barrel of a gun", became a truism for them. It made them "big men" instead of just peasants.

The Rhodesian bush war was starting to have a snowball effect. In the terrorists' favour. The security forces were finding that information which had been freely available in the past was starting to dry up.

The observation posts in hilly country were still finding terrorist groups as they moved through the country. But it was not easy. Sometimes they had to wait for weeks to locate a group. The terrorists had a fairly set procedure when in or passing through an area. They would make their base in thick woods not far from a village, usually near a river. They would lie up during the day and do their dirty work at night.

Once the village had been subverted the insurgents could take it easy until it was time to move or complete a task. Often the first indication of a terrorist presence would be shots fired in the night or screams as the villagers were beaten or tortured. Other indications were the women of the village carrying food to a camp, or taking much more washing to the river than normal.

It might take days or even weeks for the men in the OPs to build up a picture of a terrorist group's habits and numbers so that they could call in Fire Force troops to bring them to contact. Many times these OPs were compromised by "Mujibas" — young boys who acted as eyes and ears for the terrorists. They would roam the hills, ostensibly searching for stray cattle. Once an OP had been compromised, it had lost its value and would have to be abandoned for a while.

Children "searching" the hills was a good indication that there were terrorists in the area but unless they could be pinpointed, they could not be brought to contact.

In 1973, the Rhodesians formed a regiment to counter the terrorists' activities from within. The Selous Scouts were, to all intents and purposes, a tracking unit. But one of their major roles was much more bizarre.

They operated as pseudo-terrorists and infiltrated the real guerilla network so successfully that they not only gave the Fire Forces an incredibly high kill rate by locating and pinpointing them accurately, but also sowed discord, disharmony and distrust among the terrorists to such an extent that they were often too busy fighting among themselves to be a problem for the security forces.

By the end of the war, a substantial number of Selous Scouts were ex-terrorists who had changed sides and were working against their former comrades.

THE AIRSTRIP AT Grand Reef, not far from the town of Umtali, is quite a beautiful place with its rugged backdrop of the Vumba mountains rising majestically to the south-east. The sealed runway, gently sloping with the contour of the land, gives the impression of following the curvature of the earth. In peacetime it would be a pleasant enough place to idle the time away waiting for a plane.

War had transformed the place into a rough, stark fortress. On the western side of the runway, earth revetments surrounded the Fire Force base, dotted at intervals with bunkers and machinegun posts. At the northern end, high walls constructed from fuel drums filled with sand protected the aircraft from attack, with ceilings of wire netting to stop mortar bombs from landing. Inside the base were buildings and tents found in any camp to house the personnel required to operate a military establishment. Surrounding the whole area was a minefield with a barbed-wire fence.

At the southern end of the base, One Commando, The Rhodesian Light Infantry was settling in as the current Fire Force troops for the area, having just taken over from Three Commando. The Commando was parading outside the hut used as the mess.

"Right men," Major Hill addressed the troops. "I trust you have all found yourselves a place to sleep. I know conditions are a bit rough, but this isn't a holiday camp. We are here to fight a war. We have some new blokes in the Commando. I will put you with experienced men, so they can keep an eye on you.

"Just remember, you are in the bush now and there are lots of nasty people out here who are going to try and kill you. So stay switched on and you might stay alive. Right, now we are going to organise the Stop Groups for tomorrow, so I'll hand you over to Sergeant Hunter."

The Rhodesian army used sections of four men because that was all the Alouette helicopters could carry in addition to the pilot and door gunner. The term "Stop Group" was used because during most contacts troops were deployed around the area to stop terrs who were running away. These Stop Groups accounted for the majority of kills during Fire Force exercises. Also, using a simple "stop one" or "stop two" made radio communication easy.

"Right, listen up buggers," Ray shouted to the waiting men. "Stops One to Four will be chopper sticks. Stop One will be myself, Trooper Ellis, Trooper Koos and one of you new boys, Trooper Hart. Stop Two will be....." One by one he organised the groups until the forty men had been allocated a place.

"Right," Ray continued. "Stops Six to Ten will be vehicle transported. You will be driven towards the contact area and the choppers will come and pick you up when they can. The trucks will also carry fuel for the choppers. Is that understood? Any questions?

"Okay, after tea there are some nice cold shumbas (beer), so we can have a few, but don't overdo it. I don't want to see any of you with hangovers tomorrow. Before you go, Corporal Kerr has a list of people for guard duty tonight. Those on duty will not drink. Is that understood?"

There was a groan from the troops.

"Also, I will be doing the rounds during the night and if I catch any of the guards asleep, watch out, there will be trouble."

THE HOOTER SOUNDED for breakfast and the troops gulped down their food, picked up their weapons and raced to the side of the strip, waiting for the choppers. The Stop Leaders hurried to the briefing room for details.

In the briefing room, as well as the Stop Leaders, were the chopper pilots and the Lynx pilot. The Lynx was a light plane used for aerial support and to carry rockets, small bombs and Frantan, a Rhodesian version of napalm.

Major Hill, who was the Fire Force Commander, was also present. It was standard procedure now to have one chopper flying around the contact area controlling the scene. It was fitted with a Hispano 20mm cannon and became known as K-car — the K standing for Killer. The troop-carrying helicopters were known as G-cars.

Major Hill commenced the briefing for his men and for the benefit of the Air Force pilots. "Right, this is the situation. A Police Support Unit OP has located a camp with approximately twenty terrs in the Wedza Tribal Trust Land, north-west of here, just south of the fork in this river at Grid Reference UQ583164." He pointed to the position on the large-scale map.

The suspected camp is in fairly thick bush near the river. The most likely escape routes are here, north along the river bank, south along the river bank, and maybe the kraal, here to the west. I want Stop Groups here, here and here.

"It is a fair way from Grand Reef and I appreciate it will be a while before we can get more than four Stop Groups in. So I want three Stop Groups in those positions and one Stop Group acting as a sweep line. It's not much but perhaps we can use the K-car to chase them around a bit. The G-cars will just have to pick up the others as soon as possible. Any questions so far?

"Right, I want the K-car to approach over the hill where the OP is and fly directly to the terr camp. Drop smoke when you think you are at the right spot and the OP will direct you from there. Got that? The Lynx will take off ten minutes after the helicopters so it will arrive overhead just after them. Any questions gentlemen? Okay, good luck and good hunting."

Ray ran to where his Stop Group was waiting by the airstrip. "Right, boys, this is the situation. We have twenty gooks near a river line and we will be the sweep line. Initially, the other three Stops will be waiting further up the river, so be careful you don't shoot at them by mistake. Trooper Hart, what is your first name?"

"William, Sergeant."

"Do they call you William or Will?"

"Usually Will, Sergeant."

"Right, Will, when we land I want you to my left where I can keep

45

an eye on you. Do you have a full magazine on your rifle?"

"Yes, Sarge."

"Okay, cock your weapon, but make sure you have the safety catch on."

"Yes, Sarge. Er, Sarge!!"

"Yes."

"When we get on the ground, do I leave the safety catch on, or do I take it off?"

"Off, lad. The split-second it takes to flick it off could mean the difference between who shoots first. Remember, it's not your job to die for your country. Your job is to make the other fucker die for his, okay?"

"Okay, Sarge."

"Right, here come the choppers, let's make it a good one boys."

The sixteen men clambered aboard the little Alouettes and they took off, heading north-west towards a date with death.

Will Hart looked around at the faces of the men he was about to accompany into combat. Koos, beside him in front, seemed to be lost in his own thoughts, a wistful look on his face. Mark, the machine-gunner, was facing out, his MAG pointing downwards out of the door opposite the helicopter's gun, doubling the aircraft's firepower. Mark was alert, watching the ground below, ready for anything. Sergeant Hunter was sitting in the middle with the spare headset, listening in to the radio chatter, his eyes twinkling with amusement as though laughing at some big joke. But behind that the eyes were hard and mean.

They seemed so calm, these tough experienced men. Will hoped his nervousness wasn't showing too much and that he would not let them down on the ground.

Ray had noticed Trooper Hart's nervousness. He caught his eye and smiled.

"Poor bugger, he doesn't know what to expect," he thought. "It's always hard the first few times. I hope he doesn't get taken out in his first contact."

One of the other helicopters had drawn up close and the troops were laughing and making rude gestures to each other; it was a good way of goofing off and relieving tension. Ray leaned forward and stuck his middle finger up at them. No matter how many times they flew, he never tired of seeing the other aircraft flying in close formation. It gave one a sense of combined strength, a feeling of power.

The other aircraft dropped back into its proper place and the men settled down into their own world under the perspex bubbles, with the whoosh-whoosh of the rotor blades above their heads.

Jason Ncube was angry with the men under his command. He still had a few of the old boys with him, but they had been whittled down during their frequent meetings with the Boers. This new breed of freedom fighter was lazy and arrogant.

A few nights ago, they had come to subvert the nearby kraal. The villagers, although not welcoming them with open arms, had been compliant and ready to do as they were told. One of the new boys, Toby Mabhunu, had taken it into his head to rough up the village headman, just for good measure. The roughing up became a beating which ended with the headman dead. The violence was infectious and a couple of other villagers were badly beaten. When the headman's younger wife had tried to intervene, Toby shot her with his Russian-made Tokarev pistol.

Jason understood the value of keeping the people cowed, he had no problem with that. But these men were doing it for pure pleasure. He could see the naked blood lust in Toby's eyes as he stood over the headman's corpse, his club wet with blood and brains as he surveyed the stunned crowd around him. The raping of the young female in full view of the villagers by Toby and three others made Jason angry and he put a stop to it, but with some difficulty. Toby and his followers had worked themselves into a frenzy and it was some time before they could be brought under control.

The occasional murder and rape were part of life as a freedom fighter, Jason had no qualms about that. He had done it himself, but these men had no control. They were a rabble and he doubted their courage. It was one thing to beat a defenceless old man to death and bully peaceful farmers, but how would they react when those determined white men in their helicopters came to hunt for them, as they surely would.

Toby's followers were content to laze around and do nothing since the villagers were waiting on them hand and foot. These men were not here for the cause, but for themselves. Jason's natural leadership had swung some of them towards him, but there were squabbles and discord. It was going to be a tough job welding them into a cohesive unit.

At the moment something was troubling Jason, he could not quite make out what it was. Toby's men were arguing about something and it was distracting him from thinking properly. He stood up.

"That is enough," he said, not loudly, but with such authority and menace that they looked at him. "You, Toby. You have tried me far enough." With that, he swung the butt of his AK across Toby's head and he pitched headlong into the dirt.

"Now listen," he hissed, cocking his head to the sky. The sound was like the beating of a thousand wings. Helicopters.

"ONE MINUTE OUT," shouted Ray above the noise of the chopper. His men's eyes widened in anticipation and they clutched their weapons tighter. Ray could see the K-car rising above the hill to fly over the OP as their own chopper flew round the base of the hill to the right. Thirty seconds later, he heard, "throwing smoke now" as the K-car took position in a wide orbit over the terrorist camp.

"I see blue smoke." This was the OP confirming his sighting to the K-car. The terrs sometimes threw different coloured smoke to confuse the Fire Force.

"Roger. Blue smoke."

"Add fifty, K-car," the voice from the OP corrected.

While this was going on, Ray could hear the Stop Groups being put down.

"Stop Four is down."

"Stop Two is down."

"Stop Three is down."

Their own chopper banked to land in a small clearing. Ray took off the headset. The aircraft touched down and the pilot raised his thumb. The four of them scrambled out and went to ground.

"Stop One is down," he said into the handset. He could hear the chopper disappear as it headed off to pick up fuel and more men.

Major Hill's voice crackled over the radios: "Stops Two, Three and Four, get to your positions. Stop One, your location?"

"We are to your south, near the clearing by the river," Ray replied.

"Roger, I have you visual. I want you to sweep north up your side of the river. Watch out, the bush is thick there. The Charlie Tangos' camp should be five hundred metres to your front."

"Roger, K-car."

The excited voice from the OP came through: "K-car, there are gooks breaking west towards the kraal line. More are gapping it up the river line towards Stop Three."

"Roger. Did you copy that Stop Three? Charlie Tangos on their way to you. We're going to take them out."

The K-car flew towards the village.

As soon as they heard the helicopters, Toby's men disappeared. It was not the orderly "bombshelling" they had been taught, rather a panicked exodus.

"Ha, you cowardly hyenas. I knew you would run," Jason shouted after the fleeing figures. He had seen the helicopters put down Stop Groups to the north and knew they would be blocking any likely escape routes. He had seen the Rhodesians in action often enough to work out their methods. He gathered the more steadfast of his.

"Listen comrades," he shouted. "Soon there will be more of them coming from the south. Stay here until we see where they land, then we will try to dodge them through the thick bushes. Those fleeing jackals of Toby's will keep the Boers busy for a while. While they are chasing them, we will make our escape."

Jason was surprised when he saw only one helicopter land. He knew now that there would only be four men coming.

"Listen, my brothers, there are only four white men. We will go and hide in those rocks we talked about near the river. Hopefully, those men will miss us and we can make our escape to the south. Remain hidden and remain still, unless you are spotted. If the helicopter flies over you, stay very still until it has gone. If you are spotted, shoot at them. Now, let's go."

With that Jason loped off, beckoning his men to follow.

"K-car, K-car, Oscar Five. We have two Charlie Tangos visual. They have just reached the kraal line and are heading towards the mealie field to your west," called in the OP.

"Roger, we're on to them now," came back the calm voice of Major Hill. The K-car was two hundred feet above the fleeing terrorists and closing fast. The pilot skilfully altered the blade's pitch to slow forward momentum and swung the aircraft side-on to the running men.

"Right, Mick, it's all yours," he said to the gunner.

The tech sighted on the man to the left, raising his aim slightly to compensate for the forward movement, and squeezed the trigger. The 20mm explosive shell hit the running man squarely in the back, blowing out his spine and internal organs as though they had been surgically removed.

"Jesus fucking Christ ... you beauty," Mick yelled as he switched his aim to the remaining terr who was entering the maize field. The aim was slightly hurried because the man would be out of sight in two more strides, but the effect was just as devastating. From the waist down he was a bloody smear in the maize.

"Good shooting, Mick," the Major said into his mouthpiece. "Stop Three, K-car, do you have Charlie Tangos visual?"

"Not at this time."

"Okay, we'll be over there to chase them up for you shortly. Stop One, Sitrep."

"K-car, Stop One. We're sweeping north along the river line. About a hundred and fifty metres in front of us, there is a rocky hillock, thickly vegetated. If there are gooks around, they will be in there."

"Stop One, K-car, Roger. We'll have a look for you."

Somewhere far ahead, Ray heard shooting. Then over the radio, "K-car, Stop Three. We've dropped two CTs".

"Stop Three, Good work. Any more visual?"

"K-car, negative."

"Okay, stay put. We have another job to sort out."

The OP called up again: "K-car this is Oscar Five. There are gooks gapping it all over the place. One group is crossing the river to your north and more are heading west. Your Stop Groups are going to miss them."

"Okay, we haven't enough Stops on the ground to catch them all. Advise if any of my groups on the ground can move to intercept them, over."

"K-car, Roger. The Stop you put down near the hill to my west ... if they move south across the dirt road, about three hundred further on, there's a small gully. The Charlie Tangos are headed for that."

"Roger, copied that. Stop Four, did you get that message?"

"K-car, affirmative. We're on our way," said Corporal Dipps.

"There are three, possibly four of them, Stop Four," added the voice from the OP.

"Stop One, K-car. Ray, I'm going to hand you over to Cyclone Four for air support while I sort out Stop Four. Pete, are you there?"

"Yes, I'm here," came the faintly bored voice of the Lynx pilot. "I was wondering when you were going to give me some work."

"Cut the chatter," came the reprimand. "I want you to give Stop One air cover. Work with him."

"K-car, Roger. Stop One, confirm your location."

As the Lynx circled lazily overhead, Ray talked him on to the target.

"Okay, got that. Throw smoke to confirm."

Ray took out his pencil-like miniature smoke launcher and fitted an orange capsule into it. He pointed it in the direction of the rocky outcrop and fired the projectile.

"I see orange smoke," called the pilot.

"Cyclone Four, Roger, orange smoke. Add one hundred."

"Roger, adding one hundred, running in for the attack," said the pilot, and banked the light plane into a dive.

JASON HAD SEEN the stick of four men approaching and it looked as though the leader knew what he was doing. The helicopter pilot didn't seem to have seen the seven men hiding among the rocks, yet this group was sweeping not only towards this very spot, but were approaching with caution as if they knew someone was waiting. The men were out of view now, but he knew they would be planning their next move, and he knew that move would be good.

Jason had a nagging feeling that he had had dealings before with the man in charge of the stick coming towards him. With a sudden clarity he knew who it was. The man at the waterhole in Mozambique. A superstitious chill ran down his spine.

"This man has the inner eye," he muttered to himself in dread. "He can see into me, he knows where I am."

There was no magic. The white man had picked out the terrorists' position for the same reason Jason had chosen it. From a military point of view, it was ideal: high ground for defence, good cover from both observation and small arms fire. There were plenty of other places that might have been suitable but this one was the most easily defended, plus there were escape routes through the thick bush towards the river. No, it wasn't magic, it was just two military minds running along parallel lines.

That Jason "knew" his man, was not a form of ESP either. Jason was a better soldier than he realised and had subconsciously filed away in the back of his mind details of the firefight at the waterhole. Included in that data was Ray Hunter's *modus operandi*. He had merely sized up his opponent. But to his superstitious African mind, there was witchcraft in the air.

When he saw the four men's line of advance, his initial reaction was to make a break for the river and escape. He realised more men would be arriving before long and it was prudent to disappear now. Added to this, his fear of the supernatural made him want to bolt in panic. He was about to take off when his warrior background came to the fore.

"This white man knows I am here. If I go, he will follow, so I must fight him. If he can see my mind, I must show him that I am not afraid. I must make him fear my courage." With that, Jason gathered his men.

"We will stay and fight" was all he said.

He positioned men among the rocks and lay down. He wasn't just fighting his opponents, he was fighting his own fear. He couldn't see the white men, but he saw the smoke projectile arc towards their position and flare up. The Lynx, with its distinctive twin-tail and push-pull propellers, had maintained an orbit of the contact area at 800 feet. Following the orange smoke indicator, its pilot banked the aircraft sharply towards them and start its dive and run in.

Jason took an involuntary gasp of breath and gripped the stock of his rifle. He knew what was coming.

"Get into cover," he screamed, and crawled under the rocky overhang beside him.

Three seconds before the Lynx would have passed over Jason's position, the pilot released a pod of deadly SNEB rockets before banking high and to the right to avoid running into the devastation he had caused.

As soon as the rockets detonated, Ray was up and running. "Let's move," he shouted, pointing his arm in the direction of advance. "Don't bunch and keep up a steady rate of fire."

The four of them approached the rock-strewn slope, keeping their dressing by the sergeant, firing at likely cover as they went. About eighty metres from the outcrop, Ray gave the signal to go to ground.

"Change magazines," he ordered the two riflemen. As soon as they were ready, he called to Mark, "put on a hundred belt".

"Ready Ray," shouted Mark.

The Sergeant changed his own magazine. "CHARGE," he screamed, running up the hill.

The first SNEB streaked to the ground and blasted two terrorists into the spirit world, leaving the bodies twisted grotesquely among the boulders. A split-second before it would have detonated in the centre of the rest of the group, the other rocket glanced off a branch and veered over the top of the cowering men before detonating at the base of a baobab tree. The shock wave stunned them.

Dazed and groggy, Jason crawled to the lip of the ridge and looked down. From the corner of his eye he could see the rest of his men, just as dazed, struggling to join him.

"Fire," he croaked hoarsely. The men began to fire a ragged volley towards the four enemy soldiers running up the slope towards them.

The eighty metres seemed to take forever. Everything appeared to happen in slow motion, like a movie being run at half-speed. AK rounds cracked around their heads, shredding branches and leaves, but there was no alternative to continuing the charge.

Slowly, ever so slowly, Ray Hunter saw the Chinese-manufactured stick grenade as it tumbled over and over in an arc towards Trooper Hart.

"Grenade!" Ray heard a scream he hardly recognised as his own. The new boy dropped to the ground, his eyes swivelling in their sockets in a desperate attempt to locate the danger. His last thoughts were confused as the grenade rolled through the dust and settled against his right thigh. The blast lifted Hart off the ground and flipped his torso at 90 degrees to what was left of his body below the waist.

Having dived for cover, Ray was now back on his feet. There was no time to check out Hart's condition, they were exposed and the assault must go through. The three ran on, firing from the hip to keep the enemy's heads down. They were close to the ridge now, very close.

It was not physical fear that made Jason break and run. He just could not understand why this aggressive white man was running straight for him, as though he wanted Jason Ncube and Jason Ncube alone.

When two leaders place themselves in the middle of their men to keep control, and the focal point of their attack and defence is the same, then they must inevitably meet. Jason did not see it that way. He had been taught the white man's ways of fighting in just a few short years, and he did it well. But the man coming towards him had a powerful spirit inside. Jason could see that from the fire blazing in his eyes. He could see them from far away. This man was a devil, a devil coming for him.

A bullet ricocheted off a rock near his head, sending a stinging shower of granite chips into the side of his face. That was enough for Jason. Like the waterhole encounter, he broke and ran, shouting for his men to follow.

Mark and Koos reached the ridge just in time to see the last three terrorists darting away through the trees. Mark swung his MAG towards them and let rip a "walking" stream of high velocity rounds into the group. One of them jerked and tumbled to the ground. Another staggered and fell but got up and continued running. Koos, meanwhile, fired in the direction of the last man, who slammed into a large boulder and lay still.

As soon as it was obvious the enemy had fled and the area was clear, the Sergeant led his men back to where Will Hart lay, deathly pale and barely breathing. The membranes of his lower intestines were already dry and cracked and Hunter angrily swatted at the swarm of opportunistic flies. He tore the sleeve from his shirt and soaked it in water from a canteen before placing the damp cloth carefully over what remained of the boy's insides. Ray Hunter called for the radio.

"K-car, Stop One. Priority."

"Stop One, K-car, go."

"K-car, we have a badly wounded man here. Request immediate casevac."

"Stop One, Roger. The G-cars are approximately four minutes out. Talk your pilot into position. We are out of fuel and will have to land shortly, over."

"K-car, Roger. Out. G-car, did you receive that last transmission?"

"Stop One, Roger. Where are you in relation to where I put you down?"

"About five hundred to the north. There is a clearing not far from us to the west. I will talk you in."

"Stop One, affirmative. How bad is he? Over."

"Pretty bad, he's lost a lot of blood, we are trying to put a drip into him now."

The helicopter landed in the small clearing. Stop Five unloaded a canvas stretcher from behind the rear bench and doubled back to where Sergeant Hunter and his men waited. Trooper Smith looked at his wounded colleague and managed to whisper, "do you think he will be all right Sergeant?" They had been through training troop together and Will was his best mate. The Sergeant put his hand on Smith's shoulder.

"I hope so, lad, I hope so." There was no false hope in the Sergeant's tone.

THAT EVENING AT Grand Reef, a post-op debriefing took place in the Ops Room. Present were the air force officers and pilots who had taken part in the contact, Major Hill, his officers, and NCOs including Sergeant Hunter. The hut was crowded. Major Hill and Squadron Leader Thorn chaired the meeting.

"OK, guys," began Major Hill. "We have a few problems to sort out. We are not getting enough men on the ground quickly enough. We have to iron out that particular item. But first, let's see what happened today. Were there any problems in the initial stages? The choppers put everyone down okay?"

Sergeant Wells spoke up. "The choppers are doing a first class job. No problem there. We just need more of them."

"Yes, we know," replied the Major. "You were Stop Four, Sergeant Wells, what happened when you tried to cut off the group gapping it up that gully?"

"By the time we got there, the gooks had long gone. If you remember sir, at the briefing before we went, that area was one we nearly chose as a likely spot to put us down. It was a toss up between that and where we did put down."

"OK, Sergeant. Stop One. Sergeant Hunter, what were your problems?"

"Initially none, sir, but I believe that for a sweep line in a situation like we had, we must have at least two Stops doing the sweep. We could not cover anything like the ground we should have."

"Yes," agreed the Major. "It all points to getting more men on the ground sooner."

"Also, we needed a chopper above us to sort out a situation like the one we had. Even a G-car giving fire support might have kept their heads down enough to save Hart. The Lynx was good, but the extra manoeuvrability of a chopper would have made the day."

"Once again, point taken. But the K-car can't be everywhere at once." The Major was scratching his nose, a sure sign he was becoming agitated. "It was a choice between covering an actual sighting or chasing a maybe."

Realising he had touched a sore point, Ray changed tack. "There is no blame to be laid, sir. It is simply a fact that we don't have enough aircraft to do the job. There should be at least one spare chopper available."

"For fuck's sake, Sergeant, we don't even have enough helicopters to get the men to the scene. How are we going to have spare ones to cover all the Stops?"

"Hunter's right, sir," remarked Lieutenant Courtney. "We do need more choppers at each scene. Is there any way we can get more? Perhaps we can cut the number of Fire Forces. It will give us more men and aircraft, even though it will mean a lot more distance to travel."

"Good idea, Lieutenant, except that the terrs are pouring across like water. Our Fire Forces are spread out to cover the whole border with Mozambique. We can't reduce the number of Fire Forces or we will let too many terrs through. At least this way we are hitting more groups, even if we are only killing some of them instead of all of them."

Corporal Kerr spoke up. Short, wiry and insignificant to look at, he was nonetheless a hard and dedicated soldier. "It seems that the only time we have this problem of covering the ground with troops is when the scene is a long way off. When the contact is near, the choppers can ferry troops quite quickly. We have even been able to use G-cars for air command when the K-car has had to refuel."

"Well, we know what the problems are," drawled Squadron Leader Thorn through his bushy moustache. "What is the answer?"

Ray, who had been sitting quietly for a while, said: "Why don't we use paratroops?"

"That has been suggested before," Major Hill replied, "but we are told by the hierarchy that the logistical problems of training troops and keeping Dakotas in the air is too much to handle".

"What's wrong with those shiny-arsed fuckwits sitting behind their desks in Salisbury? Are they really prepared to let us go on dying in the field because they can't be bothered to organise a bit of paperwork?" Ray was angry now.

Major Hill lifted his hand for silence. "The cost of raising an airborne unit is high, very high. Top brass will need to be convinced that it is worthwhile."

Warrant Officer Read stood up. "The SAS are para-trained, why can't we be?"

This time it was Captain Watson who spoke. "The SAS are a small, highly specialised unit."

"What the hell are we, shit-house cleaners?" shouted Corporal Kerr.

"QUIET" roared the Major. "Right, there will be no more insolence." He lowered his voice: "You blokes are right, but I need facts and logical reasoning to convince the brass. Remember also," he added, before anyone else could start, "we are short of men as it is. How are we going to spare valuable troops?"

Ray got to his feet. "Well, sir, if we could convince Salisbury to let us train a small number of men on a trial basis, we might get somewhere. If we're ever going to even look like holding our own in this war, we're going to have to stop pussy-footing around."

"How are we going to use them?" Captain Watson asked. "We can't just go dropping them into riverbeds and rocks. The injury rate would be unacceptable."

"Couldn't we drop them in the nearest clearing? Then the choppers can pick them up and put them where they are needed."

"WO Read's idea would work," said Sergeant Wells.

"Right, if I'm to push for para-training, how many do you think we should ask for initially?" The Major left the question open.

"We need to fill the plane. There's no use going at it half-cocked. A Dak takes twenty-four paras. But we only have four choppers usually. If we can get sixteen men down, we have doubled our presence."

"A round of applause for our resident mathematician," laughed Captain Watson.

"Sixteen paras it is," smiled the OC.

As the men filed out, the OC caught up with Ray Hunter. "Congratulations, Sergeant. You did well today." He lowered his voice. "I'm sorry about Trooper Hart."

"Them's the breaks, sir. We could do a lot better if those staff heads got off their fat behinds and listened to us guys in the field."

"HEY, RAY," CALLED Captain Watson, after breakfast two days later. The Sergeant walked over to the Captain.

"Morning, sir. What's up?"

"It's not what's up with me. More to the point, what have you been up to?"

"Beg pardon, sir," Ray replied, looking puzzled.

"Well, it's strange, but the Afs on the base have started calling you "Isizo". It means "The Eye" or something like that. It's some weird, mystical thing – like there was some kind of magic about you."

"I can't think of any reason why they would do that. But come to think of it, they have been looking at me a bit strangely for the last day or two."

"Well, you've done something to spook them," the Captain replied. "What, I don't know."

"The only thing I can think of is the guy who was leading that group of terrs we took out the other day. Intelligence reports say it was the same bloke we had a punch up with at the waterhole in Mozambique two months ago."

"That might explain it, Sarge. Jason Ncube doesn't normally run, but he has done on both occasions up against you. Why, I wonder?"

"I've no idea, sir. But it has to be a plus for us. We might be able to exploit it somehow."

Chapter Four

THE OLD WITCHDOCTOR'S rheumy eyes gleamed at Jason through the smoke from the fire. "What is your problem, Jason Ncube, that you must come all the way here from the dirt-eating Shona — those who you try to make into soldiers?"

"My problem is a difficult one, old man. There is a man among the Boers. He has the magic eye. It seeks me out. I am afraid. I need magic to counter his."

"Tell me what you know of this man," said the witchdoctor.

Jason pondered for a minute. "They say he speaks like a man who comes from distant shores. But it is also true that his heart is African."

"What name do they call him?"

"He is called by the name of Hunter," replied Jason.

The witchdoctor stared at Jason for a minute. "Of these things you have told me, I have listened. It is indeed a problem. Things of such importance must be thought upon carefully. Return after three days and I will have an answer." With that the witchdoctor stood up and melted into the darkness.

Dwizo was a cunning, crafty old man. One does not attain such a position by conjury alone. He already knew a great deal more about Jason's dilemma than he let on and would let Jason stew for a while. Dwizo had heard about Jason's fear of Ray Hunter's eye by the same means that the African workers at Grand Reef had — through the "bush telegraph".

Most rural Africans believe mental telepathy carries messages across the land, but Africans, like any race, like to gossip. The speed at which gossip travels is amazing.

THREE NIGHTS LATER Jason squatted before the low fire, facing Dwizo. The old man did not speak for many minutes and when he did, his voice was shrill and disturbing. Jason's skin crawled with dread.

"Jason Ncube, I have thought much on this matter you have brought to me. In my dreams came the answer. Do you remember hearing of the journey the father of your mother took many years ago to a country far to the north? A place they call Kenya?" Jason nodded.

"Your grandfather went there in the service of the missionary Taggart."

"Yes, I know of this," replied Jason.

"Before he returned, your grandfather coupled with a local woman, who bore a son from this union."

Jason listened intently.

"That son grew up to be a freedom fighter like yourself, with the people called Mau Mau. There was an attack on a house owned by a man of law. This attack was led by a man called Kamau, your grandfather's son. Your uncle. The white man and his wife were killed, but the Mau Mau could not find their child. The freedom fighters believed this boy had become invisible by magic."

Dwizo paused, to maximise the effect of his next words.

"That child's name was Hunter."

Jason uttered a low moan, his eyes bulging in their sockets.

Dwizo continued: "My dreams tell me that Hunter has now come kill you in vengeance for the deeds of your uncle."

The witchdoctor had already known most of what he told Jason, not by witchcraft but by maintaining an informal, but highly-efficient, network. Many of the things he "prophesied" over the years were merely an assimilation of gossip filed away in the storehouse of his memory, which was quite incredible.

Like a modern-day politician, Dwizo was in the power game and used such situations to retain a strong hold on his people, and his position as a revered elder. Furthermore, Jason was a respected man, both as a leader and soldier. If and when the country became Zimbabwe, Dwizo wanted a patron on the inside. Jason was sure to be given a high position in the new government and the witchdoctor was going to make sure he was Jason's behind-the-scenes man.

He didn't know whether Ray Hunter's presence in Rhodesia was a coincidence, and he didn't care. It was a situation too good to pass up.

"Here is what we must do," he told Jason. "First, I will make a ceremony to purify you. Then I will make a magic potion to keep you from harm."

The witchdoctor gazed intently into the fire for a few moments.

"I will also prepare muti (medicine) which will make the man they call Hunter very sick, and he will die."

Dwizo did not say it, but the "medicine" he had in mind was ground glass disguised in plain sugar. Simple but potentially lethal.

THE SIXTEEN MEN from One Commando were divided into two groups of eight for ground training. The large hangar which had been converted into the training area for the Parachute Training School at New Sarum Air Force Base was warm and humid, despite the gentle breeze entering through the open doors. Eight men sat on a bench in the "A" side of the hangar: Sergeants Hunter and Kerr, Mark, Koos, and four other volunteers.

The instructor came out of the crew room. "Good morning, gentlemen. I'm Sergeant Hogan. I'll be your instructor on this course. All I ask is that you work hard and achieve a good standard. The course should be fun. The Parachute School's motto is 'Knowledge dispels fear'. That's exactly what it's about. By the time you do your first jump, you will know everything by heart. It will be automatic. Right now, I want your names and numbers – then we can begin."

The instructor came up to Ray and smiled. "G'day Ray, remember me? We used to skydive together in Queensland."

"Shit ... Howzit, Pete? I recognise you now, mate. Yeah, long time no see. I didn't know you were here."

"Been here for ages. I'll expect you to set a good example for the next three weeks."

"Thanks, Staff, that's all I need," replied Ray, but he was smiling.

For the next five days they learned all the skills needed to carry out a successful parachute jump.

Using the mocked-up interior of an aircraft, they practised the drills required to move from inside the aircraft to the door. They then practised the jump itself, learning how to deploy the parachute properly. In a flight harness they went through the manoeuvres required under canopy, including emergency drills for malfunctions and collisions. On the mats, ramps, and wheel-swing trainers, they practised landing rolls designed to absorb the impact of fast landings on their bodies. Over and over they drilled and practised until they were perfect and swore they could do it in their sleep.

That weekend the group hit town to drink, carouse and forget the army for a while, even though the course was a welcome break from the hardships of the bush.

On Monday morning, back in the hangar, they were ready to start again. For most of that morning, they practised and revised the skills they had learned.

After morning tea, Sergeant Hogan lined them up. "For the rest of today we're going to rehearse for tomorrow's jumps. The first will be 'slow' sticks of four from one thousand feet. The second jump will be 'faster' sticks of six from one thousand feet. Any questions?"

There were none.

"Right. Kit up with the dummy parachutes, go and get the short static lines and wait for me at the mock-up."

By three o'clock they could perform the drills perfectly. The last job they had to do that afternoon was collect "live" parachutes from the store for the following day's jump and lay them out on the mats.

THE TRAINEES WERE kitted up and ready to go — despatchers checking each man to make sure parachutes were fitted properly.

"Righteo, listen in Course," boomed the voice of Warrant Officer Boyne. "Shortly, you're going to be doing your first jumps. For most of you it will be a bit unnerving so remember, as long as you do what you have been taught you'll be okay. So, let's make it a good one. Don't forget you'll be individually critiqued from the ground. Any questions? Right, course. Right turn. Quick march."

They marched out to the waiting Dakota.

"Halt," bellowed Warrant Officer Boyne. "Starboard stick, emplane."

As the stick boarded the plane, Mark turned to Ray. "They tell us that 'Knowledge dispels fear'. If you ask me, it's more like 'Fear dispels knowledge'. I'm shitting myself."

Ray smiled. "It's a piece of piss, mate. Just do as you've been taught. You'll be okay."

"Easy for you to say, Sarge. How many jumps have you done?"

"Aw, only six hundred or so."

"Mad, stark ravin' fucking mad you are, Sarge," chuckled Koos.

"Yeah, modest too," joked Mark.

"Port stick, emplane," came the order.

One by one they climbed the steps and sat down on the bench seats.

"Fasten seat belts," called the number two despatcher.

The plane's engines coughed into life and began their warm up. A few minutes later the old Dakota taxied on to the runway ready for take off. The engine revs increased to a roar and they were off down the tarmac, building up speed until the plane lifted off the ground and began its climb to a thousand feet.

"PREPARE FOR ACTION," shouted the number two, above the noise. The sixteen men unfastened their seatbelts and unsnapped the static line hooks.

"DRIFTER. STAND UP, HOOK UP AND CHECK YOUR EQUIPMENT."

The drifter on a training jump is an experienced parachutist used to check that the drop-off point is correct — so that troops are dropped in the right place. He completed his checks and shuffled to the door. Number two despatcher watched the lights above the exit. The red light came on.

"STAND IN THE DOOR." The drifter shuffled one pace forward. The green light came on.

"GO," shouted the despatcher, and the man was gone.

"FIRST STICK. STAND UP. HOOK UP AND CHECK YOUR EQUIPMENT."

Ray Hunter's stick stood up and snapped their static line hooks over the cable.

"SNAP, HOOK AND PIN. STATIC LINE CLEAR OVER THE LEFT SHOULDER. HELMET. RESERVE. QUICK-RELEASE BOX. SAFETY CLIP. BODY BAND."

Then they checked the man in front.

"SNAP, HOOK AND PIN. STATIC LINE CLEAR TO THE LEFT. CORRECTLY STOWED. CENTRE PACK TIE."

When the checks were completed the despatcher checked them again. Then, "TELL OFF FOR EQUIPMENT CHECK".

The last man in the stick tapped the man in front's shoulder. "FOUR OKAY."

This went on down the line. "THREE OKAY." "TWO OKAY." "ONE OKAY."

"STICK OKAY," shouted the first man and gave the thumbs up. The number one despatcher swept his hand forward; the number two yelled, "ACTION STATIONS", and the stick shuffled down the aircraft and waited by the door. The red light came on.

"STAND IN THE DOOR."

The stick shuffled one pace. The green light came on.

"GO," shouted the despatcher. The first man disappeared. The stick took one pace forward.

"GO." One pace forward.

It was Ray's turn. "I don't know how the others feel" he thought, "but Christ, it's good to be doing this again."

A biting wind whipped past his face. Ray felt a tap on his shoulder and launched himself from the door.

He felt a tug as the parachute opened. He shouted aloud to himself: "Look up, check canopy. Looking down to assess the drift. Drifting forward, pull down on the backlift webs."

The ground rushed up to meet him; he landed in the classic, feet and knees-together style and rolled. The jump was over.

Ray collapsed the 'chute and field-packed it as taught before doubling over to the instructor who had been critiquing him.

"728634 Sergeant Hunter," he reported.

"Not bad, Sergeant. Carry on," said the balding instructor, who smiled as Ray ran back to the truck.

The next three jumps were to build up stick numbers and deployment rates. The last jump of the course was a "fast" stick of twenty-four from only eight hundred feet. They were conducted using CSPEP (Carrying, Straps, Personal Equipment, Parachutist) — a device attached to the parachutist's harness when exiting the aircraft. After the canopy opens, the equipment is lowered fifteen feet on a line, leaving the parachutist unencumbered for landing.

Following the last jump, when parachutes and gear had been handed in, the Parachute Training School's Officer Commanding, Squadron Leader Cooke, addressed the wings parade in the hangar.

"Good afternoon, gentlemen. Congratulations on passing the course. You were a good course; there were no injuries and the standard was high. You blokes from One Commando are here on a trial basis, we hope it works successfully out in the bush. So the best of luck. Now, before I hand out the wings, there is one thing I have to tell you.

For the last two weeks, since you started jumping, you have been at liberty to refuse to jump. Now that you are qualified, it is a court martial offence to refuse to jump. Before you board a plane to carry out a training or operational jump, you will be given this warning: 'When the red light comes on, it is an order to prepare to jump. When the green light comes on, it is an order to jump. Refusal to do so will result in your court martial or imprisonment, or both.' Is that clear?"

"Yes, sir," the course replied.

Out of the corner of his mouth, Koos muttered: "Now he tells us."

After the wings had been presented the course went to the base tailor to get them sewn on to their sleeves.

"I scheme the ouns will be green with envy when they see us with these," declared Mark proudly, showing off the winged parachute neatly stitched to his shirt.

Back in the hangar, Captain Watson spoke to the men. "Right, listen in, you fucking heroes. We have the rest of the day off, so you can do as you please. We are getting a ride out to the bush in style tomorrow — flying in the Dak. It leaves here at 0500 hours. I want you all back at the barracks at 0400, kit on, ready to go. The truck will be waiting. God help any of you who's late. Got that?"

"Roger, sir."

"Right, piss off and have a good time."

"Hey, Ray." Ray turned round to see Sergeant Hogan walking towards him.

"I've been talking to the boss. We are doing a staff training freefall this morning and I've managed to talk him into letting you come along if you're interested."

"Shit, yeah. It's been too long since I've done a freefall."

"Okay, but the boss laid down the condition that we give you some ground training to cover our procedures. It's only a formality, but we have to cover our backs."

Two hours later the eight freefallers walked over to the waiting aircraft. A few minutes later the plane was up, circling to gain height.

One of the African labourers assigned to grass cutting duties around the airstrip watched the plane get smaller as it droned around and around.

The plane reached ten thousand feet and began its run in. Squadron Leader Cooke knelt by the door with his head sticking out, talking to the pilot through the headset and guiding him to the drop-point. Ten seconds out, he took off the headset and put his helmet on. He looked out of the door to make sure the spot was right.

"Okay, boys, let's go for it," he yelled. The other seven lined up behind him. "Ready, set, go!" he called and was gone. The others followed suit.

Ray was last out. As he dived through the door he could feel the slipstream rush past his body and head until freefall speed was reached and it felt like he was floating on a cushion. Below him, he saw the figures of the others.

He watched as Squadron Leader Cooke and Flight Lieutenant Mills closed in to link up. Putting his hands back and straightening his legs, Ray swooped down towards the base. Flight Sergeant Granger linked up to make a three-way star. Sergeant Mick Duff made an approach but was too fast; he turned away for another attempt. Sergeant Frank Prentiss closed fourth; Mick closed in fifth, his second attempt succeeding. Flight Sergeant Tony Wilkins broke into the star sixth but was a bit rough and nearly took it out. Ray flared out of his swoop and looked around to see Sergeant Peter Hogan grinning at him from the other side of the formation and waiting for Ray to make his approach for them to enter the star together.

Ray moved forward into his slot and he and Pete broke in to make it a perfect eight-way star. They flew the formation down to three thousand five hundred feet, smiling and poking their tongues out before executing a turn and separating to make room to open the parachutes.

At two thousand five hundred feet, Ray waved off and pulled his ripcord. He watched the canopy deploy. Something was wrong.

"Oh shit, a line over," he said aloud to himself. A line over happens on the odd occasion, no time to mull over it. He must cut away.

"Look down and remove the Capewell covers." He went through the emergency drill. "Locate the rings and lock the thumbs in. PULL."

The connector links came loose and the canopy shot away. Ray was back in freefall. He turned over and deployed the reserve on his chest. It billowed out and he was under a canopy once more. After stowing his ripcord away down the front of his jumpsuit, Ray reached up and took the steering toggles out of their stows and steered the canopy towards the drop zone. The spot had been good and he landed near the others.

The African labourer had watched the plane fly over and the tiny figures appear in the sky. He picked out Sergeant Hunter straight away. He was the only one wearing a black jumpsuit, all the others wore green. The black one had been the only one left available to Ray. The African had seen everything as it happened.

"Dwizo must know of this," he thought to himself. "It is true, the man called Hunter is a wizard. He can fly and he can make two umbrellas appear."

The witchdoctor's ears and eyes stretched far and wide.

ONE COMMANDO HAD relieved Two Commando at the FAF (Forward Air Field) Mtoko and were already two weeks into a six-week stint. Their sixteen newly para-trained colleagues arrived from New Sarum, just outside Salisbury, around 6.30am. They were not left idle for long.

By 9.30am they were aloft and heading to a confirmed sighting of sixty terrorists in thick riverine bush in the Uzumba tribal trust land. A Selous Scouts call sign on a kopje three kilometres to the south of the river had spent two days observing the tell-tale patterns of locals bringing food and supplies before radioing in a "confirmed sighting" message.

G-cars had placed Stop Groups in position while the K-car maintained a high orbit over the scene. The rookie paras were about to find out just how an operational deployment varied from training, where jumps are usually conducted in the cool of early morning when the wind is light.

The air was already hot and turbulent and the Dak dipped and yawed on the run in. Most of the men were soon reaching for sick bags — the turbulence only heightening their nervousness at the coming action.

"Jeez — why did I volunteer for this?" said one man, bringing up stale beer and Pronutro breakfast cereal.

The trucks were still a long way off and Captain Watson, who had been listening in on the spare headset, sat upright. "Para unit, K-car. I want you to follow Golf Two to a clearing west of here. He will throw smoke at the exit point. I need all four Stops on the ground ready for pick-up by helicopter."

"K-car, Roger. On our way," replied the pilot.

The co-pilot switched on the internal intercom. "Number one

despatcher, could you get the men ready as soon as possible please."

Sergeant Wilkins pulled the mouthpiece down and spoke over it. "Steve, all four sticks please."

Number two bellowed: "ALL FOUR STICKS. STAND UP, HOOK UP AND CHECK YOUR EQUIPMENT."

As they did so, Sergeant Wilkins unclipped his mouthpiece and shouted: "Non-tactical drop, fellows, the choppers are coming to pick you up."

As soon as they were checked, Sergeant Wilkins clipped up his mouthpiece: "Troops ready."

"Right, bring them down to action stations please."

Number one gave the signal to number two. "ACTION STATIONS."

Sixteen sweaty, nauseous and nervous men shuffled to the door, stumbling along the heaving plane.

"Watch the lights," came the pilot's calm voice. As number one pointed to the lights, number two said: "Get ready." The men stood waiting, their parachutes made bulkier by the webbing worn under the harness. Rifles and machineguns were strapped to their sides.

"STAND IN THE DOOR. GO, GO, GO, GO," shouted number two as he tapped the paras out of the door.

"Fourteen, fifteen, sixteen," counted number one into the mouthpiece. "Troops gone, bags coming in."

Contrary, gusty winds resulted in hard and heavy landings for most of the men. They were scattered over a seven hundred-metre radius, resulting in a delay meeting up. Both Mark and Koos came limping in, Mark's shin bled where the foresight of his MAG had dug in on impact.

"Fuck this for a joke. I had all the breath knocked out of me, my head still hurts and I think I broke my ankle."

"Quit whining. What are you, a bunch of old women?" retorted Ray. "Where's Jannie?"

The fourth member of Ray's Stop Group, Jannie hove into sight, holding his ribs.

"You all right?" Ray called. "Ja, but my side hurts and it's hard to breathe ek se."

"Anything broken?" "Nie man, just winded, I think."

"Right, here come the choppers," said Ray. "Now, are you all sure you are okay to carry on?"

"Ja man, we are RLI," replied Koos through clenched teeth.

By the end of the day, thirty-two of the sixty terrorists had died. It was considered a good kill rate. The paras had proved their worth. They were here to stay.

TWO DAYS LATER, they were floating down to earth when Ray saw a lone terrorist running along a riverbed. The fleeing ZANLA cadre looked up in amazement to see the white man approaching him silently and instinctively let rip with a burst of AK fire.

"Oh, shit, I hope his aim is poor," thought Ray just before he crashed into the ground and performed a fast backward landing. After the contact, as they were retrieving their parachutes, Koos looked in amazement at Ray's canopy. There were seven holes in it.

"Holy Jesus, will ya look at that," he said in disbelief. Ray shrugged it off. "It takes a lot more than that to affect the rate of descent."

Sergeant Hunter was already thinking of ways to overcome the problems they were encountering.

Later, at a briefing of all concerned, the OC, his men and the air force pilots gathered to discuss ways to iron out problems.

"As I see it," said Major Hill, "the biggest headache is the time lost regrouping the men. Half of them are landing right off the drop zone. Also, Sergeant Hunter' nearly got drilled the other day. So far the injuries have been acceptable. But sure as eggs, the injury rate is going to get higher."

Ray spoke up. "Unfortunately, there is nothing we can do about the weather, and the only way we can solve the problem of injury is to train more paras.

"But there is one way we can land the men closer together and give the enemy less time to shoot at us — we can lower the jump height."

There was a stunned silence.

"Holy hell, Sergeant," said Major Hill. "Eight hundred feet is already too close to the ground for my liking."

Sergeant Kerr chimed in: "Shit, I'm getting ground rush three windows from the door as it is, never mind coming in to land."

"And what height did you have in mind, Sergeant?" asked the Major.

"Five hundred feet."

"Well, it'll save wear and tear on the parachutes," retorted Sergeant Kerr. "We won't use 'em, we'll just step out of the aircraft and on to the ground."

"Sergeant," breathed the Dakota pilot, "you realise you'll only be under canopy for a few seconds."

"That's the general idea, sir. Our groupings will be closer and the terrs won't have time to shoot at us. Jumps from this height have been done successfully before, so there is no reason why it can't be done here."

"Any idea how long you will be under canopy?"

"Approximately seventeen seconds, sir."

Sergeant Wilkins, the number one despatcher, spoke up. "We'll have to clear it with New Sarum and order extra parachutes for the trial jumps."

"Right then, we had better get on with it. When we are going to get time for these trial jumps, I don't know," muttered the OC.

Late afternoon was the time chosen. The air was cooler and there was less chance of a call out.

As they were kitting up, Ray spoke to the other three volunteers, Captain Watson, Mark and Koos. "For this first jump, we'll go out in a slow stick. That way, we can dispense with the all-round observation. The purpose of this jump is to assess how we cope with the shorter timespan under canopy. Just check your canopy, kick out of your seat strap and assess your drift. Okay?"

"I don't know how I let you talk me into this, Sergeant Hunter," said Captain Watson, but he was grinning from ear to ear.

Onlookers said later that the wingtips of the Dakota nearly touched their heads as it thundered past; the four men tumbling one by one out of the door. It might have been an exaggeration, but to both parachutists and spectators, it sure felt far too close for comfort.

Within a week, all sixteen parachutists had learnt how to be very low altitude meatbombs.

THE CALL OUT came late the next day, just after noon. In the briefing room, Major Hill was talking.

"Fifty gooks this time, blokes. If you look on the map, we have been to this location before. It's a disused kraal near a PV (Protected Village). However, the scenario is a bit different this time.

"There's no OP to direct us. A Selous Scouts callsign has infiltrated the group and has only just been able to get word back to us, hence the late call out. The reason we are going to have a go this late in the day is because the group is splitting up and moving on tonight so we have to take them out while they are still together. For this reason, I am going to change tactics.

"Apparently the terrs are moving freely about the area. The fact that they're wandering about armed during the day indicates they feel pretty safe and probably have mujibas out checking for OPs. Watch out though, the Scouts' callsign reports there are elements of hard core with them. So be prepared for a fight.

"Now, on to the battle plan. The scene is reasonably close so I want the truck Stops to take off thirty minutes before the choppers. That way they will be close enough for a fast pick-up by air. From the last contact we had in that area, I think we can work out their likely escape routes, so I want the chopper Stop Groups here, here, here and here," the Major said, pointing to places on the map.

"As soon as you drop the first wave off, I want you to go and pick up the next wave and put them here."

When he had finished discussing the helicopter groups he turned to the paras.

"I am going to use you for a tactical drop. If you remember from the last time, there is a large cleared area to the south of the PV. I want you dropped in a line from east to west along here, and an extended sweep line moved north through the site. Got that Steve?" the Major asked the Dak pilot.

"Roger, I know where to put them," he replied.

The Major continued. "You guys in the sweep line, expect resistance. You might have to slog it out among the old huts. Judging by the amount of terrs moving through the area it seems as though the locals are active sympathisers, so if you have to take out a few of the locals to get at the terrs, do it. I want that area cleaned out. It might make a few collaborators think twice about harbouring the gooks if they get a bit of a slap. Any questions?

"Right, let's go for it."

The Major was right, no sooner had they landed than they were involved in firefights which erupted in several places at once. The fact that the terrorists were still in the village showed they had been surprised, so the Selous Scouts' method of infiltrating the terrorist groups was working. Major Hill had also been right about the hard core elements.

"K-car, Stop Six, we are being fired on from the hut to our front."

"Stop Six, Roger"

"Cyclone Four, I want you to drop Frantan on the hut fifty metres to the east of where you see the red smoke."

"K-car, Roger, target visual, running in now."

"K-car, Stop Niner. We are getting stiff resistance to our front. Estimate seven Charlie Tangos in the riverbed by the big rocky outcrop."

"Stop Niner, Roger, we'll give you covering fire while you assault."

"K-car, Stop Eight. We have a man down, I say again, we have a man down. Require urgent casevac, over."

"Roger, Stop Eight, patch him up as best you can, the G-cars are two minutes out."

"K-car, Stop Eight, we're pinned down and could use air support."

"Stop Eight, K-car, Roger. Cyclone Four, are you free?"

"K-car, Cyclone Four, affirmative."

"What armaments have you left?"

"Rockets."

"Cyclone Four, Roger, support Stop Eight."

The firefight lasted two and a half hours. At the end, thirty-seven ZANLA were dead, with three captured. The RLI lost one man, with three wounded. Both Ray and Koos had cuts and lacerations from shrapnel. It was late afternoon before things began to return to a semblance of normality.

The dead and wounded Rhodesians had been airlifted out, the captured terrs taken away for questioning by Special Branch officers on attachment to the Selous Scouts, and the bodies hauled to clearings to await uplift. Eight dead civilians were left where they lay. Time was running out, the choppers could not fly in the bush at night and there were four Stop Groups still on the ground.

"Stops Two, Three, Five and Six, this is Golf Two." The G-car had taken over control while the K-car was refuelling.

"Go ahead," replied each stick.

"We won't be able to pick you up until first light. You will have to stay. We have been informed that some of these groups return to their camps after a firefight, when they think we have gone, so you have been instructed to ambush the base tonight."

"Golf Two, Roger."

"Good luck and good night."

"That'd be fuckin' right," grumbled Trooper Venter, in charge of Stop Four. "The rest of the ouns get home to a cold chibuli and we get stuck out here in the fuckin' kungen, roughin' it."

"Ja, life is harsh for us RLI schollies. We kill long floppies for them and what thanks do we get, eh? Ja, you stay out there and sleep on the hard ground they say."

"I will tell you one thing, young Jordan. We won't be sleeping on the hard ground tonight," remarked Sergeant Hunter. "Cos, if you do go to sleep, I'll kick your arse till your nose bleeds. We are here to ambush and that is what we are going to do."

"Ja, what is wrong with you okes?" This was Corporal Wessels from Stop Seven. "Who would want to go back and have a nice shower, a hot meal, some lekker cold beers and a nice soft bed to sleep in when we could be out here in the freezing cold, killing gooks?"

"That's enough, ouns," snapped Ray. "Do all you riflemen have full magazine on your weapons?"

"Yes, Sarge."

"Right, when we get to the ambush site, I want you to take out a spare full magazine and put it on the ground beside you. Machinegunners, I want you to make up one hundred-round belts and make sure they are set in the links correctly. We don't want any stoppages."

"Right, Sarge."

"If you want to eat or drink, do it now, before we move out."

When the men were ready, Ray led them into position near the vacated terrorist camp. The smell of death — roasted flesh and woodsmoke — hung heavily over the scene in the rapidly approaching twilight. Positions were taken up in a small clearing among trees and rocks forty metres from the camp. A natural killing ground. Ray positioned his men, giving the machinegunners the best field of fire. When he was satisfied he lay in his spot.

"Now I lay me down to wait and trust the pricks will take the bait." He couldn't help a wry smile at his own joke.

THEY CAME AT two in the morning, flashes of white from the bandages covering their wounds received in the contact the day before giving them away. The fight lasted only a few seconds.

"CEASE FIRE," roared Sergeant Hunter. There was no movement from the terrorists — they were dead or had escaped the withering fire laid down by the MAG gunners.

Dawn revealed five terrorists lying where they fell, with no signs of outgoing spoor. The ambush had been a total success. Ray Hunter seemed to have the knack of managing night ambushes.

"WELCOME BACK, BOYS," said Major Hill as the four Stops clambered off the trucks. "Congratulations on last night's work. That, and yesterday's contact, was a great way to end a bush trip. Or had you all forgotten that we are going home today?"

"Is the six weeks up already?" asked Corporal Johnny Wessels. "My, doesn't time fly when you are having fun?"

"Right you lot, you've got twenty minutes to get ready to get on the trucks back to Salisbury," bellowed the CSM. "The rest of the Commando is waiting."

"YAHOO," yelled the men in chorus as they ran off to their billets.

"And don't forget to clean your weapons, you slack and idle soldiers," shouted Ray, laughing after them.

The men were paraded beside the waiting trucks, the CSM addressing them.

"Right, listen in One Commando. When we get back to Salisbury, don't forget we have to clean up and boil the weapons. So we will be late finishing tonight. We would have been almost there if certain individuals hadn't wasted our time by wandering around the bush till all hours."

"Ja, boo, hiss," laughed the rest of the troops.

"As soon as we are finished," continued the CSM, "you can piss off on leave. But before you get too excited, Trooper Zietsling's funeral is the day after tomorrow and you will be there for the parade. So you had better make sure your uniforms are jacked up for that. Is that understood?"

"Yes, CSM."

"Right, get on the trucks and let's go."

The convoy was hurrying back to Salisbury and the troops were happy and laughing.

"Sarge," said Mark, leaning over the seat," have you anywhere to stay while we are in town?"

"Shit, mate, I thought I'd book into Meikles or Monos and get shit-faced for a couple of days and see if I can't get some lovely redhead to see me purely as a sex object."

"Oh, okay. It's just that my parents would like to meet you and they said it would be okay for you to stay at our place. I can't guarantee you'll get any jig-jig, but the meals are good and the beer's cold."

"Actually, I'd like that Mark. If I may, I'll take you up on that for a couple of days, but after Bob's funeral I'm going to book into town and cut loose."

"I reckon we might all get together and make it a big shindig. What do you reckon, guys?" Mark asked the others in the truck.

"Ja, I scheme we'll all go to Le Coq D'or on Thursday after the funeral and get lekker pissed."

"Make that late on Thursday arvo," said Sergeant Kerr.

ONE COMMANDO

CHAPTER FIVE

MARK, KOOS AND Ray were sitting on the step at Mark's parents' house, overlooking the lush green lawn which ran down to a small brook. The day was warm and as they sipped at bottles of cold Lion lager, it was hard to reconcile the quiet surroundings with what they had seen and done only 48 hours earlier. The jackets of their dress uniforms were undone and their berets had been discarded on the swing settee.

"Well, that's the end of Zietsling," mused Mark. "Fuck, but I hate funeral parades. Makes you wonder when it's going to be your turn."

"Ja, poor old Bob's parents were crying the whole time and his sister took it hard. Today was the first time I've seen her and not wanted to take her to bed," said Koos.

"Shit man, how stupid is this war? Everyone running around killing each other and for what? Because a bunch of half-baked gooks want to run this beautiful country. Hell, man, look at the mess the Afs are making of all the other countries they have taken over."

"Yes, but unfortunately politics and sense seldom make good bedfellows," replied Ray. "We know what a lot of bullshit all this is. But who else does? Not many I'll bet."

"Ja, our job is not to think or make decisions. We just here to slay floppies," remarked Koos.

"But shit man, don't we do a fucking good job of it. Jesus, we slew long gooks this last trip," quipped Mark.

"Talking about that," Koos said, looking slyly at Ray. "What's your story, Sarge? All the ouns in the Commando really respect you. You're a really dedicated soldier. No one has ever seen you back down from anything; not a contact — or an officer. With you it's push push, all the way. It's like something is really driving you. How come you're here fighting for us when you don't come from Rhodesia?"

"For a start," answered Ray slowly, "don't call me Sarge when we are off duty. The three of us have been together for a long time, we're good mates and a good team."

"Okay, Sarge, I mean Ray, you going to tell us what gives?"

"It's quite simple, really," he said without expression. "My parents were killed by the Mau Mau in Kenya when I was a kid. It has nothing to do with politics. It's a personal thing. I just hate to see people running around killing women and children to get what they want."

There was a moment's silence.

"But what do you think of Ian Smith, Ray?" asked Mark.

"I think he has the right idea. What amazes me is that a lot of Africans believe in him. There are a lot of Africans who know that they are going to lose out if the country is run by blacks. At the moment, things are quite orderly and even if the Afs aren't rich and don't have cars, they aren't too badly done by either. I think they know that under a black government things will get chaotic and they'll be a lot worse off than they are now.

"The problem is that the outside world believes what a few power-hungry megalomaniacs are telling them. I will tell you now, we will win the war, but we'll lose the country. The writing is on the wall."

"Fuck, that's heavy stuff, Ray. No wonder you're a sergeant and we're only troopies," said Mark. "Hey, let's grab some graze and then get into town to meet the boys!"

"We'd better change into civvies, then," laughed Koos. "We don't want the RLI to fall into more disrepute than it already is."

THE TALL MATABELE walked into the camp early one morning. It had been a long journey and he was grey with fatigue, but he refused any food or drink until Jason had been summoned.

He stood proud and aloof while he waited. He was a Matabele and the people in this camp were Shona, eaters of dirt, below his dignity. A Matabele would rather die than show any sign of weakness in front of these people — his ancestral enemies. So he waited, staring disdainfully at the hostile glances directed at him.

The camp was a fairly rough affair, situated thirty kilometres inside Mozambique next to an oxbow in a river. Crude huts made of grass and mud were well concealed among the trees. The only place that stood out was the parade ground, a large area of hard earth flattened into dust by the tramping of many feet. The camp doubled as both a training base for terrorist groups, and as the last staging post before before infiltration into Rhodesia.

"I see you, Comrade Jason," the tall Matabele acknowledged as Jason strode into view.

"I see you, Comrade Mbozo. You have news?"

Normally when Africans greet each other, etiquette demands a fairly long drawn-out exchange of pleasantries: "How are your wives, how are your cattle" and so on. However, revolutionary ideals say business comes first. The small talk could come later.

"I have news from Dwizo himself. Is there somewhere we can talk, away from these ears?"

"Yes, we can talk at my hut."

As they walked past the cooking area, Jason called to the woman nearby: "Bring food to my hut. Quickly."

When they were seated outside the hut, Mbozo asked: "How does the training go with these Shona dogs?"

"I tell you this brother Mbozo, it is difficult to instil discipline or courage in these people. They are not warriors like our people, they are just farmers. Teaching them is like trying to push against a large rock. Now, what news do you have from Dwizo?"

"The great Dwizo would have me tell you this, Jason Ncube. The attack that is to happen at the strong place the white men call Grand Reef, where their planes take off. Do you know that the man they call Hunter will be there?"

Jason did know. The amount of information ZANLA had amassed regarding Grand Reef was staggering. They knew that on the 17th of December, One Commando would be relieving Three Commando. The enemy would be at their most vulnerable on the first day as they settled in and established a routine.

The terrorist hierarchy and their Chinese instructors had decided that to boost ZANLA morale, and to show the world that they were capable of inflicting a heavy blow to Rhodesia's security forces, they would mount an attack on one of the major Fire Force bases and annihilate one of the most aggressive units in the army.

They also knew the names of all the officers and NCOs of One Commando and where they would most likely be staying in the camp. Much of this information had come from the labourers and cooking staff at the FAF, but a great deal of the technical information had come from high up in the army itself. Some men who were in positions of trust were actually working for the British and American governments who were trying to win the terrorists' favour and bring about the downfall of Rhodesia.

Jason had known Sergeant Hunter would be there and it worried him. But he trusted Dwizo. Ncube was working tirelessly to train the men under his command for the coming attack. They had practised and rehearsed for months and believed they had a fair chance of success. The only fly in the ointment as far as Jason was concerned was Isizo. If that man was there, his inner eye would see them coming and the attack would fail.

"Yes, I know of this," replied Jason.

"Dwizo says you are not to worry. When you attack them, if Hunter is not already dead, he will be very sick and his magic will be weak."

Jason's heart soared. With Hunter out of the way, not only would the attack go well, but he, Jason, would never have to run from the white man's magic again. There was no shame in running away from magic, but his warrior's soul detested any form of cowardice, acceptable or not.

INITIALLY, DWIZO'S PLAN to poison Isizo looked as though it might not come to fruition. The African staff often travelled with the Commando to and from the bush and the camp cook had overheard Ray's mention of staying at one of the hotels in town. The two-day stay with Mark had shortened the time Dwizo's man needed.

TROOPER ZIETSLING'S WAKE turned into a mammoth drinking session and One Commando did indeed fall into disrepute. The more they drank, the louder and more boisterous the men became and some of their antics shocked even the hardened drinkers in the pub. The occasional fistfight with civilians broke out and there were many complaints.

"Shit, man. We spend most of our lives in the bush fighting for the bloody civvies, then they get upset when we let our hair down. They expect us to be bloody hard killing machines one minute and meek and mild law-abiding citizens the next. Well, they can all go and get fucked. In fact, I think I will go and fuck that bloke's wife over there, in front of everybody," said Trooper Wood, as he made his way unsteadily across the room.

He would probably have attempted just that except the woman in question's husband was far more sober than the soldier and Trooper Wood ended up flat on his back with a split lip.

A general brawl then raged for some time before the Military Police stormed in and broke it up. The rest of the evening became very hazy and the next morning saw Ray with a sore head and feeling very sorry for himself.

The African waiter had only been working at Meikles Hotel for a short while. He had been told to look out for Ray Hunter. It was with satisfaction that he saw him sit down gingerly to order his meal.

After ordering bacon and eggs, Ray wandered over to the cereal table for a bowl of Pronutro and a cup of tea. He had just sat down again when Lieutenant Courtney came over and joined him.

"Ray, don't put any sugar in your tea," he warned in a low voice. Ray looked up. "Eh?" was all he could say.

Lieutenant Courtney was short and bordering on chubby, his round face making him look like a choirboy. But underneath the soft-looking exterior was a tough, dedicated warrior who could outshoot, outsoldier and outlast most men. A trained lawyer who had forgone a promising career at the London Bar to volunteer to fight for his country, Paul Courtney was also extremely observant.

"Don't put any sugar in your tea," he warned again. "While you were up at the table, that waiter over there by the door put something in your sugar bowl. My guess is that they are trying to poison you. It could have something to do with that mumbo-jumbo with Jason Ncube everyone is talking about."

Paul had sat down with his back to the waiter so the African's view was obstructed. After the first few seconds, Ray managed to look as normal as possible and tried to make the conversation seem like everyday chit-chat.

"If the sugar is poisoned, what about the meal I ordered?" he asked in a conversational tone.

"I know a fair bit about African superstition and magic," Paul replied. "They will only try one thing. If it's the sugar, they will try to poison your tea. They believe if they try to do more than one thing, the magic will not work. It's just the way they think."

"Well, let's go and grab the waiter and question him."

"No, that won't work," cautioned Paul. "We won't get the truth out of him. Not when it's something like this.

"I have a better idea. Pretend to put sugar in your tea and on the cereal. If it's supposed to poison, let's make out it is doing just that. After you have eaten, look as though you are feeling a bit sick. After last night, that won't be difficult.

"When the waiter goes to get your bill, we will take some of the sugar and find out what's in it."

After breakfast, they stood up to leave. Ray clutched his stomach and leaned over, as though in pain. "Ooh, my guts, they hurt. I hope it's not something I ate!" he said with a grimace. He was only half joking. It had been a hell of a night.

The two men walked out of the dining room, completely ignoring the waiter.

"AHAA!" exclaimed Paul in Ray's room a bit later. "Just as I thought. Ground-up glass in the sugar. Shit, mate, you really would have been sick if you had eaten that."

Paul had run a simple test. By dissolving the sugar they had taken in water, the ground glass was left in the bottom of the cup.

"Right, we know they are trying to kill you or make you very sick." Paul was talking aloud, but thinking more to himself than anything. "But why?" He was pacing the room like an expectant father.

"Let's take all the facts as we know them and see what we come up with. One, we know it has something to do with the fact Jason Ncube is scared of some kind of magic he thinks you have. Two, we now know that they are trying to kill you or make you sick. But they could have done that at any time. So the timing must be important. Why?"

The pacing continued while Lieutenant Courtney mulled.

"We are taking over Fire Force duties in a couple of days from Three Commando at Grand Reef. There is nothing unusual about that. They could be planning an attack, but we know the terrorists usually hit soft targets, so that doesn't seem likely."

Paul was sitting on the edge of the bed now, scratching his head. "Ray, I'm going to get in touch with the boss about this, to see if Intelligence has any info about anything unusual going on. In the meantime, carry on as usual. Make the Afs think you are getting sicker, have plenty of tea and cereal but for God's sake don't eat any sugar. At least we have got one up on them at the moment."

THE TRUCKS CARRYING One Commando rolled into Grand Reef at midday. The formalities of changeover were completed two hours later and Three Commando drove out.

Ray Hunter seemed very sick indeed and was put to bed by the medic, who gave him some medicine for his stomach.

"What's wrong with the sarge? He should see a doctor or be in hospital. Bloody stupid to come out to the bush as sick as that," remarked one trooper.

Only a few people knew what was really going on. The fewer in the know the better.

That afternoon, only one unusual incident took place, an African labourer made a phone call. It was very seldom indeed that any African made use of the phones on the base.

By six-thirty that evening, all the Stop Groups had been organised and the roving guards and gun pickets detailed. Tea was over and the African servants had been sent to their quarters. In the "Green Beret", the hut used as the all ranks' boozer, the troops were just opening their first beers of the night. The door opened and the OC walked in.

"Evening, chaps."

"Evening, sir."

"Listen in, buggers," the Major said. "Make this the only beer tonight. We have info that the gooks are up to something. We don't know exactly what, but we are going to be on the alert.

"I want three men in every bunker all night. Two-hour shifts, with one man waking up the next shift. This is as well as the normal roving guard."

There was a groan from the men.

"No point in groaning," said the Major. "That's the way it's going to be, and I want every shift to report to the duty Sergeant at the start of every stint. If any one of you go to sleep on watch, look out, there will be trouble. Okay?"

"Who is the duty Sergeant, sir?"

"Sergeant Hunter."

"But he's sick, sir."

"No he's not. In fact, I'm quite fine," said Ray, standing in the door grinning.

"Shit, that was a quick recovery, Sarge," said Mark.

"Actually, I haven't been sick, but that's a long story. I'll tell you another time."

"Right," finished the Major. "Sergeant Hunter has all the details for tonight. Over to you, Sergeant."

"Thank you, sir. Okay. I've spoken to all the other guys already, here is the list of guard duties and bunker numbers." Ray detailed the men off.

"As you can see, the guard starts at 2000 hours. All the NCOs and officers have been briefed, and the mortars have been given their likely targets.

"Two things before I go. One, you make sure you stay bloody well alert. Two, keep it as quiet as possible. If the gooks have planned something, we don't want them to know we are on to them. So if nothing happens tonight, keep quiet about it. Also, if nothing happens tonight, you will all see me sick again tomorrow. Don't ask why, just don't talk about it. That is a direct order. Understood?"

"Yes, Sarge."

"Right, when you have finished your beer, switch to Coke. Stay here for a couple of hours to make it look as normal as possible."

At ten o'clock that night, the first change-over went ahead without any drama. The men took their positions quietly and kept a sharp eye out as they had been told.

At ten-thirty, Ray went and checked the bunkers. All was quiet. He went and lay down. He might as well get a bit of shuteye while he could.

FOR SOME MONTHS, arms and ammunition had been smuggled over the border and cached in various places a few kilometres from the Grand Reef airstrip. Mortars and rockets were stashed in caves and down antbear holes. Rifles, machineguns and bullets were hidden in huts and in grass roofs in the villages.

Although the base was only twenty kilometres from the

Mozambique border, three hundred men marching across it loaded down with a staggering amount of weaponry would have been compromised too easily. So bit by bit the arsenal was built up: carried in scotchcarts; hidden in water containers on women's heads; driven in on vans and trucks until it was all secreted away, ready for collection.

Four days previously there seemed to be more Africans than usual wandering about the place. Nothing startling, just more of them. Two days earlier, many of them had made themselves comfortable in the villages in the area; still more were hiding in the bush.

On the day before the changeover, local sympathisers had brought much of the weaponry to the groups scattered in the area. During the day it was hidden. There was not much to be seen.

After Three Commando had departed, just before dusk, Jason Ncube watched as a gunship orbited the airfield, conducting the evening clearance patrol. He was only 2000 metres away, watching from the cover of thick bush. Once the chopper had finished, he knew that the security forces would post their pickets and guards, but there would be no more movement outside the base for the night. The helicopter would see nothing, because there was nothing to see.

Right now, on dusk, there would be men moving in towards an assembly point; a further group would be force-marching, lightly armed, from the border. They had worked out a route which would avoid any security force patrols in the area.

Jason was fairly contented with the set up. Things seemed to have gone well — the porters would be bringing the heavy arms soon and the groups would be arriving shortly. Earlier that day, he had had word of Sergeant Hunter's condition. It was as Dwizo had said, the white man was very sick. His magic would be weak.

"Yes, this attack will go well," he thought. His reverie was interrupted by a low cooing, like that which a wood pigeon would make as it came to roost for the night. He answered with another coo and six men shortly came into view through the dark.

These were his engineers; they would find paths through the minefields from the maps they had been given and mark them with white tape for the groups that would follow.

By eight o'clock, his six section commanders had reported in — their men were assembled as planned. The two groups who had marched in from Mozambique were hot and sweaty, but keen and raring to go.

By eight-twenty, the commanders had completed their final briefing and returned to lead their groups for the assault.

Each group consisted of thirty men. The attack would go in two waves: the first fifteen in each group, followed by the next fifteen. Mortars and machineguns were to give the assault groups covering fire.

By ten-thirty all groups were in position and the mortar operators were being given their co-ordinates. To save weight, the cumbersome base plates had been left behind.

This was to prove a costly mistake as it had rained the night before and the ground was soft. The mortars would dig in and become so inaccurate that they would shell their own men. The machineguns had to be sighted again as their planned positions were found to be too low. But the whole force was ready by ten-fifty.

Jason Ncube was pleased. Things had gone extremely well, but he needed a few more minutes for the mortar captains to report in after they had encountered a few minor hitches.

Just then there was a loud clang, someone had dropped a mortar tube on to a rifle. It must have hit the culprit as there was a howl of pain. Some of the more jittery men in the assault group began firing wildly at the earthen wall across the airstrip.

"Not now!" Jason roared. "You stupid baboons!" But it was too late.

"Mortars fire. Machineguns fire," he bellowed, racing forward to lead the assault. Already little pinpoints of light were winking at them from the enemy position.

RAY FELT AS though he had only just put his head on the pillow when the sky above lit up like a fireworks display as thousands of tracer rounds zipped through the air. At first he thought the terrorists had reached the revetments and were firing down at him and could not understand why all the bullets tearing into his body did not cause agonising pain. It was a second before he realised that it was not bullets hitting him but shards of fibro and timber falling on his bed from the fast disappearing roof above his head.

He rolled off the bed, slithered into his webbing, grabbed his rifle and made a low run for the nearest bunker.

Just as he reached it, the first mortar round landed in the compound. Screams came from the tent used by the drivers as another mortar exploded between it and a parked two-five truck.

An RPG-7 rocket whooshed through the large tent where most of the off-duty troopers had been sleeping only moments earlier. It detonated against the shower hut wall, punching a fist-sized hole in the concrete and sending white hot shrapnel around the inside. A still-soapy trooper clutched his knee in agony and crawled on the floor towards the door. There would be no showers for a couple of days.

Another mortar blew apart a hut used by five African soldiers from one of the support units, killing them instantly.

In Ray's bunker, he steadied his men. The machinegunner had exhausted his 150-round belt.

"Riflemen, change magazines," he bellowed above the noise. "Now give steady fire. Machinegunner, change your belt."

Other men were diving into the bunker. Ray allocated them places. Two of the late arrivals were given the job of filling magazines and MAG belts. From the rear he heard the bellowed orders of Captain Watson as he got the mortar teams into action. Sustained, steady fire emanated from the other bunkers as NCOs exerted control and more men arrived.

The first Security Force mortars left their tubes, heading towards the predetermined targets. The Rhodesian Light Infantry's superbly honed professionalism began to assert itself.

IT TOOK JASON many minutes before he could assert control and get his assault teams in order. Only through threats and vicious kicks was he able to install any kind of discipline.

The firing frenzy began to diminish after the initial adrenaline rush wore off and his team leaders took charge. But the element of surprise was irrevocably gone. The Rhodesians were returning fire, fast and accurately, and Jason could hear the crump of enemy mortars as they sought out targets.

Hampering things further was the problem with their own mortar rounds. They weren't landing in the enemy camp. In fact, orange flashes could be clearly seen as the unsighted 82mm tubes dropped their loads on to the runway.

"I must salvage this. I mustn't fail now," thought Jason, cursing the ineptitude of his men. He ran to the centre to begin the charge. Waving his rifle above his head, Ncube, the Matabele warrior, gave a blood-curdling cry as he took off towards the security force base.

It was a measure of his leadership that most of the men followed him. During training, he had often insulted them and shamed them, calling them "eaters of dirt, women and cowards". They were deep insults from an historic enemy.

Perhaps this was why they followed him now. It might have been a deliberate ploy on his part to rile the men up enough for this particular job. If it was, it worked. The normally placid Shona cadre followed the Matabele into a wall of fire.

"Holy Jesus Fuckin' Christ, will you look at that," shouted a trooper as the first wave of terrorists rose up and began to run towards the revetments. "There's hundreds of them." "Riflemen," Sergeant Hunter shouted. "Select your targets, aim and fire. Gunners, lower your sights a notch. Raking fire." He looked at the two who were loading. "You two, up here, we need you."

Major Hill, in the command bunker, also saw the charge. He picked up the handset. "Captain Watson, parachute flares please, on the double."

Before the charge, the ZANLA men had been protected from the Rhodesians by a small hollow in the ground, but now they were exposed to the full brunt of extremely accurate return fire and they started dropping. By the time the first wave had reached the middle of the runway, they had been cut to ribbons.

The human brain is a funny thing. Self-preservation is usually a priority in most minds. But sometimes a certain madness takes over — it is called battle lust. In the right conditions it can run riot and be infectious. Such was the case with the second wave of terrorists. They ran as fast as they could; charging and howling in their madness towards certain death.

They might have succeeded. As they charged, the RLI's fire slackened as most men changed magazines or belts and the mortars switched to para flares. The terrorists leaped over their fallen comrades and it looked as though the impetus of the rush must bring them up to the revetments.

In the bunkers, the Rhodesians fumbled in their haste to re-arm. A less-disciplined unit might have broken at that moment but at the last second the wall of fire was up again. Para flares hung in the air, brilliantly lighting the killing ground and making the targets as clear as day. The attack wilted to nothing.

"CEASE FIRE." The orders came from the bunkers all along the wall. "WATCH YOUR FRONT!! FULL MAGAZINES AND BELTS."

The flares had gone out and wounded and dying terrorists crawled away through the bodies of their comrades. Every so often a shot rang out as an Icarus hand-launched para flare picked out movement among the survivors.

Jason came to lying on his side on the tarmac, with blinding lights and hot, almost unbearable, pain searing through his brain. A bullet had glanced off his skull, knocking him unconscious. Blood seeped from two superficial wounds in his right leg. He lay motionless, willing himself to keep still until he could gather his wits. The night was dark, he could sense dark forms lying near him and knew them to be dead comrades. "So we failed," he thought miserably.

When he had recovered enough to take stock of his situation, he started crawling away, towards the trees. Slowly and painfully he made his way through the numerous bodies, using them for cover. Every so often he would freeze as a flare lit up the sky, only to continue again as darkness descended. Once he was a bit slow in reacting to a flare and a bullet pinged near his face. He lay still, hoping whoever was shooting at him would think he had been successful.

Eventually, Jason reached the sanctuary of the tree line and lay still, fighting to keep conscious. The urge to let sleep take away the pain was overwhelming.

Dimly he heard his name being called. It was not the voice of a comrade; it was a mechanical voice coming from the enemy position.

"Jason Ncube," it boomed. "This is Isizo! Your attack has failed. Your magic did not kill me. My magic is stronger than yours. We knew you were coming."

The blood froze in Jason's veins. He lapsed into unconsciousness and did not feel the gentle arms lift him and carry him away.

THE MESSAGE OVER the Tannoy system had been the brainchild of Lieutenant Courtney, whose lawyer's mind had correctly deduced the connection between the attack and the attempted poisoning of Sergeant Hunter at Meikles. He had guessed, rightly, that it would spook the hell out of Ncube, if he had survived.

They had known Jason was coming, but it was not by magic. He had unwittingly telegraphed his intentions through Dwizo's crude plans. But for these actions, and the accidental dropping of a mortar tube at a crucial moment, the attack on Grand Reef might have had a very different outcome.

For some reason the terrorists had not seen fit to try to take out the planes and helicopters. If they had, they would have done far more damage to the Rhodesian war effort than killing a few soldiers could have. Without aircraft, Fire Force deployments would have been brought to a halt. Such are the fortunes of war.

First light found the men of One Commando cleaning up the mess and trying to repair as much damage as possible. The wounded had been taken to the Umtali hospital and the dead removed. But there was to be no respite for the men. At 0745 hours, the paras were kitting up for another sortie.

"Stuff me dead, I'll be glad when some of the other ouns get para-trained," grumbled Koos. "I'm sick of lugging all this heavy gear around and then getting smashed into the dirt on a regular basis. It hurts and I want my Mum."

"I don't know what you're complaining about," countered Mark. "I hear we are going to be getting para pay soon."

"Is that true, sir?" asked Koos.

"Yup! About $2.50 a week."

"Fuck me dead, I'll be a millionaire," remarked another trooper. "I just don't know what I'll do with all that money. Har, bloody har."

"Hurry it up, blokes. The Dak's waiting," chided the despatcher.

THE SELOUS SCOUTS continued to locate the enemy and Fire Forces engaged them. But with more and more ZANLA infiltrations, and increasing ZIPRA incursions from Zambia and the new front with Botswana, it was like trying to bail a ship with a teacup.

Something had to be done. Rather than hold back on cross-border raids in an effort to prevent international condemnation — a futile attempt in any case — Rhodesia's politicians gave the green light for tentative "look see's" to confirm what everyone knew anyway: Mozambique was rife with ZANLA terrorist camps, used to stage incursions into the country.

The Selous Scouts, Special Air Service and the RLI were itching to get at the "head of the octopus" and needed no encouragement to take the gloves off.

THE TRUCKS RETURNED to Mount Darwin FAF after a contact in the Chesa African Purchase Area. The troops climbed wearily off and headed for their billets to clean up.

"Hey Ray!" the CSM was waving to him. "The OC wants to see you in his tent."

"Roger, CSM, I'll be right there.

"You wanted to see me, sir?" said Ray, ducking under the tent flaps. There was no salute. In the bush one did not salute officers for obvious reasons.

"Ah, yes Sergeant Hunter, come in."

Standing next to the Major was a large shaggy-looking man. In fact, large was not the word.

"He's huge," Ray thought to himself. The man filled the tent, well over two metres tall, with shoulders to match and a large, untidy beard tangling to his barrel-like chest. He also stank like a hyena and clearly hadn't see soap and water for a long time. Through the unkempt mass of hair and beard, a pair of intense blue eyes stared at Ray. Startlingly direct, they assessed Hunter, sizing him up.

"Sergeant Hunter, meet Lieutenant Schultz."

Ray did not need to be told the lieutenant was a Selous Scout. Most people had heard of his exploits. A very brave man and fearsome in the bush.

"Goeiemore meneer," said the Lieutenant in guttural Afrikaans.

"G'day, Lieutenant." Ray took the proffered hand. His own felt very small inside the Afrikaner's.

"Ray, the Lieutenant has a proposition to put to you. It's a bit unorthodox, but I think you two might be a bit like-minded in that regard. Lieutenant!"

"Ja," rumbled the deep voice. "Ray. Is it okay if I call you Ray?"

"By my guest," replied Ray.

The Lieutenant smiled at the politeness. "You call me Nick, okay?"

"Okay."

"Ray, I hear you experienced at freefall?"

"Just under 600 jumps," he replied, matter-of-factly.

"I want to take a look at a terr camp in Mozambique. To get there quickly I must freefall at night and we don't have anyone else trained just now. I have to be truthful. I could just about do the job on my own but I need someone to carry some of the extra gear, so whoever comes with me will just be a packhorse."

Ray smiled at the giant's basic honesty. With this man there would be no false modesty. Just the truth and straight down the line. Looking at Schultz, Ray wondered if he couldn't carry a ton of gear himself and hardly notice it.

"If it's a packhorse you want, it's a packhorse you get," Ray replied.

It was Nick's turn to smile now. "Okay, have you ever carried kit in freefall?"

"No, but I will have no trouble doing it."

Ray spent the next 10 minutes answering a string of pointed questions from Nick, quickly realising that he was being given a quick, though thorough psychological assessment by the Lieutenant.

"Okay Ray, there are just two more things for now. One, we will be going to New Sarum for training jumps. That will take a couple of days as you've got the experience but we need to get you up to speed with carrying kit on a night deployment. That's the easy bit. Second, my life depends on you. I need to know for sure that you will be up to the job when we are on the ground." Schultz pointed a thumb over his shoulder. "There's a Cessna outside which will take you to Inkomo (*the Scouts' barracks barracks 40 kilometres from Salisbury*) where you'll meet the OC and get your kit. Then you are on a shortened survival course at our training camp so I can see what you're made of. We don't have the three weeks it normally takes, but 10 days should be enough."

Ray had heard about the Scouts' survival course. Less than 15% of the volunteers passed. He was careful not to show any emotion in his reply. "Sounds good to me".

VERY LITTLE IN his life had prepared Hunter for the sheer physical and mental stress he underwent during the next 10 days at the Scouts' training camp on the edge of Lake Kariba in the Zambezi Valley. Virtually starved for the first five days, he and 40 other men were put through gruelling, 20 kilometre runs in daytime temperatures that exceeded 45 degrees centigrade; "jungle lane" shooting drills and assault courses.

On the sixth day, offered a choice between a few mouthfulls of a foul-smelling, decomposed, but thoroughly boiled baboon, or another day of hunger, Ray, like everyone else who had stayed thus far chose the baboon. It was delicious.

His last three days were spent with the 11 remaining participants on a 125-kilometre cross-country march. In addition to weapons and full kit, each man carried a 40-kilogram pack of rocks. This seemingly pointless task was enough to weed a further three dispirited men from the course. A small tin of bully beef and a few handfuls of *mealie meal* were all the rations they were allowed — except for any lizards or snakes they could catch for themselves en route.

At the end of the 10 days in the hot, wild Zambezi Valley, Ray climbed aboard the Bedford truck for the four-hour drive back to Inkomo. He slept the whole way.

That evening, Schultz and Hunter met at the barracks. Ray drank his beer and listened while Nick spoke. He got straight to the point. "The instructors reckon you OK. Now we see what you're made of in the air." Ray smiled. It appeared he had cleared the first hurdle. "Now we go to New Sarum. We can spare a day or two and we have to brief and rehearse, but we need to get to Mozambique pretty soon, okay?"

THE FOLLOWING MORNING, Nick drove Ray to New Sarum airfield in Salisbury. After sitting for a while in silence, Ray turned to his new companion.

"Hey, Nick, what do you know about Jason Ncube?"

"That gook, he is a cunning one. We have been trying to nail him for a while. So far he has slipped through our fingers, we can't get near him. What's your interest?"

"Oh, nothing much, he just seems to be afraid of me, that's all."

"Yussus, so YOU the one they call Isizo, the eye. I heard about Grand Reef. Ja, he is afraid of you all right. What you do to him?"

"Dunno, we have been up against each other a few times now; he seems to think I have some magic and he keeps running away."

"Make no mistake, that Jason is a good soldier and he certainly is not a coward. You must have done something to spook him up."

There was a look of respect in the big Afrikaner's eyes. "And you such a little guy, hey," he mused aloud.

Ray smiled. "Compared to you, my friend, everybody's little."

Lieutenant Schultz grinned into his beard.

UNLESS ONE IS a fairly competent freefaller, jumping with equipment can be a problem. The bergen is slung behind the legs and held up under the main parachute by two quick-release hooks. The legs are threaded through leg straps to stop the bergen flapping in the wind. Although the larger surface area tends to make one fly head down and a tendency to move forward develops, the weight of the bergen negates this to a degree. Even so, the freefaller has to adjust his body position to compensate.

Many a freefaller without sufficient freefall time has stability problems with unintentional turns which tend to accelerate as greater velocity builds up. This can create problems when the time comes to open the parachute. Added to this, the rifle or machinegun is strapped to the right side, creating possible tangling hazards.

Schultz and Hunter did three jumps during the first day and, that night, two training drops.

Night freefall, because of limited visibility, presents its own difficulties. Even with luminous tubes attached to helmets, judging relative height and distance in the dark is not easy. Ascertaining one's height above ground is done by attaching small lights inside the altimeter.

"Okay, Ray, we go in tomorrow night," said Nick after they landed and he was sure that Ray could cope with the jumps. "Tomorrow, we rehearse and brief for the job."

Under Nick's orders, Ray had not washed, shaved, brushed his teeth or changed his clothes. He was even made to stand in the smoke of a fire.

"I want you to look and smell like you belong in the bush," he said. "Clean bodies and the smell of toothpaste are a dead giveaway out there and there will be times when we are pretty dammed close to those bloody terrs, let me tell you."

In the briefing room the next morning, the Dak pilot and three Canberra bomber pilots listened intently. The sortie was hush-hush and the fewer people in on it the better. Lieutenant Schultz was giving the briefing.

"Okay, gentlemen, this is the situation." The Lieutenant was speaking in the most precise English he could manage because there must be no doubt as to the instructions. Even so, his accent could be cut with a knife.

"At this point in the river here," he said, pointing to an area on a map of Mozambique, "there is a terrorist training camp. It is a large camp with upward of three hundred terrs in it at most times. This number can fluctuate depending on how many groups have been trained and are being infiltrated into the country, but generally speaking, three hundred is about the right number. I can vouch for this information because I have been there. Several times.

"Up to now, we have not been allowed to take these camps out, but now the high-ups are giving us the go-ahead on a limited scale. The reason we are concentrating on this one is because we have very good intelligence that an important terr leader will visit the camp three nights from now and our top brass want him out the way.

"I am not allowed to tell you his name, big hush-hush, but he is supposed to be staying the night and addressing the terrs on the parade ground at 0700 hours. This way, we can kill him and slay a lot of his boys into the bargain. This is going to be purely a bombing raid, using you three Canberras," he said to the pilots. "Sergeant Hunter and I are going in to take a look. If it is a go-ahead, we will expect you overhead at exactly 0710 hours, while they are on the parade ground.

"For your run in, I want you to fly over the southern peak of the Train," he said, pointing to a range of mountains on the map. "Fly on a bearing of 70 degrees. We will be putting out a radio beacon to the west of the target for you. I think one thousand metres is about right. On that last internal raid, I put the beacon too close and the bombs overshot.

"Right, if you can work out your running time from the Train to the target, we can work out when you should be circling to the west."

The pilots calculated the times on their maps. "Twelve minutes," they concurred.

The details went on. Take-off times, radio frequencies, call signs, code words and so on, until Nick Schultz was sure the Canberra pilots knew every tiny bit of information they needed.

Next it was the Dakota pilot's turn. "Okay, Pete. This is where we want to get off. We want to jump just after dark, so if you can work out your times so that you can navigate until last light and give us approximately three minutes to run in the dark. That should be accurate enough."

During the entire war, the Rhodesian Air Force had almost no navigational aids and had to rely on map-reading and compass headings to get to their destinations. Such was the calibre of the pilots that they seldom went wrong.

"Okay, Ray, after we land we will have about twenty-two kilometres to walk in the dark. The drop zone is the closest we can get in an unpopulated area to the target. We will be lying up on a gomo near the camp and you'll be my radio man. You will stay there and pass on messages. I will be doing the running around to the camp and back. You get the easy job, ja!"

"Yeah, that's true, but we are going to stir up a hornet's nest. How are we going to get out if we get compromised?"

"All taken care of; there will be a chopper waiting for us at the border, ready to pick us up. How is your hot extraction drill?" Nick laughed.

He wouldn't have laughed as much if he had known how badly they were going to need it.

CHAPTER SEVEN

AFTER THE BRIEFING the pair checked their kit, Schultz paying meticulous attention to the smallest details: radios, batteries, radio beacons, ammunition, food, water. They donned felt hats and blue denims, and "tackies" — footwear identical to those worn by ZANLA to confuse any enemy trackers. They also carried captured folding-butt AKMs and webbing with Chinese stick grenades so that at a distance, with blackened faces, they would resemble the people they had come to destroy. They wouldn't stand close inspection, but anything that would increase their chances of survival in a hostile environment would be a bonus. By masquerading as the enemy Schultz and Hunter knew they were stepping beyond the tenets of the Geneva Convention which forbade such activities. But, this was not a gentleman's war. Guerilla wars never are.

Thirty minutes before last light, the Dakota left the runway; its wheels retracted with a thud and the ageing warhorse began its climb to fifteen thousand feet. The PJI (Parachute Jump Instructor) who was to despatch the pair had not been in on the briefing; he was there merely to check their parachutes before the jump and to help them out of the door. At ten thousand feet oxygen was turned on and the three men placed the masks over their faces. They sat in silence, lost in their own thoughts. The air blasting in through the open door got colder as they climbed.

"TWENTY MINUTES OUT," called the PJI.

"TEN MINUTES OUT." Schultz and Hunter stood up, hefted their bergens on to the seat, slipped their legs through the shoulder straps before hooking the bergens to the parachute harness and tightened them up. A lowering line was attached to the harness and they were ready to be checked by the PJI. After the check, they half stood and half sat on their bergens on the seat.

"FIVE MINUTES." They gave the thumbs up.

"ONE MINUTE! The two of them stood up and took the oxygen masks off, but held them to their faces. It was almost dark outside, a fiery tinge on the western horizon showing where the sun had set. Ray figured that it would be three in the morning in Australia and wondered what his old mates in Queensland would say if they could see him now. He sure was a long way from anywhere right now, fifteen thousand feet above a hostile African country, about to embark on the most dangerous episode in his life. He snapped out of his dreaming as the PJI waved them towards to the door.

Dropping the oxygen masks, they shuffled slowly towards the black hole. The red light came on, then the green. Within seconds they were gone, into the freezing night air.

Lieutenant Schultz went out facing the aircraft heading. Ray dived out of the door to keep him visual and nearly flipped over; the bergen acting as a sail in the slipstream. He managed to bring it under control and concentrated on the red glow of the luminous tube on Nick's helmet some way below him. He worked in closer. Their whole world was narrowed to two faint lights in the inky black void as they hurtled towards earth at over two hundred kilometres an hour. One was Nick's helmet light, the other was the dim red light that showed the altimeter needle winding down to opening height. The only sound was the air rushing past their bodies.

There was no other reference point except those two lights, only total, all enveloping, blackness. Ray could make out no lights anywhere on the ground, or in the distance, except for a few, far away to the west in Rhodesia. Mozambique was as black as a dog's guts. He shivered involuntarily, though not from the sub-zero cold.

At two thousand seven hundred feet, Ray pulled his ripcord. He felt a jerk as the opening canopy tugged him upright. There was enough glow from his helmet to see that the parachute had opened properly. He looked down trying to find Nick's light and felt a moment of panic before he located it some way off and below and followed it as the Selous Scout steered his canopy round in a slow circle. At three hundred feet, Ray opened the quick release hooks and the bergen slid down to his feet. He hooked his feet into the shoulder straps but only released his kit at one hundred feet. The bergen fell to the end of the line and dangled there. Ray knew he was close to the ground when he heard a soft thud. Seconds later he hit the ground and rolled.

As Ray field packed his parachute, he could hear Nick doing the same fifty metres away. They joined up before hiding the chutes among a rock outcrop before setting out, Nick leading. As fit as he was, Ray soon found it hard to keep up with the big man. Within an hour Ray was in a lather of sweat while Schultz appeared to be on an afternoon stroll through the Botanic Gardens. Determination and self discipline drove him on as the heavy bergen dug into his shoulders.

FIVE PUNISHING HOURS and twenty kilometres later they reached the hill overlooking the terrorist camp. Nick went straight to the little hollow in the rocks he had used on his previous visits and with his nightscope carefully checked the fishing line trip wires he had set up to determine if any unwanted visitors had called. Satisfied that his OP had not been compromised, he signalled Ray and they stowed the gear and agreed on firing positions. Within ten minutes, Schultz slipped into the night on a solo recce. Ray managed to slip into a shallow but dreamless sleep.

The big man was back well before first light and slept until the sun came up.

"That camp has grown since I was here last," he said without preamble when he awoke. "It looks as though it might be quite an important area for them. It is logistically sound. I think we are on to something big, my friend."

Although they were several kilometres from the camp, he was whispering.

"As usual, the guards are almost non-existent, the few that are on duty are slack. That is good, it means they feel pretty secure."

DURING THE DAY, the pair kept watch over the camp using a pair of high-powered binoculars, taking care not to let the sun catch the lens. As they watched, they sketched as much of the camp as possible — "for future reference", as Nick put it. By mid-afternoon they had gained extensive knowledge of the whole area and most of it was down on paper, including the enemy's dress, weapons, habits and standard of soldiering. That night, Nick was gone again, working in as close to the camp as he could. As usual he was back before sunrise.

"I wish I had some means of getting into the camp. I could get a lot more info," Schultz said as he chewed a stick of biltong.

"Why don't you work with Africans?" asked Ray. "Most of the other guys in your unit are."

Nick paused for a while as though collecting his thoughts. "Ray, all my life I have been brought up to believe that we are a race apart and that the African's place is a subservient one. I have never had much to do with them except to order them about. How can I work with someone I have never treated as an equal? I don't know how far I could rely on them. I don't even know if I could trust them. How would I know if the information they brought back to me is reliable?"

"Well, you will never know unless you try it. I hear they are proving their worth internally. If you need someone inside the camps you are watching, only an African can do it."

Nick's direct stare was unsettling, but behind the eyes Ray sensed the big Afrikaner was trying to come to a decision. "Ja my little rooinek friend, you are right, that is probably the way I must do it."

It was a measure of the man that he was prepared to put aside generations of racial conditioning and consider working with a black to get the job done. Lieutenant Schultz was a soldier first and that decision was to make him even more legendary than he already was. In time, he not only worked with them, he came to trust and respect Africans. With their help, Nick's skill at locating external camps and bringing Rhodesia's security forces on to them was indeed the stuff of legends. Men like him, white and black, many of whom were "turned" terrorists, put Rhodesia back on a winning edge. What the politicians and ditherers lost by their indecisions, the Selous Scouts regained.

THE TRACKER WAS PUZZLED. They had come across the spoor of two men late in the afternoon. The boot pattern was ZANLA and they were heading in the direction of the freedom fighter's camp. But something was wrong. Frelimo had not been notified of anyone travelling in their area. These two men had been carrying something heavy. They had not been hunting, as there was no game in the area. It certainly was not the usual route for any of the freedom fighters in the area. If the tracks had not been nearly obliterated in the last two days, he might have been able to pick out that it was not Africans who had made them. Europeans walk differently to Africans. Even so, the tracker smiled. The two men had been in a hurry, the smaller one had found it hard to keep up with the bigger one. That in itself was strange, usually Africans do not hurry, it must have been something very urgent to make those two hurry like that. He called to the section commander who came over to look at the spoor.

A few minutes later they made their way back to the garrison to notify the garrison commander. The rest of the section followed the footprints. Even if they went fast, they would not be able to catch up with the makers of these tracks tonight. It would be tomorrow morning at the earliest. But catch them they would.

LATE THAT AFTERNOON, just before last light, a Land-Rover drove into the terrorist camp, stopping outside the hut where Schultz had guessed the commander would be.

On the hill, Schultz observed the arrival and concentrated furiously. "Ja, that's him," he exclaimed. "I was right. He has turned up, and on time too!" He looked at Ray. "Take a look meneer, our prey has arrived."

Ray took the binoculars. He was just in time to see the man enter the hut.

"Who is he Nick, who is this man that he is so important?"

"You should know better than anybody else Isizo, it's none other than your friend Jason Ncube."

"Bugger me!" Ray breathed. "We meet again."

"Ja, you guys know you wounded him at Grand Reef? He got away. Believe it or not, the terrs think of that attack as a success — they killed a few Rhodies and gave us a scare. They think Jason is a pretty good leader. Make no mistake, he is climbing the ranks fast, he is an important figure now. That is why we are trying to snuff him out."

Just before midnight, Nick came back from yet another close-in recce. "He is still there Ray. It looks like he is settled in for the night."

At precisely midnight, the duty radio operator at Inkomo barracks received a short message. "Zero Alpha, this is Zulu One. The Christmas present has arrived, over." The radio operator handed the message to the Scouts' CO, a short, muscular man in his forties who had been waiting by the radio for the midnight Sitrep. A short while later he replied. "Zulu One, acknowledged. Go ahead." This was confirmation that the mission was to proceed and for Nick to place the radio beacons for the Canberras to run in on.

Minutes after receiving the confirmation, Schultz was gone again, swallowed up in the darkness as he made his way down the hill.

"With all the comings and goings he must have worn a path big enough to drive a bus up," Ray thought to himself, but he knew Nick would have covered his tracks well enough.

Dawn found Hunter and Schultz lying prone in their positions; gear packed and weapons ready for a quick exit. Ray had almost enjoyed the disgusting mix of mandarin segments, creamed chicken and corned beef he ate as they waited. He might need the energy before the morning was out.

Slowly, the camp came to life as ZANLA men and women emerged from huts and barracks. Groups wandered to the river to wash and gradually, small groups began to form around the parade square.

Schultz kept watch on the camp with binoculars held in one hand; the other was holding the radio handset set to his ear.

He faintly heard the Canberras as they sped to their holding area ten kilometres to the north of the camp. Ray who had been keeping watch further up the hill, came slithering back.

"We've got a spot of bother, Nick. There's ten Frelimo making their way towards the hill. Two of them have parted company and are making for the camp. I think we have been rumbled, old mate."

"Magtig," swore the Scout. "How long before they get here?"

"About fifteen or twenty minutes."

Nick listened into the handset. "What is the time Ray?"

"0655."

"Where are the other two?"

"They are in sight of the camp now, but they are a fair way off, walking fast but in no great hurry. I think they know we are here, but not the reason."

"Man, this is going to be a close thing. Bloody close." His ears pricked up. "Right, the Canberras are running in now. Ray, get back in position and hold them off if you have to … a Claymore will give them something to chew on. We stand a better chance of getting out after the Canberras hit. Unfortunately we have to go the way the Freds are coming, so it looks like we in the shit." Nick moved the binoculars to the left. "Ag, I see the two bods now, they are well in sight and waving. Shit, it's going to be close man."

Nick changed frequencies on the radio. "Golf Five, this is Zulu One, do you read? Over." The Alouette K-car orbiting out of hearing range eight kilometres to the west responded in the affirmative.

"Stand by for pick up, possible hot extraction. Look for us in positions Lima one, two and three at this stage. Do you copy, over," Schultz replied.

"Zulu One, Roger copied. Look for you in positions Lima one, two and three. Possible hot extraction. Over."

"Roger, and make it quick," Nick said.

He changed frequencies again.

"Four minutes to target," he heard the lead Canberra pilot say.

"C'mon, c'mon," he urged under his breath. He looked through the binoculars again. Everybody was on parade. "But where is Ncube? The bastard is playing games," he thought. "He is making them wait. Oh you fucking black bastard! Hurry up."

"Locked on to beacons," the Canberra bomber leader said.

Nick picked up the two Frelimo soldiers through the binoculars. They were talking to the guards at the makeshift entry point to the camp, gesticulating and pointing at the hill. Suddenly, one of the guards turned and began shouting at the people on the parade ground. Nearly fifteen hundred terrorists milled about — unsure what was happening.

Back on the hill, Schultz cursed in Afrikaans as time seemed to slow to a standstill. Further up the hill Ray was holding his fire. He'd been given a few short minutes' grace as the Frelimo section had slowed their ascent, cautiously moving in an arrowhead formation, picking their steps carefully. They were only thirty metres away, but still he held his fire, the bare ends of the Claymore detonator wire millimetres from his fingers. Ray had no choice but to eke out a few precious seconds before the sounds of firing gave the game away to the people in the camp.

Jason had been doing exactly what had made Schultz swear — making the parade wait. It would add to his prestige. He was on the point of leaving his hut when he heard a commotion near the gate. Running outside, he then saw the massed parade seemingly on the verge of panic. What the hell was going on? He started towards them, angry at the indiscipline, but stopped dead in his tracks as rapid firing echoed from the nearby hill, followed by a small explosion. It brought a momentary calm to the parade ground and Jason again started towards the assembly, but an icy hand gripped his guts as the umistakable sound of screaming jet aircraft could be heard. He turned and bolted towards the river.

The point man in the Frelimo section was almost upon Ray, the others spread in a line behind him. They were too close for the Claymore to be effective. At the last possible moment, Ray angled the muzzle of the AKM upwards and fired a three-round burst which tore through the Frelimo soldier's guts, tearing out great chunks of his back. He looked down at the white man in surprise, eyes wide with shock before toppling forwards, his green cap a handsbreadth from Ray's face.

Using the body as extra cover, Ray grabbed the stick grenade he had prepared by removing the screw-off cap and pulling out the copper ring attached to a strong silk thread. He placed the ring over the little finger of his throwing hand and sent it ten metres down the hill.

A satisfying crump, followed by a scream, went almost unheard in the crackle of return fire from the survivors of the Frelimo section.

These Frelimo were well trained and they had gone to ground as soon as the firing started. Ray changed magazines and fired in short bursts where he had seen men take cover. He heard a thunk and the gurgle as a man started to drown in his own blood. But the Frelimo were firing back, the hornet's nest began buzzing above his head.

"FOR FUCK'S SAKE NICK, LET'S GET OUTA HERE," he shouted back down the hill. Just then the earth shook as though a giant hammer had smashed into the ground. The noise and concussion swept through his head drowning out all sense and reason for a brief second.

He felt a giant hand grab his shoulder and was hauled to his knees. "Grab your bergen Englishman and let's voetsak," he heard the deep gravelly voice say.

There was only one way out — downhill, through the Frelimo sec-tion. In a classic forward assault, the two men swept through the Frelimo position, shouting and firing as they charged and broke through. Four minutes later, they reached the bottom as the air cracked above their heads from rounds fired by the Frelimo survivors.

RLI troopers undergo training at the Parachute Training School, New Sarum.

Troopers prepare for static line deployment from Dakota aircraft – New Sarum.

And out they go!

Training jump at 500 feet with full kit.

On the ground safely—time to do it all again!

Men of an RLI Fire Force board Alouette G-cars for deployment to scene of confirmed sighting at disused kraal in NE Operational area.

Conducting 'sweep' following contact with ZANLA terrorists

Five of 30 CT's killed during Fire Force operation.
Note result of K-car's 20mm cannon strike on CT at top of picture.

Weapons recovered at scene: Three Soviet SKSs; one AK47; one PPsh.

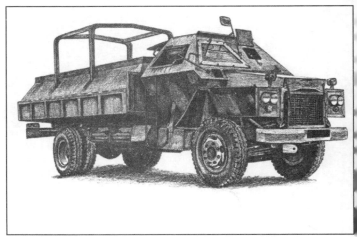

"Puma" mine-protected troop carrier. From *Wheels* by Colin Eyre.

Following operation, G-cars transport Stop Groups to clearing for uplift by road to base. Note "Puma" troop carriers at left of picture.

One Commando troops return to Grand Reef after
Fire Force deployment.

The author "chilling out" at safari lodge with companion
while on R & R.

ZANLA section prepares to leave base in Moçambique for incursion into Rhodesia.

Members of One Commando prior to cross-border raid into Moçambique. Author in centre.

Special Branch officers examine the bodies of two of four ZIPRA guerrillas killed in St Mary's Township, Salisbury. Weapons captured included a Soviet-made SAM-7 "Strela" ground-to-air missile; three AKM's; a Tokarev pistol and various explosives.

NOTICE   BEWARE   DANGER

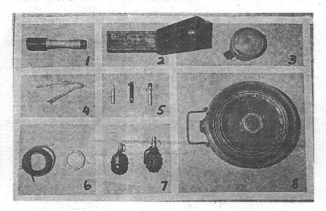

All persons should be careful of those things shown in the photograph and other similar things as they might be unexploded weapons.

In areas where there are known to be terrorists these things are often discarded or abandoned by terrorists fleeing from Security Forces.

The photograph shows some examples of terrorist weapons which, if seen, should be reported to the authorities. They should not be touched or tampered with at all because they might explode thus killing people.

Parents and teachers are particularly advised to warn their children and pupils against playing with these things otherwise they might be killed or injured by the object exploding.

The picture shows grenades (No. 1 and No. 7), mines (No. 2, No. 3 and No. 8), detonators and fuses (No. 4, No. 5 and No. 6).

Remember—do not touch these things but report their whereabouts and you will be rewarded.

Reward posters were displayed to encourage co-operation from black civilians.

The Rhodesian Light Infantry on parade: Cranborne Barracks, Salisbury.

The Sunday Mail

RHODESIA'S NATIONAL NEWSPAPER
SALISBURY, MARCH 9, 1980.

MUGABE SPELLS OUT POLICY ON SOUTH AFRICA

Nkomo's powers a key issue

PM in charge of defence

CO-OPERATION OF ZANLA MEN GOOD SAY POLICE

RLI ON PARADE

Nixon regrets boycott

BACK NEW PM, SAYS BISHOP

Melontosh out on Tuesday

Chopper chappie's cheeky cheerio

RLI ON PARADE

Sunday Mail Reporter

SEVERAL hundred troops of the Rhodesian Light Infantry staged an impromptu parade through central Salisbury yesterday morning.

It was part of the regiment's withdrawal from dozens of key positions in the city that soldiers have manned since Tuesday.

"It was impromptu," said informed sources. "Partly, they were exercising their rights to parade through Salisbury because they have been given the 'freedom of the city'."

The troops wound their way back to Cranborne Barracks in Land-Rovers and armoured cars.

A bagpiper stood on a Puma troop carrier and played "When The Saints Go Marching In", the regiment's adopted tune.

A combined Operations Headquarters spokesman said: "It was probably a show of good spirits."

The *Sunday Mail*, March 9, 1980, five days after Mugabe's election win was announced.

The author at extreme left with fellow members of One Commando at Grand Reef Fire Force Base, 17th December, 1977, the day after it was attacked by over 200 ZANLA terrorists.

Reaching the shelter of a huge leadwood tree, Schultz stopped.

"Get your pack off, leave it here," he said breathlessly. They shrugged the bergens on to the ground. Schultz pulled the pin on a grenade and carefully placed it under one of the packs with the other bergen on top. They waited for a few seconds, regaining their breath.

"I heard the instructions for a situation like this is 'Mag off, pack off and fuck off'," said Ray, "but I've never practised it." "Well you going to now my mate" replied the Selous Scout.

Then they were off and running again, this time with only rifles and basic webbing. Behind them came shouts and regular bursts of fire.

"I'll never complain about those training runs again," puffed Ray.

"Save your breath for running man," came the terse reply.

The sound of vehicles racing through the bush made Nick spin round. "They've got reinforcements. Now we in deep shit," gasped Schultz. Sweating freely, their breath came in short, sharp pants — as much from exertion as the pumping adrenaline. Schultz checked his compass. "We are running too far to the north, veer to the left a bit." They continued running.

THE TWO VEHICLES, both Land-Rovers, had driven from the Frelimo garrison attached to the terrorist camp to check on the section commander's report from the previous day. They were too far away from the camp to be affected by the bombing and caught up with the section after hearing the action on the hill.

After a hurried report, the remainder of the section climbed on to already full vehicles, they didn't want to miss out on the chase. Their quarry were obviously Rhodesian infiltrators who would be made to pay dearly for their actions.

The vehicles drove west but it was soon realised they'd missed the pair. The leader of the chase group banged on the roof for his driver to stop.

"Turn around and go back. We must pick up the spoor," he shouted.

Four hundred metres away on a small rise, Schultz and Hunter lay motionless beneath an acacia bush. "They have lost us for the moment," wheezed Schultz. "Let's go."

This time their Frelimo pursuers had a tracker running beside the vehicle and he quickly re-established the Rhodesians' line of flight. Whenever the spoor was clear, the tracker leaped on the bonnet and the chase would sped up.

They came closer. Schultz was almost too tired to speak and waved for Ray to follow him in a circle before they came back upon their own tracks.

"Wheels," was all the big man could get out.

Within seconds, one Land-Rover pulled to a halt in a cloud of fine dust almost obscuring the scene. They didn't see the exhausted white men who instantly opened fire, raking the vehicles as the occupants scrambled to debus. The second vehicle suddenly shot through the thick bush and slammed with sickening force into the rear of the first Land-Rover, crushing one man against the tailgate. The other men leaped from the back like ants from a frying pan, straight into a withering hail of fire from Schultz and Hunter who then charged, running through the confusion, "double-tapping" the Mozambicans at random.

The Frelimo soldiers died where they were shot or crawled under the vehicles, one of which burst into flames from a ruptured fuel tank. The white men were through and gone and it was a while before their dazed and shocked black adversaries were able to compose themselves. The one surviving commander, Gorge Chisambo, a veteran of the sixteen-year guerilla war against the Portuguese, ordered his soldiers into the other Land-Rover and they drove a short distance to recover and regroup. Meanwhile, their tracker cast for spoor and having located it heading to the north-west, ran back to report.

The Frelimo commander hadn't lived to enjoy his late thirties by sheer luck. He knew from bitter experience that they were up against desperate, hard men who, like cornered mambas, would fight to the death. This alone made the odds more even. He radioed to base and ordered two Berliot troop carriers with forty men to advance immediately to a point three kilometres towards the border where he guessed the Rhodesians would be heading. Aboard one of the vehicles was a 12.7mm anti-aircraft gun to counter the possibility of a helicopter assault.

The charge had given Schultz and Hunter a brief respite, but it wouldn't be long before Frelimo came back at them. On the point of exhaustion, they stumbled towards the border only fourteen kilometres away, their breath coming in short, painful gasps.

The midday sun beat like a hammer on an anvil, its strength-sapping heat reducing both sides to an agonising slowness. The Frelimo troops would have given up long ago but for the iron will of their commander who railed abuse and threats at any slackers.

"C'mon, let's go," slurred Schultz, staggering to his feet as the sound of the follow-up came nearer.

"Thanks, you bastard, I wouldn't have missed this for quids," mumbled Ray, getting to his knees. "What's that, Rooinek?" Schultz gasped as they stumbled to their feet before moving off. "Just an old saying from Australia, mate. It means "Thanks for inviting me." They ran, having discarded most of their webbing, each with just one water bottle and a spare magazine containing thirty rounds, strapped to their belts.

The helicopter had searched the areas Schultz had radioed until almost out of fuel before returning to the border to fuel up and wait further instructions. The pilot sent his sitrep.

"There has been no sight of them and no radio transmissions," he reported.

"Have you searched your whole area?"

"Affirmative," replied the pilot. "I need fuel for another three sorties. Over."

"We will send more up to you. Over."

By mid-afternoon Lieutenant Schultz and Sergeant Hunter were on their last legs. They found the only possible defensible position they could given the strength left in their pain-wracked bodies and lay in a sandy, shallow depression in direct sunlight.

"We will stop them here," Nick said, the words coming out slurred like a drunk's. "Take a few of those bastards with us."

Chisambo took his time ordering the assault. He knew they had run their quarry to ground. There was no need to rush. They could take their time and rest for a while. The white men were as good as dead. He removed his sunglasses, wiped his face with the neckerchief he constantly wore, and replaced his glasses. He wanted to look cool and in command when he took those whites out. Back at the Frelimo garrison, he had a few points to score with the hierarchy. The troops loved a hero and this was an opportunity too good to miss.

He correctly deduced that the Rhodesians were short of ammunition and ordered two of his men to maintain frequent, short bursts of fire towards the position where they lay, maddeningly concealed in the depression. This would surely induce the white soldiers to return fire.

To the south, the lone chopper turned for the last leg on its fourth and final search by the "grid" when the pilot caught a flash of reflected sunlight.

"Steve, to the north of us," he spoke to the technician through his "Bone Dome" microphone attachment "I just saw a flash ... going to have a look. Keep your eyes peeled." The flash came again, giving the pilot a positive position.

Dimly, Ray heard the noise of rotor blades beating the air.

"Hey mate, I think they've found us," he croaked.

"Well let's keep these Freds' heads down a bit then." Schultz managed a sickly grin through his filthy beard.

They began firing short bursts at the enemy.

Judging the wind direction to perfection, the gutsy RAF 7 Squadron chopper pilot kept his craft downwind at treetop level, skilfully turning the chopper to give his tech a good field of fire as he "crabbed" sideways towards the area in which he'd spotted the flash.

Coming over a rise, he saw the Frelimo section a matter of a few metres from two huddled men and instantly weighed up the situation. The tuned-in tech needed no instructions and immediately raked the by now running Frelimo soldiers. Gorge Chisambo turned and fired blindly. His last conscious moment was of a puff of smoke from the large, black barrel poking from the left side of the helicopter as a 20mm cannon shell entered his cranium just above his left sunglass lens. The Frelimo veteran's decapitated body stood for a split-second before slumping to the ground, bright arterial blood gushing from the severed neck. His glasses lay in the sand, untouched.

The Rhodesian gunner continued to belch death from his cannon at the remaining Frelimo soldiers fleeing through bush in every direction. Satisfied the coast was clear, he spoke through the mike to the pilot, who settled his craft in a hover four metres over Schultz and Hunter and the head-high scrub.

With fumbling, shaking hands, expecting a bullet in the back at any moment, both men grabbed one of the thick ropes played out by the tech and wrapped it around their chests. The tech gave the pilot a thumbs-up signal and the little Alouette rose with the men swinging underneath like trapeze artists. Six minutes later, the chopper settled in a small clearing, Ray and Nick undid the ropes and clambered aboard for a rather more comfortable ride back to base.

The pilot turned and yelled at the men he had rescued. "For fuck's sakes guys, you were way north of your supposed position."

"Yeah.. the Freds made us take a small detour and didn't want to give us a lift home so we had to hitch," Ray replied.

After another lengthy silence, Ray turned to his even smellier and more dishevelled new colleague. "Well, you big bastard, if I ever see your ugly mug again, it'll be too soon. You can stick this caper up your arse and keep it."

"What you bloody complaining about rooinek? We Scouts do this sort of thing every day," Nick joked. You weak or something?"

They grinned at each other from ear to ear. They had come within minutes of a nasty death at the hands of a seriously pissed-off foe and were both very happy to be alive. They sat in silence for the rest of the journey, lost in their thoughts.

AT 11AM THE next day, after a clean up and a good sleep, the pair of them were back in the briefing room. On this occasion a Lieutenant-Colonel from COMOPS (Combined Operations) conducted the debrief. Present were Lieutenant Schultz and Sergeant Hunter, the three Canberra pilots who had conducted the bombing raid, and the Canberra pilot who had carried out a photo reconnaissance after the strike. Representatives of Special Branch, Selous Scouts and other COMOPS staff were also present.

"Good morning, gentlemen," said the officer in clipped, precise tones. "Firstly, from a military point of view, yesterday's little jaunt was quite a success. The photos we took late yesterday of the camp showed at least two hundred and seventy bodies in or adjacent to the parade ground. One hundred and ninety-three others are clearly visible in the immediate vicinity. We estimate that as many as two hundred others may have drowned in the fast-flowing river next to the camp. On this basis, we estimate that at least as many again have been wounded and put out of action...possibly a lot more. In all, over one thousand ZANLA terrorists have been killed or wounded as a result of the operation. We have been monitoring radio transmissions from Mozambique and it appears there are wounded walking in from all over the place, so the enemy has been dealt a serious blow.

The terrorist leaders are already talking to the international press, claiming that we have attacked a refugee camp, but most of the photos the Canberra took are quite clear, and show without doubt that it was a military camp.

"Secondly, and to the other component of the raid. We are not sure if Jason Ncube was killed and have had no info on him as yet. Lieutenant Schultz, anything you can tell us?"

"Ja, I think we missed him. He wasn't on the parade ground when the bombing started. In fact, I am pretty sure I saw him taking the gap just a minute or so before the planes were overhead."

"Any idea what tipped him off?"

"Ja, a company of Frelimo picked up our tracks, they must have put two and two together and realised what we were up to, they were warning the camp just prior to the attack."

"Are you sure it was Frelimo?" The question was not to cast doubt on Lieutenant Schultz's ability, but to make sure of their facts.

"We should be, they chased us for nearly the whole day."

"That's good. At least now we have proof that the Frelimo are actively supporting the terrorists."

"Gentlemen," the COMOPS officer said, addressing everyone in the room. "We can now prove beyond a doubt that the ZANLA are using

Mozambique as a launching pad for their incursions into Rhodesia. The question now is what do we do with this information?"

"That depends on whether we want to sit around and let world opinion dictate our moves or whether we want to get out there and boot some backsides," said Ray.

"I suggest, Sergeant," said the officer staring icily at Ray, "that you keep your comments to yourself."

The officer was not used to being told basic truths from a mere NCO. The hierarchy knew they were pussyfooting around, but they did not like to be told that by a subordinate.

"The Sergeant is right," injected Lieutenant Schultz. "We have all known about these camps for a while now. Why are we still fooling around? We should be taking them out, not talking them out."

"Gentlemen, I understand your strong feelings, coming from the ground level so to speak. But believe me, it is not easy to make aggressive decisions when the rest of the world is breathing down your necks. Sanctions are hurting and world opinion is mounting against us. We are doing a hard juggling act as it is."

"Well meneer, if you're happy to stop treading on outsider's toes when our own women and children are being murdered and raped and our soldiers are getting killed, let's carry on killing the odd terr as he shows himself and leave it at that," drawled Schultz.

The senior officer opened his mouth to reprimand the Lieutenant for his insolence but found himself staring into eyes that bore right through him. Despite the impertinence, he found himself respecting these rough, rude men. Their views might be simple, but he admired them for the men they were; the type of person he could never be.

"Lieutenant. I would appreciate it if you moderated your language in this room. Now, if, and this is a big if, we were to give the go ahead for any raids of this nature, how would you go about it?"

Within an hour, the Officer had collected a lot of information that might be useful if any big raids were to take place, but before they finished Nick Schultz gave them a dire warning.

"Now that they know we are willing to have a go at them in their bases, don't think they are going to just sit there and let us kick them about. Especially with blokes like Jason Ncube in charge. They will start digging trenches and tunnels and if they can they will get anti-aircraft guns from the Frelimo. So if we are going to do it, we must make sure that our info is current, accurate and correct."

NICK SCHULTZ HAD been right. The camps that were of most strategic importance to ZANLA were fortified much along the lines of those dug by the Vietnamese only a few years earlier in their war against the

Americans. This was no coincidence; many Soviet "advisers" to the North Vietnamese were in Mozambique to pass on battle-tested methods — which included tunnel systems and judicious use of the highly effective 12.7mm anti-aircraft gun.

Under leaders like Jason Ncube, the camps' occupants became sharper and more efficient as the training improved. Even the many hundreds of female and child porters used for daily camp duties were drilled to a high state of alert against possible Rhodesian attack.

Despite these efforts, the Selous Scouts were still able to infiltrate men into the camps. They filtered vital information back to be fed into ever-growing dossiers. The SAS was also busy: mining roads and ambushing convoys bringing food and weapons to the camps; blowing up arms and ammunition dumps; and generally harassing the enemy. The Frelimo was finding it a costly and troublesome task to continue harbouring the freedom fighters from Zimbabwe.

Meanwhile, the RLI stepped up its Fire Force role and the kill rate climbed with every passing raid. More and more men were being trained as paratroopers. As one observer put it: "It looks like every man and his dog is being para-trained. Soon the whole bloody army will have wings on their sleeves." He was right, towards the end of the war even officers and men from rear echelon units were putting in for para training.

While these men were being trained, it left a shortage of available troops on the ground and the soldiers of One Commando found themselves pushed to the limit.

CAPTAIN WATSON, RAY, Koos, Mark and the others were kitting up for yet another operational jump. This time on an airfield in the middle of nowhere.

"Jeez, stuff me up the arse with a pineapple," grumbled Mark. "If I'm not getting into a harness, I'm getting out of one. If I'm not getting in or out of one, I'm sitting in the Dak in one. If I'm not in one at all, I'm chasing floppies around the bush."

He was right. Often the paras would finish at one scene only to be driven to the nearest airfield to be kitted up ready for the next. It was common now for the Fire Force Dakotas to carry two spare parachutes for each man in the cargo compartment.

Many airfields dotted the countryside around Rhodesia, some of them designed only for small cropdusters. The Dakota pilots found themselves landing in or taking off from dirt airstrips that barely deserved the title. Paratroopers' log books often had two and sometimes three entries in red in one day.

The influx of terrorists mounted rapidly and to counter the expanding incursion, other units began to be used in a Fire Force role. The two Battalions of the Rhodesian African Rifles — African troops led by white officers — were foremost in this new role and, although they did well, no one matched the expertise of the Rhodesian Light Infantry. It was not for nothing they were called Rhodesia's killing machine.

As the war hotted up, the men of the RLI became hard and detached as they coldly and efficiently dealt out death to the enemy on a daily basis — one day blending into another as they went out time and again. They lost men too, but, whereas the ratio for the security forces during the war was ten to one, for the RLI it nudged a hundred to one.

CHAPTER EIGHT

THE FIVE-DAY R&R period was over as the men of The Big Red assembled on the parade square outside the OC's office. Something was up as they would normally have been on the trucks, ready for deployment to a FAF somewhere in the operational areas. Two months has passed since Ray's "external" with Nick Schultz in Mozambique.

"ONE COMMANDO. ONE COMMANDO 'SHUN," bellowed the CSM. One hundred and twenty boots thudded into the ground in unison. This was a lot of men in one place at one time — some had been dragged off courses and from leave. Thirty-two of them had just completed basic para course.

"There's something big happening," thought Ray.

The CSM spoke again. "As of this moment, all of you are confined to barracks. Later, you'll be drawing weapons and kit and we'll be going for a nice little drive in the country. There will be no pissing off anywhere and no phone calls. I want you all to wait in the barrack rooms until further notice. Is that understood?"

"Yes, sir."

"I can't hear you."

"YES, SIR."

"That's better. Commando dismiss."

The trucks rolled into the makeshift camp just after midday. Two, Three, and Support Commandos were already there, and "C" Squadron, The Rhodesian Special Air Services Regiment.

"Shit," breathed Mark, "this is a big one all right."

The troops milled about for an hour in the traditional military "hurry up and wait" syndrome. Finally a COMOPS officer addressed them. "Right. I want all officers, NCOs and Stop Group leaders to follow me." They followed the officer to a secluded area among the trees near the barracks.

When he saw the model of the camp laid out before them, Ray knew where they were going. It was the same camp he and Nick Schultz had visited eight weeks previously. However, it had grown so much it was hardly recognisable. Many of the features were the same but where there had been only bush, there was now an elaborate bunker system with trenches and clearly defined anti-aircraft positions. It was a different ballgame all right.

When everyone had settled, the officer brought the group to order. "Right. Gentlemen, before you is a scale model of a camp in

Mozambique." He paused a moment for effect before adding: "We are going to attack it." There were murmurs of approval.

"As you can see, it is a large camp. As of now, Special Branch believe there are upwards of five thousand terrs there, plus some elements of Frelimo and, we are reliably informed, several Russian advisers."

Someone piped up: "How many of us are going in?"

The officer looked at the speaker for a moment. "Five hundred and eight of you are going in as ground troops."

"Aag man, only ten to one ... it'll be a piece of piss!" one of the RLI sergeants laughed. A snigger went up from the assembled men.

"Don't forget, we'll have heavy air support," said the officer. "Now, let's have some hush and get on with it. As I said, there will be five thousand-plus in the camp to oppose us. Of these, many have only just been trained and are expected to run as soon as contact is made. However, there are some elements of hard core and they will put up a fight.

"The latest int from SB, who've been grilling a recent capture, indicates there's at least one company of Frelimo manning the anti-aircraft positions and mortar bases. Some of them will be under the supervision of the Russians, so expect discipline, aggression and some resistance. As you can see, there is a trench system around the camp, plus bunkers. Any questions so far?

"Right. The format of the attack goes as follows. An hour after first light, 0659 hours, the Hunters and Canberras will make a bombing run to soften up the target. Exactly one minute later the Dakotas and helicopters will drop their Stop Groups. The pilots will be having a special briefing later on."

The officer walked over to a large easel and uncovered it. "Right, here is an enlarged photo of the area taken two days ago. To the west of the camp on the other side of the river, which is almost dry, is where the para Stop Groups will be dropped. You will be briefed in more detail later. To the north and east will be the helicopter Stops."

As the officer filled in the details, Ray learned that his Stop would be one of the first to land and their initial position would be on the bank of a dry riverbed leading off the main river line. Captain Watson would be on the other side. When things had settled down after the initial engagement, they were to advance towards the anti-aircraft position to the south-west of the camp. Heliborne troops would be attacking the AA positions from the other side.

It was late afternoon before final details had been arranged. There were to be three K-cars, controlling different sectors, with General Walls having overall charge from the command Dakota flying high overhead.

"Right, gentlemen, that just about sums it up. Oh, one last thing, there will be choppers not far away ready for casevac. After they drop the heliborne Stop Groups off, they will be flying to a refuelling point. We are going to be a bit cheeky here. We're dropping some fuel drums off by parachute from the DC10 and blokes from a territorial unit will be driving over to guard it and refuel the choppers when they arrive. This fuelling point is not more than fifteen minutes' flying time from the camp. Any questions?

"Right, tomorrow morning, I want the Stop leaders to bring their men in for briefings. RLI para-stops first, SAS Para-Stops next, then heli-Stops."

The troops slept by their trucks that night and the next morning the briefings continued. Ray was talking to Mark, Koos and Trooper Beck, just recently finished his para course. They were standing beside the model of the camp.

"Okay, listen in guys, this is the scenario. We are going to be dropped off here to the west of this river line running in a southerly direction," he said, pointing to the area on the model. "Corporal Wessel's Stop will be out first, then us. Stop Three is Captain Watson. Corporal Wessel's Stop will be watching the fork in the two rivers here. Stop Two, which is us, will be on the south side of this dry riverbed here and Captain Watson will be on the other side.

"Okay. The sides of the riverbed are pretty steep and overgrown. Where we're going to lie up is here — right next to this bend. Apparently this will be one of the major escape routes so we should have a bit of a turkey shoot because by the time the terrs see their mates lying dead on the ground it'll be too late; the bend will have hidden them until the last moment. But don't get complacent, stay switched on. As I said last night, there are five thousand of the buggers, so there is going to be plenty of shooting.

"That is going to be the easy part. Later on, we have to cross the main river, which should only be thigh-deep because it is the dry season, and attack the AA position here. Now, the Lynx will be dropping Frantan and rockets just before we assault the position and Support Commando will be setting up a mortar base to cover us. But if you look here, see these trenches at the base of the hill?... we're going to have our work cut out taking them out. Then we still have to get up the hill and sort the gun position out, and we have been told that there are at least two machineguns guarding it.

"Now. While the rabble will already have left or been killed by us, the guys that are left will be either hard core or Frelimo, or both, and they are supposed to have Russians with them. So it's not going to be a walkover. The hill is about thirty metres high, but it is fairly bare, so we are not going to have much cover and must get up there fast, okay. Any questions so far?"

The men shook their heads.

"Okay, the Stops doing the assault are One, Two, Three and Four, with Sergeant Kerr. The organisers of the raid have been a bit cunning. This gun emplacement is going to be assaulted from two sides and they have ensured that the Stop Groups taking the other side are heliborne Stops from One Commando. That way we know who we are working with. The K-car commander for our sector is Major Hill, so we will be working with all our own blokes. For fuck's sake blokes, when we get to the top of that hill, no shooting at our own boys, okay?"

"Right, later on we will be doing a walkthrough on the ground; the area near here resembles the topography of the camp, that is why they chose this place."

All that day the units rehearsed for the attack until they knew every aspect of the coming raid. Later, they were issued with full kit for the next day, then it was an early night ready for a big day ahead.

JASON NCUBE WAS not happy. After the bombing raid the camp was being used again, but he would have preferred to move somewhere else. He had had to fight to get his superiors to give the go-ahead to fortify the place. However, this place was logistically sound and had water all year round.

"Why bother," they said. "The Rhodesians will never dare attack a camp again. The Western press has made such a big issue of their raid on a 'refugee camp' that the Boers are still smarting from the criticism rained on them."

After the bombing raid, the press had been taken to the site to "see for themselves" that it was a refugee camp. All weapons had been carefully removed and the traces of it being a military base erased as far as possible. The press had a field day photographing piles of rotting bodies with not an AK in sight. The aerial photos released by the Security Forces immediately after the raid, showing positive evidence that it was a heavily fortified military camp, were disbelieved or ignored.

Nevertheless, Jason was adamant about improving security. He knew that now they had a taste of blood, those tenacious whites from across the border would be back, world opinion or not. He had a strong gut feeling and was seldom wrong about things like that.

Jason bullied and cajoled his men. If the trenches weren't to his satisfaction, they were dug deeper. The Frelimo were happy just to have one machinegun guarding the big anti-aircraft weapons; Jason insisted on three to one and made them build bunkers for each machinegun which, if they weren't completely bomb-proof, would at least ensure they were mortar-proof.

He knew that many of his men could not stomach a hard fight, so put them in the first line of defence with as many able commanders in charge as he could find. His hard core soldiers and the Frelimo were allocated the vital positions. At least they would slug it out. He had Frelimo mount and man the AA guns, and the big, unsmiling men from the cold country far away began training the cadre in bunker defence.

This was a difficult task as groups were constantly coming and going. One seldom saw the same group of men twice because infiltration groups were now being directed to enter Rhodesia by one route and exit by another. This tactic was a fairly recent ploy by ZANLA. Groups inside Rhodesia were being handed such a mauling by the security forces that ZANLA commanders didn't want them accidentally meeting up with incoming groups and letting them know what was in store. Otherwise, they might not have had the temerity to continue, or at least would have been reticent to take up the fight.

Bit by bit, Jason secured the camp to his satisfaction. If the Rhodesians did come back, he was not going to make it easy for them.

THE BIG MATABELE sat in his hut, mulling over the reports that had been coming in. The Rhodesians were up to something. No-one knew what, but the messages were disturbing. None of the usual units were operating the Fire Forces at the moment and only a few helicopters were flying them. The Commandos and that other specialist unit had gone to a secret place. But why?

Jason rubbed the deep scar that ran across his skull. It still hurt when he was tired or worried. Thinking back on that night at Grand Reef caused a frown of annoyance. He hadn't been thinking about Sergeant Hunter, but he thought about him now. From the information the Frelimo section gave him after the bombing raid, one of the two men they had chased that day fitted his description. Jason was sure it was him. It seemed as though the man was dogging his every step.

They had found the parachutes Ray and Nick had used, but no-one had heard any planes fly overhead and Jason wondered if it were true that men could fall through the sky as the comrade who worked at the air force base said. Jason had seen parachutes used when the enemy

110

attacked them in Zimbabwe, but to him it seemed as though the plane had something to do with making them open.

How could a man fall so far without crashing to the ground and killing himself, especially as they said it must be night-time when they came? It had been very dark that night. How could they see? He had asked the Russians if it were possible and they had told him that many men did this thing. There was so much he still did not understand. Perhaps it was part of the magic that this man Hunter had. Jason did not know, and his head hurt. Anyway, he was going to post more guards for the next few nights, just in case.

THE HANGAR AT the Parachute Training School resembled something out of the film A Bridge Too Far. Parachutes and gear were laid in rows covering every square centimetre of the floor; dozens of men were milling about, organising last-minute details and gear checks. Although it looked chaotic, there was order to the frenzy.

There were thirteen Dakota loads of twenty-four paras — each load laid out in two neat rows of twelve — with three despatchers to each aircraft. The planes would be close to overloaded, but the men had to be put on the ground somehow. Despatchers had been called off leave and reservists summoned; even the OC of the parachute school was going along.

"Righteo, gentlemen," boomed the loud voice of the school's warrant officer, a large ruddy man with an English accent and a huge handlebar moustache to match. "This is the moment you have been waiting for. Let's get kitted up."

Row by row, the paratroopers worked in pairs. First the main parachutes were fitted, with their partner holding the parachute on their backs. The leg straps and the chest straps were then fed through the harness and locked into the quick-release box, the safety clip fitted, then the back straps tightened and stowed away. Next, the rifle or machinegun was strapped to the right side of the para with a body band. The sling was fed through the shoulders and underneath the lift webbs and finally looped over the reserve D-ring, where the reserve was clipped on to hold it in place.

Once both rows had completed this stage, the despatchers checked each man. If satisfied, the parachutist hooked up the other side of the reserve and waited for the despatcher to check his back; he would then undo the snap hook of the static line and hand it to the para-chutist. When the despatcher was totally sure that his men were prepared, they sat down and waited. It seemed ages before the English voice boomed again.

"Despatchers. Are your men ready?" He looked around and waited for confirmation from each chief despatcher. "Right, I want you to leave in order of your aircraft number, with number one first. And good luck with today's venture."

The men stood up and followed their despatchers out to the waiting aircraft.

The engine noise of the thirteen old Dakotas was deafening as they warmed up in the darkness. The men filed off to their designated plane.

"HALT," called the despatcher. "Left turn." The men waited in the propblast as the despatcher climbed aboard to check last-minute details.

Mark turned to Ray. "Hey, Sarge," he shouted above the roar of the engines. "The last time we took off from here was on the course. Seems like a hundred years ago."

"Yeah, funny isn't it? We were standing in the same order, too. In fact, I think we have been jumping in the same order all the time."

Captain Watson shouted across to them: "You three guys have been so close for so long, I'm beginning to wonder whether you have strange tendencies."

Koos shot back as quick as a flash: "Hey, Sir, I think there is a poofter around here somewhere. If you give me a kiss I'll tell you who it is."

Those within hearing laughed at the light-hearted banter.

The despatcher came out. "Pay attention guys, I have to give you the warning now. 'When the red light comes on it is an order to prepare to jump. When the green light comes on it is an order to jump. Failure to do so will result in your imprisonment, Court Martial, or both. Now on you get, starboard stick first."

When all the men were on board, the Dakotas taxied on to the runway and lined up in staggered formation. The pilots adjusted throttle settings and checked gauges while waiting for takeoff. As one, the aircraft increased revs; brakes were eased off and the squadron of ancient workhorses of the sky began to build up speed before taking off and heading east towards the rising sun and the terrorist camp in Mozambique.

The sun began to creep through the open doors where the men were sitting patiently. Some laughed and joked, most were quiet and pensive and chewed gum. The other Daks slowly became visible, creating an impressive, invincible sight flying in close formation.

Ray felt Mark looking at him and turned to smile at his friend. Mark was not his usual cheerful self. He looked tense and drawn.

"What's up, mate, got the jitters?"

"Hey, Sarge. After this is over, will you make sure you go and visit my Mum as often as you can?"

"What are you talking about? I always come over to your place when we are on leave."

"Just promise me you will."

"Don't talk shit, man, nothing is going to happen to you."

"Promise me."

"Yeah, yeah, I promise, just stop talking that way, okay."

"Thanks, Sarge. She likes you, you know."

The planes droned on into the gathering light.

"STAND UP, HOOK UP AND CHECK YOUR EQUIPMENT."

There wasn't a lot of room left in the aircraft; its full load of burly, bulky paratroopers all jostling for space as they snapped their static lines on to the cables. The checks took a while because the cramped conditions left little room available for the despatchers to move up and down the plane. Even so, the men had to wait a long time before the lights came on.

"GO, GO, GO," shouted the despatcher. Ray found himself running down the gangway into the door, then he was tumbling out.

"Look up, check canopy." He went through the drills automatically. As soon as he had completed them, he looked around to see para-chutes blossoming all over the place as more than three hundred men floated to earth.

In the distance Ray could see columns of dust and black smoke where the Canberras' bombs had hit the camp. G-cars were deploying Stops and he could clearly hear the whoosh and boom of the rockets released by the Lynxs as they began their initial sorties and pounded their targets. K-cars prowled the camp like hungry cats. Ray looked down to see terrorists running only metres below him before he hit the ground and rolled in the dust.

Two terrified terrorists, one a denim-clad woman carrying a 1916-manufactured Russian Ppsh machinegun, came running towards him while casting glances over their shoulders at the carnage in the camp. Ray didn't have time to unstrap the rifle from his side. He pulled out the 9mm Star pistol issued to all paratroopers from under the pack-opening bands on his reserve, and took careful aim at the two ZANLA combatants who were almost on him. They were so panicked they scarcely seemed to have noticed him.

Ray's first shot entered the woman's head just below her right eye. Her legs buckled but her momentum kept the body upright for all of three metres before she pitched forward. Her companion made a vain attempt to lift his SKS rifle from the hip but Ray's second round caught him in the throat; a third shot stilled his thrashing limbs.

All around, Ray could hear the crack of pistol fire. The others were also engaging terrorists before they had a chance to get out of their harnesses. A third terrorist came bounding towards him. Ray fired, the man went down and tried to crawl away. Ray fired again. He was still lying on his back with his canopy billowing, so he undid the body band, unhooked the safety clip, turned and pressed the quick-release box and wriggled out of his harness.

He cocked his FN and called out: "Mark, Koos, Beck, over here." Within minutes the three of them had arrived, panting and breathless.

"Fuck me, there's hundreds of the bastards. They're everywhere," gasped Koos.

"Follow me," ordered Ray, and they were gone.

Ray led them to the dry riverbed and they went to ground. He could see Captain Watson and his Stop arriving on the other side. He waved, the Captain waved back. They knew the other was there, so they wouldn't shoot at each other.

The two Stops did not have long to wait. Terrorists began appearing round the bend in the river almost immediately and the bloody slaughter began.

All morning the sound of small arms fire could be heard. By ten o'clock, fifty-two bodies lay on the sandy floor of the dry river; the numbers being added to every few minutes. The men's rifles were uncomfortably hot, but still the fleeing ZANLA cadres kept coming. The heavy boom of airstrikes continued as the Lynxs kept up their SNEB and Frantan drops while the K-cars' 20mm cannon raked river lines and dense bush in an attempt to flush out those hiding from the withering fire.

By eleven o'clock the number of terrorists running into the Stop Groups' guns had slowed to a trickle.

Major Hill's voice came over the radio: "All Stop Groups in sector one, this is K One. Sitrep, over."

After the sitrep, the Major gave the next orders. "I want all Stop Groups to sweep up to the river line and wait on the western side until you get further orders."

Ray got his men up and they advanced to the river, where they again went to ground. Across the river, they could see the hill they were to assault.

"There she is, boys," Ray called to the other three. "Now remember, when we go in don't bunch up, go in a straight line just like in rehearsals. Remember to keep your dressing on Captain Watson, he is the assault leader. Have you all got a full magazine on your rifles? Remember, we have to take the trenches first."

All up and down the line, Stop Leaders were giving last-minute instructions to their men.

"K-car One, calling all assault groups. In one minute, Cyclone Four will be doing a strafing run over the target. I want you to cross the river under cover of the air support and go to ground on the eastern side of the river, prior to the assault. Over."

"K-car One, Roger," the leaders affirmed in turn.

The Lynxs flew overhead and dropped their payloads. Great blazing "hands" of ignited diesel and liquid soap detonated and leaped towards their targets. Seconds later, the assault leaders were up and shouting: "C'mon, let's go!"

The men followed them into the river, the SAS forming the northern part of the advance, the RLI the southern. They went to ground on the other side. Erratic, desultory fire came from the trenches.

"K-car to all assault groups. OK, it's your show now."

The leaders called in mortar fire and the advance began. The line walked at a fast pace, keeping its dressing. They walked through burned huts and scattered bodies. Two hundred metres to go. The mortars kept up their barrage. One hundred metres.

"Cease fire." The mortar barrage stopped. "CHARGE," came the cry and nearly three hundred men broke into a run, firing as they went across the blackened ground. The momentum picked up and the line became ragged as the men reached the slope. The firing from the trenches intensified and here and there, a man in the line dropped. Thirty metres ... twenty ... ten ... and the men were up to the trenches and firing down into them. Bodies lay everywhere in the various attitudes of death. From some parts of the trenches, frightened eyes looked up, offering no resistance. The fight was gone out of them.

Mark looked down into the trench at the heaped-up bodies lying there. One figure was huddled against the rear wall. Mark could not work out whether the man was dead or not; he was crouched over his rifle, head bowed.

The young terrorist must have seen the shadow of the lanky machinegunner, or perhaps felt his presence. In panic or fear, or both, the terrorist jerked on the trigger of his AK without even looking up, before dropping it. Two rounds from the burst caught Mark full in the chest and he pitched forward into the trench.

Ray bounded over the bodies towards his friend. "Oh, Jesus, Mark. NO," he whispered in despair. The ZANLA man looked at Ray with dead, expressionless eyes. Without a word, Ray fired. He knelt down and cradled his friend in his arms. "MEDIC," he shouted at Koos. "For fuck's sake get a medic."

Mark looked up at his Sergeant. He had that expression of surprise Ray had seen so often in dying men. "Jesus, Mark, hang on mate, we'll have you out of here quick smart."

Mark mumbled something. Bright blood bubbled from his chest.

"C'mon Mark, hang on, mate." Mark's body went rigid for a second, then started to relax as Ray watched the life leave his friend. He reached for his handset. "K-car One, this is Stop Two, I have one man KIA," he said. His voice was flat and toneless.

"Stop Two, K-car, Roger. Are you okay to carry on?" The Major's voice was concerned.

Ray reached up from the depths of despair. The grief that had clouded his eyes was replaced with the look Bridget the air hostess had noticed so long ago. Sergeant Hunter was ready.

"Roger K-car, Stop Two is okay to carry on. Right, Koos, you are the machinegunner now," Ray said. He went and took several belts out of Mark's pouches and handed them to Koos. "Ready?"

Captain Watson was calling in more mortar fire on the gun placement on top of the hill. Out of the corner of his eye, Sergeant Hunter noticed Beck was white and shaking. He was on the point of breaking, of losing control.

"TROOPER BECK," he yelled above the din. "If you let me down now, I'll tear your innards out and use them to drag you up the bloody hill. Switch on."

Beck looked over at his Sergeant and what he saw frightened him more than the ordeal he was about to face. That look could kill. Hunter was a dangerous man. Grief had transformed itself into temporary madness and the man appeared capable of killing anyone in his path at that moment, friend or foe.

Beck took several deep breaths and gathered his wits. He looked steadily at the Sergeant. "I won't let you down."

Along the line the assault commanders were giving the signal to advance.

AS SOON AS he heard the baboons becoming agitated, Jason knew his intuition had been right. Something was wrong. Some camp guards kept baboons tied to trees as an early warning system. Whenever a plane flew close to the camp, the ape's acute sense of hearing would send them into a chattering frenzy long before any human ears could detect a sound.

For the past two days Jason had made the men sleep in their trenches and bunkers. They complained bitterly. Like most people, they wanted to sleep in comfort. He had caught several of them asleep when they were supposed to be on guard during the night. Some of the men were becoming sullen and resentful for not only was Jason a hard taskmaster, he was also of another tribe. It was only Jason's leadership qualities that saw him through ... even so it was touch and go at times.

Jason had made them stand to until well after sun-up. This created more hostility. He despaired how he was ever going to turn these people into soldiers when all they wanted to do was eat and sleep.

The order to stand down had been given and the men were starting to drift towards the huts and kitchens when the monkeys began their high-pitched chattering.

"STAND TO," roared Jason. Men looked up at him in confusion. "GET BACK TO YOUR POSITIONS. KURUMIDZA (hurry)," he shouted again. In other parts of the camp various commanders were also trying to rally their men. The better trained terrorists and Frelimo quickly scrambled into their trenches and bunkers, but the rabble were beginning to show seeds of panic and breaking into a run away from the camp.

Thirty-five seconds later, the bombs began to fall. Jason and the Russians had planned well. The trenches and bunkers had been built properly and most of the men who went into them were saved from the initial bombing run. Even so, the noise and concussion blasts drove the breath and the senses out of them.

After the first wave, Jason climbed out of his bunker to see what had happened. In places where the bombs had scored direct hits, the trenches had collapsed, but in the main they had held up. To the west he could see hundreds of parachutes dotting the sky, while to the east the helicopters were flying in. He looked up to see the wave of Lynx light aircraft approaching.

"So the bombing is not over yet," he thought to himself as he climbed back into the bunker. "A lot of good the anti-aircraft guns were doing. The first wave caught us by surprise and the second was so close behind there was no time to get them into action."

They endured the bombs and the rockets; they endured the oxygen-sucking petrol jelly bombs that burned and scorched the ground and the very air above. Somehow, they survived.

Jason watched the strafing and the mortars falling all around the trenches just before the assault on them. Although there wasn't much fight left in the men after the shock of the bombing, Jason saw a

Rhodesian soldier fall occasionally. "At least they are putting up some resistance," he said to the Frelimo soldier standing beside him. "It will be our turn next."

The machineguns guarding the AA position began opening up but they weren't much use; the Rhodesians were already in the trenches.

"Back in the bunkers," shouted Jason as the first mortar bombs started pounding the hill.

The thin line of Rhodesian soldiers were up and out of the   trenches before the last mortars had landed. At first, the line was ragged and uncoordinated but good training and leadership began to show as it quickly steadied into an orderly advance. The Rhodesians effected controlled fire as they went, keeping the guerillas' heads down. Even so, return fire was beginning to crack and every so often a portion of the line would stop momentarily as the machinegunners changed belts; the others in the stick giving covering fire. The   magazines on the rifles were changed without a pause, on the move. The ground was getting steeper now and the enemy's fire heavier.

At seventy metres the assault commanders screamed "CHARGE" and the line broke into a run, gaining momentum even over the increasingly sloping ground. The line wavered but still kept going, the distance was getting shorter.

Sergeant Hunter and Trooper Beck had changed magazines just after Koos renewed his belt. They broke into a run with the rest of them.

So consumed was he with the fires fuelling his battlelust that Ray hardly felt the tugs at his body or the blood which flowed freely as the bullets hit him. The only thing he did notice was a perceptible slowing of movement; everything seemed to require an effort. He stumbled in slow motion as the scene before him became hazy and indistinct. The top of the gun emplacement didn't seem to be getting any closer. He felt giddy and weak, but he kept going.

Just when Ray Hunter felt as though he had run a hundred kilometres towards the base of the mountain that seemed always just out of reach, he and his men arrived at the lip of the gun emplacement. He peered cautiously over the edge to see a man directly in front of him whose eyes were wide with fear — or was it anger?

Ray felt he should know the wild-looking man before him, but he was too tired to care. He was also too tired to care that the man was shooting at him from point-blank range. Ray stared dumbly at the terrorist shooting and screaming at him.

Jason recognised Isizo as soon as he saw the Rhodesian assault line break into a run. Fear and superstition filled him and he had to fight hard to quell the panic. He emptied a full magazine in the white man's direction before regaining control of himself. The soldier in him changed magazines quickly. He took a deep breath and began to fire as accurately as he could, the adrenaline rushing through his body making everything so clear it amazed him.

He could see the red splashes as his bullets found their mark. He knew he was hitting his target but the white man kept coming. Jason mustered every ounce of courage he had. He knew he was shaking badly from fear-induced fatigue; he squeezed every muscle tight to try to stop the violent spasms, and continued shooting. More and more of his bullets were hitting their target, but still the man kept coming.

"How could he fight a man who would not die?" his mind screamed, and his aim started to go wild. His magazine was empty and he fumbled for another. Shaking and screaming, he jammed the fresh magazine into his rifle just as Sergeant Hunter appeared above the lip of the embankment.

"IT IS YOU, WIZARD. GET AWAY FROM ME." He heard a voice he dimly recognised as his own screaming at the man who simply stood there, looking at him. The "wizard' just looked at him, his rifle hanging by his side. It seemed as though the man could not be bothered trying to kill him. His magic must be strong. Jason pulled the trigger of his AK and the bullets poured in the direction of the white man.

TROOPER BECK SAVED his Sergeant's life that day. He reached the top before everyone else and for the first few moments was busy engaging a Frelimo soldier who was frantically trying to reload. The trooper shot the man twice and watched him topple over. He heard a high-pitched scream to his left and saw Jason open fire. Simultaneously, he saw Ray standing there, doing nothing.

"What's wrong with the Sarge?" he thought as he swivelled his rifle barrel towards Jason. He fired two shots in quick succession and Jason spun round and slammed hard into the earth. Trooper Beck would have fired more rounds except his rifle was empty. He saw his Sergeant topple into the pit just as he was reaching for another magazine.

Sergeant Hunter landed on top of Jason Ncube, their bodies crumpled together in an untidy heap. Blood from their wounds ran in rivulets, joining together to form larger pools that mingled as one until the thirsty earth soaked it up.

IT CAN BE said that in battle one sees all, and one sees nothing. Although Koos and Beck would have noticed their Sergeant in their peripheral vision, because that is what they had been taught to do, their whole concentration was in front of them where the danger lay. Even a well-trained, hardened soldier values his own life above everything and will do as much as he can to stay alive. This means that his whole being is focused on the enemy.

If Ray Hunter had gone down the others would have noticed, but as he kept going his wounds were not spotted until he toppled over. By then, the gun position had been taken.

The two men rushed over to their Sergeant. "MEDIC ... MEDIC," they yelled as they tried to staunch the blood pouring from his many wounds. They worked frantically with bandages and torn shirts to save the life of the man they so admired.

CHAPTER NINE

THE BRIGHT LIGHTS hurt terribly and Ray tried to screw his eyes shut to avoid them. His whole body was on fire. He wanted everything to go away; to sleep, but the pain kept nagging at him. Occasionally he could hear voices; he did not know where they came from but it seemed far away. Sometimes the voices called his name but he did not answer. He didn't want to be there, he wanted to hide away in the darkness where no-one could find him. The pain got worse and worse until he felt he could bear it no longer, then he would drift away in a state of euphoria where, for a time, the pain was only a dull pounding. Then it would return, stronger and stronger, until the medics gave him another shot of morphine.

On the second day, he opened his eyes to find a concerned face looking back at him. He knew the face, but did not know from where. He then drifted back into oblivion.

On the third day, things began to come into focus. His first conscious thought was of the smell; the antiseptic stink of a hospital. So he was not dead. Ray slowly opened his eyes, the light making the pain in his head worse, but he squinted and took in his surroundings. He was in a ward, there were several other beds and each bed had a resident. Some were in traction, others had bandages around their heads. Not a pleasant place to be, this place of suffering. Ray closed his eyes and drifted back off to sleep.

He woke to feel a cool hand on his wrist and caught a faint whiff of perfume. He registered the crisp white of the nurse's uniform from the corner of his barely open eyes. His gaze moved slowly upward and once it reached the nurse's face, he realised with a shock why the perfume was familiar.

"Bridget ... what are you doing here? This is not an aeroplane."

"So, you've had enough rest," Bridget joked. Her voice was calm and professional, but he could see the concern on her face. It could have been the genuine concern of a nurse for her patient, but he felt that it was more than that. He was too tired and sore to think much more so he drifted once again into sleep.

FIVE DAYS AFTER the raid, Ray was more alert and able to sit up in bed. Bridget was with him as often as work would permit, as well as when she was off duty.

"You still haven't told me what you are doing in the nursing profession," Ray said one afternoon while she was changing a dressing.

"Well, I thought I was needed more doing something like this than being a glamour waitress. Seeing as you boys are so determined to get yourselves all torn up playing your stupid games." There was a hint of anger mixed in with the concern in her voice.

"Talking about getting torn apart, you did a rather good job yourself. We thought we had lost you a couple of times. Boy, you took a lot of bullets in that cute little body of yours."

"How many exactly?"

"Seven."

"Holy cow. No wonder I hurt so much," Ray breathed. "How many bones are broken?" He had no casts on and had wondered about that.

"That's the amazing thing," she said. "Apart from a few chips broken off, all your wounds were flesh wounds; some deep ones and the muscle tissue is badly torn and will take a while to mend. Your main problem was the loss of blood. By all accounts you should have died. You sure are a tough one."

Bridget's mention of death brought Mark flooding back into his mind. "Bridget, I want to ask you a favour. Could you get a message to someone for me?"

"Gladly."

"Could you contact a Mrs Ellis for me and see how she is."

"If you're talking about Mark's mother, she has already been in to see you several times while you were unconscious. She is going to come in again as soon as you are well enough to receive visitors."

Mark's memory brought on a different type of pain; the pain associated with the loss of a close friend. It left a hollow feeling inside him; an emptiness that was hard to bear. Much as he pined for his friend, his heart went out to Mark's family. It was always those left behind who suffered the most.

Ray had been dozing as peacefully as he was able when he heard a faint rustling by his side. He looked up to see Mark's mother standing by his bed. She seemed drawn and tired, the anguish on her face obvious. She still managed a smile for him, however.

"Hello, Mrs E," he said quietly, raising his hand. She clasped it tightly.

"Hello, Ray. How are you feeling?" The tears were already falling from her face.

"I am as well as can be expected, I think is what the doctors say." Tears also began filling his eyes. They stayed together for a long time, holding hands; drawing strength from each other, not speaking.

Then Mrs Ellis wiped away her tears and they began to talk. "The doctor says you will be okay. He thinks you will mend pretty well."

"Right now it doesn't seem to matter about that," Ray croaked. "I wish it had been me instead of Mark. He was a good man, Mrs E, the best. How are you coping?"

"Oh, I've had a few days to try to get used to it," she replied. "I still can't quite believe it's happened. I think I'm still numb from it all."

"Yeah, it happens like that. It's a funny thing, Mrs E. Mark asked me to get in contact with you if anything happened to him. He knew. He knew before we even landed. He was a very brave man. When things get bad, just remember that. Your son was courageous."

They sat a while longer, still holding hands.

"Tell me something, Ray. ... Was he... did he... I mean, did he take long to die. Was it bad for him?"

Ray looked directly at her so that she could see the truth; that he was not telling her a lie just to ease the anguish.

"It was over before Mark realised what had happened. I can tell you with complete certainty, he would not have felt a thing."

Mrs Ellis nodded. She could hear that Ray was telling her the honest truth — and he was. Even though Mark had taken a minute or two to die from his wounds, all he would have felt was shock and surprise. The human body is a strange thing; shock is a safety mechanism which blocks out severe trauma for some time. Most people when badly hurt, even if conscious for the whole time, do not remember anything about the incident or its aftermath.

Ray and Mrs Ellis talked quietly, still holding hands, until visiting time was over. She got up to leave, promising to come often. "And, Ray, please call me Doris, not Mrs Ellis," was her parting message.

Ray knew that the visits would be important for the healing processes of both of them during the coming months.

The next visitor Ray received at the Andrew Fleming Hospital in Salisbury was Captain Watson.

"Howzit Ray?" the Captain said cheerfully. "I bring you some great news."

"G'day, Sir. How goes it? I could use some good news."

"Well, the first bit is that our raid was a bloody success. We killed over fifteen hundred of the buggers and captured so many documents and weapons, it will be a bloody long time before they can get them-selves back into gear."

"How many did we lose?" asked Ray.

"There were three killed and seven wounded," the Captain replied. Then looking concerned, he added: "Ray, I am really sorry about Mark, he was a top oun."

"That's okay, Sir. How was the funeral, did you go to it?"

"Ja, as many as could get to it went. It was a good funeral. We laid him to rest pretty decently and with honour. The wake was a lekker piss-up, I can tell you that. All the ouns were there, it was a noisy send off. Bloody good shindig."

"I will have to have a wake of my own when I get out of here," Ray said wistfully.

"I think you will find a few of the ouns will join you in that, Ray. We know how close you were. They will have a second send off for him with you, my buddy."

"That's good. Mrs Ellis is taking it pretty hard. Has anyone been to see her?"

"Ja, loads of us. She came to the wake for a while, too. Has she been in to see you yet?"

"Ja, she will be coming a fair bit. How is his Dad taking it?"

"He's doing okay, he's a hard bugger, he'll tough it out."

"That's good, Sir."

"Now I must tell you the best part," said the Captain. "Jason Ncube is in hospital under guard."

"Holy snappin' duckshit," whistled Ray. "That is good news indeed."

"Ja," the Captain continued. "It was Trooper Beck who shot him. He saved your life, man. It was Jason who was shooting at you at the top of the hill."

Memories were beginning to crowd back into Ray's mind. "I remember now. I thought I knew the bloke when we reached the top, but I was too stuffed to do anything."

"Ja, it was him all right. But we've got him under lock and key now."

"Shit hot," said Ray.

"I thought you'd like to hear that," the Captain said. "Okay, I am going to check on the other ouns in here. Have you had a chance to talk to any of them yet?"

"No, I haven't. None of us have been well enough to get about up till now. Some of the guys got really fucked up, didn't they?"

"Ja, unfortunately they did. The only consolation in that is that we really stuffed the terrs up something fierce. It doesn't make it any better for you guys, but we did hurt them .... bloody hell, we hurt them."

"Yup, we sure did that. Okay, Sir, thanks for coming. Say 'howzit' to the ouns when you get back out in the bush."

THE DAYS WENT by and Ray began to mend. Gradually, the other men who had been wounded in the raid got better and they would sit outside the ward telling stories about their part in the attack. The close comradeship formed a strong bond which helped them to overcome the trauma of their experiences. They laughed, joked and took the mickey, drawing strength from each other to get through the despair at the loss of their mates which might otherwise have been overwhelming. As well meaning as help from outsiders might have been, their mental recovery was dependent on sharing their experiences. As the boys themselves would tell you: "If you weren't there, you wouldn't understand."

Ray often felt guilt during these sessions. Although he had been wounded quite badly, they would heal and, apart from some heavy scarring, he would be able to continue his life fairly normally. Piet Grobler had lost a leg and his testicles. He would never make love again. He was nineteen. Mark Pilbarr had lost both eyes and would never see again. Their battle would last the rest of their lives. He could only admire the courage and determination they showed.

As well as the jaw-sessions with the boys, Mrs Ellis visited often. Ray found it hard to call her Doris at first, but soon grew more comfortable. Bridget spent as much time with him as she could. Sometimes they would sit together, the three of them, and talk for hours. The topics of conversation were wide and varied, and included a lot of soul searching.

On one occasion, Bridget asked: "What is it about you men that you have to go about killing each other? You start wars, destroy everything around you. Not only do many of you end up wrecked in body and mind, but innocent civilians get caught up in it as well. Not only the ones who get in the way, what about the wives and mothers who wait at home, and the children? It is so stupid and senseless and yet you continue to do it. Why?"

Ray thought for a while. "You are quite right,' he said. "War is mankind's ultimate stupidity. The trouble with the human race is that because we are intelligent, or think we are intelligent, we have an over-inflated sense of our importance on this planet.

"We have a certain degree of control over our environment; we can send rockets to outer space, we can talk to anyone in the world just by picking up a phone, we can travel by air to anywhere in a relatively short time. But for all our sophistication, we still haven't grasped the basic fundamentals."

Ray paused to gather his thoughts. "Because we think human life is so precious, we have found ways to check diseases, we have found ways to produce more food, we have found all sorts of ways to save lives. The trouble with that is now the balance of nature has been put out of kilter. I believe that nature knows what is best, not necessarily for us but for everything as a whole. Disease, droughts and famine all do their part to keep this balance in check."

Ray saw that the two women were completely fascinated by what he was saying, so he continued. "This 'cleverness' of ours is actually crass stupidity. We are pretty chuffed with ourselves, we think we are smart. 'Look what we can do,' we say, 'we are saving all these lives'.

"Unfortunately, the more people there are in the world, the more garbage we throw out. More and more factories are being built to produce more goods for sale and they pour their waste into rivers and the sea. So what we are doing, in actual fact, is taking what was a beautiful place and turning it into a giant garbage dump."

"So what do we do about it? asked Doris.

"Yes, and what has this got to do with war?" added Bridget.

"What do we do about it? Nothing," replied Ray. "The people in power — the economists, bankers and builders — don't want to do anything about it. To them a growing population spells money. They have to produce more if there are more people to produce it for. Greed and selfishness cause most of the problems we are seeing."

Ray was enjoying himself now and warming to the subject. "As to your question of what this has to do with the war." He looked directly at Doris. "Those same emotions that cause men to hunger for money and power also cause wars. Greed, selfishness and another thing — fear. If you look at all the wars that have been fought since man learned to lift a rock in his hands, you will find that they all have just a few things in common.

"To take over someone else's territory is one. They want what someone else has got. Ghengis Khan, the Romans, Hitler — they all wanted to gain control of vast tracts of land. Greed and power.

"Religion is another oldie but a goody. Look how many wars have been fought over religion. The Catholics hate the Protestants. The Christians hate the Moslems. What people don't understand they fear, so a lot of the time they go out and kill the others because, as we know, most religious fanatics believe that they are right and everybody else is wrong.

"You see, war is one of nature's little tricks to keep the population down. It uses our greed and selfishness against us. War is a very effective way of thinning us humans out. It doesn't help us blokes in here and it certainly doesn't help people like you, Doris, who have lost so much. But it is doing its job."

"Phew," muttered Bridget. "You're becoming quite a philosopher, Ray. If the answer is so obvious, why don't we go out and snip everyone after they have a couple of kids?"

Ray took a sip of his lemonade. "Because there is no money in it. Who wants to pay doctors to go around and operate on millions of peasants when there is no financial gain? War, on the other hand, is a multibillion-dollar industry. It generates economies and gets money flowing."

"Are we really that stupid, Ray?"

"Yup."

"What brings you to our little war, Ray?" Doris asked suddenly. "You don't come from Rhodesia."

"I was born in Kenya," he replied. "My parents were murdered by the Mau Mau when I was a kid."

"Ah ha ... I knew it!" exclaimed Bridget. "As soon as I saw you on that plane, I knew there was something pretty bad in your past. Your eyes were so cruel and hard, they frightened me."

"So, is that what you are here for, Ray. Revenge?" Doris asked, looking concerned.

Ray smiled at the woman who had lost so much and whom he had come to love as a mother.

"No, it's nothing like that. Mark asked the same question once. As I told him, it's more of a moral thing with me. I just don't believe that anyone has the right to go around murdering and terrorising a population in order to get what they want. It's an advanced form of the bullying you see at school. Once again, it's greed. Someone lusting for power."

"Do you think we will win the war, Ray?"

He sighed and took another sip from the bottle. "If the military was given a free rein, we could take the terrorists out in a fairly short time. We are well-organised, disciplined and highly motivated, whereas the gooks are mostly a disorganised rabble. They have plenty of factional infighting and cause as much trouble to themselves as us. Even though they have an unlimited supply of recruits and weapons, we are still holding them down, even with the political and hierarchical dithering and indecisiveness.

"No, we won't lose the war. It is all the outside influences that will bring us down."

"Explain please," said Doris.

"Most of the outside world sees this as a race war," he said. "Racism is very much in fashion at the moment. Everybody believes that whatever a black man says must be right. Not many people look into what is behind things, they just go with the fashion. The terrorists are telling the world that they want one man, one vote.

"To the western mind that is a good thing and they can't see beyond that. Because voting is a right most of us have, we believe in it. They don't want to, or can't, believe that Africa is different. You see, in most civilised countries, voting is comparatively fair and people get to change governments if they want to every few years. If you look at most of the Third World countries, you will find that they have one election and that's it. Then they have a dictator for life. From then on, they have to put up with it. They have to put up with a crumbling economy, unemployment, crime, secret police and a system where imprisonment and execution without trial are commonplace.

"A select few reap all the goodies, while the rest of the country lives in poverty and starves. In this country, at the moment, they might not have the vote, but at least they are under a stable government. Many of them have some sort of job and they receive medical care and education, even if they are poor. If they go to jail, they at least get a trial.

"Make no mistake, the people who will really lose out under a black government are the black Africans. Most of us whites will do okay, our skills will be needed and we will be as well off as we are now."

"It seems ironic that the very people this war is supposed to be about will be the ones who lose out from it," remarked Doris.

"There is more to it than naive ideals," continued Ray. "The Commonwealth is made up of a lot of black-run countries and they are using political skulduggery and economic pressure on the UK and other countries to get them to bow down to Mugabe and Nkomo's demands. The country will change hands, but it won't be the military that lets it happen, it will be sanctions and pressure from the rest of the world. The same thing will happen to South Africa before the end of the century, you'll see."

"No way," laughed Doris.

"At the end of the day, the 'civilised' countries will have assuaged their consciences and say 'justice has been done, the Africans have been given the vote'. Then they will get smugly on with their lives, not even realising that all they have done is brought a lot more poverty and hardship to a great many people."

"And the winners lose, Ray. Is that what you are saying?"

"Yup."

As well as keeping their minds busy, there came a time when the wounded soldiers began their program of healing their bodies and the physiotherapists started their work. It was going to be hard, not only for the injured men but for the people who were going to try and help them mend.

Doris had been a nurse before starting her family and she volunteered her services to help the men she had come to regard as `Her boys'. She had lost a son and because she was a brave woman, she gave back more than she had lost. She became an unholy terror as she bullied and urged and encouraged them to greater and greater efforts. She threw herself completely into her work. She laughed with them, cried with them, she cajoled them when they had had enough and tried to give up.

"Get up you bugger. I'm not going to waste my time if you are just going to lie there, feeling sorry for yourself. Get up and at least try to be a man," she would snarl when one of her charges, through pain and despair might have given up with anyone else.

They loved her. When they had put ninety percent effort in and they felt they could do no more, Doris shamed them into putting in that last ten percent. Through the sweat and the tears and the anger and the pain there came the seeds of pride. They worked hard, at first for her, and then gradually for themselves. They built up confidence and the tears became laughter as they started to clown around and try to outdo each other. The joshing and good-natured ribbing was also a good sign that they were running the race.

Nicknames like `Hoppy' or `Stumpy' came into being. If Mark Pilbarr stumbled into something trying to find his way about, one of them would call, "What's the matter Mark, you blind or something?" Or they would tell jokes like, "Why did Ray Charles' wife divorce him? She was fed up with him coming home blind every night." Or to one of them who had lost a leg, "Hey Piet, you might have a big pecker, but they sure as hell can't call you tripod anymore."

Throughout the recuperation, Ray worked harder than anyone else. He knew his recovery would be more complete than most of the others, but he set an example by his uncomplaining approach. He worked with grim determination, as though driven by some inner fire. Both Doris and Bridget noticed it.

"He's going back out to fight, isn't he" Bridget said one day when she and Doris had a moment together.

"Yes, it looks like it."

"Oh, the stupid man, he knows he can take it easy if he wants to, he knows he won't have to fight again. Why? What is he trying to prove? Oh the stupid, stupid man."

"Why! Young lady, I do believe you love him," Doris remarked, looking at Bridget with a smile.

Bridget blushed a tiny bit and answered, "Yes I do, I have loved him from the first time we met."

"You know he will probably be embarrassed by all the scarring don't you?"

"It's him I love, not his scars."

"Yes but he might not know that."

"That's if the stupid bastard doesn't get himself killed before I get a chance to even let him know."

Ray had worked out his own program so he could bring his body back to strength. He developed hard bunchy muscles and thick tissue around his scars. Where the damage was bad, he developed other muscles to compensate for the weaknesses. As soon as he was ready, he started back into a fitness routine and got himself back in shape much sooner than most people thought possible.

Ray had noticed that Bridget seemed to care for him, but he put it down to a friend who felt sorry for him. Being a dumb male it didn't occur to him that she might love him for his own sake. He couldn't understand that she didn't care about the scars. So it was Bridget who asked him out and Bridget who wooed him. They went out together and as Doris had predicted, he was embarrassed by the scars and it took patience on her part for him to accept that she liked him for what he was, not what he looked like. Through Bridget, Ray learned about love. Real love. Their love grew, but there was always a shadow there. Bridget wanted him to stay out of the bush, but he was determined to get back as soon as possible.

"What is wrong with you Ray, there are plenty of others to do the fighting, you have done your share, and nearly died for it. For God's sake let others do the dirty work. You have earned a place out of it all," she flared one day.

"Experienced men are sorely needed out there Bridget," was all he said.

"You said yourself that the country will be given to the Africans eventually anyway, so why risk your life again for a lost cause?"

How could he explain to her that it was not just a country that spurred men on to fight. He could not explain about pride in a regiment and its men to her. She could not be expected to understand that there is a special bond between men who fight and face danger together. In an elite regiment or unit, the men will fight for that unit first and foremost, before anything else. The men in it form a very strong brotherhood. First comes the regiment and then the country. To him it was simple. But he knew he could not make her understand that.

"It's that Jason Ncube fellow isn't it?" Bridget snapped.

Jason had escaped from jail about a month before. Almost fully recovered from his wounds, someone had spirited him out of imprisonment. Some said it was white sympathisers who got him out. The fact was that he was at large and would soon be creating problems for the security forces once more. Ray still didn't fully understand what all the fuss over him and Jason was. It had built up into quite a story and everyone in Rhodesia seemed to know about it. To most people there was a mystique surrounding the issue. To Ray it just seemed that African superstition had put two and two together and come up with five. Sure, he had used it to advantage a couple of times, but to him it was still just a misunderstanding. Then a thought struck him. Bridget might not understand the camaraderie between fighting men, but she might believe the Jason thing, even though it really meant nothing to him in its own right.

So he lied. "Yes it is. There is a thing between us that must be finished."

Through the tears that streamed down her cheeks, Ray could see that she believed the lie and he felt guilty for being deceitful to the one civilian who really cared about him.

JASON DIDN'T REMEMBER much after the battle. He remembered the fear when he saw Isizo standing on the crest of the hill. He knew he had hit him several times — he saw the blood spurt as the bullets hit. The man was covered in blood when he arrived at the top. But when he got there, he did not even seem to be bothered to lift his rifle to shoot at him.

"His magic must be strong," he thought. After seeing him standing there, Jason felt like he had been punched in the chest and he went down. The next sensation was the heavy weight as Isizo fell on top of him. He vaguely remembered lots of shouting, the white man's body being lifted off him. There seemed to be an argument between two men, one of whom wanted to shoot him. Another man, possibly an officer, had stopped it. The helicopter ride with a drip in his arm was a blur.

Jason woke up some days later in a hospital, under guard. He found out that he had been shot twice in the chest. Although one of the bullets had gone through the right lung, the doctors had been able to save it. The other bullets had shattered ribs, and they had been wired up. He knew he was going to be in pain for a while but he suffered it in silence.

Gradually he got better. He found it hard to believe that he was so well treated and except for the guards and secure ward, there was no other indication that he was a prisoner. There was no animosity towards him. He had expected to be treated harshly — torture at the very least. What he found was quite the opposite. The men who came to question him were really pleasant and almost respectful.

They did ask him questions, which he refused to answer. Their tactic was completely different from what he had expected. They seemed more interested in getting Jason to change sides than anything else. Their reasoning went something like this.

"Hey Jason, you know that according to the laws of this country, you will be tried for criminal offences. Because of what we know, you will be found guilty and hanged. You know the penalty is death, don't you?"

Then came the carrot.

"If you decide to work for us, not only will you escape jail and execution, but you will have a full-time job in the army. You will be paid a regular salary, you will have a place to live, for both you and your family."

They left him to think about it for a few days, then they would come back.

"How are you today Jason? Have you thought about the proposal we put to you the other day? You know that as soon as you are better, they will put you in jail."

It didn't take Jason long to work out that the people who he was talking to were the Selous Scouts and Special Branch. Selous Scouts — the dreaded `Skuz'apo', the nickname given to the Scouts by the terrorists literally meaning `excuse me here', much like a pickpocket would say as he bumps into a person he is about to rob. The bump takes the person's attention while a hand delves into a pocket. They had infiltrated ZANLA and ZIPRA ranks using captured "turned" terrorists with enormous success.

The Scouts caused massive discord among the terrorists by their actions which included straightforward operational deployments; Fire Force call-outs from OP's; flying columns into camps in Mozambique with sabotage and bridge destruction en route; and the most insidious (as far as ZANLA and ZIPRA were concerned), their posing as regular terrorist groups to sow distrust and discord in the field. Often, fierce firefights would develop between genuine guerilla groups as a result of a Scout callsign's action.

Other lines of persuasion put to Ncube included questions such as "Jason, when you were in the camps, what was the food like? Did you eat well? Did you get paid regularly? What was the medical care like?"

Jason had the feeling they already knew the answer to that. In fact the conditions were dismal. They were very seldom paid. Most of the food and blankets were supplied by various overseas charities and organised by the World Council of Churches. Even then, there was never enough food for everyone and they often had to go foraging and hunting for meat. The surrounding villages were often raided to supply the camps with food.

Jason said nothing to these questions but they persisted.

"If you work for us, you will never have an empty stomach. You will be paid on time" and so on.

Often, black Africans would come in and talk to him. They were always cheerful and happy and looked well fed.

"Greetings Comrade Jason. How are you today? You may not know us, but we were freedom fighters once. The best decision we ever made was to join the ranks of the Skuz'apo. They treat us well and they pay us well. Many of the men in your organisation are working for our side."

Jason was tempted; the choice of facing certain death was not pleasant and these people seemed to be genuine. He knew he was too well known in the guerilla ranks to be sent out in the bush again. They knew he had been captured, so the job they would more than likely give him would be to train others in the ZANLA tactics and methods. Life would be easy if he did that. But until recently he had believed strongly in what he was doing, unlike many of the others who had been abducted from schools or coerced into the ranks. Jason was beginning to have doubts about how right he had been, but still something held him back. He knew as well as anybody that this country would go to the black people and he wanted to be on the winning side. He knew he would have a place in the new government. So he held back from giving the Rhodesians the answer they wanted.

When he was well enough, and because he had not capitulated, he was sent to Chikurubi Prison's maximum security wing outside Salisbury to await trial. They kept him there for longer than normal before taking him to court because he would be a valuable example at trial. This was to prove the white man's mistake.

One night, two men dressed in Military Police uniforms came to the jail. They had all the necessary paperwork for a transfer. The two men were large, blond and blue eyed, they spoke with the guttural accent of the Afrikaner.

"We have come to pick up Jason Ncube. We have reason to believe that there will be an attempt to break him out of this prison. So we must take him to a safe place," they said.

The warders took the two hard-looking men to Jason's cell.

"Hey Ncube," the taller of the two said. "We have come to take you to a new prison. We coming in to your cell. Now you be a good Kaffir and let us put these shackles on you. If you cause any trouble we will have to fuck you up, man. Now we don't want that, hey?"

Jason looked at the two men. Even if he was completely fit, he would have had a hard job taking on even one of them. Although he was well on the way to recovery, he was still weak and out of condition. So he did not have much choice except to comply with their request. They shackled his legs as well as his hands, with a length of chain running between the leg and hand shackles.

"You an important munt. We don't want you running away on us do we," they explained.

They led him out into the courtyard and into a Land-Rover. Something did not quite ring true with these two. Jason could not figure what. They had done everything properly, but there was something not quite right. As they were driving along, Jason pondered about what was troubling him. He had the impression that they were probably going to kill him but he could not understand why. If they wanted him dead, surely they would just try him and execute him. Perhaps it was too much trouble to go through the cost and time of a trial. Maybe they were going to kill him and leave him somewhere so that the comrades would find him as a lesson of some sort. Whatever happened, he was going to try and make it difficult for them when the time came.

The Land-Rover had been travelling along a dirt road for some time and they appeared to be going not towards any real destination but to the bush.

Although his two guards only spoke once in a while and in low tones, he noticed that the accent was no longer the harsh grating sort the men had used in the jail, but had more of an English lilt. It was becoming more and more of a puzzle. Jason tried to stay relaxed, but he was keyed up and hoped he would get a chance to at least inflict some damage on his captors before they killed him.

After what seemed hours, the Land-Rover slowed down and came to a halt. It was pitch black, but Jason thought he saw a white van parked on the other side of the track they were on. What was going to happen now?

The man in the passenger seat turned round and unlocked the padlock that held Jason shackled to the frame between the seats.

"Slide to the back of the vehicle Jason," the man said. The tone was neither hostile nor friendly. Jason did as he was told. The man came round to the rear of the Land-Rover and undid the shackles. Jason was tense, he still did not know what was going on. The man stood Jason up, took the chains, walked back to the passenger's side of the vehicle, got in and the Land-Rover took off. The former prisoner looked around. An African was walking towards him from the white van he had seen.

"Welcome back Comrade Jason," the voice said. With a rush, Jason realised that he had been rescued.

"Who were those men?" Jason asked as the van bumped its way through the bush.

"British agents," Comrade Phiri answered.

"They were very good at their job," Jason thought. "Real professionals." He knew that the British government was being pressured into bringing about the downfall of the Rhodesian Government, but he did not know they were going to this length to assist the freedom fighters. He had felt that his two rescuers were not overly happy about the job they had been assigned to, but they had carried it out.

Jason thought about that for a while. He had heard a rumour that the British Government had been going to send the parachute regiment over to fight against the Rhodesians. The regiment had refused point blank. There was no way they were going to fight against their brothers. He had heard that the para's future as a regiment was in jeopardy because of it, but they were adamant. No way were they going to compromise their honour. Jason admired that. He might be against the politics of the white man's government here in Africa and he was doing all he could to bring it down, but he respected the soldiers he was fighting. World opinion was against them, sanctions were hitting hard and they were outnumbered, but they kept fighting, and by God, how they fought, specially those boys in shorts — another nickname the RLI had been given. In fact if it was not for all the outside help the liberation movements were getting, the Rhodesians would have won this war long ago. Yes, he admired and respected them. But he must get on with the war and bring black rule to the country.

CHAPTER TEN

"STOP THREE IS down," said Sergeant Hunter into his handset.

Although he had done a couple of continuation jumps at New Sarum a few days ago, there were now several other para-trained men in the Commando, and Ray was allocated a chopper stick for his first ride into combat since being wounded. Koos had been promoted to corporal and was leading a stick of his own. The other three men in Ray's Stop were new to him. They had joined the Commando while he was convalescing. Although they had all been in combat, Ray didn't know how they would work as a team. He hoped his leadership skills had not deserted him and he could see them through the next few contacts while they worked each other out.

"Howzit Sergeant? We have heard about you and we are proud to be in your Stop," they had said the previous afternoon when the Stop Groups had been detailed. Ray hoped that he could live up to his reputation. He was as fit as he could be, but it had taken a while. He also hoped he still had the courage to get the job done. Yes, it had been a while and today would tell. He also hoped that the three men would come up to his expectations. The two 18-year-old riflemen, Mick Grant and Sam Hall, seemed so young. Perhaps he was getting old — at 27 he sure felt like it. They were both fair-haired and slim of build. Only time would tell if they were tough enough to keep going. The machinegunner, Pat Coome, was solid of build — as the majority of gunners seemed to be. Ray did not think he had a great deal in the intelligence department, but he had an animal alertness about him that told Ray he would be a good man to have about in a tight situation.

"Stops, One, Two and Three," came the voice of the OC in the K-car. "I want you to sweep in a north easterly direction, through the small Kraal line in front of you, then go towards the kopje behind the mealie field. When you get there, call in."

"Roger K-car."

Ray put his arm out in the direction they were to sweep, the three went straight to their positions without being told.

"Good," thought Ray. "They at least know what it's about."

"We're going to sweep through the kraal in front of us, up to that kopje," he told them. To his left, he could see Koos in Stop One organising his men. Koos saw Ray and waved to him. Ray waved back and smiled. Trooper Beck was in Koos' Stop. "Looks like they have teamed up," thought Ray. "Good for them."

They came under fire as soon as they cleared the long grass. Ray went to ground and noticed with satisfaction that the other three had done the same. Coome was returning fire. He looked calm and his fire appeared accurate.

"K-car, this is Stop Three. We have come under fire from two of the three huts to our front."

"Roger Stop Three. We'll take them out."

The K-car's blades clattered and beat the air as it executed a 180 degree turn on its side to begin a run on the target. The tech manning the 20mm Hispano cannon talked to the pilot through his head mike to make minor corrections before releasing controlled, but murderous, fire into the huts where the terrorists had hidden. Phosphorus shells mixed in with the standard HE (high explosive) heads of the projectiles set what was left of the huts ablaze.

As soon as the helicopter had finished, Ray shouted to Coome. "Cover us, we are going in." With that he waved to the riflemen and they were off. Ray had almost reached the centre hut when the door burst open and five people ran out. He and Coome dropped to the ground and within seconds, the five were cut to ribbons.

Ray examined the bodies — all of which had severe burns to the head and upper back. They included three civilian females.

"Those fucking spineless bastards," he said aloud. It was obvious what had happened. The terrorists had used the civilians as a human shield in the hope that the security forces wouldn't try to take them out. Unfortunately, neither Ray nor the K-car commander had been able to distinguish this. Hundreds of ordinary rural civilians were dying because of it. Ray was saddened at the waste of life. The tribespeople of Rhodesia were the real victims of this so-called war of liberation.

Every day, the RBC would deliver a security force communique. A typical one would say "In the operational areas yesterday, forty-five terrorists were killed by security forces. Twenty-two civilians were killed in crossfire, while Combined Operations regret to announce the deaths of.....," followed by the names of three or four security force members.

There had been public consternation about `civilians caught in crossfire', so communiques were amended to say, "and such and such number of civilians were killed who were running with, and actively assisting, the terrorists". It didn't matter what was being said, the fact was that civilians were being killed. Although very few of the Security forces enjoyed killing civilians, if one had to do it to get at the terrs, it happened.

Sad as he was, there was a job to do and Ray pressed the switch of the handset. "K-car, Stop Three. We have two Charlie Tangos and three female civilians dead."

"Stop Three, Roger."

Ray heard Koos reporting two terrorists and one civilian killed.

Once the huts had been cleared and the bodies searched, it was time for a sweep up the hill. They rested at the bottom and Sergeant Hunter's stick waited for the other two Stops to catch up.

Although he was on the right flank, Ray automatically took charge being the senior rank and the most experienced. He pressed his handset. "Stops One and Two. I want your machinegunners to take up a good vantage point and give us covering fire while we head to the lip halfway up."

"Roger Stop Three," came the reply. Ray could sense the question in the Stop Leaders' voices. Normally the three Stops would sweep up in a line. There had been no confirmed sighting on the hill, it was more a routine sweep to clear the area and Ray hoped he was not being overly cautious. He somehow sensed that there was trouble up on the hill. He could have called in an airstrike but the K-car and Lynx were busy with a confirmed sighting and the Stops involved were slugging it out. He realised that the others might think he was afraid to go in after being wounded and that was why he was possibly overreacting, in fact he was wondering the same thing himself.

"Oh shit, have I become a coward? Is there really something on the hill or is it just plain fear that has me imagining it?" The thoughts tore at his insides. But he had made a decision and he would stick by it. Time would tell.

The powerfully built senior NCO gave the signal to advance and the men stepped out into the open. Ray suddenly felt the fear as it clawed at his bowels. "Oh Jesus, I am really scared," he thought, but he kept going. The machineguns opened fire and Ray could see the dust spurt and the chips fly as the bullets raked the wooded line on the hill. Halfway to the nearest cover the hornet's nest began to buzz round his head. He had been right, there were gooks up there and they were accurate despite the covering fire he and the other Stops were putting down.

Sergeant Hunter broke into a run and was relieved to see that the others had followed suit. As they neared cover he noticed that the machineguns had shifted their aim and were doing a good job. The enemy's fire was not quite as accurate as before.

They reached the small cover of the lip and went to ground.

"Coome, rev the fuck out of them," he shouted.

The others in the sweep began opening fire. "Give 'em heaps guys," Ray roared.

"K-car, Stop Three. We have come under heavy fire. Request air strike."

But K-car was having troubles of its own. "All Stops, this is K-car, we have taken a hit and will have to put down. Cyclone Four has gone back to rearm and the G-cars are refuelling. You will have to slog it out for a short while."

"Oh shit," Ray thought. Then he shouted, "We have no air support for a while guys. Rapid fire, keep their head down." With that, Ray frantically waved the two machine gunners to come up.

FROM THE TWO-way messages it looked as though they had hit a large force of terrs, and most of them were hard core and fighting back. Ray got the riflemen to give covering fire while he put the two machine-gunners out on a flank; he would need one in the sweep to put down heavy fire. As soon as they were ready, he shouted "Let's go", and they were on their way.

At the end of the contact, twelve terrorists lay dead with blood spoor indicating many more had fled. They had fought well. Ray stood panting and breathless. Koos was calling for a medic. One of his riflemen had been hit. Ray heard another call sign reporting one of his men KIA. "Jeez, this war is hotting up," he thought. "We are losing men nearly every contact now."

As soon as he had regained enough breath Ray pressed his handset. "All Stops. We have five Charlie Tangos heading north or east from the kopje near the kraal line. Some of them may be wounded. Over."

Ray's next scene two days later was just as hectic. The winds were high. Normally, paras would not be dropped in high winds unless absolutely necessary, but they needed men on the ground urgently. In the hurry, the Dak pilot dropped the men off target and some of them landed in a dry rocky riverbed. Ray slammed into a clump of loose rocks. He lay there stunned, his breath coming in short agonising gasps.

"Hey Sarge. Are you okay?" He dimly heard the concerned voice. Sam Hall was shaking him. "Hey Sarge, the K-car is calling you," he said.

"Stop Six, are you okay? We need four Stops now. The G-cars are coming to pick you up."

Still not able to speak, Ray passed the handset to Trooper Hall. "Tell him we'll be there," he gasped. Trooper Hall took the handset but it took him a while to answer. He had been in combat a few times now but he had never had to use the radio. The thought of talking to the big boss in the sky unsettled him. He was only a trooper, this sort of thing had always been the responsibility of the NCOs and officers.

"Get on with it man," Ray wheezed.

"Stop Six, Stop Six, do you read?" asked the voice.

Trooper Hall pressed the switch and spoke nervously into it. "Er.. K-car, this is Stop Six. The Sarge says we will be there...over."

"Roger, be as quick as you can."

Sergeant Hunter took the handset back off the trooper.

"Give us a hand up," he said.

The helicopters only picked up three Stops. Injuries had claimed four out of the sixteen paras dropped. There was one broken ankle, one dislocated shoulder, one concussion and one machinegunner had his calf torn apart where the foresight of his MAG dug into it. The fourth chopper was busy casevacing the four men.

The tide had certainly turned. The terrorists had an inexhaustible supply of cannon fodder. Time was on their side, they were infiltrating more and more men. It didn't matter that their ranks were being decimated. Like the British generals at Ypres and the Somme, and their Vietnamese counterparts half a century later, they knew the value of tying up the enemy's resources. Another benefit was that more and more junior cadres were gaining experience in bush warfare.

For the Rhodesians however, every man lost was a serious blow.

Fighting intensified across the land; sightings and contacts escalated. After every contact, the Rhodesian forces returned to their bases exhausted. To add to their worries, a further development was about to take place.

One night, after a heavy day slugging it out, the men were relaxing at Grand Reef. Most of them had had a few beers and were asleep. They were awakened at about eleven o'clock by shouting.

Colour Sergeant Keenan was bellowing. "Wake up One Commando. Everybody up. We have a job to go to. C'mon you lazy bunch of mis-fits. Up, up, up."

The weary grumbling men stumbled out of their beds.

"What the fuck is it now? Is there no peace for a man in this frigging war?"

As soon as the men had assembled, Colour Sergeant Keenan briefed them. "Okay, listen up ouns. A farm not far from here is being revved. We are close enough to get there by truck, so as soon as you're ready we're off."

When the trucks pulled up outside the farmhouse the troops leaped off. The place was a shambles; the electrified fence had been ripped down, the guard dogs were lying in the yard, hacked to bits. The house had been rocketed and was a mess. The men stood in silence. The very air was filled with dread. If the men were shocked at what they saw outside, it was nothing compared to the scene they found inside. They reeled in horror when they saw what had happened. Gaining entry after the electric fence had apparently been deactivated, a large force of terrorists had attacked and entered the house.

Once inside, they had really gone to town on the European occupants. The mother and six-year-old daughter had been repeatedly raped and sodomised — blood and faeces were every-where. They had then been bayonetted and had clearly died in unspeakable agony. Both father and son appeared to have been forced to watch the proceedings before being forcibly held down before their genitals were crudely hacked off. The terrorists' blood-lust was an act of unintentional mercy as in their excitement, they had bludgeoned the males to death before they could bleed out in agony.

To Sergeant Hunter, it was as if time had been stripped away and he was a small boy again, watching from the tiny hole in the ceiling, as his mother and father had been murdered in very similar circumstances. There was no hate for him at that moment, only numbness. A vast empty nothingness. He was not even aware of the tears streaming down his face.

Captain Watson was the first to recover. "Right, I want everyone out of here. No one, I repeat, no one else is to come in here. I want a guard on the door and the windows. Sergeant Hunter, take some men with you and check out the labourers' compound."

The soldier in Sergeant Hunter obeyed the command. His mind was still reeling with sensory overload. He automatically turned round and walked outside.

"Koos, Corporal Wessels, round up your sticks and come with me," he commanded.

"My stick, here to me. Now."

"What happened in there Sarge?" Coome asked.

"You don't want to know," came the short reply. The tone in his voice was final.

"Right, we are going to see what fun and games have been had down at the compound. I want an extended line on me. Let's go."

On the way to the compound, Trooper Van Zyl in Corporal Wessel's stick was shouting angrily. "Fuckin' Jesus, my family owns a farm. If those gooks try and take them out, I am going to kill every kaffir in the country. You see if I don't."

"Button your lip Van Zyl and get on with the job," called Corporal Wessels.

"Roger Corp. But I swear I'll murder the lot of the bastards if they try it on my family."

They walked the rest of the way in silence.

The African labourers had paid the ultimate penalty for being loyal to their employer. They had made the wrong choice. Many of them had been shot or bludgeoned to death, others had been herded into their huts and burned to death. A pregnant female had been tied up outside her hut and shot. The foetus and the mother's intestines lay together next to her inert body. She had taken a long time to die.

"Jesus!" mumbled an ashen-faced trooper. "How could they do this. And to their own people too?"

"Is this how you tell the world you want to run a country?" asked another voice in wonder.

"Quit your cackling," barked the harsh voice of the Sergeant. "Koos, John, I want every bit of this compound swept for any sign of life. Every inch. Back to me if there is anything to report."

"Right Sarge."

Sergeant Hunter pressed the switch on his handset. "Captain Watson, you had better come and have a look here too."

DURING THE NEXT weeks, many terrorists died in combat at the hands of One Commando, many more than usual. The difference was the anger and bitterness of the men. They still fought in a professional manner, but the aggression was much greater. Often they would assault a position without calling for air support. The assaults were extremely hard hitting. The fire was always accurate and there was no stopping during an assault. The terrorists found themselves reeling back before the batterings. More civilians were also being killed. In their determination to get at the terrorists the men from the RLI were taking out anything that stood in their way. Whereas before, they might try another way to get at the terrs, now they were just going for the jugular. The fight began to get nasty and bitter. The madness of war was affecting both sides. Prisoners were becoming scarce. Those terrorists caught, usually found that instead of going to jail, they were finding death the hard way. If they wanted to play rough, the Rhodesian Light Infantry was only too willing to oblige.

ONE AFTERNOON, THE troops returned from a call-out to find a Detective Inspector from the Special Branch waiting for them. They filed into the mess hall for the briefing, not knowing what to expect.

The man, tall and lanky with a droopy moustache, didn't look like much, but if one looked into his eyes, there was an intelligence and dedication that spoke of a first-class operator. DI Willis knew his stuff.

"Good afternoon lads," he began in a good-natured manner. The silence that greeted him told him a great deal about the situation and the men he was dealing with. Normally there would have been a polite "good afternoon inspector" in reply to the pleasant opening he had instigated. He knew the RLI were the country's frontline troops and they were bearing the brunt of the war, but he had dealt with them before and even though they were a rough, hard bunch, they were usually light-hearted and humorous in a cynical sort of way. Their silence told him what he wanted to know. They were angry and pissed off, and with good reason. That is why he had come to talk to them.

"I can see that you are well aware this war has taken a turn for the worse. In fact, it is getting quite nasty. That is the reason I am here, to put you in the picture and bring you up to date."

The Detective Inspector took a sip of water from the glass in front of him, and paused. "We have all witnessed atrocities committed by the terrorists, in fact, they are quite commonplace. Lately they have been getting savage. There is a reason for this."

The Inspector looked around at the faces of the men in front of him. He could see that he had their total concentration.

"As you are aware, this war is `supposedly' being fought to give everyone the right to vote. `One man, one vote' is the cry from the terrorists' lips. You may or may not be aware that the government is working on giving the Africans the vote. At the moment, we have some moderate players in the field. The government is trying to work towards an interim government where both black and white can share in the running of the country. We have a good prospect in Bishop Abel Muzorewa. We are hopeful of holding an election to that effect and most people seem to be happy with the idea. Unfortunately, Nkomo and Mugabe, the UN, the Brits and just about everyone else are not interested. They want complete black rule — and for that read the Patriotic Front. They have been invited to participate in the elections, but have refused. They don't want to share. For them it is all or nothing. Not only have they refused to come to the party, but they are escalating the war. They know that at the moment, they don't have much chance of getting many votes, so they are going to keep up the hostilities."

"So what happens now?" This was Captain Watson.

The Inspector looked directly at Captain Watson. "As far as you guys are concerned, we go on fighting the war. The politicians will go on jockeying for power in the safety of their offices. I will tell you one thing. What you blokes witnessed a couple of weeks ago will only get worse."

He could see the look of shock on the faces of the tough men in front of him.

"That's right, gentlemen. The hardline leaders are giving the go-ahead to their men to step up the atrocities. As I said earlier, there is a reason for this. Nkomo and Mugabe are telling people that they are the only ones who can stop the war. To prove this, they are hotting things up as the interim elections are coming up. It's their way of saying unless they get what they want we all suffer. It's pretty blatant, but they are doing it anyway."

"What is the rest of the world saying to this?" shouted a young trooper.

"Not much I'm afraid."

"Holy fucking Jesus. Are they really going to sit by and let innocent women and children die just because some half-smart munt wants to be the man with the big stick?"

The Inspector raised his hand for silence. He didn't want emotions to run too high.

"Okay, settle down guys. It's not quite as easy as that. People on the other side of the world only see and hear what they are told. They don't see the ugly reality as it is. This war is only a passing mention in the news for them. They probably don't even see any of the atrocities in the papers or on the news. For them it is not even real. You blokes down here in among the blood, sweat and the tears know, but they don't. All they know is that the Africans want the vote, or they think they know."

There was more mumbling and grumbling from the troops.

"C'mon guys, settle down," called the OC.

"Okay, it doesn't matter what other people say or do, the fact is we are going to get more of it," the SB man continued.

"To tell you the truth, it caught us by surprise as well. If we had known in advance we might have been able to do something about it. Our normal channels of information dried up on us. We knew that something was up, but not what." Inspector Willis took another sip of water. "The bottom line is that the people of this country are going to suffer. I'm not just talking about white Rhodesians, the black ones are going to cop it too." The Inspector looked around the assembled men. "There is another side to this issue. We are starting to get a lot more terrorists changing over to our side. Initially there was nothing, but the full impact of what is happening is pissing even a lot of terrs off too. There are two factions out there now. The hardliners who are getting savage and the others who are a bit more moderate. It is creating a rift in their ranks which is to our advantage.

This brings me to the last point... prisoners. We have noticed that there is a conspicuous lack of them from you guys lately. Okay, we know how you feel and we don't blame you. But remember, you are professionals and we expect you to do your job. We need prisoners, guys. One prisoner, on average, gives us enough information to kill at least ten others. More if they change sides. So put your feelings aside. We need that information." Willis paused. "It's going to get rough boys, very rough, but we expect you to carry on. You RLI blokes have born the brunt of this war for a long time now and I know you will carry on doing so. That's why you are called the `Incredibles'."

THREE MONTHS AFTER Detective Inspector Willis' lecture, a gang of terrorists led by a man with the colourful name of Tarzan Bazooka 'took out" a homestead in the Centenary East farming area near Mount Darwin. They went through the by now standard procedure of rape and mutilation. They then disappeared.

"Trooper Van Zyl, I want to see you in my tent," said Major Hill.

"I'm afraid I have some very bad news." he continued as soon as they were inside.

"It's about my family, isn't it Sir?" said the young trooper.

"Yes. I'm afraid it is," replied the OC.

There was a long pause before Van Zyl took a deep breath. "Were...were there any survivors Sir?"

"I'm so sorry Jim."

Jim Van Zyl stood silently before the Major. There were no tears or anguish, no outward sign of emotion. Nothing. Just a blank uncomprehending stare.

"We have arranged some leave for you, son. The truck will take you back to Salisbury in half an hour and you can make your arrangements from there. The regimental chaplain is expecting you. Come back when you feel like it."

"Thank you, Sir," was all Van Zyl said as he walked woodenly out of the tent.

He was back within the week but there was no life in him. He went about his duties as if by remote control. In battle he did not seem to care whether he lived or died. He didn't. The young troopie was an empty shell of a man. Major Hill issued quiet instructions that Van Zyl was not to be let near any captures, for obvious reasons.

The rest of the Commando covered for him when they could, closing ranks when he drank himself into a stupor and was unable to carry out his camp duties. Van Zyl was of the brotherhood and they stood by him in his time of need. It was many months before he could be a constructive part of the team — he would never be a complete human being again. The part of him that loved and trusted had been severed. The cut was irreversible.

A few weeks and several contacts after the man from Special Branch had delivered his message, One Commando finished its bush trip. They cheerfully endured the cold four-hour drive back to Salisbury. The scene that greeted them as they drove through the streets was utter carnage. Terror had visited in the form of a rocket attack on the city's main fuel storage depot. As the Commando drove through town, firefighters were frantically trying to extinguish the blaze. Sightseers milled about; the scene was chaos. The Commando watched helplessly, there was nothing they could do. The trucks took another route back to Cranborne barracks where the men cleaned up and went on their five days R & R.

The front page of the Rhodesia Herald the next day showed a visibly shaken Prime Minister surveying the scene. The war had come to town... and any last feelings of false security that Salisbury's population might have had went up in smoke along with the fuel depot.

CHAPTER ELEVEN

THE TIME SPENT with Bridget was awkward. At first it had been beautiful. Their lovemaking had been urgent and all-consuming, full of passion and tenderness. But after the intensity had worn off, the subtle campaign had started.

"Did you know that Sergeant such-and-such will never be able to use his arms again? Both his elbows are completely gone"

Yes, he knew that. It was him who loaded the man on to the helicopter. The Sergeant in question had taken cover behind a tree. A terr had fired a burst at the tree. The only part the Sergeant had exposed were his elbows. Both elbows had disintegrated.

"We had a soldier in the other day. He had been shot in the head. He will be a vegetable for the rest of his life... if he lives for long."

Ray understood what Bridget was trying to do. She was trying to preserve something she loved and held dear and was trying to get him out of the bush. What she saw in the hospital every day must horrify her and he understood how she must feel. He also saw the same things every day, but he saw them as they were happening. Ray knew better than most about the madness of the bush war, but he was not going to lie down and give up, even though he knew he could die any day. No way. The terrorists might get the country one day, but by Christ, they were going to know they had been in a fight.

He loved Bridget and knew she loved him, but it was a relief when she was at work and he could be on his own to think. On the third day of his leave he wandered into town and was sitting in the First Street Mall waiting to order a pot tea in the pavement cafe. The waiter came over. "Morning Sir... and what would the Baas like today?"

"A pot of tea please, with milk."

"Okay Sir, a pot of tea for one."

When the waiter returned he put the tea down, but instead of going he stood there for a moment.

"Ah...Sir."

"Yes, what is it?"

"Sir, there is a man over there. He wants to speak to you."

"What does he want to speak to me about?" asked Ray looking in the direction the waiter was indicating with his chin.

"Ah, Sir, I don't know, but he said it was important."

The man in question was standing next to the window of a clothing store — ironically named CT's — doing a very bad job of window-shopping. He was dressed in a shabby overcoat and a scruffy balaclava. But, beneath the scruffy exterior, Ray sensed there was a fit and intelligent man.

"What the hell does he want with me?" he thought. He checked the safety on the 9mm pistol under his jacket. "Well, here goes." He wandered idly towards the man and stood there looking at the store mannequins while keeping an eye on the stranger from the corner of his eye. Ray's right hand, hidden from the other man, held the pistol grip. The man had his hands in the pockets of his coat and would have to be damned quick to get the jump on Ray.

"Good morning Sergeant Hunter," the man said in excellent English.

Ray was astonished but didn't allow his face to register any emotion. There seemed to be no malice in the man's eyes.

"There is a man who wishes to meet you," he said simply.

"And who is this man?" Ray asked.

"The name does not matter," the man said. "But he is concerned like you at the way things are going. There are too many people who use violence too easily."

The words struck a chord with Ray, but he was not satisfied. "If I don't know who I am meeting, I am not interested."

"I cannot tell you his name Ishe, but I can tell you this. The man fears your magic. He says to tell you this. Although he fears your magic, he respects you as a soldier. He respects your courage and he hopes you respect his. He asks you to meet him as one soldier to another. He also asks me to tell you this. There is no treachery, but he has something of importance to say to you."

Jason Ncube. As soon as the man said the word "magic" he knew who wanted to meet him. Ray's mind was in a turmoil. Jason had tried to have him killed, so why should he trust him. On the other hand, why should he send a man with a message. The man had used the term `Ishe' — meaning "Chief" — a mark of great respect. Furthermore, black Africans are notoriously poor liars and find it extremely difficult to lie while maintaining eye contact. This man's eyes were clear and honest, his speech firm and clear; his body language gave no sign of this being a set-up.

If the man who wanted to meet him was Jason, and Ray was sure it was, it could make sense. From what he knew of Ncube, he was a soldier first and a terrorist second. Ray thought about Detective Inspector Willis' discussion of a division in ZANLA ranks with one faction concerned about the escalation in atrocities. If Jason wanted to meet him, then it would surely be in relation to that. It fitted. The man's next words clinched it.

"This man who wishes to meet you Ishe, he says that you can bring your rifle, but he also says that your magic eye will tell you if there is trickery."

"Why is it that the man wants to meet me and no one else?"

"Because he trusts you Ishe."

Ray thought for a while. "When and where does he want to meet me?"

"Do you know the road that leads to the lake you call McIllwaine?"

"Yes, I know of it."

"After the tar finishes and the dirt road begins, there is a rise where the two men catch birds and sell them to the whites to set free again."

"Yes I know those two," said Ray thinking about the schemes poor people dream up to make a bit of money.

"Tomorrow morning at 9 o'clock, drive there and stop to talk to those two men. They will tell you where to go next."

Ray nodded his head.

"And Ishe..."

"Yes?"

"This man, he says you must come alone."

FOR THE REST of the day and all night Ray wondered if he had done the right thing. During the meeting with the stranger in First Street that morning, his gut told him things were above board and honest. But the mind plays funny tricks and with so much time to think he wondered if it was a ruse to get him into an easy killing ground. He knew that the "magic" thing between him and Jason seemed important to Jason, and a few others too, so it was quite conceivable that it was a plot to murder him. He wondered whether to tell someone about it. Jason would be an important capture. But something held him back. A man like Jason would not waste his time with something unless it was important, something of value. It would have to be of value to both Jason and the security forces. That "something" could only be information that would be of use to the security forces — there could be no other explanation.

In the end, Ray compromised. He wrote a letter to Captain Watson outlining the meeting that was to take place, including his where-abouts as far as he knew them.

At 7.30am, he rang Captain Watson while Bridget was in the shower.

"Hi ya Bruce. It's Ray here. Could you do me a favour. I've got a few things I have to do today. I will be using Bridget's car. If I am not home by three-fifteen this arvo to pick her up, could you race over and give her a lift home."

"Be glad to Ray. Three-fifteen you say?"

"Ja, thanks mate, I hope it's not too much trouble. If I am home in time I'll ring you."

"Glad to help out, my mate."

"We must get together for a beer. Maybe tonight."

"Okay, see you."

Ray hung up.

Trying to remain as casual as he could, Ray waited until Bridget was putting on her uniform.

"Hey honey, would it be okay if I use the car today? One of the boys from the Commando is fixing his car and a couple of us are giving him a hand," he lied. He is going to need someone to run errands for him. He said he can give us a couple of petrol ration coupons to cover the running around."

"Of course, love. Don't forget I will be finishing at three."

"We should be finished by then, but just in case I have asked Bruce Watson to pick you up."

"Don't be so silly, I can catch a taxi home."

"No way lady, I would prefer that you get a lift from someone we can trust. Anyway, it's all arranged... besides, I've asked him over for a beer."

"Oh, okay."

As he dropped Bridget off at Andrew Fleming Hospital, Ray said, "If we finish in time, I will give Bruce a call so he doesn't waste a trip, okay."

She leaned over and kissed Ray. "I love you Sergeant Hunter."

"I love you too, Hon."

Bridget got out of the car and started to walk off. Ray called her back. "Oh.. sorry, by the way, if Bruce does pick you up, could you give him this. It is a list of things he asked for a few days ago. He can peruse it while he is waiting for me. It should stop him from trying to seduce you."

"You are silly, my beautiful man. No-one's going to seduce me except you... and you can do it as often as you want."

"You'd better stop talking like that or I'll drag you back into the car and you'll have to book in sick."

Bridget giggled and dashed off, pretending to be coy and bashful.

If he hadn't been so preoccupied, he would have done just that. Bridget certainly knew how to arouse him.

"Don't forget to give that list to Bruce, will you?" he shouted after her.

Bridget waved and was gone through the main entrance.

Ray drove through the hospital car park but had to stop for a taxi which appeared to have stalled at the exit gate. Ray kept his motor running, got out and walked over to the driver of the little "Rixi Taxi" Renault. "What's wrong Shamwari?"

"Good morning Sir," the driver smiled. "Could you follow me please."

"Ah ha, the plot thickens," Ray said to himself. He had expected something like this to happen. He got back into the car and waited for the driver to take off. As he followed the car through the outskirts of Salisbury, in almost the opposite direction to Lake McIllwaine, he had time to think. It was a fairly obvious ruse. If he had told anyone about the meeting and the army was out to capture Jason, they would be looking out for him in the wrong place. Another thought occurred to Ray. This operation seemed to be exceedingly well-planned and he could only wonder how far the terrorist organisation had infiltrated the daily lives of the people of the city. If they had got to most of the locals, the country was in more trouble than anyone realised. He put the thought aside and concentrated on following the battered maroon and white Renault.

He was surprised when the driver stuck his arm out the window and gesticulated towards an African standing beside the road. The man had a sign in front of him which said "Fresh Fruit and Vegetables" with an arrow pointing towards a dirt road. Ray turned into the narrow track and drove towards a small group of huts in the distance. He was surprised because it was really quite close to town — he had expected the meeting place to be further out.

Before he reached the huts, another African standing on the track waved Ray to a gap in the verge lining a mealie field. Ray pulled to a halt under a tree, the hand in his lap holding the butt of his Star pistol. The African pulled a makeshift gate across the gap, camouflaged to appear like there was no break in the verge. Mealie stalks and branches were then spread over the roof of the car.

"Follow me please, Ishe."

Ray placed the pistol in the waistband of his trousers and followed the man to the huts, his senses jangling. The hut he was lead to was square with a corrugated tin roof, unlike the others which were round and thatched. Ray pushed the door open and stepped in. The hut was gloomy and it took a few moments for his eyes to adjust.

When they did, his blood ran cold.

Five AKs were pointing at him.

CHAPTER TWELVE

"TELL ME SERGEANT Hunter, is there anything to stop me killing you right here and now?" a deep, melodious voice spoke from the shadows in the far corner of the hut.

Ray knew who this must be. Jason Ncube.

"No, nothing....nothing at all."

Ncube stepped through the line of ZANLA men and stood an arm's length from Hunter. He looked directly into his adversary's eyes for signs of fear. If he was scared, he was hiding it well.

"Except that in a few short hours, hundreds of soldiers will be hunting for you."

"They will be looking for you around Lake Mac."

"If you think I am stupid enough to fall for that one then you have underestimated me."

"So you have told people about this meeting."

"No, as of this moment, only you and I know of it. But I have put in safeguards. If I am not back by a certain time this afternoon the place will be crawling with troops. Just coincidentally, this area was one I chose." He had lied about the last bit, but it wouldn't hurt to keep his opponent guessing.

"What time do you have to be back this afternoon?"

"That is something only I know."

Jason studied his man for a moment longer. Then, "You are truly a worthy opponent. I see you Isizo."

"I see you Jason Ncube," Ray returned the greeting.

They shook hands in the African way, clasping palm, thumb then palm.

"Come. Sit down. We have much to discuss." He motioned to the guards to leave.

Ray's guess had been right. Within a couple of hours Jason had given him much valuable information about the hardliners within the terrorist ranks, including names and future plans. Some of the information was shocking, the shooting down of a South African Airways jumbo jet at Salisbury Airport merely one of the catastrophic events designed to throw the interim election process into complete chaos. Hotel bombings, widespread murder and arson of isolated mission stations and the wholesale slaughter of any relative of a black member of the security forces were designed to ensure a place at the final negotiating table. Either that, or like Mozambique, Angola and a dozen other places to the north of Rhodesia, there would be nothing left to govern.

One of the most surprising pieces of information that came to light was the name of a senior official in the RF government who was in league with the terrorists. Jason had promised further information as it came to hand. This would be conveyed by various means, it could be one of the Africans employed by the army, or even one of the low-security prisoners that were used to keep the grass down at the Fire Force bases. The information would make big inroads into decimating parts of the terrorist network. One thing puzzled Ray though. Jason seemed genuine enough, but why was he going to these lengths to cripple parts of his own side.

"Jason, if you are so concerned about what is happening why don't you come over to our side?"

"It is not as easy as that Isizo" replied the Matabele. "Make no mistake. We blacks will be running the country in a few short years. It is a foregone conclusion. This Muzorewa thing will only be a temporary interlude. The real power will be either Mugabe or Nkomo. I will tell you this. I want to be on the winning side. If I side with you, after the war I will end up dead or in jail. This whole thing is bigger than you or I. We are but ticks on an elephant's back. I might have some say in the new government, in fact I most likely will. But let me ask you this, would you rather have me as a politician or one of the others that are right now raping and murdering women and children, both black and white."

"I see your point" said Ray.

"It is not just the fact that these people are bringing cruelty to new heights. I am an African, I understand these things better than you whites, Africa is a cruel place. But I am a warrior and I believe in a fair fight, not the sort of sneaky underhanded war on women and children that is being waged here. It is beneath my dignity as a son of the Ndebele. My motives are fairly simple. Some of these people who are behaving like animals will be in government too. It will be in my interest and the country's if they are eliminated. I know that we will need the white man to help us run Zimbabwe after the war. I am not naive enough to think that we Africans are sophisticated enough to cope without your help. Let us look at the most likely scenario. The most likely person to win the elections will be Mugabe. The Shonas are the majority tribe, they will have the numbers for the voting. If they win outright we will have problems. Not only the whites, but us Matabele. As you know, we and the Shona are natural enemies, we are only united in the fight to oust you people. As soon as it is over, we will go back to fighting each other again. If the balance of power is more even, things will be more likely to work more efficiently."

Ray was amazed that this tall warrior in front of him had such a good grasp of the intricacies of politics. His respect for Jason the man was growing. Ray also realised that Jason was using him to gain an advantage in the future. But what he said made sense, both for Ncube's cause and, more importantly, for the Rhodesians in the present.

"Tell me this Jason, why did you come to me with this information when you could go higher?"

"If my people found out about this my body would be rotting in a ditch in a very short time. I chose you Isizo, because I believe I can trust you. This thing must be kept secret, only a few must know. By helping you, I am helping myself. The people you kill will not stop the war or change the outcome, but it might save a few lives. Lives of people who don't deserve to die, and in the end it might even out the balance of power in the new order."

The two men talked for another hour. Suddenly Ray looked at his watch. "Shit, I had better get back into town quickly. We don't want a manhunt to start. Do we?"

Jason laughed. "I wondered how much time you gave this meeting." They stood up, the tall Matabele and the shorter stocky white man.

"It is a strange thing," Jason said. "We are enemies and if we see each other on the battlefield we will try to kill each other. I hope that doesn't happen, because I think we can be friends and I hope that if we are still alive after this is over we will be friends."

Ray smiled and they clasped hands once again.

"Go in peace, Isizo," said Jason.

The words seemed at odds with the facts. The two men were soldiers fighting on opposite sides in a bitter, savage war. Yet Ray knew that apart from being a formal farewell, the words were sincerely meant.

"Go in peace, Jason Ncube."

RAY SPED INTO town, narrowly avoiding a collision with a Matambanadzo bus while running a red traffic light and pulled into the hospital car park just as Captain Watson was driving out with Bridget. Ray urgently waved them over.

"Hi ya guys. Sorry I'm late," he said a little breathlessly.

"What's the rush?" they both replied.

"Nothing really," he panted trying to keep his excitement down. "Uh...Bridget, did you give Bruce those notes yet?"

"Oh no I forgot. Here they are," she said, taking the envelope out of her uniform pocket.

Ray leaped out of the car and ran over to Bruce's sedan. "Actually I gave you the wrong ones," he said trying to take the list out of Bruce's hands. Other cars were honking their horns now, the two cars were blocking the exit and several people were rushing to get home after their shift.

"What the hell is this all about?" Bruce asked.

"I'll tell you when we get home," said Ray. "Trust me."

Bruce gave him the envelope, shrugging his shoulders.

"I thought you said Bruce knew about the list?" Bridget said, looking at her man.

"Never mind that now. We are blocking the driveway, I'll tell you when we get back, okay."

"Will somebody please tell me what 's going on," Bridget demanded as soon as they got home.

"It really is nothing," answered Ray as calmly as he could. "I just made a stuff up, that's all. I wrote out a list of ideas that I thought might be important, but I've checked them out and they amount to nothing. That's all there is to it."

"That's bulldust and you know it," retorted Bridget. "Now tell me what it is all about."

"It's none of your concern darling. Now be a good girl and get the boys a couple of Castles" Ray said condescendingly.

Bridget turned on her heel, clearly furious.

"Jeez mate, that was a bit off," said Bruce. "I think you should go after her and apologise."

"I will later. I need her out of the way for a bit. I have something to tell you and it's important."

They were sitting outside on the lawn on the all-weather chairs, sipping their cold beers. It was a beautiful warm evening in the northern suburb of Greendale. The Jacaranda trees were beginning to flower and the delicate smell of jasmine wafted on the wind. Somewhere nearby, a pool party was in full swing; children screamed excitedly and the smell of braiied boerewors and steak mingled with the scent of Salisbury in spring. It was hard to believe that the country was at war with itself. Ray gathered his thoughts. Bruce did not push him, he knew his Sergeant well. It must be important all right — Hunter wouldn't be this circumspect unless there was good reason.

"Captain. I have something very important to tell you."

"Call me Bruce, Ray. We are off duty."

"No Sir, this information is definitely on duty stuff." Sergeant Hunter looked straight at the Captain. "Before I go on Sir, I want your word that until we have worked this thing out, you will tell no-one. It is to be kept between just the two of us. I want your word as an officer and a friend."

"Holy dooley, that is asking a lot until I know what it is."

"Nevertheless, I want your word."

The Captain stared at the man to whom he would trust his life above any other. "You have my word."

Ray relaxed visibly and took a sip of beer.

"I had a meeting with Jason Ncube this morning."

"You what?" The Captain sat bolt upright and his eyes bulged in disbelief. "You're pulling my leg. Bloody hell. You are pulling my leg, aren't you? Bloody hell."

"Far from it Sir. That note this morning was in case I was heading into a trap."

"Fuckin' sweet Jesus. Bloody hell. I don't believe it." The Captain took a deep swig from the bottle and swallowed. It took a while before he settled down. Then he said, "I suppose you'd better tell me about it."

Bit by bit, Ray related the details of the bizarre meeting, including the name of the senior white official person working for the terrorists. When he had finished, Captain Watson sat in silence for a long while. Finally he spoke.

"What you have told me makes a lot of sense, both from Ncube's point of view and ours. But are you sure you can trust him?" The Captain paused for a second. "It could be a double play of some sort."

"I don't think so. For some reason I do trust the bloke. He seems straightforward and honest. He could easily have killed me. He has tried often enough. Remember, he holds great store by the magic thing he thinks I have. In his mind, it seems to bind us together some-how. It's strange, even though the man is a gook he is a fine   soldier and appears to be very astute with a good understanding of politics, event though he harbours deep superstitions."

The two men sat and drank some more beer.

Captain Watson spoke next, "We'll have to let the OC in on this."

"OK, but we must keep it to as few people as possible," Ray replied.

"True, but it's going to be hard to convince the powers that be to go dashing around the country looking for terrs on some advice from an unknown source."

"We've overcome greater difficulties than that in the past."

"Also true Ray. We'll go and sort it out with the OC now."

"Jason also said that if we can find a suitable contact man in the other Commandos, we must do so."

"Okay, we will get this lot sorted out quick smart. Now I think you had better go and make your peace with Bridget. She is a lovely person. Too good for the likes of you my mate."

IN THE NEXT few weeks, things did get sorted out. As Captain Watson had predicted, convincing people was a problem — initially — but they did overcome them and it wasn't long before ZANLA groups found themselves bailed up by the barking hounds of the Rhodesian Light Infantry. Other groups were either ambushed on the way to rendezvous' or when they got there. The security force's kill rate soared.

In one of the most important events, a four-man Special Branch unit from "T" Desk at Salisbury Central killed four members of a ZIPRA group in St Mary's African township outside Salisbury and captured a SAM-7 "Strela" infrared heat-seeking missile launcher and three projectiles. Documents found at the scene revealed that an SAA aircraft taking off for Johannesburg three days later had been targeted for a hit. The carnage from the jet ploughing into the densely-packed Seke Township near the airport with 326 people on board would have been unthinkable.

The matter of the inside man was not quite so easy, because the information did not come from "correct sources". The only thing done was to move the man somewhere he wouldn't be able to do any harm. This proved to be a mistake. The man was not working for the opposition because he wanted to. There was blackmail involved. Fear made him tenacious. The darker the secret, the more leverage can be applied. The white man had a very dark secret.

"WANT TO BUY a watch Baas?" Ray turned wearily to face the African. If there was one thing he didn't want on his few days off it was a hawker selling trinkets.

"No, Changamire, I don't want a watch."

"This one can see a long way Isizo," came the soft reply.

Ray made a show of looking at the watches.

"The one who fears your magic, Isizo, he asks a big favour."

"Speak."

"There is a man you both spoke of when you had your indaba. A white man."

"Yes I remember the man we spoke of."

The African paused for a moment. "The man who fears your magic Isizo, he wants you to kill the white man."

Ray stepped back in amazement. It must have shown because a couple of passersby looked at him.

"What, you want fifty dollars for that!!" he said loudly to cover his shock. The strolling couple smiled smugly and walked on. As soon as they were out of hearing, he asked, "Can you tell me why the white man must be killed?"

"The man who sent me with this message, he says to tell you this. The white man is getting close, it will not be long before he knows the secret between you and the man who fears your magic."

"Fuckin' hell," muttered Ray to himself. "What have I got myself into here?"

"Ishe."

"Yes."

"He asks that you do it as soon as possible."

"Tell him this. That I will think on it deeply. He will know my answer soon."

"Thank you Ishe."

"No way, you bloody gororo (thief) ...your watches are too expensive," he said loudly, walking away.

Ray walked around central Salisbury, trying to collect his thoughts. He sat on a bench in Cecil Square and stared at the fountain. He jumped as a deep gravelly voice spoke in his ear.

"Howzit my little mate?"

"Nick!!! Nick Schultz. How you going? Hey, good to see you old mate. Jeez, mate, you are just the person I need to speak to."

"Come my mate, we'll go and have a dop together and we can jaw."

They walked to the Monomatapa Hotel and sat down in the lounge bar, sometimes referred to as the Merc's bar because some foreigners in the Rhodesian Army sometimes went there to be seen by the press and boast about being mercenaries. The African waiter came to their table.

"Two Shumbas, and make sure they are lekker cold hey."

"Yes Sir."

They ordered rare roast beef and green beans smothered in mustard sauce and talked for a while, catching up on the news.

"Now, what did you want to talk to me about my little mate?"

"Nick, what do you know about ....?" Ray mentioned the traitor's name.

"That jackal," Nick snarled. Then he looked thoughtful. "And why do you want to know?"

Nick's reaction told Ray what he wanted to know, but not the details.

"It's a long story and I couldn't tell you anyway, but I need to know. It's important."

"We've been trying to nail the bastard for a long time now. SB have bugged his office and home phone, we have tried to get information on him for a while. He is a wily son of a bitch, and we can't get anything on him. He seems to be protected from high up."

"Have you ever considered taking him out?"

"What you playing at, you sneaky little rooinek?" Nick said, looking hard at Ray.

Ray smiled. "What if I told you that I definitely know the man is tipping the gooks off?"

"Fuck man, if you can give us proof, then he is gone."

"That's the trouble Nick. I can't. But I know for sure that he is."

"How come you so sure?"

"Can't tell you that. But I am one hundred percent sure."

"We have tried to have him slotted, but we can't get the go-ahead," said Nick.

"What about doing it off your own bat?"

"You playing a dangerous game here my mate," Nick warned.

"You soft or something?" Ray said innocently.

Nick flared up momentarily, then remembered the time they were sitting in the chopper on their way home after being chased by the Frelimo for most of a day. They had been playing a dangerous game then. They had faced almost certain death together, the bond between them was strong.

"You asking a big thing Ray, got any ideas?"

"You guys have access to Communist weapons that haven't been tested for ballistics or fingerprints."

"We might be able to get hold of something like that," Nick said guardedly.

"Do you know his movements?"

"We know them better than he does."

"Shit hot. What is to stop some of your guys revving him up to make it look like a gook ambush?"

"It has been planned before, and it would have been done if some arsehole hadn't kept stalling it."

"Can you do it?"

Nick sat thoughtfully for a long time, weighing up the pros and cons. There were a lot of things to be considered.

"Yes."

"Soon?"

"Yes."

"It must be my turn for the beers....WAITER."

As they were sipping their second beer Nick looked at Ray and said, "You know if we get found out, we'll be in very deep shit, don't you?"

"We will just have to make sure we don't, won't we?"

THE MAN THE Sergeant and the Lieutenant had been discussing a few days earlier was driving along a dusty farm road after visiting a friend on a citrus estate in the Mazoe Valley, north of Salisbury. It was almost dusk and he was tied up in his own thoughts. In his late forties and balding, he was trying vainly to cover his dome by brushing what was left of his hair over the bare parts. Although not exactly fat, he was soft, the legacy of a working life flying a desk.

His face was almost effeminate, if not exactly girlish and he looked what he was — spoilt and self indulgent. Although he had a clever and agile brain, he had never really had to work hard for anything in his life. In fact, his success had been handed to him on a platter — positions in the civil service guaranteed as his father had been a wealthy rancher and a minister in Sir Godfrey Huggins' Federal Party government in the early 50s.

He was also bisexual with a particular craving for young boys. He liked black Africans, but not half as much as whites. He supposed it was because the African boys were easy to get and without too much complication. With the white boys, however, the seduction had to be very subtle; his *modus operandi* exact with no room for error. He preferred upper-class children and it was probably the inherent danger of getting caught that excited him. It was dangerous living, but that was what drove him to take the risks time and again.

That was what got him into trouble. He had been caught and was being blackmailed into giving secrets away. He knew full well that the information went to the terrorists — the people who were murdering his own people.

At first he was troubled by his actions, but the people who used him gave him a sweetener in the form of a half-caste prostitute. High-class, exotic and boyish-looking, she indulged in every form of perversion he could think of. Sometimes she would strap on a dildo which he would suck — he had always wanted to perform fellatio on a black man, but lacked the courage to find one. And then there were the boys — eight and nine-year-olds from the townships brought to his house in Highlands at weekends when his wife and servants were away.

Perversely, he regarded himself as lucky. Being caught was the best thing that could have happened to him — he was now protected by the bad guys as well as the good guys. He was sheltered from the wrath of the Rhodesian hierarchy by the old school tie mentality. He was sure they knew about his secret, but they had no proof that it was linked to breaches of security.

Yes, life was pretty good — what if a few soldiers died because of the information he passed — dozens were dying every week.

As he neared the main Salisbury — Mazoe tar road, he slowed to make the left turn for the 30-minute drive home. Braking and moving down through the gears, the big Mercedes started the turn. He was proud of his car and he was proud of his driving, that was one thing he could do well. He wondered idly what the popping, drumming sound was all around the car, a bit like hail he thought.

He died like he had lived, easily; even his death had been without any undue trauma. He was only dimly aware that anything was wrong as the bullets found their mark. He keeled over on to the passenger seat as the vehicle ran gently into the verge and stalled.

The man's demise caused little public concern. Although high up in government, he was a behind-the-scenes operator. The attack was mentioned in the news and his burial was done with all the correct etiquette, but he had been an embarrassment and the thing was pushed aside as quickly as possible. Of course the family grieved. That was probably the only genuine part of the whole affair.

The biggest upheaval came within ZANLA itself. The ambush, because it had been carried out without any approval or knowledge from sanctioned sources, and because it had been cleverly staged, was blamed on a renegade gang of terrorists. Ballistic tests carried out by Chief Inspector Don Hollingworth at the BSAP Morris Depot armoury showed that the doppies (spent cartridge cases) found at the scene were from weapons not previously encountered.

A witchhunt ensued within ZANLA, resulting in infighting between rival factions. Things were starting to look good for the Rhodesians. A major source of information had dried up for the "Charlie Tangos".

C.I.D. and Special Branch treated the incident as a terrorist case, but with so little evidence to work on, the "culprits" were never caught. Besides, there was so much other work to keep them occupied that the case became just another one of many. Only the Selous Scouts and a few of their most senior SB liaison men ever knew the real facts.

"I SEE YOU Isizo." Ray was getting used to Africans sidling up to him at odd moments and in odd places with the by now familiar greeting.

"The man who fears your magic Ishe, he says to thank you for the swift answer to his request."

"Tell him he is most welcome," replied Ray.

"Ishe, I am to give you this." The African handed Ray a small pouch tied at the neck with a leather thong. It was obviously to be worn around the neck.

"This is a gift from your brother, Ishe. It is strong magic that will keep you from harm. He says to wear it always." Ray placed the amulet round his neck.

"Tell my brother that Isizo is most honoured by this gift, and that he thanks him," said Ray, quite sincerely.

Ray knew the contents of the pouch would probably include the dried internal organs of some animal, powdered cow dung and some special herbs. The whole thing would have been blessed during a ceremony performed by a witchdoctor, much like the Celtic Druids of ancient Europe did. He wondered about the parallel between the modern African and the minds of men thousands of years ago when they used myth and magic to explain things they didn't understand. To the logical Western mind, magic and superstition is a load of rubbish.

But then Ray wasn't to know this particular amulet would save his life.

Chapter Thirteen

"ONE COMMANDO, ONE COMMANDO ATTEN... SHUN," bellowed the wiry Sergeant Major. Sixty boots thudded into the ground as the troops came to attention.

"COMMANDO. STAND AT...EASE."

Commando strength should normally have been one hundred and fifty but with men on courses and on leave, not to mention the wounded in hospital and the dead whom the army had not had time to replace, the RLI often went to war with only a third of its men.

"Right, listen up. Now that you are nice and rested after the lekker leave the army has been so kind to give you, you will be glad to know that we are going to Fort Victoria."

"Fuckin' hell," muttered a lanky trooper to the man next to him. "Fort fucking Victoria, that means we'll be going walkies."

"SILENCE IN THE RANKS," bellowed the CSM. "Now, when you fall out, I want you to go straight back to your barrack rooms, sort out your kit and wait there for the trucks. I don't want anyone to leave the rooms until we are ready to board the trucks. Is that understood?"

"YES SAR' MAJOR," shouted the troopers in unison.

"RIGHT, FALL OUT."

The troops fell out and ran to the double-storey brick barrack rooms.

"What do you mean by walkies, Franz?" asked the trooper who had been standing next to the lanky soldier. He was fairly new to the Commando.

"I'll tell you what it means old China. It means we'll be going external. To Mozambique, where we will be trudging around the shateen with huge fucking bergens on our backs."

"Yeah, just like bloody mules," laughed another soldier. He had been there before and knew what it was like.

Fort Victoria, a pretty little town in the south of the country, was not normally used to any great extent for Fire Force operations which was why the tall trooper guessed that it would be a stopover point for external operations. Most of the Fire Forces for that area were based at Buffalo Range, which was closer to the border. He was right. Not long after the Commando had arrived, CSM Gerr called it together.

"Right ouns, when I call your names, I want you to go over to the tent behind you and pick up a bergen each, water bottles and other assorted equipment."

"Ah ha, I told you so," Franz said.

One by one, the CSM called out twenty names. The men picked up their gear and waited outside the tent.

The CSM walked over to them. "Right. You have been issued rations for five days. Shortly, you will board two trucks and you will be off to Malapati. You will be the advance guard. I want you to set up a base camp there. There is to be nothing above ground level, so dig your sleeping places in. I want you to patrol the area thoroughly and check it out. The rest of the Commando will be there in a few days. Any questions?"

"Sir?"

"Yes Trooper Van Zyl."

"Why are we going there?"

"Ask me no questions, I'll tell you no lies. Now, any more questions?"

"Right, Sergeant Hunter will be in charge. The trucks will be here shortly."

THE RIDE TO Malapati was rough and dusty as the trucks bumped over the dirt roads. In places it was obvious that terrorists had been there — the African shops and houses were in ruins, the walls pock-marked with bullet holes.

They arrived at the dirt airstrip late in the afternoon. It was just as Ray had remembered it. A beautiful piece of Africa, wild and untamed, umbrella trees and thick vegetation. At the end of the runway, a herd of impala grazed peacefully, they looked up in alarm as the trucks drove in, but soon settled when they sensed no danger. That was a good sign. If the animals weren't jittery, it meant that the area hadn't been used by men for quite some time. The weary troops climbed off the trucks, covered in dust.

"Right gentlemen," Sergeant Hunter addressed the troops. "I am going to position you in all round defence, two men to each shell scrape. Camouflage your possie as much as you can. Clean your weapons, cook up an evening meal before last light. There will be no smoking after dark and no noise. I will give you a guard roster shortly. Any questions?"

"Eddie and Cookie... put the trucks under those trees over there out of sight. NCOs... I will brief you as soon as we settle in. Right, let's go."

DURING THE NEXT few days, they patrolled the area. There was no indication of human presence. They checked out the once-beautiful hunting lodges along the Nuanetsi River, now just empty, vandalised shells. Places where rich men and their wives came. The men to prove their manhood by killing animals in an unequal contest, often going away believing vainly that they had conquered something in themselves. The wives... how else does a big white hunter get laid out in the wild?

Throughout the patrols they found nothing but pristine wilderness where nature had had the time to re-establish itself while humans were busy elsewhere.

WITHIN A WEEK, the camp began to look occupied as the rest of the Commando arrived. An open-air kitchen was established and a tarpaulin strung up as a mess tent. Latrines were dug and basic bucket showers rigged. The occasional buck was shot for fresh meat to supplement rations.

"Hey Sarge. What we doin' here? So far except for the patrolling and guard duties, it's been like a friggin' holiday camp."

"I don't know George, so far we haven't been told anything. I wouldn't tell you if I did know," joked Ray.

The answer came a few days later with the arrival of the OC and three helicopters. No sooner had the Major settled in than he gave the order. "All Officers and NCO's, briefing in my tent at 1600 hours."

"Right gentlemen. You've no doubt been wondering what the hell we are doing here. Well, you are about to find out."

There was a murmur from the assembled men.

The OC pointed to the map on the board behind him. "Most of you will be familiar with this place," he said, pointing to the border town of Malvernia.

During peacetime and before the Portuguese handed over Mozambique to the Frelimo, Malvernia had been a small town through which many Rhodesians passed on their way to a holiday on the beaches of southern Mozambique. The wine and prawns were excellent and cheap. Such were the cordial relations between the Rhodesians and the Portuguese that the two little towns, on each side of the border exchanged names. Villa Salazar became Malvernia, and Malvernia became Villa Salazar. Now the two customs post towns were fortified and the only inhabitants were heavily armed soldiers.

The Major continued: "As you know, Malvernia is a Frelimo garrison. Now, we are not at war with the Frelimo, so attacking the place is not on. However, we are almost certain the terrs are using the place as well. Here comes the crunch.

"Although we are not allowed to wage war on the Freds, we are trying to persuade them to move out by other means. We are going to attempt to make them abandon the place. The SAS have been busy around here for a while and have blown up the water mains in several places, plus the pumps. They have ambushed the roads and taken out the trucks bringing in supplies. Most of the bridges leading into the town have been destroyed.

"As you can imagine, the people garrisoning the town are having a hard time of it. But they are still hanging in there. The Territorials stationed in Villa Salazar are baiting them every day and they have a regular exchange of fire every evening. It keeps the enemy jittery. The only reason they are still there is because they are going out into the countryside and living off the villages and waterholes. They have to carry everything in on donkey-drawn scotchcarts. This is where we come in.

"Our job comes in three parts. One is to probe their defences, not to take them out, but to keep them spooked. Two is to poison the waterholes; and three, we are going to use the scorched earth policy. We are going to burn every village in the area, kill any animals that they can use for food and burn all the crops."

"A bit rough on the poor bloody civvies," interjected Lieutenant Mike Pittman.

"I make no excuses," replied the OC. "It is going to be rough for everyone. The poor bloody civvies as you so aptly put it, are on the rough end of the terrs' attentions as it is. We are just going to put the finishing touches to it. I don't like it, nor am I proud of what we are going to do. But that is the task we have been given, like it or not. Any questions so far?"

"Are we going to kill the civvies?"

"Our orders are to destroy everything that can be of benefit to the Charlie Tangos. I will leave who you kill up to you. I would think that by the time you get there, the civvies would have pissed off anyway. Let's hope so. Right, now on to the operational details. You will be working in three groups of twenty. I will assign leaders later. Most of the areas you will be working will be in range of our artillery. They will be set up by tomorrow. We will work out sectors for them to use in the next couple of days. You will be resupplied by air every two weeks. That is the only air support you will have.

"There are reasons for the shortage of aircraft, but I can't tell you what they are. Serious casualties only will be taken out by chopper. So there you have it, gentlemen. You will be virtually on your own. I am sorry to do this to you, but I am told this is important."

The Major looked around for a moment. "Now for the bad news. We stay in the area until the terrs leave Malvernia, whether it takes one month or one year. So we'd best get our fingers out."

The next few days were spent on rehearsals. They worked out

distances to selected targets. They made mudmaps of the places they knew about. They practised contact drills and break-off procedures. They were shown what to do if they were separated from the rest of the group. They were brought up to date on the latest intelligence reports. They brushed up on anti-tracking skills and mine laying. Within three days, they knew as much as anyone about the area they were going into.

"Right," growled Sergeant Hunter. "You have all been issued with twelve water bottles. Correct?"

"Yes, Sarge."

"You make sure that you carry every bottle you were issued with ... you make sure that everyone of them is completely watertight. You check them for leaks. You are going to need every drop of water you carry. Is that understood?"

"Yes, Sarge."

"The place we are going to be working in is as dry as a nun's crotch. So you will be only allowed to drink less than one bottle a day. I repeat, less than one bottle a day. Is that understood?"

"Sarge."

"Water discipline is going to be vital. Any man who drinks more than he is allowed will be left to fend for himself. In other words, you will die. Do you guys understand?"

"Sarge."

"The only time you take more than just a sip will be at daybreak and at last light. If I see anyone gulping during the day, I will cut his balls off and use them for a tobacco pouch ... is that understood?"

"Yes, Sarge."

"A Dak will be dropping resupplies to us every two weeks. There will be extra water. Then, and only then, will you be able to guzzle. Right. Ammo. Riflemen, you all have ten magazines, right?"

"Sarge."

"Machinegunners, you will carry as many belts as you can, the remainder will be divided up between the rest of us. We will be taking fifteen belts all up."

"Roger, Sarge."

"RPG-7 rockets. Have the blokes who are going to carry them got them?"

"Yes, Sarge."

"Anti-vehicle mines. We should have four. We got them?"

"Yes, Sarge."

The list went on; the weight each man carried was tremendous. The trooper's words, "we will be just like mules", was spot on. By the time the bergens were packed with all the necessary items to wage war, there was very little room left for incidentals like food, so rat packs were broken up and only things like small tins of beans and franks and orange segments were carried. Thirst would dull hunger pains. Sleeping bags were dispensed with, as most of the walking would be done at night, and in any case, it would be too hot. Washing and shaving gear would not be carried. One, there was not enough water and, two, clean bodies can be smelt a long way off in the bush. The only other thing to be carried was black camouflage cream. Lots of it. The men were to remain "blacked up" at all times. If one looked and smelt like a terrorist, at least from a distance, the element of surprise would remain.

Late in the afternoon, twelve heavily laden men heaved their bergens into the three waiting helicopters and the little Alouettes struggled gamely into the sky; the other eight would be airlifted in the second wave.

By last light, twenty men had been deposited on the only high piece of ground in the area. The choppers lifted into the air and were gone. The men were on their own, deep in enemy territory. The men hoisted bergens on to shoulders and trudged off into the night, the shoulder straps creaking under the strain.

By 0230 hours the next morning, they had reached their first objective, a sandy road, one of the few still being used by Frelimo. The trucks which had survived the SAS's surprises were driven to the downed bridge, the trucks on the other side would unload their goods. They would be ferried across to the men waiting and loaded up again. It was hard, time-consuming work.

The only cover was fifty metres on the other side of the road. The twenty men crossed the soft sand in single file, careful to tread in each other's footprints. Once across, they went to ground to cover the mine laying team. The rear man in the file swept the sand clear of tracks. When the jobs were completed, the men filed into the cover of the thick bush, covering their tracks as they went.

They waited all night and the next day and nothing came. They lay patiently for a third night; still nothing.

Early on the fourth morning, however, the sound of men's voices came clearly to the waiting soldiers. Laughing and joking, a section of Frelimo were ambling down the road. They were a mine-clearing patrol. From the casual way they were going about their business, it appeared to be a routine job. That was surprising, because these roads had been mined several times in the past. Perhaps because it had been quiet for a while, they thought they were safe. If they had seen the twenty pairs of beady eyes gazing down the sights of their rifles at them, they might not have been quite so relaxed.

They were still laughing when they found one of the mines. They had clearly not noticed the area swept of tracks over which they had just walked; the Rhodesians had done their job well. They detonated the mine with practised ease. The soldiers hiding in the bushes were itching to take them out, but they were not at war with Mozambique so no order to fire was given.

Suddenly, a shout. One of the Frelimo soldiers pointed at the bushes — he had seen something. A ragged volley of fire cracked into the scrub. The Frelimo section went to ground. They were almost hidden from view by the pile of sand on the edge of the road. The section leader was frantically trying to talk into his radio. The rest of the section was laying down fire at the hidden men.

"Return fire!" bellowed Lieutenant Pittman. The boom of the heavier Rhodesian weapons made a marked contrast to the lighter crack of the communist assault rifles.

"Hey, Ray," the Lieutenant shouted. "We might be in range of their mortars. If we don't get out of this fix soon, we might be in the shit."

"Roger, Sir ... John ... Henri, your sticks give covering fire. Koos, get your stick ready, we are going to assault them."

"Okay, Ray," Koos shouted back.

"Ready, Sir."

"OKAY ... GO," screamed the Lieutenant.

The eight men were up and running, bullets from the fire and return-fire cracking all around them. The aggressive reaction shocked the Frelimo, some of whom tried to continue firing while others jumped up and ran. Two of them managed to escape, fear lending wings to their feet as they dodged and weaved their way out of danger. The other six were not so lucky. Two of them died before they reached the other side of the road, shot many times in the back. The other four died as they tried to rise, or as they lay there trying to return fire.

"HALT," screamed Ray. "For fuck's sake, don't run over the other mine." The momentum of the charge had nearly sent one of the men running over the remaining "biscuit tin".

"C'mon Ray," called Mike from the bushes. "Get your packs on and let's get the fuck out of here. We don't know how many more of them are around."

Puffing and panting, they reached the bushes.

"Change magazines," panted Ray. They shouldered their heavy loads and they were off as fast as the weight would allow.

"ZERO ALPHA, ONE One, CONTACT CONTACT", the Lieutenant said into his handset.

"One One, Zero Alpha. I read you twos. Send, over."

"Zero Alpha, contact at Grid Papa Quebec Five Seven Zero Eight Niner Five. No Cas. Copy?"

"Zero Alpha copied."

"Okay, boys. Let's hotfoot it, we have quite a few k's to cover in a short time," said the Lieutenant.

They had only been trudging for a few minutes when they heard the distinctive cough of a mortar being fired.

"Hit the dirt!" Corporal Wessels shouted.

They went to ground. The mortar exploded a long way off.

"Looks like they are firing blind," muttered Ray. "C'mon, let's move." They were up and off again.

By nightfall they had covered a lot of ground. There had been no follow up. They went into all-round defence, ate a hurried meal of beans and franks, took a good swig of water and were off again. They walked all night. The next morning, they rested up for a short while, not far from the outskirts of Malvernia. Their second task was to probe the defences.

At 1130 hours they hit the jackpot. A tinny sound had come from somewhere ahead. Could it have been a tin mug? Corporal Wessels and Trooper Haddock, fondly known as "Fish", went forward to investigate. A few minutes later small arms fire came zipping through the foliage. Such was the intensity of fire that the greenery above their heads was fast disappearing. John and the Fish came back, slithering through the undergrowth.

"Fuckin' Jesus. We are in the middle of a horseshoe bunker system. There must be two hundred of the pricks in there. Let's get out of here," the Fish shouted breathlessly. Seconds later mortar bombs began to fall, but far behind them.

The skipper shouted to Ray: "Sergeant, give us covering fire while we withdraw."

"Righteo, Sir. It's done." Ray looked across at his machinegunner, Trooper Coome. He was not returning fire.

"Hey Pat," he called across. "The skipper sends his compliments and could you please return fire."

Coome looked over his shoulder. "Has the Fish got back yet? I don't want to hit them."

"Yes, they are back."

"Then tell the skipper that I will be delighted to return fire." With that, the MAG opened up and the men began to file past; two of them dropped a belt next to the gunner and they were gone.

The enemy's fire began to become erratic. Soon Ray called to his section: "Okay, guys, let's get outa here."

They hoisted their bergens on to their shoulders and started walking. Mortars were crumping all round as they made their way out. It wasn't long before they heard the distinctive sound of a follow-up. They increased their pace as much as they could, but the sounds were getting closer. Within fifteen minutes Ray knew that a decision had to be made. It was obvious that the Frelimo were very cautious,   otherwise they would have caught up before this.

"Okay, guys, it looks like they are following our spoor, so we will have to ambush our tracks. Let's get to it. Follow me."

With that, Ray walked round in a circle, of necessity it was a small circle and they had only just got out of sight when they saw a section of Frelimo coming up the tracks they had made. They were in their usual section of eight. What surprised them was the Russian. They knew that the Russians had "advisers" working with the Frelimo, but they had never seen them. That explained the aggressive follow-up.

Standing stock-still, the Rhodesians waited until they were fairly close before they opened fire. For Pat Coome, it was a machinegunner's dream come true. The Frelimo section was in a line; the line was oblique to him, meaning he could cover the whole section with a very small arc of fire. The section still had not seen them. Pat glanced at his Sergeant, waiting for the order to fire. The chance would be over in a very short moment.

Ray was been waiting for the exact second. "FIRE," he shouted. The Frelimo went down like ninepins. The Russian tried to run for it. He ducked and weaved in among the trees. Ray followed him in his sights and squeezed the trigger. The Russian somersaulted into the ground. The round had taken him in the base of the skull, right at the top of the spine. Ray had been aiming for the man's back, but he had ducked at the same moment the rifle has fired. The effect was just the same. The man was as dead as a Dodo.

"Right, let's get the flock outa here. Good shooting, ouns."

They caught up with the rest of the group. "How did it go, Ray," asked the skipper. "We heard shooting a couple of minutes ago."

"Ja, we culled a section of Frelimo plus one Ruskie."

"A Russian, eh? Good work. That'll teach the fuckers to interfere."

DURING THE NEXT three weeks, all three groups reported successes. The few trucks that were still attempting to resupply the Frelimo garrison were ambushed and the occupants killed. The soldiers in the small town were jittery, firing mortars indiscriminately into the surrounding bush. Two Rhodesian soldiers were wounded as a result, but both were casevaced safely.

Next, the few viable waterholes were ambushed. Because water was scarce, men had to come to them to drink. It would have been easier to kill an animal and poison the water by dumping the carcass in, but all the animals had been shot out long ago to feed the garrison. As it was, human carcasses poison water better than animals. It was just a matter of waiting. The only decent waterhole near the town was fortified, but that didn't stop the Rhodesians. The waterhole was just in range of the artillery on the hill on the other side of the border.

One morning, just after first light, twenty men in basic webbing lined up ready to assault the position. Another twenty waited in defence, guarding the assault group's bergens. Captain Watson' team was to lead the assault. At 0615 hours, the artillery was called in. The shells screamed overhead, showering earth-shaking explosions all around the waterhole.

Bruce Watson leaped up as soon as the shelling ceased. "Let's go," he shouted. The twenty men ran down the gently sloping ground, firing steadily as they went, the two hundred metres to the target eaten up quickly as the soldiers loped across the sandy terrain. The hastily fortified position had already been abandoned. The only dead were the ones unfortunate enough to be killed by the shelling. These were unceremoniously dumped in the precious water. Sandbags were thrown on top of the bodies to keep them out of sight, at least for a while.

The Rhodesians didn't fill up their water bottles. Cholera was rife in the area. As soon as they had finished, the men began to retrace their steps.

The first hint of trouble the men waiting further up the hill had was the whoosh of the RPG-7 rocket as it zipped past their heads to detonate against a tree close by. Next came shouted orders followed by small arms fire. The Rhodesians, lying behind their bergens, were a small target. Soon a fierce firefight was in progress.

"Zero Alpha, One One. Do you read? Over."

"One One, what's happening, Mike?"

"We are being fired on by an unknown number of enemy to our east. Their fire is accurate. Over."

"Roger, Mike. How far away are they?"

"Approximately one hundred metres. Over."

"Okay, we are going to try to flank 'em. Over."

"Right. We will keep their heads down."

The Captain waved his arm. "Follow me," he called. The assault team, with no heavy bergens to hamper them, made good time to where they could hear the enemy's fire to their right. The Captain put his men in line formation, with a strong rearguard, and was about to give the order to advance when bullets began cracking about their heads, this time from the left.

"Get down," he screamed.

Another group of Frelimo had come up to give their comrades support. There were now two firefights going on.

"Mike, we are being pinned down here, as well."

"Yes, I can hear that."

The firing from both sides continued for a while. Both Rhodesian commanders wondered why the Frelimo had not assaulted their positions. It seemed like a stalemate, but the answer soon became obvious. In the distance, they could hear the sound of mortars being set up.

"Mike, this lot are being organised by the Ruskies. We had better get our fingers out. Any ideas?"

"We have rifle grenades and RPG-7s. We will have to use them for cover and assault. Over."

"Good one. Let me know when you are ready."

The two officers began sorting out the available rockets and grenades. In Mike's group the rifles were being set up to fire the latter. Sergeant Hunter was bellowing: "Every second man starting from me will be the assault team. Piet, John, Paul, you stay rear defence. The rest of you, shift your bergens so you can get a good start. Rocket and grenade men, get ready to cover our front. Ready?"

"Ready, Sarge."

Ray could see the fear in the men's faces, but he knew they would not let him down. "Remember to keep your spacing. Our ouns will be firing in between us," he called to the nervous men.

The Captain and the Lieutenant confirmed that each team was ready.

"Grenade men, fire in a fan pattern. GO!" screamed the Captain.

"Go." Mike yelled into the handset.

The grenades arched lazily in the air and dropped towards the enemy while the RPG-7s whooshed along a fairly flat trajectory in the same direction. Ray was up, waving his arm. "C'mon boys!"

The ten men from each group bounded towards their destiny; fear lending them speed, training and discipline keeping them running straight.

The Frelimo men, believing they had their enemy well and truly tied down, got the surprise of their lives when rockets and grenades came blasting into their positions. They had only just got over one shock when, to their horror, screaming demented white men were rushing at them. Their nerve broke and they fled. The ranting and shouting of the Russians was to no avail and soon they too had to retreat.

The Rhodesians did not stop until they had reached the deserted mortar positions. "Anyone familiar with these things?" panted the Sergeant.

"Ja, I've done a course on them," Corporal Wessels replied.

"Right, let's get them turned round and get a couple of rounds off."

Soon the two mortars had been manhandled roughly into the right direction. The Corporal got busy sorting out the charges and bombs.

"What's happening, Ray?" asked Lieutenant Pittman.

Sergeant Hunter pressed the switch on his handset. "Sunray, we've overrun their position. We're going to re-use their mortars."

"Don't waste any time. We think they are getting ready to counter attack. Get back here ASAP."

"Roger, copied."

Ray turned to Corporal Wessels who was waiting expectantly with a mortar in his hand. "Fire that and let's get out of here."

The Corporal slipped the bomb down the tube and ducked.

"Let's go, guys."

"Hey, Sarge. Can we chuck a grenade down the tubes?"

"Will it do any good?"

"Well, it can't hurt."

"Hurry up, then."

They were doubling back as the muffled crump of the grenades sounded behind them.

The Captain was on the radio. "Zero Alpha, this is One One, CONTACT CONTACT Withdrawing from contact with a large group. Request Shelldrake puts 10 rounds rapid on Grid Papa Quebec Five Niner Four Seven Six One when we call, over."

"Zero Alpha, Roger, standing by."

While the forty men regrouped and began trudging their way out, the four guns on the hill were being brought round to bear on their target — a point through which the running RLI callsign would pass in a matter of minutes, closely persued by Frelimo.

"Look lively men," said the artillery commander before briefing his gunners on the unfolding drama.

"Brave buggers, those RLI," muttered one man as he rechecked his sights. "I wouldn't swap places with them for all the sadza in Salisbury."

"HEY, SARGE. I like your new hat!!" remarked a trooper as Lieutenant

Pittman's group passed through the Captain's men. They were leapfrogging through each other's positions — withdrawing tactically is the textbook phrase.

"Yeah, they're on special today," grinned Ray. He had picked up a hat from a dead Frelimo soldier. With its characteristic earflaps, the hat looked quite ridiculous, but at least it kept the sun off the Sergeant's nose, which was horribly sunburnt.

The Russian "advisers" were busy organising a follow up. A creeping mortar barrage was to precede the Frelimo troops as they swept after the Rhodesians.

Although the white men had a head start, they were tired and heavily laden. The Frelimo were being psyched up by their leaders, the blood was starting to get up and they were raring to go. By the time they had prepared for the follow-up they were straining like dogs on a leash. Lightly kitted up and buoyed up by positive thinking, they set off at a fast pace; it was all their leaders could do to keep them in check. The mortars had been carried as far forward as possible, and they started their barrage well in front of the advancing troops.

The Rhodesians were far ahead of the barrage, but it would not be long before the Frelimo caught up with them. They had passed 'Shelldrake' less that a minutes earlier. Captain Watson heard the crump of the Frelimo mortars and judged when they were falling approximately in the location of Shelldrake. He waited a further 30 seconds, took a deep breath and picked up the radio handset.

"Zero Alpha, One One. Shelldrake, I say again, Shelldrake. Over."

"Zero Alpha, copied."

With great fortune, the Captain's guesswork was as good as any in his already distinguished career. The artillery shells erupted among the advancing Frelimo soldiers, now only 150 metres behind Ray and his men, flinging smashed and broken bodies into the air like rag dolls. The survivors faltered, but the ranting and cursing of their   leaders kept them going.

"Zero Alpha, STOP STOP STOP. Drop one hundred. 10 rounds rapid, over," the Captain gave the correction. Forty shells landed on the revised target, pulverising more bodies to fertilise the soil.

"C'mon guys, speed it up. Let's move it," the NCOs and section leaders were cajoling. The men huffed and puffed and pushed themselves to greater effort.

"We're going to have to drop our packs shortly if this keeps up," said Sergeant Carr.

"C'mon, ouns, move it for fuck's sake," panted Corporal Wessels.

"Sir, the boys are completely knackered. We are going to have to stop and rest, or drop the packs," said Ray.

"We stop when I say, Sergeant Hunter, and not before," growled the Captain.

"Roger, Sir."

"Drop two hundred, five rounds rapid," Bruce Watson said into the handset.

"C'mon, blokes, put foot. Trooper Hall, if you stop once more, I'll drag you along by your balls. Now move it, you gutless wonders," wheezed Ray.

The Frelimo were still following up, but keeping well behind the shells. It was giving the Rhodesians just a tiny bit of space; not much, but enough to keep them out of reach.

Ahead of the exhausted men, the terrain changed from flat ground covered with trees to flat ground with no vegetation. In the distance, the ground rose to form a small hillock, previously codenamed Plum Duff due to the circular contour lines it described on the map. It was not much more than a large sand dune, but it was defensible, and most importantly, the artillery could be quite precise when working on the area. The men quickened their pace and were soon struggling up the slope.

"NCOs, I want all-round defence. I want the men to dig in and use their bergens for cover and I want it done yesterday."

"Righteo, you heard the Captain. Let's get to it."

While the men were digging in, the Captain was on the radio. "Zero Alpha, One One. We are at Plum Duff at this time. We are still being pursued by a large force. Will request Shelldrake again shortly. Over."

"One One, Roger, standing by."

The Captain checked the map for the distance between Plum Duff and the treeline through which the Frelimo soldiers would surely burst at any minute.

"Zero Alpha, One One. From Plum Duff, add five hundred and go right one hundred. Then standby for my signal. Over."

"Add five hundred and go right one hundred, then standby. Roger, copied."

THE FRELIMO SOLDIERS had reached the edge of the tree line. There they waited. They had a lot of open ground to cover; it was going to be hard going. But they had well over two hundred men, against forty. The artillery worried them but if they carried out the charge swiftly, the enemy's shells would be useless. Weight of numbers would win the day. The Russians began organising the men into four waves of fifty.

"One One, this is Zero Alpha. Over."

"Zero Alpha, go ahead."

"We have trucks on the way to pick you up at the fence on the border. They have orders to cut the fence and drive across if necessary. We also have two Cyclone Sevens ready for casevac. Over."

"Zero Alpha, Roger that, many thanks," said the strained voice of the Captain." He continued, "Confirm Shelldrake is standing by. Over."

"One One, affirmative. Over."

"Good, could they register on the treeline, Grid Papa Quebec Five Eight Two Three Niner Niner now? Over."

"One One, registering now, standing by for your corrections over."

Bruce Watson had seen movement and guessed correctly that the Frelimo were about to assault. As well as creating confusion among the enemy, he wanted to be able to correct the fire while there was still time.

If the Frelimo had been better trained and better disciplined, they would have begun the charge earlier, but it took time to bully and coax the men into position. The shell arrived scant seconds before the charge started.

"Two rounds rapid," the Captain shouted.

The Frelimo were out in the open now and running towards the hill. The next eight rounds landed behind the charging men.

"Two rounds rapid, drop two hundred," corrected the Captain.

"Sights two hundred, await my order to fire," shouted the NCOs. "When they come into range, select your target. Don't waste ammunition." The controlled, calm voices of the NCOs made it seem like range control during training. It had the desired effect and the men steadied down.

The next salvos landed with blinding, concussing crumps and the Frelimo line became momentarily ragged. But it steadied, the gaps closed and the charge continued. Bloodlust had taken hold of the black men now and their eyes were red as the fragile thread of sanity snapped, replaced by the madness of war.

"Zero Alpha, One One. From Black Adder, add fifty, ten rounds rapid fire," Captain Watts spoke again, his voice now hoarse.

Up on the hill the artillery men were frantically adjusting the big guns, zeroing in on the new co-ordinates.

"Please, God, don't let this hit one of our boys," prayed the gunner as he kissed the shell before slamming it into the breach.

"FIRE AT WILL," shouted the NCOs on Plum Duff as the first wave of Frelimo came into range. There were plenty of men to kill and they dropped as the bullets found them. But still they kept coming.

"One hundred!" shouted Sergeant Carr. The men hurriedly adjusted the sights on their FN rifles and continued firing. The enemy were dropping like flies now, the madness had affected both sides and men were screaming obscenities at each other. The two groups of antagonists were only 90 metres apart when the first shells screamed in. They dropped all around that lonely hillock in the middle of nowhere, the concussion and shrapnel bowling men over like ninepins.

The attack faltered and petered out. The concussion had stunned attacker and defender alike. Men stumbled about in the open, dazed and disoriented. The white men in their hastily dug shell scrapes had fared a bit better, but not much. They lay in the sand, too dazed to do anything except look out on to the plain, their heads swimming, ears ringing. The smell of cordite and sickly-sweet blood hung in the air. The stillness only punctuated by the groans of a few badly-wounded Frelimo survivors wandering aimlessly in the sand only metres away, dragging their AKs by the webbing.

Lieutenant Pittman and Sergeant Hunter rose groggily to their feet, swaying like drunks as they shot the surviving Frelimo .

Later, Captain Watson said he did not remember giving the order to cease fire. But he did.

"Zero Alpha, this is One One. Do you read? Over". He repeated the message. Captain Watson' radio was dead. A scratchy voice came from the Lieutenant's set.

"One One, One One, this is Zero Alpha, do you read. All stations, can anyone read me. Over?"

Lieutenant Pittman flopped heavily in the sand and it was a while before he answered.

"Zero Alpha, One One, affirmative."

"One One, Sitrep Over?" Recognising the Lieutenant's voice, slurred though it was, the OC continued. "One One. Sitrep and Cas State, Over."

"Roger, wait five."

Like zombies rising from the grave, the Rhodesians slowly got up out of the sand and began to organise themselves. Except for the occasional metallic chink as magazines were changed, the silence was deafening. Nothing moved, only the men on the hill.

"Zero Alpha, One One."

"Go ahead."

"We have two dead and four wounded. Over."

"How bad are the wounded? Over."

"We are assessing them now. We request casevac. Over."

"Can you give us a sitrep on the enemy? Over."

"There are a large number of dead all around. Over."

"Are they likely to oppose our casevac? Over."

"Negative. They won't be doing much again. Over."

"Roger. Cyclone Sevens are on their way. We have trucks coming to pick you up. They should be crossing over now."

"Roger."

LATE THAT AFTERNOON, the remaining thirty-four men were paraded on the hill, not far from the artillery guns.

"Right, listen in, ouns. There is a lekker meal being cooked up for us. While we are waiting, I want you to clean weapons."

"Aw, Sarge, can't we rest until tea and then clean up."

"No, you can't. This ain't a fucking holiday camp. You do as you are told. You hear?"

"Yes, Sarge."

"There will be a weapons inspection before you eat. Any questions?"
Silence.

"Fall out."

As the men were walking away, Sergeant Hunter called after them: "Don't forget to drink plenty of water."

"What a grouch. Fancy making us clean up before tea. We've just been in a fucking great punch up. We fucked them up big time and he wants us to clean our bang sticks, like fucking rookies."

"You know how it is with the Sarge. Soldier first, human being second."

"Jeez, I tell you what," joked another trooper, "the hours in this job are atrocious. The conditions are terrible and the management is just so insensitive."

"Yeah, I reckon we should put in for smoko at regular times, one hour for lunch and eight hours sleep at night."

"Ah shutup, you wankers. Let's get this chore done quickly and then we can graze our little hearts out."

The next day, the OC held a briefing for the officers and NCOs. "Right gentlemen, you all did a bloody good job out there yesterday. I am sorry about our casualties but considering the enemy's strength, I think we got away with it quite lightly.

"Our biggest problem is that we stirred up a very large hornet's nest. The outside media are going to have a field day with this and the shit is going to hit the fan. I'm waiting to hear from our top brass now as to whether we can go back in there. Already the bleeding hearts of the world are crying 'foul play'. It looks like we are going to have to sit here for a day or so until the hierarchy makes a decision. Any questions so far?

"Right. Captain Watson, why didn't you drop your bergens and get the hell out of there? You could have avoided a large punch up if you had got away."

"We had already been in a couple of jousting sessions, sir. There were quite a few dead Freds before we started hightailing it."

"If you remember, your orders were to leave as little trace of our presence behind as possible."

"By keeping our bergens and recovering our dead, we have left nothing concrete for them to show."

"I respect your decision, Captain, but I had to ask. Unfortunately it doesn't alter the fact that there is a great big fuss brewing over the incident."

"Sir, I think we might be able to throw up a smokescreen here!!" Lieutenant Pittman's eyes were sparkling with amusement.

"Go on."

"Can't we let it slip that Frelimo and the gooks are at loggerheads and that the contacts were between them. That is, they're killing each other and blaming it on us?"

"By God! You might have something there. I didn't realise you were standing at the next elections, Lieutenant."

"Pardon Sir?" replied Pittman.

"Weaving a tangled web of lies and deceit, Lieutenant. You should become a politician."

The troops laughed themselves hoarse.

"Okay, settle down," said the OC. "That is a bloody good idea. It might not be totally believed, but it will cast doubt on the issue and it might let us off the hook at least partially."

The debrief went on for more than an hour. At the end of it, most problems had been sorted out.

"Okay, any questions on what we have covered?" asked the OC.

"Yes, sir. There is one question I'd like to ask," said the artillery commander. "Was it our shells that killed and wounded your men?"

The OC paused for a moment. The artillerymen had done a magnificent job, their accuracy had been commendable and they had done all that was humanly possible to avoid dropping the shells directly on to the sand dune.

"I can tell you this Lieutenant. Your blokes did a bloody good job yesterday. They saved our bacon. Of that, there is no doubt."

"Yes, sir, but was it our shells that did the damage?"

Captain Watson looked directly at the artilleryman. "No, it was Frelimo action that killed them," he lied.

While they waited for the decision-makers to act, the men were taken back to the airstrip at Malapati. Once again, except for guard duty and fitness training, it was much like the holiday atmosphere they had experienced before.

ONE DAY, A SPECIAL Branch Detective Section Officer came to the camp to ask questions about a certain terrorist. "While you blokes were wandering about in our neighbour's backyard, did you come across or hear anything of 'Tarzan Bazooka'?"

"Jesus, sir, don't mention that bastard's name in front of Van Zyl. He was the gook who took out Jim's farm and family last year."

"Tarzan Bazooka" was an enigma. His *Chimurenga* (nom-de-guerre) name was more ridiculous than most, but he savoured it and insisted on being known by it. He liked to dress in loud, flashy, clothes and was generally regarded as a braggart and a show-off. But he was also very intelligent.

To their hierarchy he was an ideal operative. He hit soft targets, effectively causing enormous psychological damage on the Rhodesians and wavering tribespeople before melting back into the bush. He was very cunning, planned his forays carefully and was permitted to range over a very wide area — from the north-east to the south-east of the country. That was why he hadn't been caught — he wouldn't operate in any one area for very long.

Tarzan did not have the liberation of his country or its people at heart when he went on his raids. In truth, he was not even interested in the liberation movement. Tarzan did it for his own pleasure. He liked to inflict pain and suffering on other people and actually obtained sexual gratification from his acts. He would often climax simply from beating someone senseless. He particularly enjoyed watching the fear in people's eyes as he tortured them, especially those white pigs. They showed their fear so much more than his people.

Making sure he slipped away without getting caught was also not for the greater glory of the movement. Tarzan was a coward. Much as he derived pleasure from inflicting pain and fear, he was more frightened of having it inflicted on him. He was a wily one indeed.

It appeared that Tarzan had been using Malvernia as a base for a while. It was an ideal place to rest and recuperate. The Rhodesians weren't at war with Mozambique, so theoretically the town was a safe haven for him. Not to mention the fact that there were plenty of body-guards around in the form of the Frelimo. He was a man the Rhodesians would like to get their hands on dearly.

The Special Branch man spent the next few hours asking questions. Unfortunately, the RLI troops had neither seen nor heard of him.

The Commando idled their days away, waiting for a decision. One morning they went to the river to swim; half on guard while the others splashed around in the muddy water. In the distance, they heard bleating. Presently, a small herd of goats and a shepherd came wandering into view. The old man in the scruffy cast-off clothes gently shooed the animals along the dirt road towards the shallow ford in the river not far from where the men were swimming. He appeared be looking for good grazing for his animals. The animals stopped for a few moments in the water to drink, then they continued on to the far side. Instead of herding them along the track, the old man steered them over close to where the men were gathered.

"That old man has been coming here every day for quite a few days," mentioned Pat Coome. "He just sits there looking at us, smiling and waving."

"Silly old bugger," remarked another trooper. "Anyone can see the grazing is shit around here. He should go somewhere where the grass is better."

The trooper's astute observation struck Ray as odd. The African would not be there unless he had a reason. He looked directly at the old man. The African was gazing straight back at him and fingering the talisman hanging round his neck. Ray put his hand up to the amulet round his own neck. The African nodded his head, almost imperceptibly.

"Just how far do Jason's tentacles stretch?" thought Ray as he pulled on his trousers.

"Greetings, mdala. The day is very hot." Ray observed the formal custom.

"Greetings, nkosi. Yes, it is very hot today."

"Your goats look nice and fat and healthy."

"Yes, but the grazing is not too good at this time of year."

Ray knew that the greetings would go on for some time before the man got round to the subject he wanted to talk about; that was the custom. Some of the younger men would cut short the formalities but the calm, simple dignity of the man commanded the respect due to an elder and Ray gave it to him.

Eventually, the real subject was broached. "Isizo, there is a man who many seek. He stays at the white man's former kraal on the other side of the fence in the place you call Malvernia. The kraal is now the home of many men with guns. Black men."

"I know of this place."

The African smiled, his face crinkled up in amusement. "Yes, it is the place you have been attacking but not attacking."

It was Ray's turn to smile. The African's analogy of their "bump and run" tactics was surprisingly accurate. "This man who many seek, what of him?"

"There are two men who can lead you to him, Isizo."

Ray thought for a while. It would be impossible to do anything while they were in limbo. But they could work out a plan in the meantime.

"These men, mdala, where could I meet them?"

"Do you know of the small village on the track over there?" He pointed in a north-easterly direction. "It is only this far." The old man raised his arm a few degrees from the horizontal in the manner of Africans who do not possess a watch, and indicated about a two-hour, or eight-kilometre, march.

"Yes I know of this place."

"These men. They can meet you there, Isizo."

"Tell them that I will come in two days. But also tell them that it may not be possible to come with them to Malvernia until we have word from our chiefs. They are having a big indaba."

"I will tell them, Isizo."

"Mdala, what is the name of this man who many seek?"

"Tarzan Bazooka, Isizo. He is a very bad man, many fear him."

It appeared as though he was quite unpopular. The fact that Jason wanted him dead was as good an indication as any that he was well up in the terrorist hierarchy.

"Mdala?"

"Yes, Isizo?"

"Who is the man who sent you with this message?" Ray wanted to be sure.

"Why, the man who fears your magic, Isizo."

"How will I be able to tell these men when I can see them?"

"I will come here with my goats every day."

"Go well, mdala."

"Fambai zvakanaka, Isizo."

Sergeant Hunter broached the subject with Captain Watson and the OC.

"It's going to be a dicey one, Ray," they both said. But they began working out details anyway.

THE MEETING WITH the two unarmed Africans went according to plan. It transpired that they had joined the terrorist ranks, both believing what they had been told about liberating the country. They had become disillusioned as time went by. Jason had picked up on the two men and put them to work for him.

"How will we get to Tarzan Bazooka?" asked Ray. They were sitting under the shade of a large tree not far from the village the old man had indicated.

"It is fairly simple, Ishe," they said. They had drawn a basic mudmap of the township.

"We can walk in through here, from the east." The taller of the two pointed to the road leading in from that direction. "It is not guarded well. We can walk straight up the road, into the main street to where the post office is. We turn up here." He drew the route in the dirt with a twig. "When we reach this big house here, we turn left. Tarzan's house is this one. It is the fifth one on the right."

"I know that house!" exclaimed Captain Watson. "It used to belong to the family that ran the post office. The wife used to make beautiful jams."

"Tell me," said Ray, questioning the two, "this house, how many rooms, doors and windows has it?

"Are the windows high off the ground?

"Do the doors open inwards or outwards?

"Is there a fence round the house? Are there any dogs there? What about people living in the neighbouring houses?"

Every question was important. Attention to detail would be the key to a successful kidnap. For instance, it would be stupid to try and break a door in when it might open outwards. If the windows were easy to climb out of, a man would have to cover them, and so on.

"When is Tarzan most likely to be home, Michael?"

"Ishe, he always goes there after dark. He has two mfazis with him. He likes to beat them and hurt them while he jig-jigs them."

"Is it always the same two women?"

"Mostly, Ishe. Sometimes he takes a new one if he can get one. But they are afraid of him."

"That stands to reason," muttered Bruce Watson.

"Will there be anyone else there when Tarzan is at home?"

"He has two bodyguards with him, Ishe. One of them is very big."

"Where do they sleep?"

"In this room here," Michael said, pointing to the sketch in the sand.

"Where do the rest of his men stay?"

"They live near the Frelimo in the bunkers over here."

Bit by bit they pieced together as much information as they could. Between Bruce Watson' memory and the Africans' naturally astute powers of observation, they soon built up a very comprehensive picture of the target. They knew the layout of the land and the target's movements and habits, but how were they going to get in and out?

Back in the OC's tent they were busy working out details.

"Michael says it will take a night's march to get from here to here," Bruce Watson said, pointing to the map on the wall. "He also says that you can hide up here during the day. It is only an hour's walk from there to the edge of the town."

"Okay, that should not be a problem," said the Major. "We can get through the fence and drop whoever is going by truck. So the route in can be done. Now we have the problem of getting to the target. We can't just walk in bold as brass and ask him to come with us."

"The best time to go in would be not long after dark," said Captain Watson. "That will give us time to get out of there during the night."

"It would be easy enough to create a diversion," Ray added. "Those Territorials in Villa Salazar usually manage to stir the Frelimo up around sunset on most days, don't they?"

"That's a point," replied the OC.

"The only trouble with that," said Bruce, "is that the exchange of fire usually only lasts half an hour or so."

"Why don't we send some of our blokes in there to boost it up a bit. Give 'em a fucking good stonking?"

"Yes, we could do that Ray."

"All we would have to do is keep the fire going every time it looked liked slacking off."

"What about the artillery. Could we move them to within range of that big bunker system we hit and give that a rev as well?"

"Now hold on," the Major interjected. "Let's not get too carried away. Remember we are still on hold at the moment."

The OC paused for a moment, then said: "Okay, I will tell you something. It is not clear at the moment, but you know that there is an election planned, don't you?"

"Yes, sir."

"Well, I'll tell you what little I know. Unfortunately, we are only getting old news stuck out here in the arse end of the world."

The two men waited for the Major to continue.

"The politicians have been gearing up for an election. So far only the moderates have consented to holding it. Bishop Abel Muzorewa seems to be the most likely candidate to win at the moment. The hardline gooks, Mugabe and Nkomo, still refuse to come to the party, undoubtedly because they have very little chance of winning at this time. So, if they can step up the war, they're sitting pretty.

"The bottom line is that everything is still up in the air, and that includes taking this Tarzan fucker out of circulation. The SB boys reckon he's due to go out again and Christ only knows what he'll do next."

Ray shuddered at the memory of the white family and their farm labourers.

The OC continued: "This snatch and grab we're planning is really only something to keep our minds busy at the moment. Until we know more, we are just going to have to stay on hold."

"Right, sir. But I say let's work it out. Just in case."

"Yeah, I suppose it can't do any harm," smiled the OC.

"MICHAEL, YOU SAID the other day that there are no dogs in Malvernia. Why is that?"

They were sitting under the tree again, talking to the two Africans.

"Ah, Ishe." Michael shook his head slowly from side to side and clucked. "Food is very scarce there now. They have eaten them."

"Ah ha, that sounds promising," said Bruce gleefully.

"Tell me. Where are they getting their water from? We have poisoned all the water in the area."

"Do you know of the place where the train used to arrive?"

"Yes."

"There is a place not far from there where they put a long pipe deep into the ground. A motor brings the water up to a tank there. It was used to put water into the train engine."

"Yes. Yes." Ray and Bruce smiled at each other. "This might be the straw that breaks the camel's back," Ray said. Bruce laughed and added "and Tarzan's vine".

"SIR, WE HAVE just found out a very useful piece of information."

They were back in the Major's tent.

"They are still getting some water from the old watering point at the siding near town. It is heavily defended, but we might be able to mortar it. We can kill two birds with one stone. It will cover our snatch and grab and do them out of the only remaining available source of water."

"Point taken," smiled the OC, as though he were keeping two children amused. "Tell me. How are you going to get away with wandering through town? Two white boys. Won't they notice? Even if you are blacked up."

"All organised, sir. Michael and Joseph are getting some clothes and floppy hats for us to wear. Also, we still have plenty of AKs from that contact on the hill."

The plan was ready to go. Now they had to wait to see if they could put it into operation.

THE COMMANDO WAS paraded on the clear ground near the airstrip. There was an air of expectancy about the men.

"Good morning, gentlemen," said the OC.

"Morning, sir."

"You are all probably aware that an election has just been held. The votes have been counted; Bishop Abel Muzorewa is now the Prime Minister and our country has a new name. It is called Zimbabwe-Rhodesia."

There was a low grumble of disapproval.

"The observers from around the world have all agreed that it was a free and fair election and have okayed it. However, Nkomo and Mugabe have refused to acknowledge it and we await news whether the UN, OAU and the Brits will. In the meantime, the war is going to continue."

There was anger in the men now and they listened in disbelief.

"What the fuck does the world want from us?" asked a trooper.

"Okay, settle down. It's a piss off, we all know that. But there isn't much any of us can do about it. We'll know what's going to happen in the next few days. Until then, keep a lid on it. You are disciplined, professional soldiers, not a rabble, so I expect you to behave as such. Any questions? Right, dismiss."

As they were walking away, Ray wondered just how much Jason had known that day they met. His predictions seemed to be coming true. It was a worrying thought that the terrorists appeared to know more about the future than anyone.

Three days later, the OC spoke to the men again.

"Right, gentlemen. You are not going to like what I have to tell you. The rest of the world has refused to recognise our country."

There was a gasp of amazement.

"Sanctions are still in force and the war will go on. But there is a glimmer of hope. Muzorewa has given us the go-ahead to go and kick the shit out of the terrs."

"Yahoo!!" the cry went up from everyone assembled.

The Major raised his hands for quiet.

"Okay, gentlemen. This war was supposed to have been waged to give the black Africans the vote. That has been done. The war still goes on. The gloves have come off. The lie has been exposed. It is now just a naked power grab by the Patriotic Front. The new government has sanctioned the use of external operations. We are going after the enemy with everything we've got."

The men were cheering wildly now. "Yaaa, let's go and fuck them up, but good. Yaa, Yaa."

"Bruce, Ray, I want to see you in my tent," the Major said as he passed the ranks. "I am going to give you two the go-ahead to snatch that son of a bitch Tarzan."

Bruce and Ray smiled at each other and shook hands.

"Instead of giving you minimal distraction as we first planned, I'm going to paste that Frelimo garrison big time. We are going to shell the whole bunker system, not just around it. The watering point is going to get the biggest stonking we can lay down and the boys in Villa Salazar are going to shoot the shit out of the western side of the town. The only place we will leave alone is the area you will be working in. Hopefully, with all the revving they will be getting, they will think they are about to be attacked from outside and will be too busy to worry you two."

The Major studied the two men in front of him for a second. "Muzorewa has set no limits on what we can do — for the moment — so we are going to inflict as much damage as we can before he gets a chance to change his mind, or is made to change it."

Captain Watson and Sergeant Hunter were mentally rubbing their hands in glee.

"Right, now we'd better arrange the details. I want every part of the op to be worked out to the smallest degree. Every emergency has to be catered for."

TWO DAYS LATER, they were back in the OC's tent. "Right, let's have it then."

Captain Watson started his briefing. "We are going to send Michael's mate, Joseph, in a couple of days early to check if Tarzan is still there and to make sure his routine is still the same.

"The three of us ... myself, Ray and Michael, will be dropped at last light at that point you mentioned the other day. We will do a forced march all night to the lying up point, here." The Captain pointed to the place on the map.

"It is roughly an hour's fast walk from there to the outskirts of town. We will lie up in hiding for the day. Joseph will meet up with us and let us know of any change in Tarzan's habits. At about 1700 hours, we will start walking towards Malvernia."

Ray interrupted him. "Sir, what time do the boys in Villa Salazar usually start stirring things up with the Frelimo?"

"Around last light, say a quarter to six."

"Can we ask them to start about 1730 hours. Just a gentle rev to keep their interest in the opposite direction from us!"

"Yes, I can organise that."

"Good idea Ray," said Bruce. "Now, we will be in radio contact with you, sir. We will have a Fire Force radio hidden in a rough old canvas bag. We will keep radio silence except for emergencies and the times we are going to set out."

"And they are?"

"We will radio in when we get to the lying up point; when we get the go-ahead from Joseph; and when we are about to enter Malvernia."

"Have you thought up a call sign?"

"Yes, sir, we have," smiled Ray. "We thought we might go with Tango Kilo. Short for Tarzan's kidnappers."

"Okay, carry on," laughed the Major.

"When we get in sight of the town we will transmit 'Tango Kilo, REVLON'. That will be the signal for you to go from a gentle shoot up to a full-on stonk. It should take us roughly fifteen minutes to get to Tarzan's house."

"How long do you estimate it will take to do the job and get out?"

"Difficult to say. Anything up to an hour."

"Okay."

"When we have our captive and have got far enough out of town, we will transmit 'Tango Kilo GREEN APPLES'. You can ease up with the stonking, but keep up a sporadic fire just to keep 'em occupied. We'll walk as far as we can with our captive until first light. Hopefully, we can be extracted by chopper."

"Okay, sounds good so far. What if you are compromised?"

"We don't think there will be too much chance of that on the walk in. There is probably not a great risk during the day. By all reports, things are pretty grim in town. There is not much movement, at least not in the heat of the day, and there will be plenty to keep them occupied during the night we are there."

"Even if we are seen in the lying up point," Ray said, "unless they come up very close, all they will see is three scruffy comrades sleeping in the shade. Believe me, sir, I am dreading putting on the clothes we are going to have to wear. They are dirty, torn and smelly."

"Ja, we will be wearing gook gear, gook webbing, carrying gook weapons and on top of that we will be wearing gungy old overcoats to hide the way we walk. Ray will be wearing his Frelimo cap with the flaps down to cover his features. I will be wearing a large floppy hat for the same reason. We will both wear black gloves and our footwear will have the same pattern as the terrs'. We will be blacked up heavily too."

"Ja, and you will notice that we haven't shaved for a while either."

"What will you be carrying besides your weapons?" asked the OC.

"Plenty of spare magazines, a pistol and two waterbottles under the coats, and only Pronutro, no biltong, it'll make us too thirsty. We'll be travelling as light as possible."

"How are you going to get Tarzan out?"

"We are going to carry a cosh to stun the fucker. After we've dragged him out of town we'll make the bastard walk. Oh, we are going to need a set of those plastic handcuffs for him. Have we got any?"

"Yes, we have, but how are you going to get him out of town?"

"Ray has kindly volunteered to carry him," smiled Bruce.

"I'm sure you used a two-headed coin, you rat."

They went over the details time and again until they had picked it to pieces and put them back together again.

THE TRUCK DROPPED the three men off just after dark and they walked into the African night. They walked hard and they walked fast. Even so, they stopped often to listen — their survival would depend on it. They had no maps, but Michael led them unerringly towards the lying-up point. They had underestimated the distance and first light found them still walking towards the clump of bushes that would serve as both hiding place and shade during the hot day.

They arrived well after the sun was up and beginning to heat the ground, but they had kept their ears and eyes open. There was nothing; the only sign of life was a few birds going about their daily business before they, too, rested in the searing heat of the day.

The three men maintained a full alert for the first couple of hours, then went to one-on, two-off for the rest of the hot, still day. There was a moment of concern around mid-afternoon when a donkey-drawn scotchcart wandered listlessly past. Both driver and donkey looked nearly as lifeless as the surrounding countryside.

So, supplies were still trickling into the town but by the looks of the transport it would only be just that, a trickle. If the driver had bothered to look into the bushes fifty metres away, all he would have seen was three men lying very still, obviously asleep. He would not have noticed the six eyes peering at him keenly through slitted lids.

Just after four in the afternoon, Joseph came silently up to them.

"What is the news?"

"Tarzan is still staying at the same place."

"Any changes to his routine?"

"No, Ishe, it is still the same."

"That is good."

"Ishe?" said Joseph.

"Yes?"

"The one bodyguard of Comrade Tarzan, he is very big and he likes to fight."

Ray looked at Bruce: "I wish we had the luxury of a silenced pistol."

"Ja, we have our 9mm's with us, but unless there is plenty of noise around us it might give the game away."

Both men hated leaving such a tight operation with loose ends, but there was not much they could do except to take it as it came.

"Okay, we play it the way we have rehearsed for the time being. Michael, you and Joseph will go round to the window of Tarzan's house. If he does manage to escape out of the window, shoot him one time .. dead. You understand?"

"Yes." The two men grinned in anticipation.

"Ray, you and I will go straight to Tarzan's room and cosh him real good. I'll take out the bodyguards. I'm going to take a chance and use my 9mm. Joseph, are you sure he doesn't lock any of the doors?"

"There is no need to, he thinks he is safe with the Frelimo."

"Good. Now is there anything else before we go?"

"Ishe, there is much talk about this Muzorewa thing."

"What are they saying?"

"They are laughing about it. They say that they are going to go out and punish the people of Zimbabwe-Rhodesia for voting for him."

"That'd be right. Anything else?"

"I think they are going to send Tarzan out very soon."

"Right then, we'd better get him tonight, one way or the other."

They began walking. At 1730 hours, they heard the first sounds of a firefight, right on time. They kept walking until they came in sight of the township and stopped to observe for a while. Then Bruce delved into the canvas bag and turned the radio on. "Tango Kilo. REVLON."

"Roger," came the reply. The barrage started almost immediately.

IN MALVERNIA, THE ZANLA Sector Commander was briefing the assembled terrorist ranks in a long, low building.

He began by shouting the standard opening of all such gatherings. "Pamberi ne Mugabe" (Forward with Mugabe), to which the terrorists replied "Pamberi ne Mugabe. Then: "Pamberi ne ZANU PF" and "Pasi ne Muzorewa" (Down with Muzorewa), each phrase shouted back.

He continued: "Comrades, fellow freedom fighters. We have all heard how the running dog Muzorewa, that puppet stooge of the colonial racist oppressor Smith, is now the Prime Minister of the so-called Zimbabwe-Rhodesia." He spat on the ground for effect.

"The puppet Muzorewa has said that he is going to attack our camps in Mozambique and Zambia. Ha, the fool thinks we are going to just sit here and wait for him to kill us. The freedom fighters will all be gone when they arrive. But that does not concern us here. We have other things to do.

"While all their real fighting men are busy chasing their tails looking for our brave fighters, we are going to send in more and more of you groups. The country will only be guarded by their part-time soldiers so attacking their farms will be easy. Plus, as more and more of them are out looking for us, the more places we can attack. We will shortly be destroying their factories and fuel depots."

The Commander then briefed the men about their specific jobs and targets. He gave them dates, times, contact men in their designated sectors, and all the other details they would have to know. "Comrade Bazooka, you will be in charge of this detachment here."

Tarzan's chest filled with pride. Finally, he was a detachment commander. He was also very pleased with another aspect of his new command. He would give his subordinates the risky jobs. He himself would make sure he got the softer targets, the ones where he could carry out a bit of rape and murder, with negligible chance of any fighting back.

In the distance, small arms fire could be heard.

"Hmm they are starting early tonight," remarked one man.

"Right. Let's go to our safe places until it is finished."

The men filed out of the room and headed towards their places. Usually there was no great danger. These daily exchanges of fire were more of a nuisance than anything else. Even so, Tarzan felt uncomfortable and was happier staying in the house. He had chosen it with care, it was well shielded from the Rhodesians' fire by other buildings and a wall from the house next door.

His thinking had two flaws. It was easy to get at from the eastern side of town and it was fairly well concealed from the view of nosy neighbours. Another reason he had chosen it; he didn't want people to see the cruel games he played with the two women he kept.

He knew the only reason the women stayed with him was because they were scared stupid, a fact he thoroughly enjoyed. Plus, he fed them a bit extra. An important factor when most of the people in the town were hungry all the time. Being high up had its advantages, all right, like having the pick of everything that came in, including food.

Tarzan had been too busy with his thoughts to notice that only one of his bodyguards was with him, until he got inside the house.

"Where is Mpofu?" he demanded.

"I don't know, Comrade Bazooka. He went off somewhere."

"Well, he will feel my boot when he gets back." What was the point of having bodyguards if they didn't do their job?

Mpofu was big and strong, but slow-witted. He could be childishly happy one minute and a raging, angry bull the next. Mpofu had been doing a lot of sulking lately. There had been a definite lack of women in the town for some time. The ones that were there were all taken by bastards like Comrade Bazooka. Mpofu had his needs like everyone else. Lately it had been getting to him. If he didn't do something about it soon he would just have to take one of his master's women and be done with it.

A few days earlier Mpofu had noticed one of the young Frelimo soldiers looking at him. Normally, he wouldn't bother with men but he was getting desperate, so he pursued the matter. The boy was obviously interested, but playing coy and hard to get. Mpofu played the game and they courted.

That afternoon things had been developing nicely. He was too engrossed in the boy to notice that he should have been guarding his boss by now. He hardly noticed the daily exchange of fire that had been going on for some time. They boy was still playing hard to get when Mpofu reached the end of his patience. He threw the boy to the ground, ignoring his cry of pain and surprise. Mpofu stripped the boy's clothes off and roughly mounted him. He cried out again, this time in agony, but Mpofu was too far gone. He thrust himself wildly into the young body. In his excitement, he spent himself quickly.

As soon as he had calmed down, he realised the boy was sobbing. Gently, he put his arms round the boy's shoulders. The youngster turned to him and they lay together gently rocking to and fro. Mpofu made a promise to himself to be more patient and gentle next time.

It was some time before the big man realised it had become quite dark. Comrade Bazooka would be angry. What was more, the world around him was very noisy. Realising that this was a much bigger pounding than they had ever had before, he frantically pulled up his trousers and ran towards the house and the man he should be guarding.

Comrade Bazooka was crouching in the corner of the bedroom. He was scared, very scared. The flashes of artillery shells hitting Malvernia lit up the room almost continuously. The house rattled and shook with each explosion.

"This isn't supposed to be happening," he shouted aloud to himself. "They told us the Rhodesians wouldn't dare attack the town like this." He held his head in his hands as a shell landed uncomfortably close, showering the roof with dirt and rocks. "Where is that stupid baboon

Mpofu? He should be here." Somehow the big man's presence made him feel safe. In his anger and fear he lashed out at one of the two females crouching beside him. The open-handed slap banged her head against the wall as she tried to cover her face.

"Stupid fat cows. You are going to suffer for this when the noise stops," he snarled at them. He was just about to strike the woman again when he heard the front door opening. "Mpofu, is that you? Get in here you fat oaf! Get in here now," he screamed.

There was the sound of a scuffle and a sharp retort, followed by a gasp.

"Mpofu, what is it? What is going on?" Tarzan screamed at the door. The door banged open and a scruffy-looking man stood in the frame, his silhouette backlit from the flashes.

"Who is it? What do you want?" Tarzan screamed. "Mpofu."

At the last moment, he tried to scramble on to the bed to leap through the window, but tripped on the bed frame. Then he felt heavy blows rain on his head and shoulders. He tried to cover his head but the blows kept coming. He was only just conscious when the blows stopped and his assailant was flung from him.

FROM A DISTANCE Mpofu saw two men go into the house. He ran faster. He was not aware of the other two round the far side of the building. As soon as he got inside he saw two things simultaneously. One man was coming out of the room used by himself and the other guard. The man had a pistol in his hand. The door to Comrade Bazooka's room was open and he could clearly see a scuffle going on. For a slow-witted man, Mpofu thought fast. He knew the immediate danger was the man in front of him, but he knew he must get to Tarzan quickly. He charged towards the man holding the pistol and swung a huge arm towards his head.

AS SOON AS the small arms fire intensified and the shelling started in earnest, the four men loped into the outskirts of town and began ducking and weaving their way through the streets. The dodging was not put on, the chance of being hit was real enough.

"I hope our guys are aiming high," Ray said to Bruce Watson as they took shelter behind a building.

The town, once charming and colourful was now a dirty, scruffy tribute to Frelimo and ZANLA, a fortified dump of fear and mistrust.

They followed Michael and Joseph up the street to the house. The two Africans disappeared round the side. Bruce and Ray opened the front door and walked in. It was important not to rush. They located their assigned bedroom doors and charged at the same time.

Bruce's door burst in and he took aim at where the big man should have been ... nothing. Panic started to rise in his throat. The other bodyguard was hiding under the bed; he tried to stand up, terrified. Bruce swivelled towards him and shot the man in the chest as he was reaching for his rifle. He went down. Bruce turned, moving towards the open door, when Mpofu ran in, a massive arm raised to strike.

For a vital second, Bruce was confused, then the man was on him. Mpofu's huge fist struck Bruce on the side of the head, but luckily his pistol went off — the barrel pushed into the man's vast body. Bruce was sent flying across the room, stunned and barely conscious. Mpofu staggered back a few paces, shock registering on his face.

The big man was tough and his only thought was to save Tarzan. He charged through the door to see Ray battering Comrade Bazooka. He bounded across the room and flung Ray off his master.

He glanced to see if Comrade Bazooka was still alive before bounding towards Ray, who was attempting to get to his feet. For such a big man Mpofu moved fast. A mighty kick to the body sent Ray sprawling again.

Mpofu was astride him now. He grabbed the Sergeant's shirt, flipped him over and raised his clasped hands ready for a hammer-like blow which would surely crush Ray's sternum and ribs. Just then, a flash from a bursting shell highlighted the amulet Jason Ncube had given the white man.

The blow froze in mid-air. There was powerful magic in that amulet. Mpofu lurched back in confusion. Whoever had given the man on the floor that charm was obviously a medicine man and a feared medicine man from the look of the amulet. Mpofu began to feel tired. Bruce's bullet had gone deep into his internal organs and he was fading fast. Fear and pain was written on the huge man's face. "A black man's medicine on a white man who was trying to kill a comrade", it was all too much he thought.

Bruce crawled all round the door, dazed and hurting. He saw Mpofu kneeling astride the inert body of his Sergeant. Slowly... ever so slowly, he raised his pistol and squeezed the trigger twice. The bullets slapped into the giant body, seemingly without effect. Then with a gentle, almost feminine, sigh Mpofu toppled over and hit the floor with a loud thud. He was quite dead.

Bruce crawled over to Ray, who was trying with only limited success to draw oxygen into his lungs while frantically pointing towards the bed. Tarzan was halfway out the window. Bruce staggered to him and pulled at his waistband until he fell back on the bed. The Captain picked up the cosh and with a sickening thud laid the terrorist unconscious.

It took several long moments for the RLI men to realise there were two women crouching in the corner, sobbing hysterically.

"NYARARA — be quiet," Bruce shouted in Shona. "Do you also want to be killed?" He put his finger to his lips. It had the desired effect — they instantly fell silent, though their eyes were still wide with terror.

A mortar erupted nearby.

"Quick mate ... get the cuffs on that pile of shit," Ray said painfully as he dug the plastic constraints out of his pocket.

Getting the unconscious terrorist out of town was not as easy as they had anticipated due to the condition of both white men. They took it in turns between the four of them. Even so, the task took a long time. At one stage Tarzan regained consciousness and started struggling, so Ray slugged him again.

Bashing the man was very therapeutic. "Don't want him alerting his mates," Ray said as he slipped the cosh back into his coat pocket.

Later, when they had well and truly cleared town, Bruce gave the all clear on the radio and they stopped for a rest.

Tarzan came to and started bleating.

Ray showed him the cosh. "Now listen here, old china. You are now our prisoner. It would be better if you come along willingly, or we will just have to keep bopping you with this, okay?"

Even so, Tarzan stumbled about and made a good show of holding up the march. He was stalling for time, hoping his friends would follow up. Eventually, Joseph took out his knife.

"I will show this hyena a good reason to walk quickly. I will start by cutting off his muchendes, then his mboro." He pulled Tarzan's trousers down swiftly, grabbed his surprisingly small balls and penis and put the knife blade against them.

"NO! NO! Please, don't do it. I will walk," he pleaded.

"You just remember this, comrade. The next time you don't feel like keeping up with us, you will have to squat to piss, like a woman," grinned Joseph.

Tarzan was no trouble after that. They walked on in silence for most of the night. By now, Bruce's "Tango Kilo GREEN APPLES" message had been transmitted and the Rhodesian artillery's barrage had ceased. Desultory small arms fire could be heard to their rear, indicating that Frelimo and ZANLA were still shooting at shadows.

"Who are you? What do you want with me?" Tarzan had asked the question several times now. It was not far off daylight. There was no answer. Tarzan's mind was working frantically, trying to find a way out of his predicament. Who were these men? What were white men doing dressed in the clothes of the comrades. He knew the Selous Scouts did this sort of thing. His mind was in a whirl. He knew the Scouts often tried to get the boys to change sides after they were captured. If that was the case, he might have a chance. It would be better to change sides and live than be put in jail and hanged.

"Are you Skuz'apo?"

There was no reply.

But Captain Watson was thinking. "Yes, we are Skuz'apo," he said eventually.

"Ah, in that case I would be quite willing to change sides; I can give you a lot of information about the freedom fighters."

"There is a lot we want to know, Tarzan," came the reply.

"I will tell you all you want to know."

With that, Tarzan poured out his soul. He sang like a bird. By the time the Alouette arrived at first light to pick them up, they wished he would shut up.

The helicopter didn't take them back to Malapati, instead it put them down some kilometres away in a large clearing.

Major Hill had recalled the Special Branch man. Soon, he had more information than he could have dreamed of. Tarzan was a gold mine. A lot of terrorists would be stopped in their tracks.

"Right, I have all I want from him now. We can get him off to jail," the Inspector said with a satisfied smile. "You blokes did a bloody good job, even if it was a tad ... ah... unorthodox."

"Inspector, what will happen to him now?" Ray asked innocently.

"Well, he will be tried and, I imagine, hung," replied the policeman.

"He will definitely hang?"

"I wish I was as sure of winning the lottery."

"We have a special request to make," Bruce added.

The Inspector frowned, he didn't like the look in the men's eyes.

"We have a man who is anxious to meet him, that's all."

"I can't just let people do what they want. I have a job to do."

"C'mon, Inspector, think about it. This war is continuing when it should have been over weeks ago. Now, is that playing cricket? Of course it's not. What do you think will happen to Tarzan if Nkomo or Mugabe get into power before you put him away and string him up? He will get off, that's what. He will be one of the people who dictate to you when the country goes black. Instead of being a criminal he will be a politician, and he'll tell you what to do."

The argument went on for 10 minutes. Against his will, the policeman gave in. "What is going to happen to him?"

"Just write in your report 'shot while trying to escape'."

"I don't want to know about it."

"Okay, why don't you get a chopper ride back to the airstrip and we will get a truck to pick us up later."

"Okay, but I don't like this one bit. I've a good mind to change my mind."

The two men hurried the Inspector to the helicopter. "Bill, take the Inspector back to Malapati, will you," said Bruce.

"Trooper. Over here," said Ray to a young man. "I want you to stand guard while we question the terrorist a bit more."

They walked over to where Tarzan was sitting under the tree. Michael and Joseph were sitting next to him, grinning wickedly.

"What is going on? Why wasn't I on that helicopter? Why am I still tied up here?" Tarzan wailed.

"We will let you go shortly, comrade. But first we have to ask you some more questions," Ray lied.

"I have told you all I know," said Tarzan sulkily.

"Yes, but we need to know a bit more about that farmhouse you attacked the year before last, that one near Mount Darwin."

"I told you all about that, too."

"Was it you personally who shot the man and raped his wife?"

"I have already told you. Yes, I shot the man and I raped the girl. I did not rape the older woman, some of the others did that."

"How did you kill them?"

"I beat them to death. I have already told you. Can I go now?"

"What was the name of the family."

"You know who it was. The Van Zyls."

"Do you know where the Van Zyl's son is?"

"No, I don't. He wasn't there."

"See this man here, Tarzan... his name is Van Zyl... he is the son of the family you killed. He is going to guard you now while we go and rest."

"NO! NO!" Tarzan shouted. His eyes shot open, there was real fear in them now. There was a sudden spurt of liquid between his legs, from both orifices. "NO! NO!.. please, you promised. I told you everything. I will change sides. Please, please."

"See you, Comrade Bazooka," said Ray as they turned to go.

"I don't think so," added Bruce as they walked away with their rifles on their shoulders.

The screams started soon after.

Beyond a small ridge, Ray picked up the radio. "Zero Alpha, Tango Kilo. Could you send a truck for us?"

"Roger. Do you still have your prisoner?"

"Negative. He tried to escape."

"I presume he is dead. Where's the body?"

"I believe the hyenas have got him."

THE COMMANDO WAS paraded by the airstrip again. Major Hill addressed the troops. "Well done guys. In the last ten weeks we have forced not only the terrorists to vacate Malvernia, but Frelimo as well. The place is now a ghost town. The top brass calculated it would take several months. You boys did the impossible, with only minimal support. Not many armies would ask that, but we did and you came up with the goods. I have a message from the top. It reads 'Congratulations to the brave men of One Commando. You have the sincere thanks of your country. Well done'."

"Well, you know how it is with us RLI okes, sir. The difficult takes a short while, the impossible just takes a little longer," remarked one Corporal dryly.

The Commando cheered.

The OC smiled, but his smile was sad. "Now for the bad news .... we are not going on leave, we have more work to do."

There was a loud moan from the troops.

"Okay, you blokes have earned a spot of leave. Heaven knows you deserve it. But Muzorewa had decreed that we hit the enemy and we hit them hard. To put it into simple words, 'if the gooks want a shit fight, then we'll give 'em one' is what I think he is trying to say."

There was a half-hearted laugh from the men.

"Some way to the north of here, there is a belt of inhabited area, most of it farmland. What we are going to do is create an area of wasteland on the other side of the border. We are going to wipe out anything that can be used or eaten by the Charlie Tangos .... a shit of a job and one that I know most of you will not want to do. But we have been ordered."

The Major stood in silence for a second. "For the last ten weeks, I have asked you to go into hell. Not once but several times. This you have done uncomplainingly. Now I am asking you to go back there."

"That's not too much of a problem, sir," said the Corporal, this time with respect in his voice. "If YOU want us to go back there, we'll go."

"Hear, hear," said Sergeant Thomas.

"Thanks, ouns," the Major said quietly.

BACK INTO HELL they went, but this was a hell of their own making.

199

For three weeks inside Mozambique, the three groups walked and walked; they burned and killed and walked and burned and killed. Everywhere they went, black pillars of smoke from terrorist camps and caches reached up into the heavens while the stench of death reached down into their souls. The Devil walked behind them in respectful silence. Satan was no longer the master of this hell on Earth — One Commando of the Rhodesian Light Infantry had taken over. They walked and burned and fought for what seemed a thousand years until the job was done.

The filthy, exhausted men crossed back into Rhodesia to the mammoth task of cleaning up, ready for the long overdue leave. In other parts of the country, the other RLI Commandos, "C" Squadron of the Rhodesian SAS, and any unit which could be carried by helicopter or dropped by parachute, were busy attacking camps all over Zambia and Mozambique.

It was the death throes of a nation. Zimbabwe-Rhodesia was going down fighting with every breath it had left. The terrorists were hurting badly but for every camp that disappeared, another sprang up in its place. There were simply too many of the enemy. They outnumbered the Rhodesians nearly eight to one.

JOSHUA NKOMO WAS putting his army on a conventional war footing. His ultimate aim was a direct attack on Zimbabwe-Rhodesia. He might have succeeded had the SAS and Selous Scouts not destroyed every bridge that could be used to get his vast army to the border with Zambia. The invasion never got off the drawing board.

The country ground its way inexorably towards total black rule, even as its defences were being held — albeit tenuously — by a small, valiant security force.

However, what Zimbabwe-Rhodesia maintained with sheer blood and sweat was being rapidly eroded, not by lack of military effort, but by the internal and external politicians and the results of fourteen years of sanctions.

After so long, the country was weary of hardship and bitterness. They were tired of the pain and anguish. It was time for peace.

CHAPTER FOURTEEN

FIRE FORCE OPERATIONS and external raids continued for a time until the Lancaster House agreement between the warring parties led to a ceasefire in December, 1979.

A monitoring force comprising many nations arrived in the country to oversee the "new elections". Vast assembly areas were set up to accommodate the estimated 50,000 "guerillas" expected to flood into the country from Mozambique and Zambia. In terms of the Lancaster House Agreement, both the ZANLA and ZIPRA forces, for the time being united under the "Patriotic Front" banner, were supposed to be confined to these points until after the elections on March 3, 1980.

The British Government believed it had the perfect plan to establish a stable coalition government in an internationally recognised Zimbabwe. And it didn't include the ultimate winner, Robert Mugabe. The belief was that Joshua Nkomo's ZAPU faction would win enough seats in the new 100-seat parliament to warrant the senior position in a coalition which would also contain 20 constitutionally-entrenched white seats and several dozen for Bishop Abel Muzorewa's UANC party.

Neither the British nor, ironically, the Rhodesians for all their knowledge of Africa, had grasped the basic concept of African rule. While the Rhodesian authorities complained bitterly, they were unable to convince the newly installed temporary British governor, Lord Soames, that wholesale intimidation was being conducted by Mugabe's men in the rural areas where eighty percent of the voters lived. This intimidation was brutal, widespread and very, very effective. It was later estimated, and corroborated by several ZANLA officers, that up to sixty per cent of all "guerillas" in the Assembly Points were, in fact, "mujibas" — local youths armed with rusting, unworkable weapons.

This gave the impression that PF forces were abiding by the rules, while in reality the hardened men of the terrorist ranks were in the field doing what they knew best — coercing simple peasants into voting the "right way".

By permitting the intimidation to continue, the British lost control of events and out-smarted themselves. When the results were announced, Mugabe had swept the board with 57 of the available 80 unreserved seats.

As one German observer put it: "If that was a free and fair election, I am a Chinaman."

The people who really lost out were not the whites, but the Africans themselves. At no time were they ever given a real say in what they wanted; rather, they were told what they would get. True, they were given the right to vote, but that one vote put them under a much harsher yoke than the white men ever did.

"One man, one vote is what the people want," the slogan went. One man, one vote is all the majority of the population has really received since that day in March, 1980. In the 16 years since Zimbabwe was born, the country has still been a de facto One-Party state; with the now-President Mugabe listed as the 11th richest man in the world.

THE WAR WAS now officially over. The RLI and the SAS struck their colours and sent them down to South Africa. The two units ceased to exist.

The Selous Scouts had become extinct a few months earlier. Its members had been badged to other regiments to avoid the violent recriminations that would follow. Any mention of them, except in the state-controlled press, was banned by the new order.

Three magnificent units, each unique in its own way, simply vanished into the air. Gone with the winds of change. Many men from these regiments drifted to South Africa and joined that country's defence forces; broken in spirit, but sticking as far as possible to each other in the brotherhood.

Sergeant Hunter, now Ray Hunter, civilian, stayed on in Zimbabwe for a while; waiting partly for the small commutable pension that Mugabe had been forced to honour as a condition of the settlement. He was owed plenty of back pay and holiday remuneration.

There was another reason he stayed; he had not seen or heard from Jason for a long time, although he had heard Ncube received a minor post in the new government.

After a month's holiday at Kariba and Wankie National Park, he returned to Harare; soon to be the new name of the capital city. Ray mooched about, spending too much time in the pubs, looking for he knew not what.

One day, as he was sitting in a bar in town, an African sidled up to him.

"I see you, Isizo." The man was a stranger but Ray knew he had come with a message.

"Can I buy you a beer, my friend?" Ray asked.

"There is no time for that. There is a man who must see you and he asks that you hurry. There is not much time."

Ray knew it must be urgent for an African not to observe the normal niceties. He followed him out into the street and they climbed into a taxi waiting on the corner. There were no words between the two as the taxi drove through the streets to a township on the road to the eastern highlands.

After what seemed an eternity, the taxi pulled up in a rough area full of corrugated-iron houses. Houses that had not been there for long.

"Follow me," the African said. He led Ray along dusty, windy streets. As they rounded a corner, Ray heard several shots being fired; they raced towards the sounds, just in time to see two men running away from a house. They dashed into it.

Inside, Jason was slumped on the floor, blood pouring from many wounds. Ray rushed over to him. Jason tried to rise, but the effort was too great. "I see you Isizo," he greeted weakly.

"I see you, Jason Ncube." Ray was beside him, trying to stem the flow of blood.

"I think it is too late for that," Jason smiled. "they have won, my friend," he said, clasping Ray's hand.

"Who was it?"

"Mugabe's men. They are killing us Matabele — eliminating as much opposition as they can. They don't want to share power."

Ray forced a smile: "That is not considered constitutionally correct, old chap."

Jason's voice was becoming feeble. "We have lost, my friend. I wanted to believe that we could share this country, black and white. I wanted to believe that there was a future, where we could have learned from each other and gone ahead to make a good country. We have lost that. This will be no better than the other African countries, with one dictator and a crumbling economy."

"Did you ever really believe that, Jason?"

"I had hoped, Isizo."

"We white boys have a saying, 'If you take a country by force, you will have to keep it by force'. That is exactly what Mugabe is doing."

"Yes, he is murdering as many of us as he can, so there won't be enough power to oppose him. We have sent warnings but it is too late, he is getting to us."

There was a heart-breaking silence for a while, before Jason looked up. "Raymond Hunter."

Ray stared hard at the dying man; he had not been called Raymond for many years.

"I had an uncle in Kenya during the Mau Mau. He was part of the gang that killed your parents."

Ray's eyes flashed.

"You have a right to be angry, Isizo," he said.

That cold, icy stare that had frightened so many people bored into Jason's eyes.

"You would have only been a boy then," he said.

"That is correct. So this is what all the magic nonsense was about."

"If you think back, Isizo, was it nonsense?"

Ray blinked furiously. The anger was gone.

"We could have been good friends, you and I," Jason said; his voice now barely audible.

"Yes, we could have been, given the chance."

"You had better go now, my brother, before you are also killed."

The clasped each other's hands tightly.

"Go in peace, Isizo."

"Go in peace, Jason Ncube."

Ray stayed until the lights went out in Jason's eyes.

"Rest in peace, my brother."

As he walked through the door, he turned to face his former enemy one last time. "Yes, they have won, haven't they?"

THE TEARS WERE to no avail.

"Why can't you stay in the country? There will be plenty of work for people like you. You could get a job as a park ranger. Anything like that."

Bridget was not prepared to leave the country of her birth, but Ray would not — could not — stay in a country he felt had betrayed its people. It might be legal in the eyes of the world but in his eyes the morality was wrong, so to him it was illegal. There was nothing here for him any more.

"Where will you go?"

"London, for a start."

"What will you do?"

"I don't know."

He didn't really care, either. He wasn't interested. He just wanted to leave. It would take him a while to come to grips with the betrayal he felt; not just with the country, but with the interference from other people.

If the country had been left alone to sort out its own problems, there was a chance it could have worked; a chance to show the world that two peoples from different races could work together and progress. That was gone now, so he was going too.

Ray looked back as he was about to board the plane. Bridget was waving tearfully from the balcony. He returned the wave. For some reason, at that moment he thought of the poster that had hung on the orderly room wall at the One Commando barracks. It proclaimed: "Fighting for peace is like fucking for virginity.'

He laughed out loud, making his fellow passengers stare in amazement. Perhaps all that was needed to survive in this world was a sense of humour.

THE AIR HOSTESS on the flight from Johannesburg to London had noticed the stocky man in seat 12B. He looked as though he had seen the rough side of life; the lines etched on his face testimony to that. She took in the eyes which could be dangerous or kind — as the owner chose. He wasn't young any more but he had a toughness she found attractive. She smiled at him a few times during the long haul.

RAY ENDURED THE questions of the immigration officer at Gatwick.

"What were you doing in Zimbabwe, Mr Hunter?"

"I was a maintenance diver on the Kariba Dam wall."

"Have you any proof of that, sir?"

Ray dug out a forged reference, typed for him by a friend who had done some diving work. He had heard it was possible to receive a jail sentence if they knew one had been a "mercenary" in Rhodesia.

"We haven't heard of this firm, Mr Hunter, it is not on the files."

"They went bankrupt a few months ago."

In the end, they let him go.

He left the checkpoint to merge with countless others, just one among thousands of nameless faces.

For the first time since his childhood he felt alone — a nobody — a nobody with no direction.

As he walked outside Terminal Three into the cold London air, he noticed an air hostess at the taxi rank, smiling at him; she was the one from his flight.

"Are you new to London, Mr Ah ..?"

"Hunter. Ray Hunter," he replied.

"Do you want to share a lift?"

Perhaps life wasn't going to be that bad, after all.

THE END

AA	Anti-Aircraft guns
BAAS	Afrikaans for "Boss"
BERGEN	Military pack
BILTONG	Dried strips of meat
BOERS	Self-descriptive term used by Afrikaners for their people (of Dutch/Huguenot descent). Used as derogative by terrorists to include all white "settlers" in Rhodesia
BWANA	Respectful term for European man
CADRE	Expression used by CTs for group of own fighters
CASEVAC	Casualty Evacuation (usually by helicopter)
CHARLIE TANGO	Phonetic spelling of the first two letters of Communist Terrorist (also gooks, terrs etc)
CHIBULI/DOP	Slang for beer
CLAYMORE	Portable anti-personnel explosive device
COMOPS	Combined Operations (Rhodesian Military Command)
COMRADE	Expression used by CTs for member of Cadre
CONTACT	Firefight or skirmish between opposing forces in bush
DAK	Dakota aircraft
DOPPIE	Spent cartridge case
EK SE!	Afrikaans for "I say!"
FAF	Forward Air Field (Fire Force base)
FRANTAN	Rhodesian-manufactured napalm
FREDS	Frelimo (Mozambique Army)
GOMO	Mountain or hill
GOOK/FLOPPY/	Terrorists
GRAZE	Eat or food
IA	Immediate action
INDABA	Meeting or talk
ISHE	"Lord" term for respected elder)
JAMBO	Swahili for "Hello"
KAFFIR/MUNT	Derogatory terms for black Africans
KIA	Killed in Action
KOPJE	Small hill
KRAAL	Rural village
LEKKER	Good or nice
LONG	Many or lots. Can also mean good
MDALA	Old man
MEMSAHIB	Respectful Swahili term for European woman
MFAZI	Woman/wife

MUJIBA	Young, mainly herdboys used as lookouts by CTs
MUTI	Traditional medicine
NDEGE	Aircraft.
NKOSI	"Master"
OC/SUNRAY	Officer Commanding
OP	Observation post
OUN/OKE	Person
OUNS/OKES	Collective words for group of people
PANGA	Machete
PARAS	Paratroopers
PV	Protected Village – kraals concentrated behind wire to deny support to terrorists
PJI	Parachute jump instructor
RBC	Rhodesia Broadcasting Corporation (Radio & TV)
RECCE	Reconnaissance. Preliminary study of enemy positions prior to attack
RF	Rhodesian Front – party led by Ian Smith
R & R	"Rest and Recuperation" (short leave)
ROIINEK	Afrikaans for "Red Neck" — friendly expression for people of English stock
SB	Special Branch of BSAP
SCHEME	Think. "I scheme I'll see the boss about the graze"
SCHOLLIES	Rascals, bad boys
SHAMWARI	Friend
SHATEEN/BUNDU KUNGEN	The bush
SHUMBA	'Lion' brand beer
SITREP	Situation Report
SPOOR	Tracks
2IC	Second in command
TUNE	Explain or tell. "I scheme I'll go and tune the boss about the graze"
TTL	Tribal Trust Land set aside as black reserve
UANC	United African National Council – party formed by Bishop Muzorewa to fight election
WO	Warrant Officer
ZANLA	Zimbabwe African National Liberation Army – Mugabe's Chinese-backed faction
ZANU (PF)	Zimbabwe African National Union (Patriotic Front) – party formed by Mugabe to fight election; still in power in the country
ZAPU	Zimbabwe African People's Union mainly — political precursor to ZANLA and ZIPRA
ZIPRA	Zimbabwe People's Republic Army – Nkomo's Russian-backed faction

A BRIEF HISTORY OF THE RHODESIAN ARMY
by Richard Allport

THE BEGINNINGS OF the Rhodesian Army go back to 29 October, 1889, when a Royal Charter was granted by Queen Victoria to Cecil John Rhodes' British South Africa Company, authorising it to raise a police force for the territories that were intended to come under its control north of the Limpopo River.

One hundred men were enrolled initially, almost entirely from the BBP (Bechuanaland Border Police), to accompany the Pioneer Column and this force was officially designated the "British South Africa Company Police". For the march into Mashonaland this number was later increased to 500.

By 1892, a couple of years after the successful occupation of Mashonaland, the number of men in the force had decreased and the BSACP was replaced by a number of volunteer forces — the Mashonaland Horse, the Mashonaland Mounted Police and the Mashonaland Constabulary.

The peace did not last for long, however, and the outbreak of the Matabele War in 1893 saw the total number of volunteers for police service rise to about 1000 men in a number of new units — the Salisbury Horse, Victoria Rangers and Raaf's Rangers. With the assistance of the BBP the power of the Matabele was broken in a three-month campaign in which the most memorable event was the last stand of the 34 men of the Shangani Patrol. Cornered by a large Matabele force near the banks of the Shangani River, the patrol had no option but to fight to the last man, refusing to surrender. The battle lasted from sunrise to sunset when the Matabele paid tribute to the bravery of the men of the patrol.

The volunteer regiments were disbanded in December 1893 and a new force named the Rhodesia Horse was formed. For the policing of Matabeleland another force named the Matabeleland Mounted Police was raised.

Many of the police accompanied Dr Jameson on his raid into the Transvaal in 1895 to help the Englishmen who were rebelling against the Boer government there. The raid failed and Jameson and his men were all captured. The raid, having left the colony almost undefended, led indirectly to the Mashona and Matabele Rebellions in 1896.

The fighting lasted until 1898, with British troops arriving from Natal and the Cape to help the beleaguered colonists. The two forces of police were amalgamated into the Rhodesia Mounted Police and in 1909, much expanded, this force became known as the British South Africa Police (BSAP), the name it was to retain until 1980.

The population of the territory increased rapidly and a purely military force, as opposed to police, was raised in 1898 and called the Southern Rhodesia Volunteers (SRV). This unit was divided into an Eastern Division, based in Salisbury, and a Western Division, based in Bulawayo.

The SRV served in the Boer War and took part in the relief of Mafeking, where a division of the BSAP were among the defenders. A new unit, the Rhodesia Regiment, was also formed at this time, mainly for the defence of Rhodesia, but this unit was also sent to serve in the Boer War.

With the end of the Boer War, a fledgling Rhodesian Army was in being, based on the British Army, and the first King's Colour and Regimental Colour were awarded to the SRV.

The original Rhodesia Regiment had been disbanded shortly after the siege of Mafeking, but the unit was revived in 1914 to form two regiments to fight alongside the Commonwealth troops in South West Africa and East Africa (and later in France) during the First World War. The Rhodesia Native Regiment, which was formed at the same time, earned the battle honour "East Africa 1916-1918", this honour later being transferred to the Rhodesian African Rifles, which later absorbed the RNR. The Rhodesia Regiments were also awarded their first battle honours.

The Southern Rhodesia Volunteers were disbanded in 1920, although a few rifle companies were retained in each of the main towns. The Defence Act of 1927 finally created a Permanent Force and a Territorial Force for the colony, although little progress was made in the period up to 1939, at which time the police were finally separated from the military, and conscription for the latter introduced.

The war years of 1939-1945 saw the rapid expansion of the Rhodesian armed forces, with the addition of a number of full-time units, including the 1st Battalion RAR, an artillery unit, an armoured car unit, and training schools in Gwelo and Umtali. Rhodesians served in many British units during the war and supplied three squadrons to the RAF. After the war, the King conferred the title of "Royal" on the Rhodesia Regiment.

In 1951 a volunteer group called the "C" (Rhodesia) Squadron, 22 Special Air Services Regiment (Malayan Scouts) was raised for service with the Commonwealth troops in Malaya, and in 1952 Rhodesia again supplied troops for service abroad in the Suez Canal zone.

During the period of Federation, the army was totally reorganised and each corps now received the prefix "Rhodesia and Nyasaland". In 1955 units of the RAR were sent to Malaya to replace the Northern Rhodesia Regiment serving there. It was also during this period that the Rhodesian Air Force finally became established as a separate service with its own HQ. In 1961, a unit was formed that would later to play an important role in the bush war of the 1970s, namely the 1st Battalion, The Rhodesian Light Infantry.

With the break-up of Federation in 1964 the army again underwent a large-scale reorganisation, with the units reverting to their original territories, two of which had now gained independence from Britain.

Southern Rhodesia took matters into its own hands in 1965 with its "Unilateral Declaration of Independence" (UDI), signalling the start of a prolonged effort by communist-supported guerillas to force the whites to relinquish power.

From April 1966 onwards groups of guerillas infiltrated Rhodesia from neighbouring Zambia in steadily increasing numbers, but the bush war is generally considered to have started in earnest on 21 December 1972 when an attack took place on a farm in the Centenary District, with further attacks on other farms in the following days.

As the guerilla activity increased in 1973, "Operation Hurricane" started and the military prepared itself for war. During 1974 a major effort by the security forces resulted in many guerillas being killed and the number inside the country reduced to fewer than 100.

The year 1974 also saw the fall of Portuguese rule in Mozambique and the eventual opening of a second "front" in the bush war, necessitating the creation and expansion of a number of specialist units. The Selous Scouts, named after Rhodesia's most famous big game hunter, was a mostly black unit which conducted a highly successful clandestine war against the guerillas by posing as guerillas themselves.

Their unrivalled tracking abilities, survival and COIN (Counter Insurgency) skills made them one of the most feared and hated of the army units. Another new unit, the Grey's Scouts, reintroduced cavalry into the Rhodesian Army, forming a highly mobile and aggressive unit which could follow the enemy into otherwise inaccessible areas with greater speed than infantry. A ceasefire in

1974 gave the guerillas time to regroup and resupply, but produced no political solution to the war.

In 1976 Operations "Thrasher" and "Repulse" started in order to contain the ever-increasing influx of guerillas. At the same time rivalry between the two main guerilla factions increased and resulted in open fighting in the training camps in Tanzania, with more than 600 deaths. The Soviets increased their influence and began to take a more active role in the training and control of the ZIPRA guerillas. New tactics were developed on both sides.

Perhaps too late, the Rhodesians decided to take the war to the enemy, and cross-border operations, which had started in 1976 with a raid on a major base in Mozambique in which the Rhodesians had killed more than 1200 guerillas and captured huge amounts of weapons, were stepped up. Attacks on large guerilla camps such as Chimoio and Tembue resulted in thousands of guerilla deaths and the capture of supplies sorely needed by the Rhodesians. In 1979 as the war increased even more in intensity, the Rhodesian army was able to take delivery of eight T54/55 heavy tanks which the South Africans had confiscated from a Libyan freighter when it mistakenly docked at Durban while en route to Tanzania.

In 1978 the Rhodesian Air Force launched the daring "Green Leader" attack on a ZIPRA camp outside Lusaka, the Rhodesian fighter aircraft completely taking over Zambian air space for the duration of the raid. In September the guerillas again took the offensive by shooting down a Rhodesian airliner with a SAM-7 missile. Eighteen civilians who survived the crash were subsequently massacred at the crash site by ZIPRA guerillas, increasing calls for massive retaliation by the Rhodesian security forces.

In 1979 another airliner was shot down and the Rhodesians launched more raids on guerilla bases, successfully avoiding air-defence systems and the Soviet MiG-17s based in Mozambique. A raid was made by the SAS and the Selous Scouts on the ZIPRA HQ in Lusaka, where they narrowly missed being able to kill the ZIPRA leader, Joshua Nkomo.

Towards the end of 1979 talks had begun at Lancaster House in England, with both sides seriously interested in stopping the war, but Rhodesian cross-border raids continued in the meantime, hitting supply lines, strategic bridges and railways in an effort to convince Zambia and Mozambique to put pressure on the guerilla leaders to end the war. Rhodesian losses in men and aircraft were increasing, whereas the supply of equipment and recruits to the guerillas seemed endless.

By the end of 1979 it was becoming obvious that the Rhodesians would be unable to bring the war to a speedy end, despite the fact that their troops were winning every battle and skirmish they engaged in, and that the guerillas had not yet "liberated" any part of the country.

A political agreement was finally signed in December 1979, and new elections took place. Commonwealth troops monitored the proceedings, but for a while it seemed that the Rhodesian army, still in control, might stage a coup to prevent a Marxist takeover, with troops and tanks on standby at strategic points in the capital. When it became clear that ZANU leader Robert Mugabe had won a decisive victory at the polls, however, the military reluctantly accepted that there was no point in resuming the war and a new crisis was avoided.

The first year of Independence saw the dissolution of the Rhodesian security forces as the agreement to integrate the former guerillas into the regular army was implemented. Lack of discipline among the guerillas caused problems, but the major cause of friction was the fact that the two main guerilla groups distrusted each other and formed their own rival "camps" in the army. When ZANU introduced the "Fifth Brigade", a new unit trained by North Koreans and loyal only to Mugabe, which later gained a reputation for killing up to 7,000 civilians in Matabeleland, the writing was on the wall for the army as the Rhodesians had known it.

The Commander, Lt. Gen. Peter Walls, was dismissed by Mugabe, and as the traditional British-style discipline broke down in the army, many whites left the country. In the course of 1980 most of the front-line units were disbanded or simply faded away. Disillusionment among the troops was great and the departure of many men to find employment elsewhere contributed to the lack of ceremonial disbandment of some of the units.

The prime example of the fading away of a unit was the case of the Selous Scouts. Because of their clandestine operations and since many of their troops were ex-guerillas who had been "turned", it was not surprising that after the election an order was immediately given for the Scouts to dispose of their regimental insignia and wear other badges instead. Many Scouts elected to disappear over the border, taking their weapons with them. The majority eventually enlisted in the South African Defence Force in comparable elite units, such as the "Recces". There was no parade and no public acknowledgment of their services to their country. Their regimental standard was taken across the border and in 1990 was laid up at Phalaborwa in the unit chapel of the SADF's 5 Recce Regiment where it remains.

The RLI was officially disbanded on 25 July 1980 at a last parade before a small crowd, with the troops that had constituted the most formidable unit of fighting men in Rhodesia marching past their War Memorial — the "Trooper" statue. The Roll of Honour was read out and the bagpipes played "Last Post". The regimental colour was marched past for the last time, and three days later the Trooper statue was dismantled and spirited away to South Africa along with the rest of the regimental memorabilia. It now resides in a South African museum.

The Rhodesian SAS also held a simple flag-lowering ceremony and then mounted their last top-secret operation, in which they smuggled their 25-ton plinth across the border to South Africa for safekeeping.

The RAR, composed mainly of black troops, was the only unit not disbanded in 1980. Because of the rivalry between the guerilla factions, it was fortunate for the new government that the highly-disciplined troops of the RAR remained on hand. In November full-scale fighting broke out between the rival guerilla groups near Bulawayo with over 500 casualties, and ironically it was the RAR — his former enemy — that Mugabe sent in to quell the fighting among his and Nkomo's own former guerillas. In February 1981 fighting again broke out, this time involving more than 10,000 ex-guerillas. The RAR, which Mugabe had now wanted disbanded, was again sent in to separate the combatants, which they did very efficiently. By December, however, the situation in the Zimbabwe military had deteriorated and many troopers left the RAR, rendering it largely ineffective. On 31 December the order was given to integrate the remainder of the RAR with other units and the last remnants of the Rhodesian Army faded away.

Extract from "RHODESIAN INSURGENCY " by Professor J.R.T. Wood

THE BRITISH DROVE through their solution. Most difficult to arrange was a ceasefire, but in the end a plan for the gathering of the insurgents into assembly points and the monitoring of them by a British-led and dominated Commonwealth force was accepted. Until a government had been elected, a governor, Lord Soames, was to exercise executive and legislative power. Smith predicted that the outcome would be a transference of power to Mugabe. The British and everyone else pinned their hopes on a hung election and a   coalition which would feature Muzorewa, Nkomo and Smith.

It is curious that the Muzorewa Government accepted the ceasefire arrangement without any adequate mechanism to prevent the inevitable violations.

Furthermore, the assembly point arrangements favoured the Patriotic Front. ZIPRA used the ceasefire to establish a series of heavily defended strong points to constitute the bridgehead for the force with which they hoped to recover the initiative from Mugabe. ZANLA ignored the restraints imposed by the ceasefire. They kept a significantly large proportion of their forces outside the assembly points while sending in mujibas (young supporters) to make up the numbers expected.

ZANLA infiltrated 8,000 guerillas into the eastern border area alone. They brought in large quantities of arms and ammunition and cached them near the assembly points. Inside the assembly points the mujibas were given intensive training. Thus ZANLA managed to re-stock with arms and ammunition and to treble the strength of its forces inside the country. The guerillas outside the assembly points went to work on the population to ensure victory at the polls.

The plan worked. The Commonwealth forces were too weak to intervene and there was nothing that Muzorewa's Government could do but protest to the British Governor, Lord Soames, after he arrived in early December. Soames rejected demands for the disqualification of Mugabe's ZANU(PF) or the declaration of the result as null and void. General Walls approached Mrs Thatcher but was ignored.

The signs of what was going to happen were clear even if few of Mugabe's opponents wanted to believe them. Neither Muzorewa's UANC nor Nkomo's PF(ZAPU) could hold meetings in the Victoria Province or in Mashonaland East.

The British, however, had come so far that they were not prepared to turn back. They would pretend that what had happened was for the best. Mugabe's trump card was to threaten to continue the war.

When the election was held Mugabe, to his evident surprise and the dismay of his opponents, was the outright winner with 57 seats. Securing only three seats, Muzorewa was eclipsed, Sithole was eliminated, gaining none, and Nkomo only secured 20 in his traditional areas of support.

The whites were taken aback because they had thought that Muzorewa stood as good a chance as any. Furthermore, the white males, called up to protect the election, had been assured by General Walls and his senior officers that Mugabe would not be allowed to take power even if he won the election. He would be eliminated, it was hinted, in a coup. As has since been revealed the demise of the ZANLA/ZIPRA command was plotted with precision and assaults on the assembly points planned and, in one case, rehearsed.

On the day the election result was announced, 4 March 1980, key points were seized by Rhodesian forces but the order to act never came. Whether 'good sense' prevailed or doubters hesitated, is not known. Officers trained in the British tradition, and from British stock, are virtually programmed against illegal action. It is something that they never contemplate. The consequences of a coup, of course, are incalculable. Even with the elimination of the leadership would a replacement

African leader have been found? And the world was hardly likely to accept him.

Instead, Soames embraced Mugabe as the winner and the Commonwealth Monitoring Force extricated itself rapidly from its exposed and dangerous position in the middle. The whites were left to vote with their feet, leaving the Africans to endure Mugabe's bungling 'scientific socialism' and all that it entails.

From "Rhodesian Insurgency" by Professor J.R.T. Wood. Homepage: http://ourworld.compuserve.com/homepages/RAllport/wood1.htm

ZOOM-AWAY LIFESTYLE OF ZIMBABWE'S NEW KING
Jet-set Mugabe behaves like old-style tyrant.

The Sunday Express (UK): November 24 1996
From Jeremy Martin in Harare, Zimbabwe

PRESIDENT ROBERT MUGABE is the new emperor in Africa — a former Marxist-Leninist who has acquired an insatiable taste for power and the good life.

His local admirers believe his 16-year reign heralds a new Golden Age after 200 years of invasion and conquest. But his many enemies think the President of Zimbabwe has turned into an old-style tyrant. When the former Jesuit-trained schoolmaster won British-sponsored elections in 1980 he was a model of leftist correctness in his austere high-buttoned Mao Tse-tung suit. Last April Mugabe — by then a free enterprise capitalist — was sworn in for the third term as president. The ceremony had all the trappings of a tribal emperor's coronation. While school children sang and tribal musicians drummed, traditional chiefs gave him a leopard skin, symbol of African royalty, and the ceremonial axe, spear and Knobkerrie of Kingship.

"Everything will be all right now, we have got a Shona King and Queen once more," said a Mugabe official, referring to the emergence from years of concealment of the president's "secret" second wife, Grace. She bore him two children before the 1992 death of Mugabe's childless first wife, Sally. Even before the couple's two-million pound Catholic church wedding in August,

Grace, 31, had started jetsetting round the world with Mugabe, 72. Sometimes their children, Robert, six, and eight-year-old Bona go too. Grace a former secretary, seems to have replaced not only the flamboyant Sally but also Mugabe's domineering mother who died aged 90 a month after Sally.

When one of Grace's cousins stole some wedding presents she, not Mugabe, took responsibility for getting him a nine-month jail sentence — a massive breach of Shona male culture. The reception itself raised eyebrows in the land of a million homeless and two million unemployed. It took four days to clear up and almost as long to sober the 8,000 guests and 1,500 gatecrashers. Mugabe lavishly dishes out patronage to any rivals and now faces no credible opposition. Grace was given a 500,000 pound state loan to build her own private mansion — money which could have provided homes for up to 10,000 Zimbabweans now living in backyard packing case shelters.

Two new presidential helicopters cost 30 million pounds each. A 25 million pound presidential jet is on the shopping list. With Grace at his side, Mugabe flies to one world summit after another, denouncing the remaining 70,000 whites, the West and the International Monetary Fund. But local commerce chief Danny Meyer says simply that government extravagance is the cause of failed economic reforms. Inflation touched 40 per cent as budget over spending soared. The state put bank loans beyond the reach of struggling businessmen, triggering a wave of bankruptcies. Mugabe exploited presidential immunity from libel laws to warn a white banker that he would have to forget money owed to him by a party loyalist. Mugabe also pronounces on criminal cases, deciding on guilt or innocence before police have even had time to investigate. Then he and Grace are off again "shopping up a storm", to Geneva, Accra, Sofia, Budapest, London, Mombasa, Yaounde, Kingston in Jamaica, Pretoria and Cape Town — where they stayed at the 500 pound-a-night Cape Sun Hotel.

To take Grace and a 30-strong delegation to a conference in Ougadougou, capital of impoverished Burkina Faso, Mugabe evicted passengers from a 193-seat Air Zimbabwe Boeing 767 who were flying the lucrative European route. Unable to switch bookings, many passengers were left stranded. His last trip to Britain and Italy was undertaken despite his country's worst labour unrest since independence in 1980. Mugabe said he was baffled that doctors and nurses — earning less than 100 pounds a month — had gone on strike, paralysing a state hospital service flooded with Aids cases.

Last year Mugabe and his ministers took backdated rises, largely exempt from tax rates which hit 47 per cent of incomes above 2800 pounds a year.

The presidents favourite target remains the white population, particularly the 4,500 farmers who make Zimbabwe one of the few African states able to feed itself. They live under constant threat of being "designated" for takeover on Mugabe's terms, without right of appeal to the courts. In June, the family of a one-time guerrilla claimed he died of wounds 20 years after a gun battle with Ian Smith's Rhodesian security forces. "You", Mugabe told whites in a televised graveside statement, "are the murderers of this young man. "The harshest penalties should be meted out to you. You deserve to die from a hail of bullets, your carcasses being thrown to dogs and vultures."

A visiting American investment delegation which heard the TV broadcast quickly took the next plane to neighbouring Botswana.

THE LAST WORD

"IT WAS SAD that Rhodesia/Zimbabwe finished up with a Marxist government in a continent where there were too many Marxists maladministering their countries' resources. But political and military realities were all too evidently on the side of the guerilla leaders. A government like that of Bishop Muzorewa, without international recognition, could never have brought to the people of Rhodesia the peace that they wanted and needed above all else.

From the British point of view the settlement also had large benefits. With the Rhodesian question finally solved, we again played an effective role in dealing with other Commonwealth — and especially African — issues, including the pressing problem of the future of Namibia and the longer-term challenge of bringing peaceful change to South Africa. Britain had demonstrated her ability, by a combination of honest dealing and forceful diplomacy, to settle one of the most intractable disputes arising fon her colonial past."

Margaret, The Lady Thatcher OM PC FRS
From her memoirs "The Downing Street Years"